A Bedroom

"You're supposed to be in bed," Angela said. Oh, he was impossible!

"And as it is cold by the window, I will certainly return to it." Phillip took a step and grimaced at the pain.

Crossing the room to help him, she wrapped an arm around his waist, and he draped his arm around her shoulders. In this half embrace, she felt hot all over, from her cheeks to her toes and everywhere—*everywhere*—in between. A heat so intense it was as if the flames of hell were licking at her heels. Except that it felt so very, very good . . .

The ROGUE and the RIVAL

MAYA RODALE

BERKLEY SENSATION, NEW YORK

THE BERKLEY PUBLISHING GROUP
Published by the Penguin Group
Penguin Group (USA) Inc.
375 Hudson Street, New York, New York 10014, USA
Penguin Group (Canada), 90 Eglinton Avenue East, Suite 700, Toronto, Ontario M4P 2Y3, Canada
(a division of Pearson Penguin Canada Inc.)
Penguin Books Ltd., 80 Strand, London WC2R 0RL, England
Penguin Group Ireland, 25 St. Stephen's Green, Dublin 2, Ireland (a division of Penguin Books Ltd.)
Penguin Group (Australia), 250 Camberwell Road, Camberwell, Victoria 3124, Australia
(a division of Pearson Australia Group Pty. Ltd.)
Penguin Books India Pvt. Ltd., 11 Community Centre, Panchsheel Park, New Delhi—110 017, India
Penguin Group (NZ), 67 Apollo Drive, Rosedale, North Shore 0632, New Zealand
(a division of Pearson New Zealand Ltd.)
Penguin Books (South Africa) (Pty.) Ltd., 24 Sturdee Avenue, Rosebank, Johannesburg 2196,
South Africa

Penguin Books Ltd., Registered Offices: 80 Strand, London WC2R 0RL, England

This is a work of fiction. Names, characters, places, and incidents either are the product of the author's imagination or are used fictitiously, and any resemblance to actual persons, living or dead, business establishments, events, or locales is entirely coincidental. The publisher does not have any control over and does not assume any responsibility for author or third-party websites or their content.

THE ROGUE AND THE RIVAL

A Berkley Sensation Book / published by arrangement with the author

PRINTING HISTORY
Berkley Sensation mass-market edition / November 2008

Copyright © 2008 by Maya Rodale.
Cover art by Tim Griffin.
Cover design by George Long.
Hand lettering by Ron Zinn.
Interior text design by Laura K. Corless.

ISBN: 978-0-425-22452-6

BERKLEY® SENSATION
Berkley Sensation Books are published by The Berkley Publishing Group,
a division of Penguin Group (USA) Inc.,
375 Hudson Street, New York, New York 10014.
BERKLEY SENSATION and the "B" design are trademarks of Penguin Group (USA) Inc.

PRINTED IN THE UNITED STATES OF AMERICA

10 9 8 7 6 5 4 3 2 1

*This one is for my girls
and for their valiant efforts
to reform rakes everywhere.*

ACKNOWLEDGMENTS

I'd like to thank my editor, Wendy McCurdy, for her insightful comments and for being a pleasure to work with. Thanks also to the team at Berkley.

Special thanks to: Linda Loewenthal, Jen Parkinson, Ann Bleakley, my family and friends, and Penelope.

Prologue

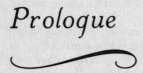

ASTON HOUSE, BEDFORDSHIRE, ENGLAND
MAY 1822

Time had been good to Phillip Kensington, Marquis of Huntley, even though he certainly did not deserve it.

He had been a rake, a rogue, a drunk, a gambler, and a danger to virtuous young women everywhere. He had nearly been a duke. He had been a disgrace. He had almost died and definitely deserved to.

But Angela had saved him anyway.

Presently, he was nothing more than a man in love with nothing to lose and everything to win.

And yet, he was no longer sure if he was the gambling man he had always thought himself to be.

The hour was late, and Phillip sat before a dwindling fire in the library of Aston House, his unexpected inheritance. In his right hand he held a glass of brandy, of which he did not partake. With his left hand he pushed his hair back from his face. He squinted, looking at the fire. There were lines around his eyes now, ones that spoke of age and wisdom he did not possess. He was not in the slightest bit wise, but at least he now knew that he was a fool, whereas before he hadn't a clue. He considered that knowledge of himself progress.

His hands were not those of the nobleman he was. They were rough and calloused from long days of laboring to improve his home and estate. That work had transformed his body as well, and it was now tanned, taut, and muscular, like the build of a common laborer.

His nose, which once had a perfectly aristocratic slope, had, years ago, undergone a permanent transformation due to a run-in with his twin brother's fist. It was now crooked with an odd bump. It was a distinct flaw and a regular reminder of the man he used to be.

As per his new nightly ritual, Phillip mused upon the changes in himself for a moment before turning his thoughts to the reason he had become a new man. It was, of course, because of a woman. He tormented himself by recalling her soft honey-hued hair and how it had felt between his fingers. He imagined, yet again, how the curves of her figure would look without the awful frocks she wore, how she would look in the beautiful gowns he wished he could buy for her and—oh God—how she would feel, naked, beneath him. He imagined her appearing in the doorway of the library, telling him to quit his brooding and to come to bed.

He smiled at that thought. He looked at the glass of brandy in his hand. Not a drop of alcohol had crossed his lips in the past eight months. Now the only thing he craved upon his lips was the mouth of one particular woman. Angela, his angel.

As he did every night, Phillip poured the liquid onto the fire, admiring the burst of flame that disappeared as soon as it had started. Just like their time together, he thought wryly. He paused then, still astounded at how much he ached for her. Did she—? No, he would not allow himself to wonder if she still thought of him. If she did, it was probably without the slightest tender feeling. He would go to bed and miss her with an intensity that shocked him still, until he finally fell asleep.

Or, he could read the letter. The one he had never expected and had never even dared to hope for. The letter he couldn't yet bring himself to read. Until tonight . . .

BOOK 1

EIGHT MONTHS EARLIER

Chapter 1

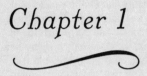

Phillip opened his eyes to an unfamiliar sight. Squinting at the strange, soft, silken light, he realized that it was morning, and he could not recall the last time he had seen morning light. To him, it was something to be shut out by heavy velvet drapes and slumbered through after a long night spent drinking, gaming, and wenching. He blinked a few times, and his eyes adjusted.

What did one do in the morning?

Breakfast, he recalled, rolling onto his side while wincing at the pain of doing so. He reached for the bellpull beside the bed, groaning at the strain that it placed on his aching muscles and the subsequent crushing pain in his chest. His hand grasped helplessly at the air, finding no braided cord to tug on. There was no bellpull! How was he to eat if he could not alert a servant and inform them that he wanted food? He was going to starve to death.

Phillip shifted once more to lie on his back, a shockingly painful activity. What the devil had he done? And where on earth was he? Looking around the narrow, rectangular room, he thought there was a good chance he was in prison. The walls and floor were gray stone. There was one door, and on the wall opposite, one window with a view of nothing other than sky. No carpet, no curtains. Nothing, really, other than bare necessities: the narrow bed on which he lay, a table by the bed, and a chair, both of which were of such poor quality that Phillip wondered if the carpenter had been foxed when he made them. That was all.

It was a far cry from any residence he had ever inhabited in his nine and twenty years. Cliveden, the ducal estate where he had spent his youth, wasn't as grand as it once was, but it at least had carpets in every room. And the Parisian apartment from which he had recently fled (that much he remembered) was on the smaller side, with only ten rooms. But each of those had been exquisitely decorated. Even the maid's rooms had curtains.

But everything begged the question of where the hell he was. He couldn't even ask anyone, because there was no bloody bellpull to summon a servant to answer his questions.

Phillip could only conclude that he had not escaped the men that were after him. His head started to throb viciously as he tried to recall what had happened, to no avail. But he could recall the relentless darkness of midnight, the constant drumming of his horse's hooves, the cold rain slapping his face and soaking him to the bone. And always, always, looking back over his shoulder to see if he had lost them. His memory was blank after that, and judging from the pain and cell-like chamber he was in, he could only conclude that he hadn't been able to outrun them after all.

But he was too tired and in too much pain to give a damn. He didn't even have the strength to worry about the footsteps he heard in the hall that eventually paused outside the door. Phillip did, however, feel a spark of interest when a woman entered bearing a tray that he hoped contained food.

"You're an angel," he said without thinking. Phillip did not believe in angels, and he certainly did not believe that he would ever make it to a place inhabited by them. Heaven, in all its eternal vastness, had no space for Phillip Kensington. But she looked like one. Her golden hair was pulled back into a thick braid that was coiled atop her head like a halo. Big blue eyes, under thick lashes and light brown arching brows, stared at him. Her complexion was pale. Upon a closer look, her expression, in contrast, was anything but angelic. She looked quite peevish, in fact.

"You must have hit your head harder than I thought," she retorted. She did not have the voice of an angel; hers was low, smooth like velvet, intoxicating like brandy. She had the voice of a devil with the face of an angel.

Phillip was intrigued, pleased, and confused. Who was she? And where was he?

The tray she carried was placed on the bedside table with a thump as it hit the wood, and with the sound of glass and cutlery clattering against each other. She told him to sit up, and he did, hoping she didn't notice him wincing in pain, and then she unceremoniously handed him a bowl of porridge.

"I hate porridge," he said, handing the bowl back to her. She did not take it. "Fetch me something else. And I want tea with a generous splash of brandy. And while you're up, I could use another blanket. It's damned drafty in here." When she didn't make any move to leave, he added, "Go on then."

"Oh, *really?*" she asked, with such obvious sarcasm that even Phillip, with his apparent head injury, could not miss it. "Oh sure," she continued, "I'll just go tell the cook, who has just made breakfast for fifty people, and now has to prepare luncheon for fifty people, that the ungrateful invalid we've been keeping alive for the past week only out of Christian charity now wants 'something else.' And we don't keep brandy here."

No brandy? Oh, that was too horrifying to even contemplate. He focused his attention on the dish in his hand instead.

"Porridge will be fine," Phillip said.

Her smug expression wordlessly communicated that she thought so, too. The face of an angry angel, he thought. The voice of the devil. And the bedside manner of a prison warden. He thought it best if he took a bite of the damned porridge. It tasted as awful as it looked. Made a man consider starving to death.

"Perhaps you could tell me where I am," he said, forcing himself to take another bite.

"Stanbrook Abbey," she replied.

Phillip choked. She smacked him on the back, between his shoulder blades. And then the evil wench laughed.

"Last place you expected to find yourself, I gather. Well, we didn't expect the likes of you, either. But since we are good Christian souls here, intent on redeeming the most worthless specimens, we couldn't very well turn you away when the Sloan brothers brought you in, after finding your nearly lifeless body in a ditch."

"I presume you know who I am then," he said haughtily, shocked at her impertinence and treatment of him if she was aware of his status as a peer of the realm. That should at least entitle him to some respect, if not a decent meal.

"We come across a news sheet from time to time, Lord Huntley. And besides, the abbess here is the Dowager Countess of Bamford, and she recognized you." Phillip had no idea who Lady Bamford was, but this didn't surprise him. It had been years since he had been in England, years since he had even attempted to remember a name of someone he met. And being the notorious scoundrel that he was, more people were familiar with him than he was personally acquainted with.

"I see. Well, I shan't be staying long. I could leave this afternoon, in fact."

"As much as I wish you would, I'm afraid that is impossible," she said briskly. "You have a gunshot wound in one leg, three broken ribs, and a nasty gash on your head. It seems you broke your nose, too."

"Again?" he wondered aloud. She looked confused. "Or not. My nose was already broken," Phillip added wearily, rubbing his jaw. It was in need of a shave. He must look like a complete barbarian.

"You must be in the habit of provoking many people," she observed, and he did not contradict her. "You don't like your porridge?" she asked, after looking down at the nearly full bowl he still held.

"No," he said. "It's revolting. I doubt even the pigs will eat it."

"I'm beginning to see why you have so many injuries," she

answered, taking the bowl from him and setting it on the tray, from which she picked up linen strips and a small jar of ointment. To his surprise, the angry angel placed one small hand on his chest, urging him to lean back against the pillow so she could tend to him.

She didn't speak as she worked, starting with an application of ointment at the cut on his forehead. He didn't speak, either, although he was tempted to swear and complain because the ointment stung. Phillip was acutely aware of her fingers gently brushing his skin. He was far more aware, however, of her breasts as she bent over him. She wore some horrid, ill-fitting gray dress that covered everything up to her neck. A white apron was pinned to the front. He could see her breasts strain against the fabric. The hint of round, full breasts just inches away from him. From his mouth.

Phillip did not avert his gaze. He may be a gentleman in title, but generally, he was not a gentleman in his actions. After all, admiring the view never hurt anyone.

Phillip thought she was finished, and he was slightly shocked and more than a little pleased when her fingers began to undo the buttons on his shirt and push it open. The shirt was not his own, for the fabric was coarse and rough against his skin. In fact, he thought it looked rather like a woman's nightgown.

"What am I wearing?" he asked suspiciously.

"You can thank the cook, Henrietta, for lending you her extra nightgown. It was the only one that would fit you. And the only thing we had for you to wear."

"Yes, do give her my eternal gratitude," Phillip remarked dryly. He would have rather she provided a decent meal, instead. One quick glance at his angry angel's face, and he thought it best not to voice that thought.

It was a relief to have the blasted female garment off, if only partially. Her hands were warm against his chest as she examined the bruises from his broken ribs. He closed his eyes. For a fleeting second, everything was right and perfect in his world: her hands on his skin. The thought vanished as quickly as it came.

"What is this from?" she asked.

He looked down at the old gray scar on his left shoulder that she traced with one fingertip.

"The usual," he said, his voice sounding rough to his ears. "A duel over something stupid."

"A stupid woman, I presume," she said sarcastically.

"Game of cards," he corrected.

Her cheeks reddened as she pulled the blankets aside so that she might check on his gunshot wound. It was in the middle of his thigh, covered by a long strand of linen wrapped around his leg. She began to unravel it. She talked as she worked, and between her hands and her voice, he couldn't help but become aroused.

"The doctor removed the bullet. He said as long as the wound did not become infected, you should be fine. You might limp, though."

Limp. He wanted to laugh, but he knew it would hurt. Phillip had on nothing but a shirt and a pair of smalls, and thankfully, blankets covering his lap so that she wouldn't see that he was far from limp.

She worked quickly, applying the ointment and wrapping a fresh bandage around his leg. He inhaled sharply as she touched a sensitive spot that caused an intense shock of pain. He couldn't hide a wince.

"Sorry," she said quietly. Phillip was sorry when she began to pull the blankets back in place and button up the horrible dressing gown. "How often do you have to do that?" he asked when she was finished.

"Once a day," she replied.

Once every hour would be preferable, he thought. She placed the bowl of porridge and jar of ointment on the tray, in preparation to leave. He didn't want her to go, because he didn't want to be alone.

"I could use another blanket or two. It's awfully drafty in here. Curtains would help, too. And I should like some brandy."

She ignored him.

"You haven't told me your name," he said as she opened the door.

"You haven't asked," she replied pertly.

Insufferable wench, he thought. She was going to make him ask. So he did.

"My name is Angela," she answered. "But I'm no angel." And then she left, banging the door shut behind her and leaving him all alone.

Phillip had never cared for being alone. He found it rather dull, so he always went out instead of staying in, and surrounded himself with friends, acquaintances, or companions. And now his only option for company was a mean but attractive woman, and she had left him alone. There was nothing to do but think, an activity he generally avoided.

He thought that his choice to starve rather than eat the nasty porridge was a bit foolish. Hunger pains joined his other ailments. He certainly would not be leaving this afternoon, or the next, or even the next after that, which was just as well, since he had no place to go. Or rather, there was nowhere he wanted to go. Might as well get used to life in an abbey.

Phillip couldn't help but smirk that a worthless bounder such as he was in a house of God.

Who knew that nuns were pretty? They were supposed to be pinched old spinsters that did foolish things like pray for unredeemable souls like his. Angela was likely praying that he would leave soon, and preferably feetfirst. Angela was certainly not a pinched old spinster, either. No, she was young, luscious, and lovely, with the mouth of the devil.

There was one sort of thinking that Phillip was fond of. And so Phillip imagined her unbuttoning his shirt and running her hands over his chest. But in his mind, she didn't stop there. The dress went first, and then the pins holding her hair in place. His fists clenched around the sheets, but in his mind his hands roamed freely over her. She would slip into bed with him. And he would run his fingers through that mass of golden hair, tugging lightly to pull her mouth to his and then . . .

He didn't know why, but he looked up at the wall behind his bed. A small wood carving of Christ on the cross looked down at him.

"Jesus," he said, not sure of if it was an acknowledgment or a curse.

~

It is still too hard to be good, Angela thought as she made her way to the kitchen. Six years in the abbey, and still she could not control her tongue or her temper. Six years here, and she still wanted to shout in frustration or sometimes for no reason at all other than to hear her own voice echo endlessly in the stone halls. Anything to break the unrelenting silence. She longed for music, dancing, and laughter. Six years here, and she still could not get used to the rough woolen fabric of her practical gown against her skin. She missed the finely spun cottons, silks, and satins of the exquisitely tailored dresses she used to wear, even though she knew it was a frivolous and useless desire. Six years here, and her body still hummed with desire at the sight of a man.

Worse yet was that her body betrayed her with a quickened, excited pulse at the sight of a very bad man. All of England knew that Lord Huntley was bad. He ruined women left and right, gambled away the family fortune, and drank to excess regularly. His temper was notorious as well, as were his numerous duels. It was a huge scandal when his twin inherited the title instead of him, contrary to everyone's expectations. He had fled to Paris, and tales of his debauchery had crossed the channel. In short, he was a legend. A paragon of sin.

Three days earlier, she had watched as the Sloan brothers unloaded his battered body from their cart, along with the usual assorted items from town. Her heart had lurched at the sight of him, not in disgust, but because something so beautiful had nearly been destroyed. That, and the fact that she hadn't had any contact with men since she had arrived at Stanbrook Abbey six years earlier—other than Johnnie and William Sloan, and they were mere lads so they didn't count. And then this one arrived, handsome and wicked, and in desperate need of some tender, loving care.

The abbess, otherwise known as Dowager Countess of Bamford, familiarly known as Katherine, assigned Angela to administer that care, in spite of her pleas and protestations to the contrary.

When Angela entered the kitchen, she saw Penelope Sloan and Helena Smith, her two best friends, or, if one was being too specific, her only friends. But that didn't matter. More than occasionally, Angela thought their friendship was all that got her through the day.

Penelope was one of six children, including four daughters, born to a vicar. Having grown up in the church, and with few marriage prospects because she lacked a dowry, it was only natural that she join the abbey. She was happy here and certain of her path. Angela occasionally envied her certainty but more often admired her for it.

Helena was older than Angela by a few years. After a short marriage left her a widow, her only option, other than a religious life, had been to live as a housekeeper with her only remaining family, a miserly and lecherous old uncle. She declared that if she must bind herself to another man for the rest of her life, it might as well be the good Lord.

Angela's two friends must have seen from her face that she was in a foul mood. After a quick greeting, they continued with their work, Penelope popping peas out of their pods and Helena peeling potatoes.

Angela had told a small lie to Lord Invalid. The cook, Henrietta, did have to prepare luncheon for fifty people, but not for another half hour. Angela set down the tray with a bang on the large, rough-hewn table in the middle of the room. She began to clear the tray, and the sight of the full bowl of porridge made her angry. *I won't do it,* she thought as she scooped the contents into the scrap bin for the grateful pigs.

"What are you doing?" Penelope asked. Cooking was not one of Angela's usual chores in the abbey.

"My good deed for the day," Angela replied dryly as she began assembling ingredients and started to boil some water.

"Did Lord Invalid not like the porridge?" Helena asked with feigned innocence. Angela had checked on him earlier and saw that he was stirring. Thinking it best to be fully prepared when she went to tend to him and his wounds that morning, in case he woke fully, she followed Helena's suggestion to serve him yesterday's porridge.

It had also been Helena's idea to call him Lord Invalid. The name had stuck. They had referred to him as such for the past three days that he had been lying unconscious in his room.

"Oh, has he woken?" Penelope asked eagerly.

"He must have done. Why else would she be making breakfast so late in the morning?" Helena said before Angela could answer. She was too absorbed in her own thoughts. "*I won't do it*," she muttered to herself as she slammed down a cast-iron skillet on the stove. She repeated this phrase as she vented her frustration on cupboard doors and the like while gathering the necessary ingredients and supplies for cooking Lord Invalid a feast.

"I heard a racket, so I knew I would find you here," the lady Katherine said as she strolled into the kitchen with her usual expression of eternal serenity. She sat down at the table, smoothing out her dark skirts and running a hand over her gray hair, which was always pulled back into an immaculate bun.

"How is our patient?" the abbess asked.

"In a word, despicable," Angela stated.

"So he has woken."

"And I wish he hadn't," Angela said, picking up a large knife.

"Angela . . ." The abbess sighed in disapproval.

Angela began to cut thick slices of bread that had been freshly baked that morning. She set them on the plate and added a few slices of ham and cheese.

"I don't wish him dead. I didn't mean it that way. But why do I have to be the one to take care of Lord Invalid?"

"Yes, why did you choose her?" Helena chimed in, placing her arm protectively around Angela's shoulders. "Considering what sort of man he is, and what she has suffered, it's more of a hardship for her than any of us."

"It is because Angela has not taken her orders yet," the abbess answered. "She may still be in the company of men, though we may not be. I'm sure, however, that as long as he is here, we might have to make exceptions to that rule. Because we are caring for him, I'm sure God will forgive us."

"You said to take all the time I need before I take my orders," Angela protested. "And now I'm being punished for waiting until I was ready."

"You are not being punished. It's only practical. And furthermore, I think it's for the best. You need to learn compassion and forgiveness for exactly the kind of man Lord Huntley is." The kind of man who had ruined her, Angela thought, knowing the others were thinking the same thing.

"He doesn't deserve it. No man like him does," Angela said, cracking an egg into the hot skillet.

"Everyone deserves compassion and forgiveness. You, too, Angela," the abbess said softly.

"I know." Angela sighed. She turned her back to the room to pay attention to the stove. Tears were stinging her eyes. She blinked them back and added two more eggs. Six years here, and she still hadn't forgiven herself for ruining her family. She had blood on her hands that just wouldn't wash off, no matter how many prayers she uttered or, she suspected, no matter how many very bad men she nursed back to health.

"What are you making?" the abbess asked. "Breakfast was two hours ago, and you know that we fast between meals."

"I am making breakfast for his lordship. Porridge is not to his liking."

"You didn't serve him the porridge from yesterday's breakfast, did you?" Katherine asked, looking aghast. Helena and Penelope ducked their heads to hide their smiles.

"Maybe," Angela replied, adding the eggs to the plate. She placed the food on the tray, along with a glass of water, a cup of tea, cutlery, and a napkin.

"Angela." The abbess murmured her name, as she often did, in a voice laced with disappointment.

"I'm trying," Angela said, pointing toward the plate. "But I'm not giving him the brandy he asked for."

"I should think not," Katherine replied. " 'Tis the last thing he needs."

I cannot believe I am doing this, Angela thought as she

carried the tray back to Lord Invalid's chamber. It wasn't just that he was surly, rude, demanding, and difficult that had her in a foul mood. He just so happened to be a specimen of the most loathsome breed of humans; he was an absolute scoundrel. She had an encounter with one once before, and as a result she ended up here.

And now she was supposed to wait hand and foot on a destroyer of virtue and goodness in her refuge, the abbey. Perhaps she had half expected that this sacred site would burst into flames when he entered. But it didn't, and now she was bringing him a proper breakfast. She did feel slightly guilty about giving him yesterday's porridge. No one deserved that, and it would not help him get well. Besides, the sooner he regained his strength, the sooner he would leave, and her life would return to its usual placid state. Angela ignored the fleeting sense of dismay at that thought.

When she entered, Lord Invalid was reclining in bed with a smile on his lips. He had the nerve to seem pleased at his situation, didn't he! Oh, but he was so handsome when he shouldn't be. Part of his head was covered in linen, because of the gash, and still that did nothing to diminish his appeal. One could almost imagine him getting hurt in some noble effort to save a damsel in distress or children from a fire in an orphanage. But that was highly unlikely. In fact, she didn't know what had happened to him.

His eyes were a deep dark brown, slightly shadowed by black lashes. They promised seduction, followed swiftly by destruction. She had looked into those eyes earlier and felt a stab of fear. Temptation.

His brow, his cheekbones, the line of his jaw, even though partially obscured by a few days' beard, all proclaimed *nobleman*. His broken nose, however, made him seem human or barbaric; she wasn't sure. Only he could make an imperfection seem perfect.

At least his shirt was buttoned, covering his chest that, in spite of the bruises over his broken ribs, was nice enough, tempting even. And as his nurse, she had to touch it. She shouldn't look at it, let alone place her bare hands on it. But she did. And she had liked it.

"This is for your apology," she said. At the sound of her voice he opened his eyes.

"I didn't apologize," he answered, sounding perplexed.

"Well, I think you ought to," she said. Angela knew that he must be in pain, was likely confused, and certainly was unaccustomed to life in an abbey. She knew he could have been worse this morning. But if he was even half the man his reputation declared him to be, she found it essential to show him that she was not to be trifled with. So she would make it clear that he was at her mercy and not the other way around.

"I'm a man. Men do not apologize. What do you have there?"

"Three fried eggs, fresh-baked bread, slices of ham, and some cheese. Water and tea."

"I'm deeply and sincerely sorry for something. I know not what, just that I humbly ask your forgiveness," he said, placing his hand over his heart for emphasis and looking pleadingly at her. She restrained a smile. She would not encourage him.

"You are sorry for being difficult and making excessive demands upon me when I have other things to do."

"I am sorry, indeed. I blame it on the severe pain and agonizing boredom I am suffering." Lord Invalid grimaced in pain as he made the effort to sit up.

"Agonizing boredom? You've only been conscious for little more than two hours in three days," she said pointedly.

"May I have the tray now?" When she did not move, he resorted to an act of desperation. "*Please.*"

"Since you said 'please.'" Angela placed the tray on his lap.

"You know, I do think that might have been the first time I ever said 'please' to anyone," he remarked, picking up the cutlery.

"Well I'll just have to get you a prize then," Angela replied dryly.

"Don't tell anyone. It would ruin my reputation." He seemed serious for a second, until she saw the hint of a sly smile, and she realized he was joking. So he was an absolute scoundrel with a sense of humor. That was even more dangerous than being just a plain old scoundrel. She should leave. Now.

"I don't think you have one to ruin," Angela answered, pulling over the chair and sitting down in spite of her better judgment. It was just that he was someone new to talk to, and it had been so long since she had engaged in conversation with someone new. Six years, to be precise.

"This is delicious," he said. "The cook can make something decent after all."

"Yes, she can."

"So what did you do to get stuck nursing me?" Phillip asked after a moment of silence in which he devoured half of the meal.

"What makes you think this is some sort of punishment for me?" she asked evasively.

"Really, Angela," he said patiently, setting down his fork and treating her to a withering stare. "I'm not as stupid as everyone believes me to be."

"Are you as wicked as they say?" Angela asked, the words out of her mouth before she could censor them.

"Probably," he answered with a shrug that made him wince in pain. "But you needn't worry. You're safe as long as I'm bedridden."

"You shouldn't say that. I might be tempted to keep you that way."

"I'm not sure I would mind if you did. I don't exactly have anywhere to be or to go."

"What, did your club membership expire while you were abroad?" she teased.

"I should hope not. That would be a fate worse than death. Living here might be a close second, though."

"It's nice here," she answered defensively. "It's quiet and peaceful, and I'm happy here."

Lord Invalid gave her a look that simply questioned her

quick response. It was quiet and peaceful here, that much was true. And most of the time she was happy here. But lately she had been getting sick of the tireless serenity. He didn't need to know that, though.

"Are you finished yet?" she asked impatiently. She was on the verge of enjoying herself and his company, and that really would not do. It was one thing to be tired of quiet and peaceful, but she had to learn to accept it rather than indulge in something potentially thrilling.

And this scoundrel before her: it was one thing if he was handsome but quite another if he was intelligent and humorous as well. Therein lay danger, and Angela had learned the hard way that it was better to avoid temptation entirely rather than attempt to withstand it.

"Yes. Here," he said, motioning for her to clear the tray away.

"Do you have to tend to my wounds again?" he asked, sounding slightly hopeful that she would say yes.

"Not now."

"What about that blanket? Please."

"If you keep saying that, you might make a habit of it, and then what will your friends think?" She didn't give him a chance to respond before she left the room, where she encountered Penelope in the corridor.

"Is he any better?" she asked. "I mean, is he still bothersome?"

"Yes. He wants extra blankets now. Next he'll probably ask for beeswax candles and cigars," Angela said.

"I thought he might be charming," Penelope said with a look of disappointment.

"Handsome men don't develop qualities like charm, because they do not need them," Angela replied.

"He must be extraordinarily handsome, then. If so many women have fallen for him and he is not charming," Penelope said thoughtfully. Having spent almost her entire life, all nineteen years of it, in the abbey, she did not have much experience with men at all.

"Lord only knows how he managed it." Angela said, though

she certainly had a clue. He was not extraordinarily handsome in his current state, but she could easily see how he would be if he were well. He had an unmistakable air of danger about him that promised thrills usually unknown to women such as herself. He could be tempting until he opened his mouth to demand this or that.

"I'll bring him the blanket," Penelope said, offering to break the rules. In return for the favor, Angela would keep her secret.

"Thank you." Angela was safe from him for a few more hours until nightfall.

~

Angela returned to his chamber with dinner during the last hour of daylight, when the sky was a lovely shade of periwinkle and the moon was just starting to appear. Just one candle was necessary, and the flame wavered as she walked.

He was asleep when she entered. Making an effort to be quiet and gentle, she set down the tray and went about checking on his wounds. A small part of her wished that he would wake up and complain about something so that she could find him difficult and despicable and thus have a good reason to dislike him. She would respond with sarcastic remarks, all to keep him at a distance.

But he slept on, looking deceptively gentle and impossibly handsome.

Angela thought of her prayer, the secret one for a wish she wasn't supposed to have. And she thought how God had misunderstood what she was asking for and that perhaps she ought to have been more specific. Angela prayed for forgiveness for her sins. She also prayed for a second chance at love. She had forgotten to specify that she wanted the love of a good man, an honest man, who would love her back this time. Because God had sent her a man who was not good, a man who was just like the first one, a man that could ruin her all over again, when she was looking to be saved.

Chapter 2

A week passed in which Angela, by divine intervention, managed to refrain from murdering Lord Invalid. But, oh, how she wanted to.

Against her better judgment, she gave him a bell to ring, should he need anything. She thought it might quiet his constant laments about the lack of a bellpull. Instead, that tinkling sound of the bell began to haunt her dreams and dog her every step. But he rang, and she answered, because he was severely injured, and the last thing she needed was another dead man on her conscience.

His reasons for requesting her presence were ridiculous. The room was too hot. Could she open a window? The room was too cold. Could she close the window and bring a blanket? He couldn't sleep. He was bored. He was hungry. He was impossible.

He did *not* complain about the food. She served him the best so that he could regain his strength sooner rather than later and quit her life forever.

She had every intention of letting him wear Henrietta's nightgown until the apocalypse came and went, but Johnnie

Sloan brought up a pair of breeches and a shirt and made her promise to give them to Phillip. She did—and while he changed into the shirt before her, she took the bell from him. It was a small victory.

Lord Invalid repeatedly asked for brandy. Even resorted to begging for it. She seriously considered sneaking to town to buy a bottle, only to smash it over his head. But that would just result in yet another wound she would have to tend to.

His other wounds, she was sure, plagued her as much as him. Every morning she had to apply ointment and change the dressings.

The cut on his head was mostly healed, thank goodness. Every time she leaned over him to tend to it, she just knew he was looking at her . . . inappropriately. She thanked God for something so trivial as the high neckline on her dress so that he could not see how his gaze heated her skin. It was as if she could feel his hands upon her. And, judging from her past experiences, she suspected she would rather enjoy it.

And she shouldn't, of course.

She refused to check the bruises on his chest, because she was sure they were fine, and there was nothing she could do about them, and because she enjoyed touching his bare, taut skin a little too much.

And then there was the gunshot wound on his leg. The doctor had assured her that it really was not that bad, as far as gunshot wounds went. The bullet missed the bone and was removed completely. So long as she tended to it regularly, it would heal nicely and, Angela prayed, quickly.

A debauched wastrel such as he was should not have the body that he did, she thought. And she had to tend to that damned wound on his lean and muscular thigh, right near, well . . . She shouldn't say it. She shouldn't think of it. She shouldn't even know about it, but she did.

She had been with a man. Once. She had enjoyed the act. It was the aftermath that had ruined her. Destroyed a little part of her heart and a big chunk of her soul. She had come to the abbey so that she might discover forgiveness or at least forget.

Angela had gotten quite good at forgetting her past, until he came along; Lord Invalid was making that a mighty challenge.

She was trying to devote herself completely and utterly to immortal, heavenly men who would forgive sins she couldn't forgive herself.

And yet she found herself completely and utterly devoted to one particular mortal man. He was handsome like the devil and tempting, causing feelings she had long tried vainly to suppress.

Oh, Phillip Kensington had become the thorn in her side, the stone in her shoe, her own personal plague. He had moments when he was funny and charming, but they were few and far between. Mostly he was a constant reminder of the darkest moments in her life, the ones she tried so hard to forget. She hated him for it.

～

"Where have you been? I've been up for hours already. I'm starving," Phillip said before Angela had even fully entered his chamber the next morning.

"Good morning to you, too. How do you even know you've been awake for hours? There isn't a clock in here."

"It felt like hours," he muttered.

"My heart is overflowing with pity for you. Having to lie abed and do nothing while some of us actually have been awake for hours doing chores and other useful activities." Today was no different than the days before it: Angela had been up at dawn. Lying in bed till midmorning was a luxury she had lost.

"Such as?" he asked, sitting up and leaning forward as Angela placed an additional pillow behind him.

"You really want to know?" she asked, making the mistake of looking into his dark eyes. His expression was honest; it seemed he actually wanted to listen to her. Her heart skipped a beat.

"I asked, didn't I? Besides, I swear I am perishing of boredom here. Listening to your list of chores in that voice of yours . . ." he said, his own voice trailing off as a smile played upon his lips.

"What about my voice?"

"It's bewitching. Hasn't anyone ever told you that? Even though you say mean things to me, I still want to hear you speak because of your voice."

"The first hour of my day is spent in contemplation and prayer," Angela said in answer to Lord Invalid's question and to distract her from the memory playing out in her head. All rakes and scoundrels were indeed the same, Angela thought. For another one, another time, had said essentially the same thing years ago, when her parents had foolishly left her alone in the drawing room with the lord of her downfall. She had been nervous and rambling, until she stopped herself. "Please continue," he had said. "It is a pleasure to hear you talk in that voice of yours, my darling. You could read my accounts book aloud, and I would be riveted." She talked until she was silenced by his lips against hers.

She had already spent enough time in thought and contemplation this morning.

"Contemplation upon what?" Lord Invalid persisted.

"My sins. Those in the past and the present. And then I pray they shall not be in my future," she recited.

"Tell me your sins, Angela," Phillip murmured with a wicked smile and a devilish gleam in his eye. A smile that made her want to tell him, made her *almost* thankful she had sins she could confess to him. Her heart thudded heavily.

"Absolutely not." Her voice was a little more breathless than she would have liked. "After that, I spend an hour tending to the garden. Then I perform penance for my sins."

"And what does that entail?"

"Tending to you," she said with a smirk.

"I can't be *that* difficult. Your sins must be small, then," he said with a little grin.

Angela, in a moment of divine grace and self-restraint, did not act on her urge to pour the cup of hot tea upon him.

She simply turned and began to walk away.

"Don't leave," he said. But she did anyway.

She didn't go far, just outside the door, where she slumped down and sat on the floor, leaning against the wall. Her head fell into her hands and tears began to trickle down her cheeks. She was sure to be quiet so that he wouldn't hear.

Their sins were the same, hers and his. Two different halves of the same sin. And it wasn't so bad for a man. Phillip had ruined four girls—that the world knew of. And he was still welcomed wherever he went—even here, in Stanbrook Abbey.

But for a girl like Angela, living under high expectations and guided by silly romantic optimism, well, it just wasn't the same. She had been ruined, and she had taken her family down with her. Like Phillip, Lord Lucas Frost still roamed free, with no repercussions and, she was sure, without even the slightest twinge of regret.

It had been a warm day, not quite spring and not quite summer, six years earlier. Lucas had been courting her for months, braving some combination of snow, sleet, and frigid temperatures to come call on her. Occasionally he dined with the family, or sometimes he would come just for afternoon tea . . . and her. As the temperature rose, and the ground thawed, so, too, did Angela's feelings for Lucas. That is not to say that she hadn't been half in love with him from the very first moment she saw him at his friend's New Year's Eve ball.

But she got to know him, and he got to know her. They had gone from discreetly holding hands to stealing kisses. This particular afternoon, he suggested a walk through the gardens. They happened upon a clearing in the woods, where they paused to rest on the grass. Resting became kissing, and that became something else.

"What are you doing?" she had asked in a voice that was breathless from his kisses. Lucas, lying on his side to face her, was pushing her skirts up. And then he was unbuttoning his trousers.

"I'm going to make love to you, Angela," he said in a voice just as breathless as her own.

"Oh," she said. That was her consent, a rush of air through her lips. He had never said he loved her, and she so wished he would. Making love, though she was not quite sure what that entailed, sounded just as good to her innocent brain. She didn't know what they were doing, because no one had ever explained it to her. It was a talk one had the night before their wedding, and Lucas had not mentioned a wedding . . .

It hurt a little at first, but it was not an unbearable pain. And then it got quite a bit better. And then it was over.

When it was over, Lucas held her. That had been her favorite part: lying in the arms of the man she loved. The sky was blue above them, the birds sang their usual chirping songs. A warm breeze stole over them. Lucas told her he loved her. She said she loved him, too.

"I had better go talk to your father," Lucas said finally. They dressed and returned to the house. Lucas disappeared into her father's study, behind closed doors. Angela paced in the hall, barely able to contain her joy. She was going to be married! And to the man she loved, who loved her back.

That was, until the study doors burst open, slamming against the wall. The marks were probably still there, but she had no way of knowing for sure, since she hadn't been home since then. She would likely never know, since she had been told not to return.

"How could you, Angela, how could you?" her father had thundered, his face—and his eyes—red. Had her father been crying?

"Papa, I—" She was so confused.

"You're ruined now! Your sisters, too. This whole family! All because of what you did."

"I don't understand. We're going to be married, Papa . . . Aren't we? Lucas?"

"You tell her," her father had said. She noticed then that Lucas sported a black eye.

"I'm already betrothed to another, Angela," Lucas said quietly. She had asked him to repeat his words, just to be sure she had heard them correctly the first time. Alas, her judgment was faulty, not her hearing.

She leaned against the wall. She looked up and saw her two younger sisters, Samantha and Claire, at the top of the stairs, witnessing her shame.

"The contracts were signed before I arrived in your village. I don't love her. I had to do it for my family. I'd break the engagement if I could afford it. But I do love you, Angela."

"If you could afford it?" Angela questioned in a small voice.

"Apparently your dowry is not so grand as he thought," her father said cruelly.

"Why? Why did you do to this to me?" Angela pleaded, looking at Lucas, who was staring intently at his feet. She looked up at her sisters again. She had ruined them, too.

. "I thought it was the only way for us to be together. But we can still be together, Angela. Just not as man and wife."

"Hear that, Angela? His mistress. His whore." Her father spat out the words and refused to look at her.

"Papa, I didn't know!"

"You will leave this house. Go with him, if you want. I don't care. I don't care what you do. And you," her father said, turning to Lucas, "I will see you at dawn."

The loss of her maidenhead was the least of it. It was the loss of her family that she grieved for the most. That and her faith in her own mind, her own feelings, her own actions. She had lost her faith in love. She had lost her faith in just about everything. And she wanted that back. That was why she went to the abbey instead of with Lucas.

Angela wiped a fleet of tears from her cheeks. It had been ages since she had relived that scene in her head. And then she was aware of someone joining her, and she was relieved to see it wasn't Lord Invalid, but Helena.

"What did he do?" she asked, after coming to sit on the floor beside her.

"He said my sins were not that great," Angela said, wiping tears from her eyes and even managing a wry smile. They may have devoted themselves to God and the religious order, but they were still women, they loved to talk, and thus they all knew each other's stories. With Helena, Angela did not have to explain.

"Stupid bounder," Helena said meanly. "And coming from a man like him!"

"What happened?" Penelope asked, joining them on the floor in the hall after setting down the linens she had been carrying.

"Lord Invalid said my sins were trivial."

"Well, did you tell him what had occurred in your past?" Penelope asked.

"No."

"But that doesn't matter," Helena said. "It just goes to show that he has no remorse for ruining all those women."

"And to think I brought him *two* blankets," Penelope muttered. This, coming from the girl that saw the good in everyone and everything, made Angela smile.

"Are you going to go back in there? Or shall I?" Helena offered.

"I will. It might make me feel better to torture him somehow."

"You know it is not up to us to give judgment or punishment to others, but it is up to God," Penelope said gravely.

"Yes, I know," Angela said with a sigh.

"But that ointment stings like the devil, especially if you use a lot of it," Helena added.

~

Clearly, she was a great sinner, Phillip thought. Clearly, he had said the wrong thing. Clearly, he had injured her feelings. But he was not as stupid or as thoughtless as he allowed others to believe, and he knew he hadn't been *that* difficult a patient until that moment, so it had to be something else.

Phillip wondered if they had met before, and if he had done something then. But she was a woman that a man remembered without effort. It couldn't be that. Perhaps he was as stupid and thoughtless as everyone believed him to be.

An apology was certainly in order, if she ever returned. That much he was sure of.

He knew she was just outside the door, for he heard women's voices, although he couldn't hear what they were saying. Phillip knew they were talking about him; only an imbecile would think otherwise. And of course, they were discussing how awful, despicable, and thoughtless he was, and what to do about it.

They could easily poison his food. Or worse, just leave him alone in this room for days or weeks, or however long it took for him to die. Which would do him in first, starvation or boredom or loneliness? Well, that was extreme and a bit ridiculous, Phillip told himself. But the fact remained that he was entirely at Angela's mercy, and he had hurt her.

Damn stupid thing to do.

The door opened.

"I'm sorry," he said immediately. She did not reply, and in her silence he was struck by four troubling thoughts simultaneously.

The first was that she had made him, a nobleman, apologize not once, but twice.

The second was that she had made him, a nobleman, utter the word *please*, not once, but twice.

The third troubling realization was that she had obviously been crying because of something he had said. It probably wasn't the first time he had driven a woman to tears, but it was the first time that he had seen evidence of it. And it was the first time that he felt guilty.

And that was the fourth terrible realization: he genuinely felt like less of a human being, a truly awful one, because he had hurt her. He cared. Thus when he said loudly and clearly, "Please forgive me," he genuinely meant it.

Within a week, she had made significant alterations to his vocabulary and inflicted new emotional states upon him. What on earth would be next?

Rambling. Was that his voice going on and on, trying to make things better? It was indeed: "I did not mean to belittle your sins. I'm sure they are tremendous. And you are quite right about me; any interaction with me must be a great trial. That's what my father always said, anyway. As well as all of our governesses. The servants, too, I'm sure, said as much behind my back. So you are right, and I am wrong and—"

"Please stop," she said, mercifully cutting him off, sounding exasperated, and rightfully so. "You're only making matters worse."

"I was afraid of that." Had he just spoken about his father? He *never* did that, not since the old man saw fit to die and leave Phillip's inheritance to his brother instead. And did he, in effect, just call her a tremendous sinner? What had happened to him? What was wrong with him?

It wasn't just her voice that was bewitching, it was her. He had never been like this before he met her. She was dangerous. And he was unable to leave.

"I appreciate the effort," she said, and he was relieved.

"You're welcome," he answered. And then the curiosity began to grow. What had she done? He couldn't ask. He shouldn't ask. He bit back the words. And Angela, his angel of mercy, offered him a distraction. She bade him to lie back so she could tend to the cut on his forehead, which didn't hurt so much today.

He was disappointed to discover that she didn't deem his broken ribs worth checking on. He would have called her attention to it, but he knew that would be pushing his luck.

Phillip propped himself up on his elbows so he could watch her as she checked on his gunshot wound. Well, mostly he wanted to watch her hands remove all the obstacles on her way to it, pushing the blankets aside but never fully exposing him, and unraveling the bandage. It was healing nicely, he saw. Though he would certainly have yet another scar.

"Do you really need that much ointment?" he asked. "You didn't use as much yesterday."

"I'm sorry, but it's necessary," she said, dabbing it on. Yesterday it had stung, but the pain had been manageable. But today . . .

"Bloody hell, woman, I said I was sorry!"

"Yes, I know. But now I am certain of it." There was the slightest smile of satisfaction on her full, pink mouth. But there was also a trace of sadness in her eyes that had not yet gone away. That ache of remorse returned. In silence, she gathered her things and began to leave.

"Wait," Phillip said, and she paused and turned to look at

him. *Stay here with me,* he wanted to say. But he didn't. He couldn't. And she arched her brow expectantly, and he had to say something. "You took the bell away."

He hadn't seen her do it, but it had vanished, and he had to admit he had abused it, ringing it incessantly, often for no good reason at all other than to see her.

"Yes, I know."

"What if . . ." *What if I need you?* he was about to ask. Instead, he asked, "What if I need something?"

"Do you need something now?"

"No."

"I'll be back."

"Even though I don't deserve it," he finished. But she was already out the door. He closed his eyes and willed himself to sleep, if only to avoid thinking.

⌒

Claude DeRue had said, in his heavy French accent, that fleeing would be futile: Phillip owed him money, so Phillip would pay. Claude DeRue accepted coin and also a man's life, but he preferred coin.

Phillip preferred parting with neither. He had exactly enough in his purse to settle his debt, but that would have left him without a farthing to his name and no way of getting more. Claude DeRue was the end of the line as far as money-lenders went.

It was raining when Phillip stepped off the boat and onto English soil for the first time in four years, but that was unremarkable, as it was always raining here. His eyes scanned the docks for men who might be employed by DeRue who might have been alerted that Phillip had fled. He didn't see them, but they must have seen him.

Phillip found an inn, where he purchased a hot meal and a horse. And then he took off in a rainstorm, in the dead of the night. He headed toward London. He never made it.

The horse's hooves pounded, thudding on as Phillip urged, even though the beast must have been tired by that late hour. The rain had not ceased nor had it gotten heavier. Just a steady, relentless wet. The drumming of the horses became louder, because Phillip was no longer alone: DeRue's men had caught up with him. He would never outrun them now. He would die. This was the last chance in his life to display courage.

Phillip urged the horse to stop, and he turned around to face them. He couldn't see them, but that meant they couldn't see him, either. Hindsight suggested he might have dismounted and silently run off into the night. But no, he turned to face the men who wanted him dead, and he waited, sitting high and still in the saddle. Waiting.

A shot rang out in the night—no questions asked, no opportunity to exchange coin for his life. The horse cried out and bucked, chucking Phillip off the saddle and into a ditch.

Phillip awoke with a start. The drumming of horses' hooves that had seemed so vivid in his dream was nothing more than the heavy beating of his heart. The sound of the rain falling sounded so real in his dream because it was raining now. He looked out the window and was unable to tell if it was just a dark afternoon or late at night.

They had left him for dead. But what would they do if they found out that he had survived? The door was opening, and Phillip felt a fleeting stab of panic that they had found him. But it was only Angela.

Only Angela, a new, different, and strange sort of danger. She didn't make him fear for his life, but for life as he knew it.

"Are you all right?" she asked, for the first time sounding actually concerned for him.

"Fine. Why do you ask?"

"Because you have sustained life-threatening injuries. Why wouldn't I ask?"

"You never asked before," he answered, becoming annoyed at the realization.

"You have never looked like you had seen a ghost before. You're quite pale." She came over to the bed, set down the tray as she always did, and placed her palm on his forehead. He didn't want to enjoy that tender touch, but he did. "You don't have a fever."

"I had a dream," he said, thinking that sounded stupid. "I remembered what happened to me."

"Tell me. I've been wondering," Angela said while lighting a few candles. There was just enough light to illuminate them both, while the rest of the room was cast into the shadows. The sound of the rain against the glass was the only reminder that there was a whole world beyond them and their little patch of candlelight.

"I was brave, or stupid. I'm not sure."

"I have my suspicions, but go on," she answered, sitting on the chair beside his bed. She needn't say more; he knew what she thought.

"Two men were following me, and I stopped my horse and turned to face them. I waited, allowing them a clear shot. I could have run away." The story sounded ridiculous to him as he recounted it. He wasn't brave; he was incredibly foolish and cowardly, if not downright lazy.

But then again, look where he ended up: in a place with a fifty-to-one female-to-male ratio and a very attractive nurse. He might have just been lucky.

"What did they want from you?" Angela asked.

"That depends. Did I arrive here with any money?"

"I don't think so."

"So my debt is settled then. They have my money, and they think they have taken my life as well." He allowed a small sigh of relief and was pleased to find that the pain from his broken ribs was diminishing.

"You were just running from creditors? And I had thought there was a chance you suffered for a more noble reason," she said lightly.

"What, like running down highwaymen?" Phillip asked sarcastically.

"Yes, but I'm glad that wasn't the case."

"Why is that?" One would think that was the sort of thing women would love to hear. How confusing. No wonder he never tried to understand them.

"The real reason makes it easier to dislike you."

"You needed more reasons, other than my blackened

reputation and that I'm a tremendously difficult patient?" he
joked, rather than asking why she was determined to dislike
him. Then she might think he cared or something embar-
rassing like that.

"You do make it easy," Angela said. Of course he did.
Making people dislike him was his sole talent.

"And yet here you are, sitting and talking to me, when you
surely have other things to do," he couldn't resist pointing out.

"You're right. I should be going." She stood to go, and he
was sorry he suggested it. To him, any company was better
than no company. But there was something about *her*. She
didn't try to flatter him, as women often did. Or, when they
weren't flattering him, they were avoiding meeting his gaze
because it had been whispered that he could ruin a woman
with his eyes. Angela wasn't afraid to look him in the eye.

And even though she only cared for him out of duty, it was
more than he had ever gotten from anyone else.

And at the risk of angering her, he dared to ask the question that had plagued him all day, if only on the off chance she
might stay around to answer.

"Angela, are you going to tell me what you did? Your great
sin?"

Her back was to him, as she was on her way out of the
room. She paused with her hand on the doorknob, readying to
pull it shut behind her. She stood there with her back to him
for what seemed like an eternity. One in which he stopped
wondering about her sin to admire the shape of her backside.
And then she turned around.

"There was a man like you in my life, once," she said
coldly, looking into his eyes.

"Like me?"

"Handsome, thoughtless, remorseless. He ruined me, and
because of that, I ruined my family."

Oh.

He looked at her again, this time seeing a fallen angel. She
wasn't any less beautiful, any less angelic. But now he understood: all those cutting remarks, quick retorts, and her admitted

determination to dislike him had very little to do with him at all. They were meant for someone else, and he was similar enough, and just happened to be around to bear the brunt of another man's failing.

Like you. She, like everyone else, confused the reputation with the man. Maybe there wasn't anything different about her at all.

"Do you always take gossip for gospel?" he asked, trying not to sound accusatory but failing. Was there nowhere on this earth he could go to just be himself? Was there anyone who hadn't heard all about him before they met him?

"What's that supposed to mean?" Angela asked, taken aback.

"That you'd rather believe the rumors than seek out the truth. No one has ever bothered to look at me beyond my reputation. You included." That marked the first time that Phillip had put words on that gray, nagging feeling that was always within him. Did anyone ever mention his name without, in the same breath, mentioning all the awful things he had done or was alleged to have done? No. No one ever saw anything about him other than whatever had appeared in the gossip sheets. He didn't like that, to say the least.

"So you did not, in fact, ruin numerous innocent women?" Angela challenged. "You did not gamble away your family's fortune? You have not spent more of your life drunk than sober?"

"I'm just saying that there are two sides to every story, as trite as that may sound." That was true. Some of the things she had accused him of were also true.

"Well, it's not like you've ever bothered to correct anyone's assumptions," she retorted. "Or were you just thinking that if you ignored them, they would go away, just like those girls you ruined?"

"I didn't say I was perfect. Just misunderstood. Overlooked."

"Am I supposed to pity you now?" Angela asked hotly.

"No. Just don't confuse me with the man who ruined you."

"Don't give me reason to."

She stormed out. It was the cowardly way to win an argument. It was practically cheating. And it really wasn't fair, because Phillip was bedridden and did not have the option of quitting while he was ahead.

Tomorrow he would get out of this damned bed if it killed him.

In the meantime, he would sleep. Or try to. *Overlooked*: the word echoed endlessly in his head. What if there was no oversight? What if there really was nothing more to him than a long list of sins?

⌒

Angela often had trouble sleeping, and tonight was no exception. When she did, she always went to the chapel to quiet her thoughts. At this late hour, the sacred chamber was empty and dark, save for a few candles that always remained lit at the foot of a statue depicting the Virgin Mary and baby Jesus.

She knelt before it.

But rather than clasp her hands in prayer and bow her head, she opened the sketchbook she had brought with her. The book, a thick volume with high-quality paper, had been a gift from Lucas Frost. She had brought it with her to the abbey not because of any sentimental attachment but because the act of drawing soothed her, and she so desperately needed soothing. She needed to get lost in line after line of pencil lead on paper, blurring them to make shadows, pressing down hard to make them heavy and dark. She loved all those little lines of worry resulting in a complete picture of something beautiful, something true.

The first page contained a sketch she had done of Lucas before everything had gone wrong. Angela had depicted him sitting comfortably on the settee before the window in the drawing room at her parents' home. If she looked like an angel, Lucas certainly did, too. His hair was dark blond, slightly curled. His eyes were a light blue color. His features were round rather than rough or chiseled but still handsome, still masculine. Still looking up at her from the page, but no longer tempting her. Beyond him, she had drawn the window and the view of the front lawn. Home. An intruder in her home.

The second page contained a drawing of the statue she now sat before. The stone Mary held her stone baby Jesus. The plump baby was wrapped in a blanket. Its mother's smile was slight but serene.

Pages two through forty contained illustrations of this statue. Some were drawn in profile; some were drawn from the far side of the room. Some were just of Mary's face; some were of only the baby. The one Angela worked on now, on page forty-two, was drawn looking up at the figure from down below, where she knelt.

As she worked, Angela wished that she might take back that last hour with Phillip.

In spite of all pride and reason, she had told him about being ruined. Why had she done that? What sort of ninny told a complete stranger that sort of information? To make it worse, Phillip was not a complete stranger; she would have to see him again. It was all too mortifying to contemplate.

Angela knocked her head against the wooden railing before which she knelt. She rubbed her forehead and returned to her drawing, shading in the hood covering Mary's head.

What was even more humiliating was she knew precisely why she told him: because it would mean a few more minutes of conversation. And because she had hoped he would say something really awful, so she could fully and completely hate him. But he didn't. And for a few moments there, he wasn't despicable at all. That was dangerous, for disliking him was her only defense against desire.

She began to outline the baby, resting in its mother's arms. She barely needed to look at her model, for she knew it so well.

They had fought, then, and it had been so long since Angela had argued with someone that she had forgotten how it made her stomach ache. As if embarrassment didn't burn enough. She was really a wreck. And she still had to face him tomorrow.

She drew Mary's hands clasping the baby to her breast. She added shadows and details to make them look real, not like the stone that they were.

Satisfied with her progress on that particular sketch, Angela turned to page forty-one of her journal. There, in the midst of the dozens of depictions of the Virgin Mary and the infant savior of mankind, was a drawing of Phillip. She had done it on one of the days before he had woken up.

In the picture, he slept. She had captured his dark lashes resting on his cheeks. And those cheekbones—like cliffs a girl might throw herself off of in a fit of despair. His mouth, full lips closed, was relaxed without a trace of haughtiness or his devilish grin. A lock of his hair fell like a slash across his forehead. She had even drawn the cut next to it, and shaded around it to depict the bruise. Getting the crooked line of his broken nose right had been a fun challenge.

Even more of a delight had been drawing his bare chest. She had never done that before. His chest was not overly muscled, but there was certainly definition there, and shadows to create. The hair on his chest had been a challenge for her, but looking at the drawing now, she thought she had managed quite nicely.

The Devil Sleeps was the title she had written at the bottom of the page. But after what he had said this evening, she wondered if he was as much of a devil as the rumors claimed he was.

Chapter 3

He was not in bed, where he was supposed to be. Lord Invalid was leaning by the window, taking in the view, when Angela and the abbess arrived the following morning to bring him breakfast.

"Good morning. I didn't realize we were having company. I apologize that I am not dressed to entertain," he said, referring to the fact that was just wearing a shirt, unbuttoned at the collar, and just long enough to cover his smalls. His legs were long and muscular and bare. One held more weight than the other one, which still bore a bandage.

"You're supposed to be in bed!" Angela said. Oh, he was impossible! If he fell, he could injure himself more and thus remain here even longer.

"And as it is cold by the window, I will certainly return to it." Phillip took a step and grimaced at the pain of putting pressure on his injured leg.

"Oh, you are such a bother," Angela muttered, handing the tray to the abbess and crossing the room to help him. She wrapped an arm around his waist, and he draped his arm around her shoulders. In this half embrace, they both froze.

Angela thought the temperature in the room must have spiked a thousand degrees. She suddenly felt hot everywhere, from her cheeks to her toes and everywhere—*everywhere*—in between. A heat so intense it was as if the flames of hell were licking at her heels. Except that it felt so very, very good.

The length of their bodies touched: her thigh to his, her hip to his. Her palm rested on his waist, feeling hard muscles. And if she tilted her head just so, she could rest it on his shoulder. The temptation to do so was great, as was her other impulse to push him away. She did neither.

"Give me some of your weight," she said. "I can take it."

He did, slowly and gently. Together, they took a step toward the bed. And then another, and Angela looked up at him and saw that his mouth was firmly set, his expression one of extreme torment. *Me, too,* she thought, as they took another step. But not for the same reason, she was sure. He couldn't be feeling that same heat, that same hum as she. Desire. Temptation. His hand slid from her shoulder to grasp just below her breasts, and she unwillingly felt the ache of wanting his hand to reach higher.

Together, they took another step toward the bed.

The abbess looked on, her expression inscrutable.

Phillip was rigid beside her, moving slowly. Too slowly. This torment was going on long enough, she thought. Because with every step they took, she remembered just how damned wonderful it was to be held by a man. But Angela wondered if it had felt this amazing when Lucas Frost held her. She couldn't remember, and she couldn't decide if she was glad of the fact that those bittersweet memories were fading or if it was dangerous to forget.

They reached the bed, and Phillip allowed his hand to slide across her back, and down, just brushing her backside as he eased himself into the bed. And that fleeting touch of his hand where it ought not be, especially in front of the abbess, brought Angela back to her senses. What a cad. A scoundrel. Taking liberties when she was helping him!

Angela scowled at him and at his sheepish, unrepentant grin.

"Lord Huntley, I don't believe we've met. I'm Lady Bamford, the abbess here at Stanbrook. I was acquainted with your parents, very long ago."

Phillip nodded. The smile faded at the mention of his parents.

"I do hope Angela has been taking good care of you."

"She does, when she comes around. I don't think I am receiving enough attention. As you have just seen, I am not entirely well just yet."

Oh, she was going to murder him.

"Well, Angela does have other duties here, Lord Huntley, but I'm sure she'll be able to devote a little more time to you. Please ask if there is anything you wish for."

"There is one thing," he said, rubbing his hand along his jaw. "I would really love a shave."

"I'm sure that can be arranged," the abbess said before excusing herself and leaving the room.

"You should go, too," Phillip said to Angela once they were alone. He was dismissing her! Or, even more alarming, was that a stab of disappointment at being asked to leave?

"But I have to check your wounds," Angela said, which was true. She also couldn't believe he was asking her to go.

"They'll still be here later," Phillip answered wearily. "I just need to be alone right now."

Phillip didn't really want her to leave, but he couldn't have her checking a wound that was inches away from his erection. He couldn't even have her in the room, because looking at her was not going to make it go away. Besides, he needed to think, and he couldn't do so with her around.

He had been standing by the window when she arrived along with the abbess. And he didn't have breeches on. That was bad. What was worse was that he saw Angela looking at his bare legs, and he liked it. Worst of all, her looking at him caused him to start to become aroused. In front of the abbess. Without breeches on.

Phillip was then struck with the genius idea to subject himself to extreme pain. So he decided to walk.

And Angela ruined his plans.

She didn't just ruin his plans. No, it rather felt like he was suddenly besieged on all sides from an attack he never saw coming.

That she came over to help him do something as mundane as walk across the room pricked his pride. He was a man, a peer, and he wasn't supposed to need help with anything. And he certainly wasn't supposed to like it.

But how could he not enjoy a beautiful woman pressed up against him? One with lush curves that begged for his touch but were just out of reach. He had taken a deep breath, knowing it would be painful with his broken ribs, and thus a distraction. But he didn't notice the pain, only the faint scent of soap and vanilla and woman.

And when she asked to take some of his weight, when she offered to help . . . well, no one had ever offered to help him before. He wasn't supposed to like it. It was supposed to be a grave insult to his masculinity. But it felt so good.

And then because he was a scoundrel, he couldn't stop himself from slowly caressing her lower back, and just a little bit lower, as he was letting go. She didn't know it, but she got the last laugh. Because that one fleeting touch undid him, until he couldn't help but give in to his arousal.

It was no surprise that the touch of a beautiful woman, whom he could not have, would arouse him. It was just that she aroused something else in him, too. He suspected that something else was his *feelings*. Emotions.

As he already knew, she was dangerous.

He had been attacked from all sides and with no defenses. Literally caught with his pants down. He might have laughed. He could even imagine telling the story for the amusement of his friends over drinks and cards at the club. But it wasn't really that funny to discover that one lusted and even longed for a woman who disliked him. Which didn't even matter at all, because she was a nun.

For the first time in Lord Huntley's life, there was something he wanted, and he suspected he couldn't have it. Oddly enough, it only made him want her more.

⟡

"No, I'll do it," Phillip said to Angela, who had arrived with all the necessary tools for a much-needed shave later that afternoon.

"I'm trying to be helpful," Angela responded impatiently.

"Yes, and I appreciate that. But there is no way I'm letting you near my throat with a razor."

"I expected you would feel that way, which is why I brought this," Angela said, picking up a mirror.

"You're not going to attempt to convince me that you won't hurt me?"

"Breath is precious; I prefer not to waste it."

Phillip grinned at that and then caught himself. He was *not* going to find her amusing. He was now determined *not* to enjoy her company. And above all, he was not going to try to discern the curve of her hips under that awful gray dress she wore. He was not going to admire the golden hue of her hair and wonder how long it was, or how soft it was, or how it would look falling around her face.

"You're staring at me," she said, and he thought that might explain the faint flush across her cheeks.

"Hold the mirror. I'll stare at myself, then." He was sitting up in bed, thinking he had never shaved in bed before. And he placed his hand over hers, holding the mirror, so that he might adjust it to the proper position.

However, it took longer than one might expect, because her hands were soft, and because he forgot to look at his reflection and instead focused his gaze on the strange sight of his hand holding hers. Because it occurred to him that he could just pull her close to him. Close enough to kiss.

"Is it really that hard . . . ?" she asked slightly breathless.

Yes, he thought to himself.

". . . to adjust the mirror and look at your own reflection?" she finished. They were not thinking about the same thing, then. Phillip let go of her hand and devoted his concentration to shaving.

"Talk to me," he said, not comfortable with the silence.

"About what?"

"How long have you been living at the abbey?"

"Six years," she said with a sigh. "Six years, plus one month and twelve days."

Phillip paused to look at her. "Really? You're older than I thought."

"Older and wiser," she replied, meeting his gaze.

"Pity, that," Phillip said lightly. "Keep talking, Angela. I like the sound of your voice." He could say that because he wasn't looking at her.

"Well, then, ask me something."

"Tell me about your family. Brothers? Sisters?"

"One brother, two sisters, all of them younger than me," Angela said. And then she had to change the subject because it made her sad to think of them. "What about your brother? He doesn't know where you are, does he? I can bring you writing instruments to write to him. He is probably worried about you."

"Doubtful. We do not speak, unless it is to argue about something. Although I can't wait for him to see this scar," Phillip said, rubbing his finger over the cut, now fading into a scar, on his forehead, just over his right eye. "He'll be livid."

"Why is that?"

"Because he has one just like it. But mine is bigger. My broken nose is the only thing that distinguishes us. Well, and the fact that he is good, and I am not."

She did not contradict him.

"Anyway," Phillip continued, "we were talking about you. And your siblings. Do you write to them?"

"I receive letters from them occasionally. I rarely write to them, and when I do, my letters are quite brief. I have little to say."

Her letters, like her days, were always the same: *Dear Family, Contemplated my sins, prayed for forgiveness, completed chores at the abbey. Hope you'll forgive me. Love, Angela.* Phillip's presence was the only interesting thing that had happened to her in the past six years, but it felt wrong to write of him in a letter home, when it would only result in more damaging gossip.

"If you have so little to write about, then you really must get out more."

"I can't leave here," Angela said and then paused. "Well, I haven't taken my orders yet, so I guess I could but . . ."

"You haven't taken your orders yet? What does that mean?" He paused in his shaving to look it at her.

"It means I have not yet taken my vows of poverty, obedience, and chastity, and thus fully devoted myself to God and life here in the abbey," Angela answered. Phillip didn't hear anything she said after vow of chastity. He didn't remember anything she had said before that, either, except the part where she had *not* taken a vow of chastity. This struck him as the best news he had heard in years.

And yet she was contemplating it. Foolish woman.

He had been contemplating something else entirely.

"What's stopping you?" He actually hoped that she would answer, *You.*

She gave a little shrug and asked if he was almost finished yet. He was.

"You look almost civilized now," she said. Phillip was not feeling civilized in the slightest. He was contemplating seducing a woman away from her vow of chastity. Or at least seducing her before she took her orders.

Phillip quickly discovered that seducing Angela was one of those thoughts that, once it took hold, it was impossible to let go. After all, someone had to save her from herself, and Phillip thought it might as well be him. There wasn't anyone else around for the job, and he was certainly up for it.

The only problem was that Phillip was not entirely sure how to go about it. Seduction was one thing when he was an able-bodied peer of the realm. It was quite another when he was a bedridden scoundrel, often confused with the loathed man who had ruined her and given her the idea to become a nun.

"Thank you," he said, handing the shaving things back to her. "You must have other things to do." Phillip secretly enjoyed watching her become flustered at his politeness.

"Why are you asking me to leave again?"

"*Almost* civilized, Angela," he said with the slightest smile and lift of his brow.

"Oh," she said, her eyes widening in understanding. She left quickly then. But for the first time in days, he was not bored. He was too occupied with planning his seduction.

That proved more difficult than he had expected.

As long as he was bedridden, his only option was to pull her into the bed with him and take the risk that she would not fall onto the more sensitive parts of his anatomy, which, thanks to his injuries, were numerous. And she was not a small woman, so if she did not take kindly to it, she could easily beat him senseless. That was the more likely scenario, since she hated him.

Clearly, he needed to get well. He also needed to soften her feelings for him. The former would be taken care of by time. As for the latter, Phillip was at a complete loss. A man like him had ruined her once. Angela would not surrender so easily again, and certainly not to a man like him. Phillip cursed the young buck who had ruined her, for that cad might have just ruined Phillip's own chances with her. And then it occurred to Phillip that somewhere there might be a man, or a few men, cursing him for the very same reason. For it was true: Phillip had indeed ruined four women, just like the gossip rags had reported.

⌒

"Where have you been?" Helena whispered when Angela arrived late to supper. She sat in her usual place between Helena and Penelope at one end of the table. Meals were to be taken in silence, but sometimes one could manage a whispered conversation, hidden by the sound of the cutlery on the dishes.

"With Lord Invalid," Angela answered quietly, as she placed her napkin on her lap.

"I thought you brought him his supper after we dined," Penelope said, joining the conversation, pushing a strand of her red hair out of her face.

"I do. And I will later, but just now I was with him while he was shaving," Angela explained. And then she took a bite of her mutton stew, and then another, before she realized that both of her friends were staring at her silently.

"What?" Angela asked, looking at them. She noticed Sister Bethany and Sister Agnes, seated across the table, staring at her curiously as well.

"You have been spending a lot of time with him," Penelope said. "It's very compassionate of you. He is probably not used to the solitude here, as we are."

"I simply stay with him while he takes his meals, because it's easier than making numerous trips," Angela said. "And it is pleasant to have company during a meal, most of the time," she added pointedly to her friends.

"Aye, and you keep him company while he shaves. And what's next? Washing his back during a bath? That's a lot of time to spend with someone you don't like. Unless, of course, you are starting to develop feelings for the scoundrel," Helena said accusingly, as if it were wrong to feel anything for a man other than disdain.

"I'll confess that he is not as awful as he was at first, but I certainly don't *like* him," Angela replied. She didn't. But she had caught herself enjoying his company far too much, now that she thought about it. But she wouldn't tell her friends that.

"Well, I hope you are only talking to the man and not allowing him liberties."

"He's bedridden. What can he do?" Angela retorted.

"He's a scoundrel, and everyone knows it. It's a question of what he won't do."

"He doesn't like that people assume all the gossip about him is true," Angela whispered back in an effort to change the direction of the conversation away from herself. But her friends' eyebrows arched up in shock and curiosity.

"Well, is it?" Penelope dared to ask. Even Sister Bethany seemed interested in hearing the answer.

"I actually haven't really asked," Angela replied truthfully, mostly because she wasn't sure if she wanted to know. And Helena, she was sure, would hate him even if it were all a lie.

"So maybe it's not," Helena answered with a shrug. "But *has* he taken any liberties with you?"

"He hasn't." Angela took a big bite of food so that she wouldn't be able to say anything else like, oh, that she wished he would kiss her.

It wasn't him in particular; she was sure of that, or she tried to be sure of that. It was just that having a man around reminded her of all the happiness she had shared with Lucas before it all went so horribly wrong. She had enjoyed a man's kiss and his touch before. And lately those memories and the longing to enjoy them again had become more palpable and more memorable than the horrible aftermath.

Chapter 4

"*You* are an excellent nurse, Angela. He is healing nicely," Dr. Hastings said after checking on Phillip's injuries. It had been a week since the doctor had visited during Phillip's first few days when he was unconscious and suffering from a fever. Phillip recalled nothing of the first three days he had spent in the abbey.

"At this point, I see no reason why he can't get out of bed," the doctor continued, "although he might require the assistance of a cane to walk at first."

"Perhaps it would be best if he stayed abed for a few days longer," Angela suggested, to Phillip's surprise.

"I thought you were praying for my quick departure," he said, noting that now the doctor and abbess seemed intrigued.

"I am. But if you walk before you are ready, you risk doing further injury to yourself, requiring a longer stay." The abbess placed her arm on Angela's, as if to quiet her.

"She does have a point," Dr. Hastings said thoughtfully.

"What about a bath then?" Phillip asked. He had been bedridden for nearly a week now, and he was becoming damned uncomfortable with it.

"That should be fine, too," the doctor answered. "Just be careful."

"Angela," the abbess said, "please have Penelope help you prepare a bath for Lord Huntley." Angela nodded and quit the room.

"I must advise against any strenuous activity," Dr. Hastings added. "At least for a few more days."

"Take all the time you need, Lord Huntley," the abbess offered generously.

"If there are no more questions, I'll be off then," the doctor said, while packing his equipment. He departed shortly thereafter. The abbess, however, remained.

"Lord Huntley, if I may have a word with you," the abbess said in a tone that did not allow him to refuse.

"Of course, madame."

"Call me Lady Katherine. When I said you may stay as long as you feel is necessary, I do mean that." She had strolled across the room to stand by the window.

"That's very generous of you."

"Of course, you would be staying for reasons relating to your health. I can't imagine any other reason why you might wish to stay. Can you?" She turned to look at him sharply, and even he couldn't miss what she was hinting at.

Yes. "Well, I—"

"Angela is very dear to us. I should hate for her to be hurt." *Translation: keep your hands to yourself.*

"Again," Phillip added.

"I beg your pardon?"

"You would hate for her to be hurt again," Phillip added. And then to answer the unspoken question, "Yes, she told me about the incident."

"She did?" the abbess asked, obviously shocked for a moment before recovering herself. "She was here for a year before she confided in me. I suppose she is closer to making peace with that catastrophic situation."

"Catastrophic?"

"I see she hasn't told you everything."

"Apparently not," Phillip said dryly. There was more, and

he didn't know what it was. And he had nothing to do all day but wonder about what that something else must be.

"Nevertheless, my point is that she had been grievously injured by a man like you. It is my wish that you should remember that. Be gentle with her, Lord Huntley. It is not easy for her to be around you." *A man like you.*

"So tell me, Lady Katherine. Would you give this lecture to any man, or just me?"

"I would give the lecture to any man who looks at Angela the way you do." And with that, the abbess gave him a curt nod and quit the room before he could even try to get the last word in.

Angela cast furtive glances up and down the hall, and was relieved to see that no one was around. She felt her cheeks become hot merely at the thought of what she was about to do. But once the idea of catching a glimpse of Phillip in the bath occurred to her, she found herself at a loss to think of anything else. She may have been ruined, but she had never seen a naked man. She felt guilty for what she was about to do, but Angela also felt this was owed to her. Just a peek.

She shouldn't do it. She was going to do it.

She twisted the knob slowly, and quietly opened the door just a bit. Just enough for her to see into the room. Just enough to see Phillip in the bath.

His back was toward her, and she was relieved. If he caught her attempting to sneak into his room, she would lie and say she thought he might be sleeping and didn't want to wake him, because he was such a bother when he was awake.

Angela watched as he poured water over his head to rinse his hair. The water slid over his shoulders—really broad, muscled shoulders. The water glided down his back, which was smooth and strong. Some water even spilled onto the floor, and Angela did not even dwell for a second on thoughts of cleaning it up.

He lifted his arm to run his fingers through his hair, and she was riveted at the sight of the muscles on his smooth, bare back rippling as he moved.

She couldn't restrain a sigh.

Phillip looked over his shoulder at her. His hair was pushed back, showing off his strong profile: the sharp, slanting cheekbones, the broken nose, the wet eyelashes almost hiding his dark brown eyes, the full yet firm mouth curving into a half smile.

Then she made the grave mistake of looking into his eyes. For a moment, he didn't move, and neither did she. They just looked into each other's eyes.

She wished he would stay in that pose, so she might draw him. Instead she memorized the scene before her to record it later, and have this image to gaze upon forever.

She didn't move. Couldn't move, really. Angela felt like she was melting. She felt like she was nothing more than a puddle on the floor, not unlike the ones that surrounded the tub. She was melting, melting into nothing more than a mess to be mopped up. But she wasn't a puddle. She was a fallen woman, preparing for a lifetime of chastity by spying on a handsome, dangerous, naked man.

Phillip turned around, once again presenting her with his back.

Still, she did not move.

"Come in, Angela, before someone sees you skulking in the hall," he commanded. She did, if only so as not to be caught spying on him. She did have the presence of mind to leave the door open, for she had long ago learned that closed doors lead to one's downfall.

"I, um, brought you some things. A towel, fresh clothes, and some clean sheets for the bed." At the mention of the bed, her cheeks reddened, and she was glad that he was still not looking at her.

"Thank you."

"I'll just, um . . ." she took a deep breath. "You stay there until I am done changing the sheets."

"Yes, ma'am."

She was just finishing up when the sound of water pouring over the edge of the bathtub caused her to look up suddenly and instinctively. *Oh, Jesus,* she prayed, *help me.*

He stood tall, mercifully with his back to her. But that was torment and temptation enough. She prayed for divine intervention, but with an equal fervor she wanted to be a drop of water on his skin, slowly traveling from his neck, caressing his back, sliding down lower over his firm backside, down his sculpted legs, and lower still until she was nothing but one drop of water among the pool at his feet.

"The towel, please," he reminded her, glancing over his shoulder. She saw his mouth curl into that devilish grin. "Unless you want me to turn around."

"I'd rather you didn't," she replied. She held the towel out to him from an arm's length away, very careful to keep her eyes focused above his waist. She thought about closing her eyes entirely, but she could not make her body obey her brain. So Angela remained and watched as Phillip used the towel to dry his hair, his back, and his chest, before wrapping it around his waist. When he turned, she noticed the unmistakable bulge of his arousal. Her heart beat faster.

Stepping out of the bathtub made him grimace and swear, presumably in pain. And then he just stood there for a moment, as did she. They were both thinking the same thing, she was sure, recalling that half embrace as she had helped him walk across the room the day before. And it dawned on her then that it might have affected him the same way it had her.

"I have to do this by myself," he said finally, taking a step toward her. He winced as he took a step with his injured leg. Angela looked into his dark eyes and took a step back. That drew a slight smile to his lips as if to say, "I see what you are doing." He took another step, and so did she.

One step forward for him meant one step backward for her. All the while, his eyes were focused on hers. And even though they did not touch, she felt as if his hands were actually upon her. It was suddenly too hot in the room; her skin became intensely sensitive, and it made her want to rip off her dress, with its itchy wool fabric rough against her skin when it should be his hands upon her bare skin.

One more step and then another, until Angela, oblivious to all of her surroundings but him, bumped against the bed and fell to sit upon it. The shock of it jolted her back to the reality of the situation: she was on a bed, with a mostly naked man, a very bad naked man, approaching. The most dangerous thing of all was that she desired him. She trusted herself to say no if it came to that. She did not trust herself to mean it.

Angela stood quickly, just as Phillip took another step closer to the bed. She bumped into him, he grasped her to steady them both, but it wasn't enough to stop their fall.

She landed on her back, on the bed, with a stunningly handsome, oh so bad, and utterly dangerous man on top of her. One of his hands was placed beside her head, another was wrapped around her waist. She felt his arousal against her, between her legs, just as she felt an intense surge of heat and desire. She did not move. She did not dare speak out of fear that she would say what she was thinking instead of what she ought to say. All she could think was, *Kiss me*.

"I'm sorry," Phillip whispered. His mouth was near her neck, his breath stole across her skin. It made her shiver. It made her arch her back so that he might remove his arm, which he did. With one hand on either side of her, he pushed himself up, and Angela immediately missed the loss of his weight upon her.

Oh, but he didn't move away just yet. He looked into her eyes, and she saw his gaze then drop to her mouth. She parted her lips to speak, to say, *Don't kiss me, because we shouldn't, and I can't trust myself to stop you.* But she didn't.

She placed her hands on his chest as if to push him away but not managing to apply the necessary pressure. She closed her eyes. And she felt him lean in closer. His lips were not on hers, but so close that she could feel his breath on her lips. All she had to do was lift her head a fraction of an inch for the kiss.

Just one kiss, whispered temptation. Years ago she remembered wondering what the harm was in just one kiss. She couldn't see it, and so she had done it, but it didn't stop at just one kiss. No, she was older and wiser now. And just one kiss was a lie, an illusion, and a step off the ledge. Angela knew how kisses ended. But the temptation remained.

All the vows of chastity and hours spent in contemplation

and prayer could not erase the desire to be held, to be touched, to be kissed, to be loved in such an earthly way. With his arms around her and his weight on top of her, she felt closer to being whole. And she wondered if Lucas had been rougher or crueler to her, would she feel this. But she had loved him and never doubted his love for her, and he had shown her the potential for pleasure. Lucas just hadn't satisfied it.

And then Phillip groaned and rolled to the side. Without him on top of her, or touching her, the haze in her mind cleared. She quickly stood up and turned away from him so that he could not see her face, which she knew was flushed. She took a deep breath and then another before turning around, and she saw that she had not waited long enough.

He lay on the bed, his arms behind his head. His eyes were closed.

"You're trouble," he said, opening his eyes and turning to look at her.

"Not as much as you are." She walked around the bed to the table beside it, where she had left the linen and ointment and all the things for tending to him.

"Where did you put my clothes?" he asked.

"They should be on the bed," she said, rearranging the things on the table.

"Perhaps you could close the door," he said.

"Of course," Angela replied. When she did close the door, she was safe on the other side. She picked up her skirts and ran down the hall, down the stairs, and through the door to the garden.

~

Phillip, dressed and standing by the open window, saw her run outside. It seemed they both had the same need for cold air to cool heated skin and clear muddled minds. At this moment he keenly craved a brandy and a cigar with a nearly palpable intensity. Like most men, Phillip was conditioned to use brandy to help with thinking . . . or rather, to help stop thinking.

Stop.

He had stopped.

He had stopped before, when the girl told him to. He wasn't *that* despicable. But, in all frankness, it was a rare occurrence that a woman denied him. And this afternoon marked the first time that he had denied himself. He had felt her shiver with desire beneath him. She had not pushed him away. But he had stopped anyway. Stopped so close that he could almost taste her.

Angela, luscious and soft beneath him, had placed her hands on his chest, closed her eyes, and parted her lips. He almost lost himself on the spot. That, too, was new. It usually took a little more time, and a lot more than an almost kiss to get close to his release.

It was just that she had closed her eyes so as not to look at him. And he thought of the rumors, greatly exaggerated, that he could ruin a woman with his eyes. And then he heard the abbess's voice his head: "*I would give this lecture to any man who looks at Angela the way you do. Don't hurt her. Again.*"

It was the *again* that got to him. It did not matter to him if she was innocent or not; he would be the biggest hypocrite in the world if he did care about that. It was just that he felt like he was always hitting his head against low expectations. And his reputation. *A man like you.*

But he had stopped. If he really was the man they thought him to be, she wouldn't be out in the cold right now. She would be in bed with him. But if he wasn't that man, then who was he? And what was it about that woman that made him think of these things?

As he already knew, that woman was bewitching and dangerous. She was also a danger to herself, sitting out there in the cold, making no effort to move, even though it had begun to rain.

He leaned out of the window and shouted her name: "Angela!"

She looked up.

"Come inside."

She nodded and stood and walked into the abbey, but she did not come to his room that night.

Chapter 5

"*Good* morning, my lord." At the strange and unexpected voice, Phillip opened his eyes to see a very young girl with flaming red hair and dark brown eyes. She reminded him a bit of Emilia Highhart. Well, Emilia Kensington now. The one time Phillip had planned on marrying a chit after being caught in a compromising position, it didn't work out. Instead, she married his twin, which was just as well. Devon was the one she had wanted all along, not him.

"Who are you?" Phillip asked.

"Penelope. I brought you breakfast."

"Where is Angela?" he asked. His first thought was that she might have fallen ill after spending so much time in the cold and the rain yesterday. The possibility had him worried. His second thought was no consolation: she was avoiding him after what had happened yesterday afternoon.

"She is in the chapel," Penelope answered, bringing a tray over to him. Phillip then recognized her as the nun that had brought him two blankets when he had asked for one. He liked her.

"What is she doing there?"

"Praying, my lord. It's what one does in a chapel," Penelope answered gravely, but the gleam of amusement in her eyes didn't escape him.

"Right," he answered. He suspected that Angela thought their moment yesterday was a sin that needed to be confessed, and that she was praying for forgiveness. But nothing had happened, really, much to his frustration.

"Can I get you anything else?" Penelope asked sweetly. She was so much nicer and obliging than Angela. He missed Angela.

"Directions to the chapel," he answered.

"What for?"

"Perhaps I have some praying to do."

Penelope laughed. "I'm sorry, my lord. I just—"

"You caught me in a lie," he admitted, grinning sheepishly at her. "I want to see Angela."

"She's not avoiding you, if that's what you're wondering," Penelope said, lowering her voice. "When I didn't see her in the kitchen this morning, I looked for her and found her in the chapel. I didn't want to disturb her. And I thought you didn't want to wait any longer for breakfast."

"That's considerate of you."

"Thank you, my lord."

"How old are you?" he asked curiously.

"Nineteen."

"And you're a nun? Took your orders and everything? Aren't you quite young for that?"

"If I hadn't promised myself to God, I would have promised to be some man's wife by this age. Both are lifelong commitments."

"Indeed. But . . ."

"Sometimes, Lord Huntley, one just *knows* what they are to do. In fact, I am inclined to think that one always knows their path, but that pain and struggle come from denying the truth one already knows."

"You're awfully young to be dispensing such wisdom."

"And you're awfully old to not already know that. Finish your breakfast, and I will walk to the chapel with you."

⁓

Penelope left Phillip at the doorway to the chapel. He paused before entering, irrationally fearing the place might erupt in flames if he stepped inside. His only concern was that Angela would be caught in the fire.

She was kneeling before the altar, particularly before a statue of a mother and child, surrounded by lit candles, the light of which made her hair glow as if it were spun gold. Phillip watched for a while until the urge to be near her won over the thought that he shouldn't disturb her. So he began the long walk down the aisle. His injured leg was in agonies now, and he occasionally leaned against a pew for a momentary respite. Kneeling down beside her was excruciating, but he didn't allow the pain to stop him.

"What are we praying for?" He leaned in to whisper the question to her. She looked up suddenly, shocked to find him here, of course. But then she turned and bowed her head again.

"We are praying that I may master and stifle my desire," she answered without looking at him.

"I am not praying for that," he said. "Quite the opposite, in fact."

"Which is why I must," she answered, bowing her head.

"Is this because of what happened yesterday? All you did was break my fall."

"But I wanted something to happen," Angela confessed. He really ought not to feel such joy at her pain. And he wouldn't have, had it been anything else. But he desired her, and she him, and now there couldn't be anything to stop them . . . except for her guilt and her thinking it was a sin and her looming vow of chastity.

"Me, too," he answered.

"But you stopped."

"That's a problem?"

"Yes. No. It's just, well, you're *you*." He winced at her

words, and she saw that. A look of something like guilt or concern took over her features. But they both knew that she was only being honest.

Phillip had never given a damn what people said about him, even when they spread horrid lies, or even when they whispered the truth of what he had done in drawing rooms and ballrooms all over town. But now he was really beginning to hate everything he had done in his entire life until he entered this abbey. It struck him all as monstrously unfair: she was changing him, and she couldn't see it. What, then, was it all for?

"You're you," she repeated and continued. "You're worse than a rake; you are an absolute scoundrel. You could stop yourself, and I, who am preparing for a lifetime of chastity, could not. Don't you see?"

"I do," Phillip said after a moment. "You want me to leave."

"Yes and no," Angela said. Phillip restrained himself from groaning and rolling his eyes. Women. Couldn't they make up their minds? Say what they mean?

"Angela," he said patiently, "I can't do both."

"I have been here for six years, and I had thought myself cured of desire. But I know now that it was only because there was nothing here to tempt me. And then you arrived," she said, pausing to allow a bittersweet smile to form on her lips.

"You want me to stay here, tempting you, so you can refuse me," Phillip supplied. She didn't answer, just lowered her head. "That strikes me as quite unfair," he said, "or at the very least, torment for me."

He turned to look at her then. And all he saw was the way she had looked below him yesterday: soft, curved, luscious, wanting. Something stirred inside him. He knew very well the desire she spoke of. A deliciously wicked idea occurred to him.

"As you pointed out the other day, my club membership has likely expired. Since I have nothing to do and nowhere to go, I shall stay and help you overcome your desire."

That captured her attention. She turned to look at him,

wide-eyed, with lips slightly parted in surprise. "What are you going to do?" she wondered aloud, looking terrified and yet curious, too.

Phillip leaned in to her, allowing his cheek to caress hers as he whispered into her ear, "I'm going to tempt you, Angela."

"You are a very wicked man," she whispered back.

Or a bloody stupid man, Phillip thought to himself. His heart was pounding, and his breathing was dangerous, for he was intoxicated by the scent of her. He became light-headed, as blood abandoned his brain for another part of his anatomy. He was about to take back his offer when she spoke.

"Very well. I accept. And you shouldn't be walking so much just yet. We should get you back to bed."

Phillip groaned quietly and lowered his head. "I need a moment first."

It was only for the noble purpose of assisting Angela on her spiritual journey that Phillip allowed her to wrap her arm around his waist to help him walk. For the same reason, he placed his arm around her, resting his hand just below her breast. She softened, and then straightened her spine. Phillip slid his hand down her side, leaving it to rest on her hip.

"You are a scoundrel."

"I never denied it."

In this completely torturous half embrace, they walked down the aisle. They exited the chapel and began the long walk back to his room. No one had put much thought into decorating the place. The hallways were long and winding, with stone floors to match the walls. Small, randomly placed windows provided some light, as did the occasional sconce.

"I'm not feeling tempted," Angela said. Phillip wasn't sure if she was glad of the fact or prompting him to take some liberty with her. He decided to pursue the latter.

"We could pause here in this dark corner," he said, leaning against one wall, and pulling her close to him. He loosed his grip on her, so she was free to walk away. But no, she stayed.

"And then what?" she whispered, leaning against him.

Phillip took a moment to rest his cheek on the top of her head before he answered. She leaned back slightly to look up at him. He could kiss her now, if he wanted. But for the first time he thought of the consequences: she might hate him more or hate him less. But something would change, and he wasn't sure he wanted it to. "Nothing," he said, smiling devilishly at her. "My leg was tired. I just needed to rest for a moment."

"Scoundrel."

"Or perhaps not," he said with a lift of his brow. Angela merely scowled in response.

They continued on in silence up a short flight of stairs, down another long corridor, before taking a left, then a right, then pausing at another flight of stairs.

"By now you must be regretting your decision to visit me in the chapel," Angela said. Phillip couldn't help but lean against her a little more, thankful she was there, as he eyed the stairs. It was not so much the prospect of physical pain that gave him pause but what was waiting for him at the top of the stairs: nothing. He'd get into bed because of his damned injury, and Angela would leave to attend to other chores, and he would sit there, bored out of his mind. The only thing he had interest in thinking about was how to tempt Angela, but he feared he would end up more tempted and tormented than she.

"I just need to sit here for a moment," he said, lowering himself to sit on one of the steps. She did not join him.

"You really shouldn't have gone walking so far just yet," Angela scolded, standing before him with her arms akimbo.

"It was worth it." He looked up at her. Her hands resting on her hips drew his attention there. He allowed his gaze to travel higher, to linger on the place where her dress clung to the swells of her breasts. The woman was all curves, he noticed. Phillip looked up to her face and noticed the curves continued: the soft, round cheeks; the plump lips; the curling eyelashes; the arched brows. The expression on her face revealed that she was concerned, presumably for him. Phillip could not recall anyone ever looking at him in such a way: caring. About him. Even though he didn't really deserve it.

That look, to him, felt like a glass of cold water after months in the desert.

He could get used to having someone care for him, he thought. Especially if that someone was Angela. Wanting such an impossibility was stupid. It was terrifying. It was time to change the subject.

"That is a really awful dress," he said, hoping she would scowl or glare at him instead. Anything other than a look of care and concern. But she just smiled.

"I know," she said. "I miss silk and satin because this itches horribly."

"You could take it off," Phillip suggested, smiling because he made her scowl.

"I certainly will," she answered to his surprise. "Just not when you are around."

"I'm supposed to be tempting you. Not the other way around."

"I wasn't trying to tempt you," she protested.

"But you do, Angela. You do."

They made it back to his chamber without any other incidents. Phillip couldn't help but sigh when he returned to his bed. It was a sigh of relief at having the weight off of his leg, but also one of disappointment.

"What is it now?" Angela asked.

"I'm bored," he said. Just looking around his chamber bored him. There was little there by way of distraction: stone walls, stone floors, a few pieces of furniture, a carving of Christ on the cross above his bed. The view from the window consisted of little more than fields.

"You could sleep," she suggested.

"I'm not tired."

"Would you like a book?"

"Have you got anything to read here other than the Bible?"

"It would do you good to read some scripture."

"Exactly. So I would prefer something else."

"I'll see what is lying about," Angela said and then she paused in the doorway before leaving. "Is there anything else you'd like?"

"Yes, actually," Phillip replied, an idea forming in his mind. "A deck of cards."

～

Angela returned after supper with some old newspapers, which was the only reading material she could find that was not the Bible. Of course, she couldn't resist bringing a copy of the Good Book to him as well. She also managed to procure a deck of cards.

He showed no interest in the other things, but she could swear his face lit up when he saw the deck. Phillip took them immediately, sliding them out of the case. He shuffled them, sifting them through his fingers, smiling, presumably, at the pleasure of them in his hands.

"It's just a deck of cards," she said, lighting a few more candles in the candelabra on the bedside table.

"No, it's more," he answered, taking one card out at random. "Ace of diamonds. I played this card to win a horse, Rags to Riches, from Lord Wexford, and then I entered her in Ascot and won six thousand pounds. God, she was a magnificent animal. I then lost the horse that night to Lord Pommeroy in a game because of the four of clubs," Phillip said, setting that card out of the deck.

Phillip drew another card at random. Angela saw it was the nine of hearts. "Ah, this one caused me to lose my hunting box up in Scotland."

"You lost a house?"

"It was practically in Scotland," Phillip said with a shrug. "What a Frenchman wants with it, I know not. But he has it now, unless he lost it to someone else." He drew another card. "Jack of hearts. Won me Lord Vincent's entire store of wine and brandy. That's long gone, of course. I could have sold it for a fortune."

"But you drank it," Angela said bluntly.

"I had some help."

"Of course."

"The two of diamonds," Phillip said with an impassive expression as he set the card down before him. "Had I not cheated, I would have drawn this card, and have won thousands of pounds and Viscount Althorp's boat."

"But you lost."

"Oh no, I won anyway. But then I got caught because of this card, the jack of spades."

"Was he the one who shot you? You mentioned that one scar was from a duel over a game of cards."

"He challenged me, yes. But I shot myself."

"You did what?"

"I was drunk out of my mind. Hadn't slept. It had been raining. I tripped and fell on my pistol."

"Oh."

"Rather shameful, I know. Fled to Paris once I recovered. That wasn't so bad, because they had card games there, too." Phillip began to shuffle the cards as he spoke. "But my inheritance was gone at that point. No, I didn't lose it. It went to my brother instead of me. To keep playing I had to borrow money from, well, doesn't matter who. Badly in debt, I kept wagering, trying to win it back. It was this card," he removed the two of hearts, "that was dealt to me. I won exactly enough to settle my debt."

"You didn't pay your creditors, and they came after you," Angela supplied.

"Yes. And now my debt is settled. And I haven't a penny to my name."

"Your life is in those cards," Angela said, looking down at the bed where Phillip had set out the selection of cards with stories. He gathered them all up. There was a snap and a whoosh as Phillip shuffled the full deck.

"Pathetic as that may be, I suppose it's true. Should we keep the tradition going?"

"What do you mean?"

"Sit down," Phillip said, motioning for her to sit at the foot of the bed, which she did. "We're going to play."

"But I don't know how."

"I'll explain the game to you. Playing is the easy part; it's winning that is a bit of a challenge." Phillip then explained the objective and rules of vingt-et-un, the easiest game he knew. They engaged in a few practice games first.

"We have to wager something," Phillip said, shuffling the deck once more in preparation to deal.

"You have no money," Angela pointed out, "And I haven't, either."

"Good point," Phillip conceded. "We could wager articles of clothing."

"We absolutely cannot."

"Yes, I suppose that would be unfair to you, as you have already seen me naked."

"That's not why, and you know it," Angela said, adjusting her position at the foot of the bed. "Besides, gambling is a sin."

"Is it?" he remarked idly. "There are so many, I can't seem to keep track of them."

"It is," Angela repeated firmly.

"But confessions are not sins, am I correct?" he asked, and she eyed him warily, wondering as to his point.

"One confesses sins, so no, they are not bad," she had to agree.

"And trading is not a sin?" he queried.

"No," she answered honestly.

"So what if we traded confessions, depending upon who wins or loses the game?"

"Well, don't you have a gift for twisted logic?"

"So is that a yes? Say yes, Angela." And then he grinned at her, and she couldn't say no.

"Fine. Yes. Whoever loses must confess to a sin or a secret."

"And the person who wins gets to ask the question," Phillip added.

"I fear this shall not be fair to me. You have more experience than I do."

"Yes," he answered, "but I also have bad luck." With that, he gave the cards one last shuffle before dealing them out. Angela looked at the cards in her hand and saw a four and a three.

"I'll take another," she said. He dealt her a king. She decided to play it safe. Seventeen was close enough to twenty-one for her.

"Show." Phillip set down eighteen. He had won.

"So much for beginner's luck," she grumbled. "What is your question for me?"

He regarded her for a moment, undoubtedly pondering his options, before he spoke. In that moment, she grew nervous. Surely, he would ask her about being ruined, and she wasn't sure how she would answer.

"How old are you?"

"That's all?" she asked, and he nodded. "I am three and twenty years old."

"You're quite young," he said and then dealt another hand. They each drew another card from the deck, presenting three cards each. His totaled nineteen this time, hers, twenty. She knew then why he had paused for a moment before asking his question. There were so many she wanted to ask, it was hard to decide which one to ask first. And there were so many delicate questions, but she didn't want to ask about something very painful, lest the game be over before it had begun.

"Do you have a mistress?"

"At the moment, no."

"No one you left behind in Paris?"

"That's another question. But the answer is no." He dealt again. She lost the next round. Phillip asked her a question she expected.

"Who was he?"

"Lord Lucas Frost." She said the name aloud for the first time in six years. She braced herself for a wave of regret or nostalgia or something to come over her, and felt nothing. A lock of Phillip's hair had fallen across his forehead, into his eyes, squinting slightly as he tried to place the name, and she wanted to brush it back. But she didn't.

"I don't know him," he said finally.

"And I wish I never had," she answered.

Phillip dealt again. Angela did not need to draw another card. Phillip did, and he lost.

"Have you ever been in love?" she asked.

"No," he answered quickly and surely.

"Really?" she asked skeptically. "Not even once?"

"Angela, do I seem like the sort of man who falls victim to love? I'm selfish and self-absorbed. I've been called heartless by more than one woman."

"You do seem like a man who leaves a trail of broken hearts in your wake. One of them could have been your own, though."

"Well, it hasn't happened," he said plainly.

"Yet," Angela added as he dealt another round.

"Don't get your hopes up," he said, this time looking intently into her eyes for a second. "Mine aren't. Would you like another card?"

"Please."

She lost that round.

"I thought you had back luck," she grumbled.

"I do. Apparently, yours is worse," Phillip said, grinning. "Since we're speaking about love, were you in love with him?" There was, of course, no need to specify which "him" Phillip was asking about.

"I'm not sure I know anymore," she answered truthfully. "When I think back, what is most vivid to me is the horrible aftermath. But I must have loved him to have lost my head so completely. I must have been so high to have fallen so low."

"Or it could just be an excuse. A justification. People are always using love to justify extreme or foolish actions. Hell, that's the one excuse I haven't used."

"Maybe it would be a justification. I'm not sure I know. But I do know that the whole world seemed like a brighter, better place when he was around. All he had to do was smile at me, and I would forget my own name. He was that . . . intoxicating. My heart beat faster every time he was near. And maybe I didn't even see him. I recall standing in a ball, and without turning around, I just knew he was there behind me because my heart thudded and my knees became weak. I was just so blinded by the reaction he inspired in me that I didn't think to question his intentions. He made me feel so very alive, until he made me wish I was dead." Angela felt ashamed to have spoken so much. And appalled that all those words had just fallen out of her mouth, and she couldn't stop them. But she was sad, too, because as she spoke of those feelings, she missed them with an intensity she did not expect.

"What were his intentions?" Phillip asked with a lift of his brow.

"You'll have to win another round for the answer to that one," she said. And then he did win another round and asked that question again. And she answered.

"He was visiting the neighborhood. He stayed for a few months and neglected to mention that he was betrothed. The friend that he was staying with didn't even know. The families had arranged it when he was quite young, and it was not a well-known fact. But there was no way for him to get out of it, at least not without severe consequences. It didn't stop him from allowing me to believe that he was unspoken for, that we might wed. So he didn't love me enough, if he even did at all."

"He might have," Phillip said. "But men in our station . . . You did mention he was a lord?"

"Yes. Viscount Frost."

"Men in our position are raised to put the title, the estate, and the legacy first. It's beaten into us, sometimes even literally. We are not ourselves; we are just the next in line to carry on the tradition, and we sure as hell better not be the last in the line."

"Did your father beat you?"

"No. He didn't care enough," Phillip said, sounding as if he didn't care, either. His gaze was focused upon the cards in his hand that he had recently dealt. They showed their cards, and Angela won.

"Did you really ruin all those women?" she asked. She had assumed the rumors were true at first, until he had asked her if she always "took gossip for gospel" and until she had gotten to know him better. But then she had wondered about the truth, and she wondered if she even wanted to know it. But she couldn't help but ask, now that she had the perfect opportunity.

"Define 'ruin,' " Phillip said evasively, and her heart sank a little.

"Were their marriage prospects destroyed because of a liaison with you?"

"Do you really want to know the answer to that, Angela?" His voice was low, warning her.

"I do," she said. Now she was quite sure.

"Yes, I did ruin four women." Was that a stab of disappointment she felt? Had she dared to hope that it had been gossip? And what did it matter what she felt, anyway?

"Why didn't you stop at just one?" It wasn't her turn to ask another question, but she did, and to her surprise, he answered.

"Honestly? Because there was nothing stopping me."

"But what about honor? Integrity? Or compassion at the very least?" she asked, aghast that those things had not crossed his mind.

"I told you, I am selfish. I am shallow. I was going to inherit one of the oldest and most powerful titles in England. No one was going to cross me." It was most likely the truth, and not very comforting at all.

"Deal the cards, because I have another question," Angela said coldly. He did, and her cards totaled nineteen. The spirit of gambling took over her. She wanted her prize, an answer to her question. So she played recklessly and drew another card, a king, which put her over twenty-one. She had lost. Phillip set down eighteen. She could have won.

"Why have you not taken your orders yet?" he asked. That question caught her off guard.

"I . . . I . . . don't know," she stammered, picking up the cards to hand back to him. Their fingers brushed, and she quickly pulled her hand away.

"I'm pretty sure you know, Angela."

"It's a big commitment. I want to be absolutely certain first," she answered, folding her hands in her lap.

"It took you a few months to commit, in a manner of speaking, to being a man's wife. That, too, is a lifelong obligation. And yet you have been here for years . . ."

Angela made the mistake of looking into his eyes. They were so dark, so intense, that it felt like he was looking past her and into her head or her heart. It unnerved her, and she spoke without thinking. "Because I want to marry. I want a husband I love and children and a home," she said, unable to keep her voice from rising in pitch, let alone stopping. "I am sure of it, and have always been sure of it. I don't want to take my orders. I just need time to accept my fate." She pressed her hand over her mouth. She had not meant to say those things. Certainly not aloud. Those were her secret thoughts, her secret wishes. They were supposed to stay secret and unspoken until they went away.

And to confess them to him of all the people in the world! He was sure to think her a fool for wanting that. He was sure to assume that she hinted that he should marry her. That was preposterous, of course. He was not the marrying kind, and she was not so deluded as to think he might change.

Phillip did not say anything. He dealt another round. This one, she was sure, he allowed her to win. For when it came time to reveal their cards, he showed the two of hearts and the two of diamonds, and she showed a jack and an ace. A perfect twenty-one.

"Why did you stop? Yesterday, and today, too, you could have kissed me and you did not. Why did you stop? And do not lie and tell me you have discovered honor, integrity, compassion, or any other noble emotion."

"Do you ever get tired of seeing yourself as nothing more than a girl that made a mistake once?" he asked casually.

"It's not my turn to answer a question," she replied, because that question was not one that she cared to contemplate, let alone dare to answer.

He shrugged, as if to say he already knew the answer, even if she didn't say it, and that he didn't give a damn if she answered or not.

"Well, maybe I'm tired of living up to my reputation," he said, leaning back onto the pillows. "Maybe I'm tired of meeting everyone's low expectations of me. Or maybe I haven't a damned clue as to why I stopped. But you didn't want me to stop."

"It's not my turn to answer a question," she replied. Again.

"It wasn't a question, Angela."

And then Phillip sat up and leaned forward. Her spine went rigid. He placed one fingertip on the soft spot beneath her chin. And with one finger he drew her into him.

And there it was again, like before with Lucas: the quickening of her pulse. She became light-headed. And then the new feelings: a constant humming within her and smoldering heat radiating from her stomach. Angela closed her eyes.

Lucas had made her feel alive. Phillip made her feel immortal. Time, space, and everything else ceased to matter.

His lips were nearly upon hers. So close that she could feel his lips part.

But he didn't kiss her.

Phillip leaned in a little more, brushing his stubbled cheek against hers. She arched her back and let her head fall back. Lightly, his lips traced over her skin—along her neck, down to the edge of her dress, and back up again.

Still he didn't kiss her.

He whispered something instead. "Perhaps I stopped because I knew you would hate me if I kissed you."

She didn't answer. Phillip placed his hand on the nape of her neck, holding her still, as he whispered more to her: "But I wonder if it's better that you hate me."

"I already hate you," she said softly.

"If I kissed you, I might make you like me. That could be far worse."

"Yes." Angela wasn't sure if that was an agreement or a plea.

"Or, maybe," Phillip whispered again, "you would only end up hating yourself."

"What do you care?" she asked. He didn't answer, and she felt him pull away from her. Angela opened her eyes. And then she just knew. "You do care."

He shrugged as if to say, "No, I don't. I couldn't care less."

Liar. She scowled at him. But he didn't see, because he refused to meet her gaze.

"You do care," she repeated. "You care what I might think of you. And you care how you might make me feel about myself. And you've been sitting here all evening telling me you are shallow, selfish, self-absorbed, and generally unfeeling. And—"

"Angela . . ." His voice was a warning for her to stop. He leaned forward again.

"You are a liar. But you do care." ·

His face was inches from hers now. "I don't care at all," he said.

And then he did kiss her.

Chapter 6

Phillip had lied. He did care very much. This new discovery of this new feeling, caring, was so absolutely terrifying that he couldn't recall ever being so struck dumb with fear in his entire life—including the moment when he sat still and tall in the saddle, waiting for them to take their shot.

He cared, and she knew it.

Instinct urged him to flee. With his injuries, that was not an option.

And so he kissed her instead. Because a kiss would make her stop talking and make her stop putting into words truths that he didn't want to know. A kiss would put a stop to the fear and would put a stop to his thoughts. He didn't want to think, and he didn't want to be afraid, and he didn't want to care.

And so he kissed her, hoping that it would make her hate him so that it wouldn't matter if he cared or not.

Phillip had never been struck by lightning before, but he imagined that it might feel something like this. The second their lips touched, he felt a hot, sharp sting rocketing through him, followed by an intense surge of heat and energy and the sensation of every nerve in his body vibrating. *Inflamed* was such an inadequate word to describe the fire he was feeling. It was a fire so roaring, so uncontainable, that there was nothing to do but let it burn.

Still, he tried to control it. He struggled not to completely consume her, because God knew he wanted to, and because she was right. He didn't want to hurt her.

His lips parted, as did hers. He slid inside, and she did the same. To taste her, to be inside her, was like adding gunpowder to that fire that was burning him up. A blinding, deafening explosion. The kiss deepened. Phillip gave himself up for lost. But if he was going to be burned alive by this kiss, then he was going to take her down with him.

She did not resist. Not in the slightest.

He cupped her cheeks in his hands—God, her skin was soft—because he needed to hold on to something. He needed an anchor, because he was starting to feel lost and adrift. And if he was going to feel lost and adrift, then she would have to go with him. Angela placed her hand on his chest, right above his heart, which was beating double time. Her hand slid higher to rest at the nape of his neck. She pulled him closer. Another explosion.

And then oblivion. Sweet, sweet, pure oblivion. No thoughts at all. There was no past and no future, just pure bliss in this moment.

It could have been an hour, or it could have been a minute, Phillip knew not. He just knew that it was not long enough.

Angela murmured his name, once, twice. It took him a second or two to recognize it.

Reluctantly, he pulled back so that she could speak.

"We . . . I . . ." she stammered and then gave up trying to form words and just looked at him, wide-eyed and wondering. Words were beyond him, too. So Phillip just nodded to say, *Yes, me, too. I can't speak because I can't think of anything but kissing you again.*

He leaned in toward her, because the idea of kissing her again had taken hold and refused to go away. Not that he wanted it to.

He stopped inches from her mouth; she placed her finger over his lips.

"I must go now," she whispered. "I must go," she said again as she stood. The cards that had been resting on her lap fell to the floor. "I can't stay here anymore."

She hurried out of the room without another word, and Phillip blew out the candle burning on the bedside table and reclined back on the bed.

Phillip closed his eyes, and all he could think was that she was going to hate him in the morning, all because of that kiss. He couldn't bring himself to regret it, but he questioned it and himself. What if he had waited a little longer? What if he had never pressed his mouth to hers at all? What if she didn't hate him in the morning after all?

Why the hell did he have to give a damn? Why here, why now, and why her?

Phillip opened his eyes, but it was so dark that he might have just kept them closed. He could see nothing. But he continued to lie on his back, eyes open, staring up at a ceiling he couldn't see.

He had never had a kiss like that one before. And that made him think of Esme. She had no last name that anyone knew of, which didn't matter. All she needed was one name: Esme. She was a Parisian courtesan and reputed to be the best lover on the Continent.

Phillip had not been in Paris long before he heard of her. He had been there for three weeks before he had seen her. Three months passed before she agreed to take him as a lover.

"I don't care for bad lovemaking," she announced to him after he had been shown into her bedroom. She was reclining on her large feather bed, dressed in some silky, lacy thing that seemed very easy to remove. Esme indicated that he should join her on the bed, and Phillip did not need much persuasion. She spoke with such a mixture of accents, it was impossible to discern her origins. Not that Phillip cared about her past at the moment. He was going to bed the best lover on the Continent.

"Do you agree?" she asked.

"Of course. Whatever you say," he answered. Phillip knew that agreeing with whatever a woman said was the quickest way to get under the sheets with her.

"Exactly," she answered with a proud smile on her rouged lips. "Some men, they do not listen to what a woman says, and that is bad. Sometimes, she does not speak with words. But still, you must learn to listen, and to give her what she wants. And then, Phillip, she will give you want you want."

He didn't understand, at first, how that made for a better romp in the sheets. But she was a legend, so he assumed that she knew what she was talking about. He wished they could stop talking, though.

"What do you want?" he asked, forgetting to make his voice husky and seductive.

"I want you to kiss me."

He did. It lasted a second before she stopped him. "*Non.* A woman knows within seconds of seeing a man if she would take him to be her lover. A kiss, however, can change her mind. You, your kiss is too strong, too fast."

"It's just a kiss."

"No, it is more. You kiss to dominate, to conquer, to obliterate an obstacle in your way. I am not a locked door you must break though; I am the key that will open that door. You must think of kissing as coaxing, convincing, seducing a woman to surrender. You must imagine, with every kiss, with every touch, that it is all you will ever have. Now kiss me again."

He did. Esme taught him how to kiss that night. Every night for a week, she taught him a great many things, too. She certainly delivered on her reputation as the best lover in all of Europe. All of Esme's teachings had done nothing to prepare him for this. And even Esme could not compare to Angela's kiss.

And as he thought about it, comparing the kisses was like trying to compare the Sistine Chapel to a drawing done in the dirt with a stick.

But Angela had cut the kiss short, Angela had stopped, and Angela had fled.

Had he done something wrong? He hadn't been able to think at all during that kiss, and maybe he forgot all the things he had learned from Esme. What if it had not been good for Angela? God knew that woman needed to be thoroughly and completely kissed. She needed to be reminded of what she was giving up with that vow of chastity.

⌒

Though Angela sat in the first pew of the chapel, facing the statue of mother and child, she did not draw it tonight. Her sketchbook was open on her lap, and her pencil lay idle as she looked at the drawing she had started recently.

It was just a rough sketch of bold lines and no shadows, depicting Phillip in the bath. She had outlined his broad shoulders and his back. She had drawn the line of his profile. (She was getting to know that broken nose of his quite well now.) His hair was slicked back. His mouth was held in the slightest smile. She had somehow managed to make him appear wicked and inviting all at once.

Or perhaps she had just managed to draw him exactly as he was.

"There you are," a voice said, and Angela shut her book and turned to see Helena.

"Right where I always am," Angela said.

Helena sat in the pew beside her.

"Sometimes I wonder at how much time we spend in this chapel," Angela said. "All the hours of one's life in this one room, when there is a whole world just outside."

"And yet we don't really tire of it," Helena added.

"Do you miss it, Helena? Your life before . . ."

"The life of a soldier's wife? Not really. Sometimes I miss John, though, even though he left me." John was Helena's husband, who had died at war on the Continent. She so rarely spoke of him, and when she did, Angela was never sure of what to say. So she simply placed her hand on Helena's and kept silent.

"I confess," Helena started, "it does feel different here with Lord Invalid. Having a man around and all."

Angela laughed, and the sound echoed throughout the room. "Yes."

"Is he still so awful?"

"No," she answered, ducking her head so that Helena

might not see her smile. That kiss had been the opposite of awful.

"Be careful, Angela. Men always hurt us in the end. But you already know that."

Angela did indeed know that, as sure as she knew her own name. But at the moment, with Phillip's kiss still burning on her lips, the pleasure a man could give a woman was far more vivid, visceral, and real than some foggy notion of eventual hurt.

Chapter 7

Contrary to all expectations, Angela was not racked with self-loathing after that kiss. Troubling as it may be, she did not hate Phillip because of it. And how could she feel guilty when she felt so . . . giddy?

There was nothing, she thought with a sigh, like a first kiss, even if it was one's second first kiss. Angela was beyond pleased to have discovered this. That she had now experienced two first kisses, when she probably should have only had one, if any, did not dishearten her. She just felt lucky.

But it would be her last first kiss, she vowed. It had to be, because she wasn't going to leave the abbey, and Phillip certainly couldn't stay. Angela might be sad about that later, but at this moment, she was just too happy. Because there was nothing like a first kiss, and nothing in the world like a perfect first kiss that made a girl feel hopeful and more alive than ever.

Thus were her thoughts the following morning as she knelt in the chapel, along with the other nuns, with her head bowed and her hands folded in prayer, until the sound of a door slamming open gave her reason to lift her head and turn around.

Phillip leaned in the doorway to the chapel. There was a

collective gasp from all the sisters and, a moment later, a collective exhale when it seemed that the chapel would not burst into flames or collapse upon them because a man, a very bad man, had entered.

The abbess, who had been leading the prayer, paused briefly and then returned to her task. She was going to ignore Phillip. A few other women did so, too, while others merely pretended to. Angela watched openly as he limped, slightly, down the aisle. He paused when he came to her pew, inconveniencing Helena, who merely arched one of her dark eyebrows at him as he shuffled past. Penelope, however, stared at him with wide eyes. There was the faintest blush on her cheeks when she moved aside so that Phillip could sit between her and Angela.

Angela was mortified. She thought of the advice not to feed stray dogs, for then they followed one everywhere. Twice now Phillip had sought her out.

Secretly, she was pleased. Just a little bit.

Phillip sat on the pew beside her. After a moment, he spoke to her in a whisper.

"Hasn't anyone here heard of upholstery? These seats are deuced uncomfortable."

"They're not supposed to be comfortable."

"Like those dresses of yours? I should like to see you in silks or satin. Or, really, I'd like to take some silk or satin dress off of you."

"Hush."

Phillip clasped his hands and bowed his head. But then he leaned in closer to her and whispered again.

"What are we praying for this morning?"

"For you to be quiet."

He took the hint, but his silence did not end her distractions. Angela maintained the pose of prayer, but her thoughts were not at all on her soul or salvation. No, she was imagining wearing a satin gown. It would be the color of pale aquamarine or the color of a robin's egg. Perhaps it might be edged in lace or embroidered with gold thread and pearls. Her stockings, and all her underthings, would be silk and lace and gently luxurious against her skin.

In her imagination, Angela wore this dress to a London ball. She had never been to one, but she had attended a few local dances. London balls must be a hundred times grander, and she had no difficulty conjuring one in her mind.

Even easier to imagine was waltzing with Phillip in an exquisite silk gown at a decadent London ball.

Never mind that the man could barely walk, let alone waltz.

Never mind that she hadn't a silk dress or the means to procure one or an invitation to an event to which she might wear one. She didn't even have a clue what the latest fashions were.

Never mind that she was not in London and had no plans to go, and no reason to go.

Never mind that she was living in an abbey, preparing to spend the rest of her days here, wearing itchy wool gowns, praying instead of dancing, and imagining kissing Phillip instead of actually kissing him.

Last night she had, by some miracle, ended their kiss. "*I must go. I cannot stay here*," she had said. Only this morning did she understand her own words: she had to leave the abbey, she could not stay here. But she had nowhere to go, because this was the only place in the world that would welcome her.

And so, even though all she longed for was a satin gown and another soul-scorching kiss, she would not have either. The giddiness she had been feeling began to beat a retreat. Angela watched it go without a fight.

"Are you crying?" Phillip asked her.

"No," she lied, brushing away one rebellious tear and blinking rapidly so that the others might not fall.

"I'm pretty sure lying is a sin. Especially in church."

"Perhaps, Phillip, you should focus on your own prayers instead of mine."

"Well, I have been praying that this damned pain in my leg would cease, but so far God has not granted me that favor."

"You might take it as a sign that you are to stay in bed, instead of rambling around the abbey."

"I tried. But then I got tired of waiting and wondering if you would avoid me this morning."

"Don't worry, I shall not let you starve."

"I know that. But I thought someone else might come instead. Because of last night," Phillip said, lowering his voice so that no one would overhear. Helena and Penelope were clearly making an effort to. Angela did not respond. The prayer service was ending, and though all the others stood and began to make their way out of the chapel, Angela and Phillip remained.

"You do remember, don't you?" Phillip asked.

"Of course I remember."

"I just wanted to make sure that you weren't thinking it was some grave sin, that you have to spend all day begging forgiveness for, instead of bringing me breakfast."

"There is the selfish, self-absorbed man I know."

"I'd just like to point out that you were the one to stop. Which means that you have either resisted temptation or that the kiss wasn't much of a temptation," Phillip said, and Angela wanted to laugh. Not much of a temptation! It was much more than that—so much more that the thought of the rest of her life without a kiss like that made her weep. Angela turned to look at him, and Phillip was looking around the chapel, as if admiring the stones or the craftsmanship of the stained glass window behind the altar, and Angela understood. He wasn't sure it had been good for her, nor was he sure if it had been a good kiss at all. She understood that he cared for her pleasure and wasn't sure if he had satisfied it.

"One of us has to exhibit better judgment in the face of temptation," she said. "And I have more practice than you."

"I could use more practice. Perhaps you might assist me?" Phillip asked, and Angela saw that gleam in his eyes again that told her he was joking—slightly.

"Oh, and so I am to kiss you so that you might practice stopping it?"

"It would be a favor to women everywhere. That, and if I can restrain myself, I shall certainly avoid matrimony, or at least any more duels."

"You know, you were supposed to be the one tempting me," Angela replied, immediately regretting reminding him of that. As if she needed to make things harder on herself!

"I'm giving you the chance to reform me. Isn't that what women always want to do? Change a man? Reform a rake . . ."

"Everyone knows that you are worse than a rake."

"Thus I am all the more in need of reformation," Phillip answered succinctly.

"You really are impossible. You know that?"

"Yes, but you like me anyway," he added with that devilish grin of his. She was going to miss that.

"I do not," she answered firmly.

"Angela," Phillip said with mock gravity, "we already spoke about lying in church."

"So I may not lie in church, but I may kiss a man who is not my husband."

"I'm sure there is a logical reason why that is so, but I can't think of it on an empty stomach."

They both stood to leave. This time when they walked down the aisle, both of them avoided touching the other. For that, Angela was thankful. Though they may joke about tempting each other for noble and spiritual purposes, she was starting to think that might be an excuse.

⌒

The abbess was waiting for them outside of the chapel doors. She wore the same gray dress as all the other women here, and it matched her gray hair. Though she was older, perhaps in her sixties, one could still see that she had been an attractive woman in her youth. It was her eyes—bright green, rimmed in dark lashes. They were stern and kind, all at once.

"Lord Huntley, perhaps I might walk with you while Angela goes to prepare breakfast." It was not a question.

"Of course, Lady Katherine," he replied, which was the only thing he could say. Angela bowed to the abbess and disappeared down the hall. When Phillip turned his attention back to the abbess, she had the faint trace of a knowing smile on her lips.

"I see you are feeling much better."

"Yes. And I must thank you for the care you have shown me."

" 'Tis our duty," she answered, entwining their arms to walk down the hall, back to his chamber. "You seem to enjoy it here. Perhaps you might consider taking orders yourself? There is a monastery not far from here."

Phillip coughed, choked on a laugh, really, before responding. "I don't think this is the life for me. That's probably the wrong thing to say, though."

"On the contrary. Knowing one's path and following it faithfully is, in my opinion, the purpose of life. A religious life, such as we live here in the abbey, is not for everyone." Phillip knew, then, that they were no longer talking about him but about Angela.

"But you welcome anyone here anyway. For any reason," he said.

"We offer safety here, not judgment."

"She told me she hadn't taken her orders yet."

"It seems she tells you a lot of things," the abbess mused.

"It's not as if there is much to do here besides talk."

"Or play cards," she added. "I happened to walk by your chamber last night."

"I suppose card games are not allowed here," Phillip said, bracing himself for a lecture on how attempting to seduce a woman was not allowed here, either.

"No," the abbess agreed. "Your mother loved to play cards."

"Really?" Phillip paused, mostly in shock. That was the last thing he had expected to hear from the abbess. And he had long ago given up on ever learning about his mother, who had died giving birth to him and his twin.

"Your father did not speak of her?" the abbess asked, when he had resumed walking.

"Not a word." His father had never said so much as a word about his late wife. Phillip only knew her name because he had looked in the family Bible at the age of ten, when he was curious and yet knew better than to ask his father. He had certainly never considered that she might be a person, with likes and dislikes, and that he might share some of her traits.

"I imagine it was too painful for him to do so. They were

very much in love." Phillip fought the urge to stop again. His father in love with something other than his house and lands? Again, a shocking revelation.

"I was under the impression that it was an arranged marriage, or one of convenience. He got his heir, and a spare, so there was no reason for him to take another wife. I never thought he actually cared for her."

"Oh, it was the talk of the town," Lady Katherine said with a laugh. "Your father was so reserved and restrained, and your mother was wild. Madeleine loved to dance and play cards till the wee hours of the morning. A pair of opposites, they were. But to see them together . . . well, it all made sense."

"Did you know her well?"

"We were on some charitable committees together, and that is how I became acquainted with her. But I knew her well enough that I recognize some of her qualities in you."

"Oh?" He didn't want the abbess to know how much he had always wanted to know about her. Yet he couldn't pass up this opportunity to learn more.

"You have her eyes. And a devil-may-care attitude, and a preference to be with people rather than alone. And while she was never involved in any scandals, she was always just a step away from it. She was great fun, though. She may have been a duchess, but she never thought herself above anyone." Phillip mused on this in silence for a few steps, wondering why he didn't already know these things, or why he had never thought to ask someone other than his father. He wondered what his twin knew of her.

After they had reached his chamber, the abbess left to take care of other things, and Phillip pulled the chair over to the window and kept wondering.

His father had loved his mother not too little but perhaps too much. So much that when she died giving birth to Phillip and his twin, Devon, their father didn't have any love left over for them. So Phillip figured love came in finite quantities.

And if he had his mother's eyes, that meant that Devon did, too, since they were absolutely identical in appearance. Only now could he begin to imagine how his father might have felt with two pairs of his beloved dead wife's eyes looking up to him, practically begging for his attention. It would have been damned hard, to say the least. No wonder his father avoided them.

And him, in particular, if he was like his mother. Phillip had always felt as if his father only paid attention to him because he was the heir, and he had to be taught estate management and all sorts of tedious things like that, because the estate was what his father loved most in the world. Or maybe his father was trying to make Phillip more like himself.

But the old man was dead, and so Phillip couldn't ask.

His mother was long gone, too. And it was Phillip's fault. He had learned that stunning fact years ago, in the same afternoon that he had learned he wasn't the heir after all. No wonder he generally avoided thinking or feeling. One might discover unpleasant thoughts and feelings.

No wonder he left England and went to Paris, where he spent four years in a drunken oblivion.

But now he was in this place, where the only thing to do was reflect and think. Why anyone voluntarily subjected themselves to this, he knew not. The only distraction was Angela, and attempting to seduce her. And that, after some damned thought, needed to stop.

Because what if he fell in love with her? Phillip had always thought of himself incapable of that finer emotion and thus like his father in one respect. And if ever there was a woman to fall in love with, it was Angela. With that face, that figure, that voice.

She wagered secrets and made them seem more valuable than the best-bred horse, a big house in the country, large quantities of the finest brandy, or an outrageous sum of money.

She made him say please, a short step away from begging, and he didn't mind. She made him say thank you, and he meant it.

Her kiss bested that of the best lover in Europe.

Yes, she was a woman he could love.

Love led to loss; that much was clear to him, now knowing what he did about his parents' marriage. Losing at a round of cards was one thing. Losing at something that might actually matter, love for instance, was another entirely. It had happened often enough that Phillip had wagered his last penny, only to win big. With an equal frequency he had lost that last penny. But when it came to this game, all he could see was the potential for a devastating loss, not the win of a lifetime.

Perhaps he wasn't as much of a gambling man as he had thought.

Phillip picked up the deck of cards from the bedside table. He gave it a shuffle and selected a card at random. The queen of hearts. He didn't have a story for that one.

And then Angela walked into his room.

Phillip slipped the card back into the deck and shuffled again.

"I brought you breakfast," she said in that voice of hers. No wonder he hadn't been craving brandy, since he got to hear that voice. But unlike her voice, brandy took away the thoughts.

"Thank you," he said with a nod. "Just set it over on the table. Please."

"Is there anything else you want?" Phillip heard the hesitation in her voice.

"No, thank you." He couldn't look at her now. Not when he was trying not to lust after her or, God forbid, fall in love with her.

"You look like you could use a shave."

He ran his hand along his jaw. She was right. "I guess."

"Phillip . . ." Her voice trailed off, but he still knew the question she was going to ask: *Is something wrong?* He didn't feel like answering that question, so he turned his back to her and looked out the window. And thus he stayed until he heard the door shut.

She would be angry, perhaps hurt by his sudden coldness. But she knew he was a self-absorbed scoundrel. She was trying so hard to be good, and he was wicked to the bone. He would have to go.

⌒

Later that afternoon, Angela was still angry. She took it out on the carrots she was chopping for supper. *Thwack thwack*

thwack. The knife sliced through them with ease and slammed into the wooden table beneath. Sometimes she hit so hard that the knife got stuck in the wood, but it was no trouble for her to yank it back out and keep slicing the poor carrots into bits.

This morning, when she brought him breakfast, he had been cold and distant. Which she might not have minded, if it hadn't been such a stark contrast to his usual flirtatious, teasing, and sly behavior.

She had brought him the things to shave a short while later, and again, it was the same: "Thank you. Set it over there." And then he stared out the window, refusing to look at her. When he wasn't looking outside, he was shuffling the deck of cards, pulling out a card, staring at it for a second before slipping it back in the deck.

She knew he was remembering stories to go with each card. Phillip did not share the stories with her this time, but she could imagine them. All the wine and women that went along with them. Women who probably just threw themselves at him, who didn't cut kisses short and flee. Who weren't about to take vows of chastity. Women who just offered themselves up to him for the taking.

Women who weren't her.

Thwack thwack thwack.

She had brought him lunch, and it was still the same. She reminded him that she ought to check on his wounds, and he declared it unnecessary.

And then Angela spent the afternoon thinking of things she could possibly bring him or, rather, excuses to go to him. And that was sick and deranged, because she was so clearly unwanted. And she so much wanted to be wanted, though it shamed her to admit it.

"Angela, are you all right?" asked Penelope, who was seated across the table and peeling potatoes.

"I'm fine."

"You really are attacking those carrots," Lady Katherine added, as she diced onions. Angela set down her knife.

"What did you say to him?" Angela demanded of the abbess.

All the others in the kitchen hushed, for no one ever challenged the abbess.

"I beg your pardon?" Lady Katherine did not seem angry at the insubordination, simply confused.

"This morning, he was . . ." She couldn't find the words. And the ones she could find she didn't want to say: this morning he seemed to like her. "He has been cold to me all day, since you spoke to him. So I'm wondering what you said to him," Angela finished and returned to chopping carrots with a vengeance.

"You are speaking of Lord Invalid?" Penelope asked.

"Of course, what other 'he' would there be?"

"You called him Phillip yesterday. In fact, you haven't referred to him as Lord Invalid for days now," Penelope pointed out.

"That's neither here nor there," Angela said with a shrug, embarrassed that the others had noticed the change when she hadn't. "What did you say to him?"

"Not that it is any of your business, but we spoke about his mother. He never knew her, and I did. That is all."

"Oh." What did that have to do with her? She bit her tongue to keep from asking. "Did he say when he was leaving?"

"No. I suggested that since he seemed to enjoy himself here, he might consider taking orders himself."

Angela laughed.

"That was his reaction, too. Speaking of taking orders, Angela, when are you going to take yours?" the abbess asked.

That was a good question. Her own words from last night echoed in her head: *I must go. I cannot stay.* But she was so cowardly; making the leap to commit to a lifetime within these walls seemed impossibly overwhelming. She certainly had reasons to stay. But she often thought she would leave on a moment's notice if she had a place to go. Home, of course, was not an option.

"I don't know yet," Angela said. She had finished chopping the carrots and started dicing the potatoes Penelope had peeled.

"Very well," the abbess said with a patience that Angela

envied. "Lord Huntley has made a remarkable recovery. He likely shan't stay much longer."

"I will be happy to ask him when he is leaving," Angela said.

"I'll miss him when he goes," Penelope said with a little sigh.

"You're the only one," Angela replied. She would *not* miss him, Angela told herself firmly. She would be relieved at his departure. Things would return to normal: life would be quiet, peaceful, and secure. She would not miss bantering with him. She would not miss being tempted by a glance, a touch, a kiss, or even merely the knowledge that she desired a man and he was always nearby. Or so she told herself.

⌒

Angela delayed bringing his supper until a later hour than usual. She had wanted to see if he would seek her out as he had done this morning. That a man disappointed her once again did not have a pleasant effect upon her mood.

Her mood was just as black and cloudy as the night sky when she brought supper to Lord Invalid's chamber. The giddy delight she had woken up feeling was long gone, and she missed it almost as much as the kiss itself.

"You must be hungry," she said upon entering his room. He was in the same place as he had been earlier in the day: in the chair by the window, looking out, though she couldn't imagine that he saw very much in the darkness. Two candles burned on the bedside table, and they did not offer much illumination.

"I am."

"I was surprised you didn't come find me to demand your supper."

He shrugged. He shrugged! She wanted to slap him out of frustration, and she might have, had she not had her hands full carrying a tray with his meal. She settled for slamming it down on the table.

"Stop that! All day, you shrug when I ask you something,

when I try to talk to you. You've been cold and distant and strange since the abbess talked to you about your mother. What does that have to do with anything? With me?"

"She told you that?"

"Yes. Women talk, Phillip. I'd think you would know that by now. How else would you have the reputation you do? How else would everyone in England know about all your ruined girls? I'm just surprised everyone doesn't know every little detail."

"Did you tell her that we kissed last night?" he challenged.

"No," she muttered.

"Why not?"

"Because I might get in trouble. I might be asked to leave, and I have nowhere to go."

"You didn't think that I might ask you to leave with me?"

"No, actually."

"Good," he said, sounding relieved. That cad. She didn't think for a second that he would ask her to go with him. That didn't mean she didn't want him to.

"Yes. Good for you. You get to leave another ruined woman in your wake. Too bad for you that someone already got there first." She turned to go.

"Don't say that," he said sharply, and she turned around.

"What? It's the truth. I've been used. I'm damaged goods."

"Oh, Angela," he murmured, the sadness in his voice all too clear. She was surprised when he crossed the room and took her in his arms. Even more surprised when he said firmly but quietly, "Shut the hell up about that."

He pressed his mouth to hers, silencing her. It only lasted a second before he spoke again.

"It doesn't really matter," he murmured. She opened her mouth to protest, but the words got lost in another kiss.

"There is more to you than one mistake . . . if it even was a mistake." This time, when she opened her mouth to protest, he took advantage and deepened the kiss.

Just to be in his room at this late hour made her feel as she did the night before: like a dam about to collapse under the pressure of a rising river. And he was like a relentless rainstorm, and she wasn't sure she could stand up under the strain.

Phillip held her close, one hand cradling her head, the other caressing her back, coming to rest on her backside. She grasped the collar of his shirt, a fistful of fabric in each hand. They leaned upon each other for balance and held on so that if one fell, the other surely was going down, too. As a fallen angel, she wondered, why not tumble down from heaven once more?

There was a rumble of thunder in the distance. The threat of a storm was not worth stopping for.

Only an absolute and utter scoundrel could kiss like this, she thought. Like the devil himself. He tasted like temptation. His hands on her, caressing and exploring, were like a fire melting her resolve and annihilating all her best intentions. And when he held her, her only thought was that eternity was not long enough.

And just when she was ready to hand her soul over to the devil himself in exchange for this kiss, he pulled away. He left her breathless.

"It was my turn to stop," he explained.

Angela stood there, too stunned to move, and attempting to gather her wits, while he calmly pulled the chair up to the bedside table, sat down, and proceeded with dinner.

"Well, are you just going to stand there, or are you going to sit down and keep me company?" he asked. He did not suggest that she leave, and she was glad, for she didn't want to go.

"There is nowhere to sit."

"You could sit on the bed," he suggested. She could, she thought, but then she might never leave it. But her knees were still a little weak from that kiss, so she accepted.

"I'll probably leave in a day or two," he said. She was supposed to feel relieved, not this hollow ache of longing, of missing him before he was even gone. And really, it was stupid to feel that way. She had known all along he wasn't going to stay.

"Where will you go?"

"London, I guess."

"What will you do?"

"Probably what I do best: drink myself stupid, lose enormous sums of money and other valuables in card games. Win it all back, and blow it on brandy."

"What about seducing scores of women and fighting duels?" Angela couldn't resist asking.

"That, too, most likely, but I'm not so good at those things."

"You seduced me," she said. The words flew out of her mouth before she could stop them.

"So, my skills are improving," he said with a half smile. "Although, you must admit, I haven't got much competition," he pointed out.

"Just my better judgment and a promise to God."

"I don't think I want to compete with that. You'll take your orders when I leave, won't you?"

"Probably. And for all the wrong reasons. But I don't want to talk about that."

"All right," Phillip said, shrugging again. There was another rumble of thunder, louder than the first.

"What did the abbess say about your mother?"

"I don't want to talk about that," Phillip answered firmly.

After a long moment of silence, Angela gave up and laughed.

"What is so funny?"

"*Us*. We both refuse to speak about certain things, unless it is in the context of a card game."

"It's because in order to talk about those things, we have to think about them, and I think neither of us wants to do that."

"I can't stop thinking about those things," Angela confessed.

"This place does demand reflection. It's driving me crazy. And I don't know how you do it, Angela. You've been here six years, I assume, just ruminating on painful subjects. It's a miracle that you are not insane."

"I guess the idea is that through reflection, one can come to accept the past, then learn forgiveness, and finally make peace with it all," she said, reciting the formula that had been explained to her time and time again.

"I'm partial to ignoring a situation until it goes away. And, surely, something must be said for letting go and moving on."

"How do you do it? And I'm not trying to be accusatory, but all those women . . . and you just walk away. How do you do it?"

"I guess I just don't think about it."

"But how do you do that?"

"It's easy in the world outside of the abbey. There is brandy, which helps tremendously. After a few drinks, you can't think clearly, if at all. And if you do manage some deep thoughts, they certainly won't be remembered in the morning."

"Is that the only way? Because I had a sip of brandy once, and I found it revolting."

"Well, there are card games, horse races, parties, and other people and their problems," Phillip added.

"I miss parties. I miss dancing and dressing for a ball and wondering who I might meet that evening."

"You had made your debut then?"

"Not officially; I haven't been to London. But I attended local balls and soirees and the like. That's how I met him." There was no need to explain which *him* she spoke of. And it was oddly comforting, having spoken of it once, so that she did not have to explain again or evade any questions about that situation.

"Your family had some prominence, then."

"Yes. My father was a viscount. I was supposed to make a good marriage. And my being the eldest made my indiscretion all the more devastating."

"Was there a duel?"

"Yes," Angela answered after a moment's hesitation. This was one of those things that she really didn't care to talk about, that she couldn't stop thinking about. The conversation was clearly turning down a path she wasn't sure she wanted to take but was helpless to stop.

"He didn't shoot wide, did he?" Phillip filled in.

"His bullet never hit my father, but my father died any-way," Angela said sadly.

"What happened?"

"My father suffered an apoplexy on the dueling field after Lucas had taken his shot. His heart gave out from the shock, or so Damien, my brother, explained. He was my father's second."

"That bastard should have never accepted the challenge, or he shouldn't have fired a shot."

"I guess I can understand," she started. "His life was at stake, too. My father was certainly going to shoot to kill."

"Bullocks. Duels are a matter of honor, and Frost had none to defend. He should have let your father shoot first."

"Is that what you do when you are in duels?"

"It doesn't matter when I fire, because I am a notoriously terrible shot," Phillip said.

"You must be lucky to be alive then. Lucky all those husbands and fathers missed."

"I was lucky twice. For one duel, I convinced my twin to go in my place. He took a bullet in the shoulder. And for another, I ended up shooting myself, which is fair enough. I deserved it."

"I daresay you did," she answered dryly.

"I'm sorry about your father."

"Me, too," Angela said, and they fell into silence once again, until she spoke. "You owe me now. We talked about one of my difficult subjects; now we have to talk about one of yours. It's only fair."

"All right," Phillip said, and then took an eternity before saying anything more. Her curiosity grew with each breath. "The abbess said that my mother liked to play cards, too."

"That's all? I just told you that I, in effect, killed my own father, and all you're going to offer up is that your mother liked cards?" She looked at him as if he were daft to even compare the two.

"First of all, you did not kill you father. He was just doing what he was supposed to do, what an honorable man would do. And trust me, not all of them do. Otherwise, I would have fought a few more duels."

"What if I wish he hadn't?"

"Someone fought for you, Angela." And that was all he

needed to say for her to understand. Someone had loved her. Loved her so much that he would still fight for the honor she had tossed to the wind. It was a small consolation, but a consolation nonetheless. *I'm sorry,* she offered up a silent prayer. And then she added a *thank you* to this small prayer. And she wondered what her father would think if he could see her now, alone in a dimly lit room with a man like Phillip. He would be livid. He would warn her.

Or, would her father repeat his words of that fateful afternoon? "I don't care what you do now," he had said.

This time, whatever happened, there was no one to fight for her except herself.

Thinking. All there is to do here is think. Ignore, and let it go. She changed the subject.

"So tell me the significance of the mutual love for cards," she said.

Phillip paused, presumably thinking, before answering. "Before the abbess told me that, all I knew about my mother was her name and that she died in childbirth. So it was my fault. And I'm just like her, according to the abbess. And my father loved her and hated me."

"You don't know that he hated you."

"Well, he certainly didn't like me very much. Then again, I am difficult to like."

"You don't make it easy," Angela agreed but couldn't bring herself to confess that she had managed the feat. "But about your mother; it wasn't your fault. It happens, and far too often. You were just an innocent baby. There was nothing you could have done differently."

"Then maybe I wasn't born wicked after all," he said, and she realized that he must have always thought that he was born wicked and that there was no other way for him to be.

He stood up from his chair, having finished with supper some time ago. She wondered if that was her cue to stand as well, and leave, and end the night. But then he sat beside her on the bed.

"No, you weren't born wicked. And I wonder if you are even so wicked as the stories say."

"I might not be. I'd hate to disappoint you, though," Phillip said, and she heard the amusement in his voice.

"So don't." She turned and looked him in the eye. His mouth curved into a grin.

"You're trouble, you know that? Here I am, trying to be good, and I don't think that's what you want."

"It's too hard to be good," she said with a sigh. It was supposed to be a deliberately overdramatic sigh, but it was all too real. For the most part it was not too hard to be good; it was easy to care for the people in her life, to say her prayers, be honest and kind, and all those sorts of virtues. But when it came to battling her desire for not just any very bad man but the one beside her on the bed, it was just too damned hard.

Oh, she knew all too well the consequences. She could anticipate the heartache, the guilt, and the pangs of regret. But just as there was no one to fight for her now, there was also no one who would get hurt by her actions—other than herself. And the thing was, she thought, she knew she could handle it. She had done it once. She could do it again.

It was too hard to be good, and frankly, with Phillip so close beside her, and the memory of his kiss still on her lips, being good seemed like a difficult, painful battle with very little reward.

"Being good is certainly not as pleasurable as being wicked," he remarked.

"I might agree," she said cautiously.

"Or you might need to be convinced?" Phillip asked.

"Perhaps," she whispered just before his lips brushed against hers. His lips lingered against hers. For a second, it was enough. Just for a second, and then it wasn't enough. She parted her lips and took it further.

There was another rumble of thunder. Louder. Closer. The wind picked up, and the rain began, slapping against the windowpanes.

This kiss was slow. As if they had all night. As if they had forever. It was all she had ever wanted and all she had ever needed. That is, until it wasn't. Until she wanted more and needed more.

"Take down your hair," Phillip said in a momentary break in the kiss. She started removing the pins, one by one, letting them fall on the bed and onto the floor. She couldn't help but laugh, trying to kiss and undo her hair at the same time. In the candlelight, she saw him grin. And then he uncoiled the braid that rested on her head like a halo. She certainly should not be wearing a halo for this. No, she was no angel.

Her hair fell around her face, and Phillip brushed it aside. "You're beautiful," he stated, sinking his fingers into her hair and pulling her to him. And then her mouth found his, and there were no words for a while.

There was nothing in the world but his mouth against hers. His lips were soft and firm against her own. His tongue tangling with hers, teasing, taunting, and indulgent all at once. He nibbled upon her lower lip. She sucked his tongue. The kiss deepened once more. The clink of tooth against tooth as they both threw caution to the wind and forgot to be gentle. This was a greedy kiss, both of them taking and demanding just what they had been needing.

Both of them giving everything they had to give. And though neither of them had much to offer, somehow it was exactly what was needed.

There was a sigh.

There was a murmur.

And Angela knew with utter certainty that she would not be taking her orders—not as long as Phillip and his kiss existed in the world.

There was another rumble of thunder. It was not nearly as loud or as powerful as the beating of her heart. Placing her hand on his chest, she could feel his heart pounding under her palm. So he felt the same way, she thought with wicked delight. She slid her hands under the fabric so that she could feel his skin. His chest had become familiar to her already, with its fading bruises and broken ribs and muscles covering them. But it was different now: stronger and hot to the touch.

Phillip had not tired of kissing her, but beyond her mouth was the rest of her, begging to be explored. So he feathered kisses along her throat. It was too short a distance from her mouth to the hem of her gown, barring him from the rest of her.

The dress had to go.

"Take this damned thing off," he growled. She arched one eyebrow and flashed him a coy smile.

"Please." He whispered the word. It sounded like the prayer that it was.

Those few seconds it took her to remove one more barrier between them were so heavy with anticipation, Phillip thought he might be crushed by it. And then there was a flutter of fabric falling to the floor and a flash of lightning.

He sucked in his breath, and at the same moment she uttered a sigh of what sounded like relief.

She was not nude, but her chemise was so transparent that she might as well have been. Nothing was hidden to him now. He drank in the sight. To look at her was more intoxicating than a monthlong drinking binge of the finest brandy in the world. And it was just as mind melting, if not more. Not one thought remained in his head. But he was overwhelmed by the urge to touch. To taste.

God, if it didn't take every ounce of control he had not to throw himself on her and devour her.

He managed not to. The distraction of her fingers undoing the buttons on his shirt one by one gave him a reason to pause. Made him feel like she was undoing him and his self-control.

Her fingers fumbled with the last button; they brushed against the waistband of his breeches, and it was just too much. He couldn't be still anymore. He pushed her honey blonde locks out of the way, cradled her cheeks in his hands, and leaned in to taste her again.

Angela leaned back, taking Phillip with her. And there was nothing, she thought, like the weight of a man on top of her. Made a girl feel protected and vulnerable all at once. But she didn't dwell on the thought, because Phillip was kissing her neck again—God, that felt amazing—and each little kiss was a little bit lower than the last. She sensed a method to this madness: after each fleeting imprint of his lips on her skin, he paused, giving her a chance to tell him to stop. But there were no protests on her lips, just quiet sighs begging him to continue, almost lost in the sound of the rain pouring outside. Almost.

Phillip cupped one breast in his hand, and she arched her back. He closed his mouth around the center of the other. Angela moaned in pleasure, and the sound was nearly lost in another rumble of thunder.

He placed a hand just above her knee, grasping, inching his way up her thigh, and shoving aside the fabric of her chemise. Sliding along her stocking, pausing at the garter, and going farther. With his fingers, he began to stroke her at that magical place between her legs.

What was he doing? Angela wondered. Didn't he know this wasn't how it was done? It felt impossibly amazing, though, this strange thing. Lucas had never touched her there with his hands. With something else, yes. That much she knew. But what was Phillip doing, stroking her, sliding one finger inside of her?

Oh, God. She arched her back. She couldn't ask him, because he was kissing her now, thoroughly and hungrily. She wouldn't ask him, because she didn't care what he was doing, as long as he did not stop.

He kissed her in a stunningly sensitive spot where her neck met her shoulder. Her hips were rocking beneath them, as if they had their own free will. Phillip's mouth roamed all over her now. Every second that she settled into the feeling of his lips against her skin in one place, his mouth moved on to another, leaving her tingling all over in anticipation.

He still caressed her in a steady rhythm. Faster. The heat pooling there was spreading all over her now, into her stomach and into her limbs. Hot. If hell were this kind of hot, she would happily spend eternity there. But it was too pleasurable to be hell. Instead, it rather felt like heaven, or how she imagined heaven might feel.

She sighed. She moaned. She couldn't help but writhe beneath him. She faintly heard him murmur her name, and God, in one breath.

Lightning flashed. More than merely flashed. The crackling

was deafening. Angela opened her eyes at the sound, and was nearly blinded by the flash of light. The brightness faded slightly but did not go away. Phillip, above her, kept stroking her there. His eyes locked in a gaze with hers, just for a moment before he kissed her once more.

There was another rumble, certainly not thunder, but she knew not what it was. She didn't even give a damn.

Between his hands, his kiss, his weight upon hers, thought of any kind was impossible. There was the heat, and now a delicious tingling sensation radiating throughout her. She couldn't breathe, but she didn't want to. Her heart was pounding so hard she thought it might burst through her chest. She didn't care if it did.

And then the feeling took over. She was wholly owned by it. Possessed. She cried out, not to fight the feeling but in surrender. The sweetest surrender.

She didn't know it, so lost in her own pleasure, but Phillip was owned by the same feeling. He was trying to fight his release. Because he was a grown man, not some overexcited schoolboy, it was supposed to take more than this to make him come. And he was supposed to be able to control it. But he took one look at her face in the throes of her climax, one that he had given her, and it was all over for him. He groaned at his release. In defeat. But losing never felt so damned good.

It took him a minute to gather the strength to move off of her. God, the last thing he wanted to do now was suffocate her by his weight. He didn't go far, though; the single bed didn't leave much extra room with two people on it.

"What just happened?" she asked in a whisper. "What did you do to me?"

"The French call it *petite mort*," he said, his voice low and rough. "A little death."

"Then I want to die again and again," she murmured.

Phillip turned to look at her and saw the smile of a satisfied woman. Of an angel who had fallen from heaven and was raised back up to the lofty place she deserved. And he felt a tremendous swell of pride and power. He had made her feel that way.

He had put that smile on her face. Her eyes were closed now, so she didn't see that his lips were curved in the same smile.

The sound of doors slamming throughout the abbey broke their quiet moment. There was a pounding on the door to his chamber, and before Phillip and Angela could disentangle themselves and dress, the door opened.

Chapter 8

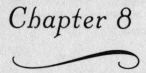

It was only Helena, with Penelope standing behind her, which was bad, but not catastrophic. Friends were better than mothers and chaperones when it came to being caught in a compromising position. Phillip, of course, had plenty of experience in that area.

"Bloody hell," Phillip muttered, as he saw the situation from their point of view. Him, shirtless with his scarred, bruised, and naked torso. Angela, in a nearly transparent chemise, long locks unbound and, now that he paused to notice, with flushed cheeks and lips plump from his kisses.

"Oh, thank God," Helena said, leaning against the door frame. Phillip was confused. He, too, had been thanking God, but he suspected for different reasons.

"What is it? Is Angela there? Is she safe?" Penelope asked, sounding hysterical.

"She's here," Helena said, still staring at Phillip and Angela as they fumbled around for clothes.

"It's not what you think," Angela said. "Really, it's not. I swear it, and oh, where are my hairpins?"

"Forget your hairpins, Angela," Helena snapped. "The chapel is on fire. We need everyone's help." She turned and started down the hall.

"Stay here," Phillip told Angela. He crossed the room while buttoning his shirt, and in a few strides, he caught up with Helena.

"What happened?"

"I should ask you the same thing," Helena said sharply.

"Lightning struck the old oak tree, setting it afire. Branches have fallen on the roof, and now that is on fire, too," Penelope explained.

Phillip swore.

"I quite agree," Helena said.

"Was anyone hurt?" he asked.

"No, but we feared Angela might have been," Penelope said.

"She wasn't in her chamber, and we thought she might be stuck in the chapel, because she goes there every night," Helena explained.

Phillip dared not speak.

"It could be divine providence that she was in your room, Lord Phillip, in deviation from her usual routine. You might have saved her," Penelope said, a little breathless now from the quick pace.

"Or ruined her all over again, Penelope," Helena responded. Turning to Phillip, she said, "I'm not going to forget what I saw."

Staring levelly at her, he answered, "And I am not going to forget about her."

"There's no time for this," Penelope reminded them, pushing open a set of doors that led outside, which they hurried through. Phillip swore under his breath again.

A massive orb of fire seemed to float in the sky; upon closer look, it was the top of the old oak tree. Flaming branches had indeed fallen onto the nearby roof of the chapel, setting that on fire, too. Phillip heard a low roar and rumble; it wasn't thunder but another portion of the roof collapsing into the chapel.

Torrents of rain were helping to contain the destruction.

The heat of the fire kept them all from feeling the cold of soaked garments against their skin. Talk about being thankful for small favors, Phillip thought grimly.

Dozens of the nuns were about in their nightgowns. Phillip couldn't recall ever seeing so many women in such a state of undress at once. Given the circumstances, he rather would not have. Given the circumstances, they didn't seem to care that a man was in their midst.

Villagers were now streaming in to help the women in lining up and passing along buckets of water from the well to try to douse the flames. Phillip estimated there must have been fifty or so people trying to control the inferno.

"Find some things to start collecting rainwater. Bowls, chamber pots, troughs, anything," Phillip said to Helena. "Set them up around the chapel, so that we needn't carry them far. It won't be much, but anything will help." Then he walked away and cut in line so that the abbess, who had been at the head of the line, was not so close to the fire.

Even though after a minute he was soaked to the skin, Phillip was not cold. The fire took care of that. It wasn't long before his skin felt scorched and dry. It wasn't much longer before his injuries began to ache for the first time all day, and soon after that, all the muscles he owned were protesting. He ignored the pain and lost himself in physical labor.

He threw one bucket after another onto the fire and watched it accomplish almost nothing. Their best hope, it seemed, was to save the rest of the abbey, for the chapel and the greater buildings shared one wall. He gave the roof up for lost, as another hideous cracking sound erupted, and a large section of the roof collapsed, landing just before the altar. Right in the spot where a man and woman might stand to recite their wedding vows. Phillip did not believe in signs, but that really unnerved him.

But not as much as the thought that Angela could have been trapped in this. To think such a thought brought on a wave of nausea. That the thought of her being hurt induced such a visceral reaction could only mean one thing: he was beyond merely caring and on the verge of falling in love.

He threw another bucket of water onto the flames. One little patch went out with a hiss, but it was nothing compared to the crackle of the rest of the fire.

Phillip had never suffered from attacks of modesty, and he did not now. She could have been caught in this inferno, if it was true that she was in the habit of visiting the chapel every night. Instead, she had been with him. He had been on the verge of ruining her all over again, but it seemed as if he had saved her.

～

Phillip was really stupid, Angela thought, if he assumed she would sit in his bed and wait for him while the chapel burned. Instead, she ran through the halls, through the doors, and outside. She stopped short then, her breath catching in her throat.

Without fail, every night, Angela had trouble sleeping. She never felt as lonely and alone as she did in her bed at night. Desire, pent up, with no way out, kept her awake. And every night, without fail, she ended up donning her robe and taking a candle down to the chapel, and she would pray and draw until she was so tired she wasn't sure she could make it back to her bed. One night she had even fallen asleep in one of the pews.

And tonight, of all nights, she hadn't been there. A small part of her wondered if it was her absence that had caused this disaster, and she wondered if perhaps it was her presence that protected the chapel. But it had remained unscathed for two hundred years without her nightly devotion.

She needed it more than it needed her.

But tonight, she hadn't needed it at all. Because tonight Phillip had conquered the feeling that kept her awake at night. His kiss and his touch satisfied her in a way that hours of midnight prayers had never managed.

And there he was, soaked to the skin, face-to-face with the flames, fighting them back from their path of complete destruction. She choked back a bubble of completely inappropriate laughter. The wickedest man in England was risking his

life to save a church. She would have never believed it if she
hadn't seen it with her own eyes.

Angela also saw all of the sisters working to fight the fire.
She saw villagers assisting, too. And she also noticed someone
had set out an assortment of receptacles to capture the rainwater. They were now near to overflowing, so she set about picking them up, hurling their contents at the fire, and setting them
right side up so that they might collect more rainwater.

It was quite nearly dawn when every last smoldering em-
ber was extinguished. Angela ignored commands not to enter
the chapel. Stepping gingerly around all the heaps of half-
burned timber and wrecked pews, she made her way to stand
before the altar, where she turned in a slow circle to survey the
damage.

The old stone walls, at least, had survived, though they were
blackened by the smoke. By some miracle, the stained glass
window behind the altar had remained intact. Angela tilted her
head back and gazed up to the night sky. The storm had ceased,
and now the clouds were passing, allowing her a glimpse of a
few stars and the moon.

"Angela, come out of there." It was Phillip, and he sounded
weary.

"In a minute," she answered, still looking up at the sky.

"*Now*. It's still not safe."

And she turned to look at him. His shirt was soaked and
clung to his body. Parts of it were burned straight through, leaving big holes in the fabric, exposing his skin. There was a black
streak of soot on one of his cheeks. He had been that close to
the fire.

He held out his hand to her.

Once she was close enough to place her hand in his, he
pulled her into a tight embrace. He just held her, that was all,
but it was everything.

It would have been perfect, had Helena not been looking
on with a fierce scowl upon her face. Penelope's innocent eyes
were wide, but when Angela smiled at her, Penelope smiled
back.

"Come on, let's go to bed," Phillip said, pulling away.

"She'll be coming with us," Helena said, taking Angela's other hand. "And you," Helena said once they were out of earshot of Phillip, "will be telling us everything in the morning."

Chapter 9

"*How* could you? I mean, really, Angela. I thought you were smarter than that. I thought you might have learned from the first time."

"Helena, I—" Angela started and then gave up, deciding to let Helena keep going until she ran out of breath. In the meantime, she would concentrate on weeding the garden. Helena certainly wasn't helping in that regard, and Penelope, in the row next to them, was more focused on her task than on coming to Angela's defense against Helena's tirade.

"You were devastated when you arrived here. When you weren't sobbing until you couldn't breathe, you were like a corpse. It took you a year to so much as smile, and here you are, making the same mistake twice."

"Helena, I appreciate your concern, but—" Really, she did. But it would be different this time, would it not? And if it was going to end badly, what was so wrong with snatching a few moments of happiness? Phillip was filling up that emptiness inside of her that had persisted for years now.

Helena cut her off and kept going. It was midmorning and already quite hot. They all had gotten a late start to the day because the events of last night had kept everyone up until the wee hours. Angela was sure everyone else felt the same aching exhaustion she did.

"Do you not remember who sat with you while you cried? Me. Who consoled you? *Me.* You may not remember what you went through before, but I do. And if you think I'm going to do the same again, once he leaves and disappoints you, you must have really lost your wits."

"Helena!"

"You could be with child, you know."

"No. I'm not, because what you think happened did not happen." Angela wiped sweat off her brow, probably leaving a streak of dirt there. She was too tired to care.

"Last night, anyway. As long as he's still here, and as long as you are a complete and utter fool about him, there is a chance you might be. And then what?"

"Then I shall love the baby, and it will love me back."

"Because Lord Invalid won't love you back," Helena said sharply, and Angela felt as if she had been slapped. Of course he didn't love her back, because she didn't love him in the first place. Being half in love was different than being fully and completely in love.

But that was beside the point. Did Helena really need to be so cruel? Angela took a deep breath. Helena was just cranky because of lack of sleep. That was all. She was speaking words of anger, not the truth.

But a seed of doubt had been planted.

"First of all, you just pulled out a tomato plant, not a weed," Angela responded. "And second of all, why the outburst? I thought you were my friend." Helena looked at the plant in her hand and scowled at it.

"I am your friend, which is why I'm trying to warn you that you are making a big mistake," she said as she dug a hole and jammed in the tomato plant.

"Who says I'm making a mistake?" Angela asked angrily, yanking out a thistle and ignoring the sting on her hands.

"Don't you know him at all?"

"More than you."

"Aye, that much is true. You're lucky I haven't told the abbess what I saw."

"And why haven't you?"

"I didn't see the point. She can't make him marry you. No one can make him marry. And why should he marry *you*? He won't have ruined you. The ton won't care if he takes his pleasure with some chit stuffed away in the country. He's not under any obligation to marry you. He has no honor, otherwise he would have been married years ago. Why should he do so now?"

"That's enough," Penelope cried out.

"Aye, I have said enough. Now you can't say I didn't warn you when he leaves you," Helena spat out before storming off.

"What is wrong with her?" Angela asked angrily.

"She's just concerned for you," Penelope said consolingly.

"And I appreciate that, but she didn't have to be so horrid about it."

"She's just tired, I'm sure. And, well, you know what today is, don't you?"

"Thursday?"

"Yes, that. It's also the anniversary of her husband's death."

"Oh. I didn't realize."

"She only wants what is best for you, and it's just a difficult day for her."

"What do you think of the situation, Penelope?"

"I should hate for you to get hurt again, of course. But if it helps you achieve a sense of peace, it can't be bad, can it?"

"I don't know. I don't know anything, really. Well, last night, with Phillip . . ."

"Yes?"

"I just knew that I couldn't take my orders."

"What will you do instead?" It was a fair question for Penelope to ask. Angela could always just stay in the abbey without taking her orders, but what was the point of that? And if Phillip did not ask her to marry him, what would she do? Follow him and be his mistress? If she wasn't going to take her orders, it had to be for a better reason than being some man's mistress. And could she even leave on her own, with no place to stay or no way to support herself?

"That, my dear, is what I don't know."

~

He was still abed, and this morning she couldn't fault him for it. He had done so much to fight the fire last night, he deserved his rest. That, and she was too tired to pick a fight this morning.

One fight was enough.

Angela thought Helena might understand if she could see him like this: looking harmless and handsome as he slept. Phillip laid on his back, sprawled out as much as one could be in a narrow bed. The sheet and blanket were tangled around his middle. One of his arms lay over his chest, the other rested behind his head.

She set the breakfast tray on the bedside table as quietly as she could. But then he groaned and opened his eyes.

"Hullo."

"Hello," she said.

He just lay there for a moment, staring at her, and she wasn't quite sure what to do other than return his gaze and smile as if everything were fine.

"How are you this morning?" she asked.

"I've been better, but I've also been much, much worse. Can't complain, I guess."

"You? Not complain?" Angela asked, mockingly incredulous.

"Well, I could manage to find something to gripe about if it would make you happy."

That made her smile. He cared, in some minute way, about her happiness. It was a start, wasn't it? Or at least a continuation of last night. "Some other time, perhaps."

"So how are you this morning?" he asked. He sat up in bed and accepted the cup of tea she handed to him.

"Fine," she said with a sigh. Phillip was being nice, which

reminded Angela that Helena wasn't around to witness that, or how he'd been changing. And it reminded her that Helena could be wrong.

"You don't sound fine."

"Just a lot on my mind, that is all." Angela handed him the breakfast tray as he indicated.

"Tell me while I have breakfast."

"Well, Lord Rutherford offered the funds to repair the roof. So that is a big relief to everyone."

"*That* is what's troubling you?"

"Not really, no. Helena and I fought this morning."

"Who is Helena?"

"A sister here. My friend. She was the one who, um, told us about the fire last night." Angela couldn't quite bring herself to say *caught us in a compromising position* or, worse, *found us mostly naked in each other's arms.*

"Right. I forgot about that."

"You *forgot* about what happened with us last night?"

"Of course not. That I remember with vivid, exquisite detail. The bit about being interrupted is what I didn't bother to remember."

"Well, she thinks I am making a mistake. With you."

"I can certainly see why she would think so. And admit it, you can, too."

"But . . ." She very well could, but she didn't want to.

"Hell, I wouldn't wager on myself, even though I could control the outcome. I'm a bad bet, Angela."

"I suppose it was foolish of me to defend you then. And now I've fought with my friend for no reason," she said sharply, feeling like a fool.

"You defended me?" He looked up at her, obviously startled. It made her think that no one had ever taken his side before. But that couldn't be true, right?

"Yes. You're changing, you know that?"

"It must have escaped my notice."

"At least one of us is paying attention," she retorted.

"So, did your friends tell the abbess about what they saw last night?"

"No," Angela said, watching his reaction closely. He sighed, and she prayed it wasn't a sigh of relief. Although, as Helena pointed out, it wouldn't matter who knew. No one could get this man to the altar. She decided to mention this to him, to test the waters.

"Helena said she wouldn't tell because she didn't see the point of doing so," Angela said, rushing out the words in one breath.

"I see," he said and fell silent. Angela counted to thirty in her head, waiting for him to say something else. And then she couldn't wait any longer.

"That's all you're going to say about it?" she asked.

"Well, that, and that I don't think it's any of her business, and I hope you told her so."

"I didn't."

"As it happens, I was planning on speaking to the abbess today anyway," Phillip said, much to Angela's surprise.

"Are you going to tell her about last night? About us?"

"I wasn't planning on it, no."

"Is that because . . . ?" Angela prompted. Because he didn't want to be forced to marry her?

"Because then she might make some other chit bring me my meals, and I've become fond of you."

～

"Come in," Lady Katherine called out in response to his knock. Phillip entered, limping slightly after the strain of last night's activities. At her gesture, he sat in a chair before her desk. The room was sparse, like every other room here; it only contained a full bookshelf on the wall behind her desk and an extra chair. And the abbess. Phillip could easily imagine her as a society matron; it was something in the way she carried herself.

"Good morning, Lord Huntley. How are you this morning?"

"Fine, thank you. And yourself?"

She sighed and gave him a half smile. "I've had better mornings. Lord Rutherford offered the funds to replace the roof. It's so very generous of him, and I confess, a great relief to me."

"I'd imagine. That is what I've come to discuss with you, Lady Katherine. We both know I cannot remain here indefinitely. And yet, I don't have any money." Phillip was surprised at how easily the words came out. Admitting to not having money was just not done in his circles.

"There is no charge for your care here, Phillip. It is our duty to God to help our fellow man."

"And I thank you for that. But I need money to leave. I couldn't even walk to London, with this leg, if I were so inclined." It went without saying that he was not inclined, nor would he ever be, so long as there were other options.

"I could arrange to loan you the funds."

"No, thank you," Phillip said, wishing she would stop being so generous and let him say what he had come to say, before he changed his mind about it. He could always write to his brother or to his friend Parkhurst and have them send the necessary funds but, well, Angela was right. He was changing.

"I have a proposal for you," he said firmly. "In exchange for the funds to leave, I will work on the roof. I recognize that I am not in the physical condition to do much, but I'm sure there is something I could do to, ah, earn what I need."

There. He had done it: *he had offered to work to earn money*. His father must be spinning in his grave. Phillip could imagine his friends at the club choking on their brandy and laughing uproariously if they heard of this.

"Lord Huntley—"

"Phillip."

"Phillip, that is so very generous of you," Lady Katherine said, positively beaming at him. "Your mother would be so proud."

Phillip winced at that; he couldn't help it. It was just that to hear those words was like being punched in the chest. He just felt like he had lost his breath for a second. And he was too stunned to think at first. And the abbess kept talking as if she didn't realize the enormity of what she had just said. He had done something right. That was new. He had done something someone would be proud of; that, too, was new. And he had, by some miracle, managed to do something that would have impressed one of his parents. It went without saying that was new, too.

". . . I think you should take today to rest," the abbess was saying, "after all you did last night. That way you can be refreshed and ready to start tomorrow with the men from the village who are coming to help. We expect that it should take about two weeks."

Phillip agreed to that.

"Now, Phillip, is there anything else you'd like to discuss?"

He looked at her curiously. Did she know about him and Angela? She couldn't possibly. She certainly wasn't going to hear a word about that from him.

"No, thank you."

"Very well, then. My door is always open to you, if there is something you should like to talk about."

"I'll remember that," Phillip said and then promptly forgot about it.

He shut the door behind him and paused in the hall, wondering what to do with himself all day, and where Angela might be, and how to get back to his room. Really, whoever had designed this place must have wanted people to get lost. All the corridors looked exactly the same and followed no pattern that he could discern.

With nothing to do, he wandered around, eventually stumbling upon the kitchens, and, even better, Angela. She and her friends were sitting around the table in the center of the room, chopping up vegetables. They did not speak.

Ordinarily, Phillip would have rather done anything than sit with three women in the midst of a fight. But he was bored, and Angela was here, so he said good morning and joined them at the table.

"Hello," Penelope said brightly. She was chopping carrots that were nearly the same color as her hair. She looked up at him and smiled.

The other one shot him a look of complete disdain and returned to peeling potatoes, clearly determined to ignore him. This must be Helena.

"Hello," Angela said, looking up from shelling peas. "Did you want something?"

"Just company. I'm bored," he answered. Helena snorted, and the others ignored her.

"Well, you can stay here with us, I guess," Angela said.

"And maybe even make yourself useful," Helena said with a daring expression, pushing some potatoes his way and handing him a knife. He looked up to find three faces staring at him expectantly. He supposed they were waiting for him to declare that such a tedious chore was beneath him. And he might have done, except that if his options were to peel potatoes or sit alone in his chamber, bored out of his mind, then he was certainly going to peel the damned potatoes. So he started, ignoring their expressions of shock, and they all continued with their work.

"How was your meeting with Lady Katherine?" Angela asked.

"Fine," he said.

"What did you want to see her about?"

"I'm going to work on repairing the roof in exchange for money to get back to London."

Angela muttered something under her breath to Penelope.

"What was that?" Helena asked.

"She said, 'I told you he had changed,'" Penelope said loudly. "I think that is very kind of you, Lord Huntley."

"Lord Invalid, you mean," Helena muttered.

"I beg your pardon?" Phillip could not have possibly heard what he thought he did.

"Nothing," Angela said quickly, giving a look to Helena. Phillip turned to Penelope and smiled at her. She blushed.

"She called you Lord Invalid," Penelope answered.

"Penelope!" Angela exclaimed, looking horrified.

"You call me Lord Invalid?" He wasn't sure whether to be insulted or amused.

"Not anymore," Angela was quick to point out.

"Just for the first few days that you were here," Penelope added.

"Before Angela started losing her wits and liking you," Helena said harshly.

"Helena!" Angela exclaimed again, looking utterly horrified.

"I've been called worse," Phillip said with a shrug, deciding to find it amusing. "Which one of you thought of it?"

"I did," Helena said proudly.

"It does have a ring to it, doesn't it?" he commented.

"I thought so," Helena agreed.

"Did Lady Katherine say how long it would take to repair the roof?" Angela asked, obviously to change the subject.

"Two weeks."

"And then you're going to leave?" Angela asked.

"Yes." He peered at her, trying to discern her expression. But she seemed utterly focused on her task.

"What will you tell your friends when they ask where you have been?" Penelope asked him.

"I could tell them the truth, but I doubt they'd believe it. They'll have a good laugh over it, I'm sure."

"And will they have a good laugh if you tell them you seduced a sister in an abbey?" Helena asked.

There were awkward silences, and then there were Awkward Silences. This was certainly one of the latter. Even Angela didn't chastise her friend. In fact, the worst of it was that she stopped shelling peas to look at him, unabashedly curious as to what he would say.

His friends would find it hysterical if he told them the truth of the situation—not only that he had seduced a woman about to take her orders, but that she had seduced him, too. Parkhurst would probably clap him on the back and offer to buy him a drink. But he had no intention of telling anyone anything. In fact, he never confided in his friends about anything—for there was no point, when they would all rather believe what is written in the papers than something so mundane as the truth.

"Contrary to popular belief and much to the chagrin of my friends, I don't kiss and tell," he answered firmly. And because he couldn't resist, "I also don't meddle in the affairs of others," he said pointedly to Helena.

"*Affairs* being the operative word," she muttered before setting down her knife and quitting the room. What was it with the women here leaving the room in the middle of arguments?

"Sorry about that," Penelope said after another moment of excruciating silence.

"It's all right. To be expected, really," he answered. And it wasn't Helena that bothered him so much as the way Angela looked at him skeptically, as if she could easily imagine him dining out for weeks on his tale of seduction in the abbey. She may have thought he was changing, but she obviously didn't think him a gentleman. He could see why she wouldn't, what with her experience and his reputation. Didn't mean he liked it, though.

Penelope and Angela then began discussing the different villagers, and who in particular might be working on the roof. For women who lived a secluded life, Phillip thought they knew a lot about the goings-on in town. They fully expected Johnnie and William Sloan, Penelope's brothers, to come help with the roof, but not Rob McCabbin, as he had broken his leg jumping off of the porch in front of the Sun and Moon Tavern. He had been deep in his cups, of course. The Fitch family probably couldn't spare their eldest boys at this time of year; too much work to do on the farm, if they were to make ends meet.

Phillip kept silent and kept peeling potatoes. Angela and Penelope seemed to forget that he was there for long stretches of the conversation, leaving him to puzzle out the strange feeling he was experiencing. He thought it might have been something like contentment.

⌒

Phillip did not join the sisters for lunch or dinner. Their rules about not being in the presence of a man were only flexible to a point.

During his midday meal, alone, he thought that his friends would indeed laugh themselves sick to hear that he was in an abbey. They would choke on laughter and mock him mercilessly if they heard that he had spent the better part of the morning peeling potatoes and listening to female chatter with some interest. And he knew that they wouldn't understand if he tried to explain about Angela's voice, and how a man could be riveted by anything she said. They would just laugh even more and call into question his masculinity.

Well, they wouldn't laugh, because he wouldn't tell them any of it. It was true that he didn't kiss and tell; he didn't need to brag about conquests or affairs or anything of the sort, because others always did it for him. They took his silence to be an affirmation.

He had ruined four women, but not as thoroughly as everyone seemed to think, because he never corrected their assumptions. No wonder he had the reputation he did.

During dinner, which he took alone again, it occurred to him that he ought to make some sort of plan about what to do when he left the abbey.

He could go to London. He had two options for lodgings, neither of which appealed to him. He could impose on Devon and Emilia. Lord knew the ducal residence in London had plenty of room. But he'd be damned if he'd ask his brother for anything. And though Emilia had obviously forgiven Devon for allowing her to be confused about his status as a twin, Phillip doubted she'd be as forgiving to him. He had, after all, tried to trap her into marriage because he needed her dowry.

And he had needed the money to prove to his father that he wasn't the hopeless case his father always told him he was. He could have taken her dowry to fix up the estate and keep it running. Because the only thing his father cared about was the estate. It was always the damned title and the lands and the house. Nothing else mattered.

And here he was, penniless, and without a father to impress. He just had a twin who had spent his life one-upping him and who now had money to spare and a wife who hated Phillip. No, he would not darken their door, asking for help.

He did have some pride, after all.

He had friends, too. Parkhurst would let him stay at his place, even though they hadn't had any communication since Phillip took off for Paris, since neither of them wrote letters unless absolutely necessary. Parkhurst could always be counted on to lend out some money for drinks and, Phillip realized, much-needed clothing.

It was decided. He would go to London and stay with Parkhurst.

And then what? It was harder and harder to believe that he had once been one of the wealthier men in England and due to inherit one of the oldest titles in the land. Well, until Devon had a son, Phillip was still the heir, with his honorary title of Marquis of Huntley. One day that would be relinquished, and he would be left titleless. It may have already happened, for all he knew.

But not necessarily homeless. He still had Aston House, and that could always be sold off, if necessary. And then what would he do?

With his meal finished and his future still uncertain, Phillip went to see if Angela was finished yet. The doors to the dining room were still closed. With nothing else to do, he waited in the hall.

It occurred to him that he hadn't touched her for nearly twenty-four hours. This struck him as grievously wrong, and he vowed he would remedy it as soon as he could. To think so much time had elapsed when he hadn't touched her, and especially when they had so little time together as it was.

He breathed a sigh of relief when the doors opened, and all the sisters started streaming out into the hall. Angela saw him immediately and smiled.

He leaned heavily on his good leg and made a show of needing her assistance to walk back to his chamber. She was clearly not fooled but did not protest. His bad leg was fine enough, really. He just wanted to touch her. But he lied anyway, so that those watching them walk off arm in arm would think he was just some poor wounded sot in need of charity, giving them less to gossip about.

Once they had gained sufficient distance from the group and found themselves in a darkened, empty corridor, Phillip stopped.

"What is it? Do you need to rest?" Angela asked, looking up at him. He smiled, because that was exactly what he expected, wanted, her to do. He didn't answer her, not with words, anyway.

Phillip took a step toward her, closing the distance. He could feel his pulse quicken in the anticipation of touching her. He allowed a few seconds to pass, and then a few more, so that they both might revel in the feeling, because he was sure she felt the same. Like falling, with the knowledge that one was going to be caught before hitting the ground, so one could just savor the momentary sensation of falling.

When he slid his arms around her waist and she leaned in to him, he was sure that it was all the more amazing because of those few seconds of waiting.

Phillip couldn't remember if—what's her name—Esme had taught him the pleasures to be gained from a long pause, or if it was something he had discovered himself. At the moment, he really didn't care, though.

They barely moved, entwined as they were. Barely breathed, as if an exhale would invite reality to intrude with its reminders of his inevitable departure and her inevitable promise to take her orders.

Angela reached up, her arms around his neck and her fingers woven in his hair. He wished he could do the same, but her hair was braided and coiled and pinned up on her head like a halo. The memory, however, of running his fingers through her long, soft locks the previous evening was shockingly vivid.

He wanted to touch her skin, her bare skin, with an intensity that made him ache. And so he pressed his lips to her bare skin just below her earlobe. It was softer than he had expected, and warm. Her head fell back, a lazy, lulled fall, so that her throat was exposed to him. He was generous with his kisses and his attentions. He was rewarded by her sigh of pleasure. Her warm breath against his skin was like a caress.

Angela was the one to press her mouth against his. She was the one to initiate the kiss and then take it further. She was the one to take one step backward, and then another, holding on to him all the while so that he had no choice but to follow. Not that he would have chosen anything else, given the option. One more step, and her back was up against the wall.

"My knees were feeling weak," she managed to say in a rough whisper.

"I'll hold you up," he murmured, but the words were lost in another kiss. And then he couldn't hold back anymore, so he let his body rest a little more heavily against hers. And then a little more, because she pressed him into her, making him groan softly. If she felt this good standing against him, fully clothed . . . He didn't dare allow himself to imagine a feather bed instead of a wall behind her, and her naked skin against his naked skin and . . .

Oh God.

Even he, Phillip Kensington, renowned absolute scoundrel, did not take women up against the wall in a hallway. Especially when the woman in question was about to commit herself to God, and the hallway was in an abbey. And especially when it would be the first time with her and . . .

Well . . .

He thought it should be special.

So he took a step back and noted that his breathing was ragged and his heart was pounding, but not as much as other parts of him were throbbing with wanting her. He grasped her hand in his and started walking down the hall.

"I don't know where we're going," he said.

"I was hoping to talk about that," she said softly.

"Right. Before we do that, I meant that I think we are walking in the wrong direction. Isn't this the way we came from?"

"Oh, it is. I hadn't noticed."

And so they turned around and walked down the corridor, hand in hand. At the end of the hall, they turned left. And encountered the abbess.

The expression on her face was one Phillip knew well, having seen it before on the faces of numerous society matrons. The eyes narrowed, while the expression remained impassive, absorbing every last detail and committing it all to memory. The eyebrow raised questioningly. The lips pursed into a thin, straight line.

Phillip kept his mouth shut, because the only thing he could think of saying was, "But we're only holding hands!" Speaking of that, he dropped Angela's hand, like getting rid of the evidence after a crime.

Neither he nor Angela dared to speak, so it was the abbess who broke the silence.

"Angela, might I have a word with you?"

And she knew, as well as he, that though it may have been phrased as a question, it was in truth a command. And it was not what he had expected.

"Of course, Lady Katherine," Angela said, glancing nervously at him.

"Good night, Lord Huntley. I am sure you hope to get a good night's sleep before you start work in the morning."

Four hours later, Phillip lay in bed, most certainly *not* having a good night's sleep. Angela had not come to enlighten him about her meeting with Lady Katherine. And now, here he was, literally and metaphorically in the dark.

It was very likely, he assumed, that Lady Katherine would demand a marriage. Hand-holding was not a grand offense, but it begged the question of what else had been going on . . . and what else had gone on would certainly have been grounds for marriage.

The thought of matrimony had the same effect on Phillip as it always did. It made his stomach ache. Like he was starving yet nauseated all at once. Like it was coiled into one giant knot that would never unravel, and so he would have to live with this agonizing pain forever.

Unless he ran.

But he couldn't run now . . . literally or figuratively. He had a bum leg and no money.

And he really needn't take such drastic action until he had heard his sentence. And so he waited for four long, agonizing hours, with this unbearable stomachache, for Angela to come to him. Except she didn't.

Panic started to set in. What if she had fled, rather than marry him? He considered that a definite possibility. She could be out there, all alone, having no idea the dangers that awaited a woman with nothing. Not a man to protect her, or a chaperone to warn men away. No money, no connections. Nothing but a figure men would die to possess and the voice of a siren.

He got out of bed, prepared to go out into the night in

search of her and save her from herself. He got as far as the door to his bedchamber when he realized he didn't know where to begin. He couldn't very well go knocking on every door, waking every sister in the abbey until he found her, in her room.

And if he didn't? Was he really going to traipse around the countryside in the dark? Look how well that had turned out the last time.

Rather well, actually, but that was hardly relevant.

She was not stupid, he reminded himself. She would take her orders, instead of marrying him. And if she was going to leave, she was at least going to wait until morning. She would say good-bye to her friends—or at least Penelope. And she would explain to him that she couldn't marry him for reasons he already knew.

The very reasons he had fled every other marriage he ought to have entered into. As he saw it, he didn't ruin those women so much as save them from a lifetime of disappointment.

He just wasn't worth it, and now he was even more worthless than he had ever been. He hadn't any money. His reputation and, he suspected, his own soul were as dark and filthy as chimney soot. He was shallow and self-absorbed and in possession of a short attention span when it came to women. His own father had declared, repeatedly, that Phillip was a hopeless case—his own *father*, who was supposed to be the one person in the world that ought to love him unconditionally.

And so Phillip lay back on his bed, imagining Angela saying all these things he already knew in that bewitching voice of hers. All of them unfortunately true. And they would part ways; she would be relieved. She would take her orders and live devoted to God.

And what about him? Oh, bloody hell, did his stomach ache now, at the thought of a life without Angela. Really, the thought made him nearly sick.

And that's when he knew. If he was going to be an utter disappointment, it would not be because he didn't *try* to be a better man. And when he left the abbey, she was going with him.

~

"Please sit," Lady Katherine said in a voice that did not belie what she was feeling. Though Angela would have rather been free to pace around the room, she did as told, sitting in the chair and bracing herself for whatever might come next.

Angela felt nervous. Jittery. She had an inkling that things were going to change after this conversation. How, she knew not.

"Well," Lady Katherine said, sitting in her chair behind her desk after lighting a few tallow candles on her desk. It was still fairly light outside, though darkness was rapidly approaching. "I had hoped to speak with you tonight anyway, Angela. I wanted to ask if you had given any thought as to when you might take your orders."

"I have," Angela said and paused. She took a deep breath. A little voice in her head urged her to just say it allready. "And I am sorry, but I cannot do it."

"I see," Lady Katherine said, but Angela wasn't sure she did understand.

"I had thought that I just needed time to get used to the idea," Angela explained. "I've been here six years, always putting it off, wanting to be sure. But I think I can admit now that I never wanted to do it. I was just waiting because I was so . . . so . . . hopeless about my alternatives."

"Am I correct in assuming that Lord Huntley has something to do with all of this?"

"It could be nothing more than timing," Angela said. But it wasn't that. At this point, she stood and began to pace around the room. The chamber being small, she did not have far to roam. But it was enough. She paced. And she talked.

"Or it could be that because of him I no longer see myself as just some stupid girl that got herself ruined. And if I am not that girl, then who am I? And how will I know if I stay here, where it's safe and unchanging?" Angela paused at the window, but she already knew the view and turned to give the abbess her full attention.

"The religious life, as you know, is not easy," Lady Katherine said calmly. "It requires sacrifice, dedication, and devotion. It is not something to be undertaken lightly. One will never attain or even appreciate its rewards if one has not undertaken this life with certainty."

"I know. I—"

"I never thought that it was the life for you," Lady Katherine said bluntly, to Angela's surprise. "When you arrived here, you were running away from a bad situation. You were not running toward your fate. The abbey was for you, I think, a place where you could tend to your wounds for a while, before returning to the outside world."

"But you let me stay anyway."

"I could have been wrong."

"I'm sorry," Angela whispered.

"Don't be sorry, Angela. There is nothing wrong with that. I think we would both be sorrier if you took your orders because you had given up on life. We do not judge here, and we welcome anyone."

"Even scoundrels like Phillip," Angela said with a wry smile.

"Aye, even scoundrels like him. But you were holding hands with him tonight. Might I assume that your feelings for him have changed?"

"Oh, I still think he is a scoundrel. I still hate that he has ruined all those girls. And he is still demanding. And in spite of all that, I think I might be falling in love with him."

There, she had said it. She had woken up this morning with the thought on her mind. All day, she had kept it to herself, not because she wanted to keep it a secret, but because who could she tell? Certainly not Helena, who would just call her crazy, and Angela might have agreed. The timing hadn't been right to tell Penelope. As for telling Phillip—she suspected she was just as terrified of telling him as he would be upon hearing it.

But now she had said it, as if that made it real.

"In love with him?" Lady Katherine echoed. Not doubtful but not encouraging, either.

"Maybe I just love the woman I am when I am with him. Or maybe I am just in love with the way he makes me *feel*."

"How has this come about?" Lady Katherine asked gently. Angela thought about this before speaking. She walked from one end of the room to the other and back again.

"I don't think I can pinpoint one moment where something changed. It just seemed that each minute I spent with him, it was a little harder to see him as the newspapers did, or to see him as one and the same as Lucas Frost. I suppose it became easier to see him for who he is and who he is becoming," Angela said.

She thought of his kiss, too, but kept this to herself. She hadn't even considered that a kiss could be so soulful, so magical, so impossible to describe. Now that she thought about it, kissing Lucas had never, ever been even close to what she had with Phillip.

And, in that exact moment, she felt nothing at the thought of Lucas. Not regret or rage, nor even a sort of fondness. Absolutely nothing—and this was wonderful. That feeling, or lack of it, was what she had come to the abbey in search of. She had found peace. And it hadn't come from opening her heart in prayer to the divine but from opening her heart and daring to love a mortal man.

Angela gave up her pacing and returned to the chair. She looked at Lady Katherine. Her expression was serene, as it usually was, but she was also smiling sweetly.

"Angela, I think you have changed, too. You are no longer as angry as you have been these past few years. But I don't think you are exactly happy, either."

"I fought with Helena today," Angela confessed. "Or rather, she fought with me. I am not certain. She, too, has noticed my change in affection for Phillip. She is sure that he will hurt me, the way I was hurt before."

"Do you think he will hurt you?"

"He might. He could." Angela looked down at her hands clasped tightly in her lap. She didn't want to say what she was about to say, but she couldn't keep the words inside. "Lady Katherine, I was with him last night. Helena discovered us. And she said she wasn't going to tell you about it because she didn't see the point."

"I had suspected you were with him."

"You did?"

"Penelope and Helena arrived at the chapel in quite a state, because you had not been in your room. We all feared that you were in the chapel, because we know of your nighttime visits there. But you weren't there, obviously. So I thought you might have been with Lord Huntley."

"I was."

"Is there grounds for a marriage?"

"There is no chance that I am with child. But people have married after being caught in less compromising positions. But as Helena said, no one can get this man to the altar, not even you. And frankly, I don't want to marry him if he is forced into it. *I* don't want to be forced into it."

"Angela, you do realize why I assigned you to take care of him?"

"Because I hadn't taken my orders, so I could be in the company of a man."

Lady Katherine threw her head back and laughed.

"I can't believe none of you have seen through that! I could have always requested that someone from the village come up here to take care of him until he was well enough to be moved."

"Yes, you could have done! Why didn't you?" Angela was stunned that she hadn't thought of this herself. *Really*.

"Like I said, I had always suspected that the religious life was not for you. But how were you ever going to know that if you didn't leave, or didn't get a glimpse of what was out there? And how were you ever going to achieve any sort of resolution about the man who had ruined you if you did nothing but curse him for your present unhappiness?"

"You were giving me a gift, and I thought you were punishing me," Angela answered.

"I had a less noble reason as well. I was an excellent

matchmaker when I still took part in society functions. I haven't had much practice these past few years. I couldn't resist."

Angela's mouth dropped open in shock. She had been set up and hadn't even realized it. She looked at Lady Katherine in a different light, and could easily see her as a younger woman, shrewdly observing the goings-on in a ballroom and seeing what others failed to notice because they were so caught up in themselves.

"Having said that, I now have a proposal for you," Lady Katherine continued. "I will not demand a marriage unless there is a chance that you might be with child. I expect that you will either refrain from such activities or inform me that we need to plan a wedding ceremony. And if that is the case, I will personally escort him to the altar with a pistol at his back, if necessary."

"Lady Katherine!" Oh, she was shocked. But she was also pleased. She had a champion.

"He has gotten away with far too much as it is," Lady Katherine said. "It's about time someone brought that man up to scratch."

A sentiment likely held by the entire population of England, Angela thought. But was she the one to reform the biggest scoundrel in a generation? If she failed, no one would be surprised, and she certainly wouldn't be the only one.

"But you must go when he leaves—either with him or without him."

Her instinct was to agree immediately, before she thought too much about it. Still, reason intruded with practical questions. What would she do if she struck out on her own? Where could she go? Perhaps she should stay at the abbey after all, living out the rest of her days wondering what might have been if she hadn't passed up the chance of a lifetime . . .

She didn't know the answers to those questions. But maybe she didn't have to know. Because maybe . . . maybe . . .

Angela nodded her agreement.

She was not hopeless. Quite the contrary, in fact.

Chapter 10

Phillip awoke at dawn. His eyes easily adjusted to the morning light, which was now familiar to him. Though he had lain awake for hours the night before, the sleep he managed must have been enough. His mind felt clear—clear enough to recall and compare all the other mornings of his life when he woke up feeling positively wretched. It seemed like another lifetime, or even someone else's life.

Funny, that.

Angela was right. He was changing. And she had better still be around to appreciate what she had done to him.

Phillip dressed quickly and went off in search of her. And it occurred to him, as he wandered the halls, his nerves on edge, that he felt rather like he was fourteen years old again.

Like he was a mere lad, wandering around the halls of Cliveden, searching for Jenny, the pretty housemaid he had fancied. OK, he had been infatuated with her. She was a year older than he, experienced, and had returned his affections enough to relieve him of his virginity. He had been heartbroken when he had discovered her with one of the footmen, though he never let anyone know it. A footman! He was going to be a duke, and she chose a footman instead.

But at the moment, he didn't recall that blow to his pride as vividly as he remembered the sweet anticipation of glimpsing her, of talking to her. He felt this now, and he hadn't felt it since he was a lad of fourteen. And when had he lost it? When, exactly, had he forgotten about that feeling? When had he started skipping over it, just to get into bed and get out before dawn came, before the woman realized that she might rather have a footman instead of him?

Where was Angela? This corridor was empty, and he was lost, but he kept going. Perhaps she was in the kitchen. He hoped so, because he was hungry now, and he couldn't manage a day of physical labor on an empty stomach.

Gah. A day of physical labor. His first day of work in his life. It took him twenty-eight years to get to this. Some people he knew, like his father, died without ever having done anything remotely resembling physical labor, unless one counted hunting. Phillip suspected most people didn't.

At the thought of this first day of work, Phillip felt as he had on the way to begin school at Eton. He had spent the entire journey there telling his twin that it was likely Devon wouldn't have any friends, no one would like him, the work would be too hard for him to manage, and he would fail out by the holidays.

Phillip had, of course, been transferring his own fears onto his twin. Devon had made friends (despite Phillip's taunts) and excelled at school (despite doing most of Phillip's work for him). But Devon wasn't around to bully today, and Phillip knew now that it wouldn't help if he were. So Phillip did what he did best, which was push unpleasant thoughts aside and think of something else instead.

Finally, he found the kitchen.

And Angela.

He leaned against the door frame, forgetting about his hunger and instead savoring the sight of her engaged in conversation with Penelope while standing over the stove. From where he stood, it didn't seem like one of those sob-filled

I-can't-believe-I'm-leaving-I'll-miss-you-so-much conversations. He felt relieved.

And then she turned around, he caught her eye, and she smiled.

❧

It was nice, Angela thought, that he sought her out this morning. Unless he was avoiding a private conversation with her. No—now was not the time to start second-guessing herself. She made herself focus on the breakfast tray she was preparing. She had just added the fried eggs to the plate, which already contained bread and slices of ham.

He was walking toward her now. His stride was sure, confident, and she was clearly his destination. Her pulse quickened. I am leaving *with* you, she thought.

"He is handsome, isn't he?" Penelope sighed beside her. "I bet he is devastatingly so when he is dressed for a ball." Angela murmured her agreement, even though she thought he seemed quite handsome the way he was now: breeches, boots, and a shirt unbuttoned at the collar and rolled at the sleeves. They were all clean but still rather worn. They were undoubtedly of a lesser quality than he was accustomed to, but he wore them well, and he did not complain. He could do with a shave, though. Or without. It didn't matter to her.

"Good morning," he said, smiling especially at Penelope.

"Good morning, Lord In—Lord Huntley," she answered.

"Call me Phillip," he said, and smiled at her expectantly.

There was a long silence.

"Oh, very well, I can take a hint," Penelope said with a laugh before she went outside into the garden, leaving them alone in the kitchen.

"You didn't come to my room last night," he said pointedly to Angela.

"I know," she said, pouring tea into a cup, which she handed to him. He didn't say anything, though certainly he must have something to say. "If you have a question, Phillip, you can just ask."

"Tell me what happened with the abbess."

"That wasn't a question," she couldn't resist pointing out.

"I'm trying, woman, I just don't know where to begin."

"Maybe I don't, either," she said. "We talked for a while. And I suppose all you need to know is that Lady Katherine and I agreed that I am leaving the abbey when you do—either with you or without you."

"Angela! Angela?" Voices were calling for her. Male voices. Ones that could only belong to Johnnie and William Sloan, Penelope's brothers.

Because of the interruption, Phillip did not have a chance to reply. Although, she noted with some satisfaction, his darkened expression at two men calling out for her might have been the answer she was looking for.

In a minute Phillip would see that they were just boys and not in competition with him for her affections. William, the eldest of the pair, was eighteen, and Johnnie was a year younger.

"There you are, Angela!" William said, coming into the kitchen from the garden door. He stopped abruptly when he saw Phillip, and Johnnie, coming up behind him, bumped into him.

"What'd you stop for?" Johnnie asked, annoyed.

"Looks like you might have competition for Angela's affections, Johnnie," William said teasingly after taking note of Phillip. Johnnie's face flushed as red as his hair—the same shade as his sister Penelope's.

"Hello, boys," Angela said. "Aren't you supposed to be working on the chapel? Or do you need something?"

"Penelope told us some fellow was in here that is going to work with us. I figure that's him," William said, jerking his head in Phillip's direction.

"Hey, isn't that the bloke we found in the ditch?" Johnnie asked.

"Yes. His name is Phillip," Angela said, and then completed the introductions.

"You look a lot better than the last time we saw you," William said. "I could have sworn you were dead when we first found you."

"Thank you for taking a closer look and for bringing me here," Phillip said. Angela watched the Sloan brothers' expressions when Phillip spoke. His accent betrayed him, making it clear he was of the upper class. The boys did seem to note that, suddenly standing a little straighter and becoming a bit more reserved.

"Do you boys want something to eat?" Angela offered. They hesitated. "It's no trouble."

"Perhaps a cup of tea, if that's all right," William answered for them both. Phillip sat down to his breakfast, and the Sloan brothers joined him. Angela straightened up the kitchen while listening in on their conversation.

"So where are you from?" William asked.

"Buckinghamshire. But I spent most of my time in London."

"What brings you round these parts?"

"I was returning to London from Paris."

"Paris? Lots of fellows around her have been to Paris. Two French blokes have been staying at the tavern, in fact. And then Frank Jones, from the next town over, was in France for a bit during the war. He said the women over there were quite different from the English ones, if you know what I mean."

"I do," Phillip said, grinning in spite of himself.

"So, could you tell us about them?" William asked in a lowered voice.

Angela caught them all casting glances at over at her. Or rather they caught her shamelessly listening in.

"Oh, don't mind me," she said sweetly. "Do carry on."

"Angela, what Phillip is about to tell us is not fit for a lady's ears," Johnnie said gravely.

"You don't know that," Phillip protested.

"Aw, don't disappoint us," William chided.

"A gentleman does not relate those sorts of things," Phillip said sternly.

"In front of other women," William added with a wink.

"You can at least tell us a bit. No need to relate the specifics. But we need to know for, um, educational purposes," Johnnie said.

"In case we are ever in France," William added, even though it was unlikely.

"Well . . ." Phillip said, looking over at Angela. And she

understood that his rank would likely work against him, because here he was an outsider, and yet he still had long days of laboring with them ahead of him. She understood that he was just trying to fit in, and if he had to talk about Parisian trollops to do so, he was going to do it.

But did they think that maybe she wanted to hear about that, too? Well, she could just eavesdrop from the hall.

"Fine. I'm leaving," Angela said, scowling at the lot of them.

~

By lunchtime, Phillip had become friends with William and Johnnie. Over lunch the two brothers detailed all the local girls that were available if a man needed some company, to put it nicely. They didn't believe Phillip when he said he had no need of the information; they insisted that it was only fair that since Phillip had told them where to go for women in Paris, they return the favor and give him some local tips.

The work was mind-numbingly simple: unloading lumber from the carts, measuring it, and sawing it into the proper lengths. But by the end of the day, the simple labor had every muscle in Phillip's body screaming for mercy.

He turned down an invitation for pints at the village tavern, preferring a bath. And Angela. He hadn't spoken with her at all during the day, though he occasionally caught a glimpse of her working in the garden. At one point, he saw her working on something in a little book. Curious, he had been about to put his shirt back on and go ask her about it, but another cart of lumber had arrived, demanding his efforts.

Now, relaxing in a bath in his room, he realized that she still hadn't told him about her conversation with the abbess, except for the whole leaving with or without him thing.

He sensed an ultimatum.

He sensed "A Talk."

Both his body and mind were too weary to worry or panic or even dwell on this looming conversation. The kind of conversation he had so far managed to avoid in his nine and twenty years. He had also managed to avoid working for that same length of time, too, but he had had enough firsts for one day.

Or not.

Angela had brought her own supper as well as his, and they sat down to dinner together. He had taken just one bite—God, he was starving—when she brought it up.

"The abbess is not going to make us marry. At least not for hand-holding."

"Hmmm." Food had never tasted so good. How had he lived so long without knowing such simple pleasures? A hard day's work, a hot bath, a good meal, and the company of a beautiful woman. And then later, perhaps, they might . . . He looked up at her but felt his smile evaporate when he saw her face.

"You weren't listening to a word I said, were you?" she asked sternly.

"This dinner is delicious."

"Looks like I am leaving without you then," she muttered. "If you won't even pay attention to me when I am right in front of you."

"Fine. I wasn't paying attention. Tell me again?" Phillip said, and then quickly added, "Please." The man could be taught.

"I was just saying that I am not taking my orders."

"Oh. Because of me?"

She sighed impatiently, as if she were trying to talk to the village idiot. He didn't know why he had even asked that, because he certainly didn't want to know. If he was the reason, he thought that might be more responsibility than he could manage to endure.

"Like I said," Angela continued, "I realized that this is not the life for me. I am leaving when you do. Either with you or without you, don't you see?"

Yes, he did see. Very clearly. This was the part where he was to drop down onto one knee and ask her to marry him. And the funny thing was, that didn't seem so terrifying or horrible. The thought that did ruin his appetite was after the wedding, when he had no home to take her to and no money to even buy her dinner, let alone the gowns and jewels that she deserved. Society wouldn't welcome either of them, so she would be stuck with him, and only him, without even friends to complain to about what a horrible husband he was. All these truths nullified the resolution he had made the previous evening.

"Angela," he started, "I have no money. I suspect you don't, either. I have a house, but I have never been to it. In fact, I don't think anyone has been there in years. If the thing is still even standing. Furthermore, society will not be kind to either of us."

"Because I'm ruined," she muttered, looking downcast.

"No, because you'll be attached to me. But that doesn't matter, because I simply cannot get married now. I can't even support myself, let alone a wife and children."

"But I could still go with you. We'll find a way to make things work."

"No, but not because I don't want you to. I was quite nearly sick at the thought of not seeing you once I've gone. But I'll manage, and you will, too," he said. It was the right thing to do; he was sure of it. But he didn't necessarily like it.

"Maybe I'm tired of just managing. I've been doing that for years."

"It'll just be more managing with me. Managing to get by. Managing not to be completely disappointed in me. Managing not to completely regret choosing *me* over God."

"Did you ever think that maybe I don't care about all that so long as I am with you?" Angela cried. From the look on her face, Phillip could have sworn she hadn't meant to say that. Or maybe, he couldn't believe it. He didn't even have a title to offer her now. Just himself, and that really wasn't much.

"No, I didn't," he said softly.

"Well, think about it," she snapped, in that brandylike voice of hers. Oh, he would miss that voice. Almost as much as he might miss other things about her.

"Later," he replied. He would certainly miss kissing her.

"Later? Next week? Next month? In ten years' time?"

"Just not now." And then he stood up a bit, to lean over, across the table, over their dinner, and he pressed his mouth to hers. There were so many things in the way—the table, the plates, the glasses—that it was not the most convenient position for kissing. But the need to kiss her at that moment was so urgent and overwhelming, the obstacles between them be damned.

He coaxed her into a deeper kiss, running his tongue along the seam in her lips so that she parted, letting him in. She sighed a bit, perhaps in vexation, pleasure, or surrender. He knew not. He treasured it all the same.

"You think if you just kiss me, you'll make me forget everything else?" she murmured.

"If I'm doing it right."

Phillip rested his palms on either side of the table to support himself, still leaning over the table, still reaching out to her in the only way he knew how.

"When you stop kissing me, I start thinking again."

"I guess I'll have to keep kissing you then."

He leaned in for another kiss, this one all too brief.

"Only until you leave. Without me," she said.

Phillip sat back down, abandoning that strategy for ending the conversation in favor of another.

"I'm too tired to talk about that any more tonight." That was true. He was just too tired to have a conversation about how inadequate he was. How unsuitable he was for marriage, and how he couldn't make her happy and couldn't make her see that. And he knew he had to make her see that now, before it was too late, and he was miserable from making her miserable.

"I'll go then," she said.

"Stay," he said firmly, flashing that suggestive grin of his. "I'm not too tired for other things."

"You should know, Phillip, that the abbess said that if I am carrying a child, she will personally march you down the aisle, at gunpoint if necessary."

"I don't doubt that."

"So perhaps I ought to go then." To make her point, Angela stood up and stepped to the side of the table. He stood as well.

"No," he said, smiling wickedly. "There are other things to do. Or there are ways to prevent conception."

"There are?" That, of all things, caught her attention and made her pause.

"Some more reliable than others."

"Such as?" she demanded.

"You're awfully curious about this."

"Well, no one's ever told me. No one tells young women anything they might actually need to know," she said angrily.

"You shouldn't need to know this kind of thing."

"I might."

"I'll take care of it."

"And if I'm not with you?" Angela asked with an eyebrow arched in challenge.

"Who the hell are you going to be with?" he quite nearly yelled. He swore his heart had stopped for a moment.

"I don't know," she replied with a little shrug of her shoulders. "But you seem intent that I shan't be with you. And I will be leaving here. I might meet someone else."

He hadn't even considered Angela with another man after him; thus far he hadn't had to. He most certainly didn't want to.

"Oh, no," he said firmly. "If you are going to be with any man, it will be me."

"So I am going to be with you, am I? But I won't become pregnant, so you don't have to marry me."

"Well . . ." He couldn't think of anything to say that wouldn't result in something thrown at his head.

"You just want to have your cake and eat it, too, don't you?" she said angrily, stomping her foot for emphasis.

"What I really want is to kiss you." Best to distract her, he thought, closing the distance between them and placing his hand on her waist.

"The gentleman tries to be charming," she retorted, folding her arms across her chest.

"The gentleman is just a man who wants to kiss you while he still has the chance." He kissed the soft spot of skin just below her earlobe.

"You aren't a gentleman. I take it back. You are an absolute scoundrel."

"One who still wants to kiss you." The words were a bit muffled, as he was now feathering kisses along her neck.

"You will, if you can tell me why I'll let you, in spite of my better judgment."

"Because you want to," Phillip murmured, pressing his lips to the hollow of her throat. She arched her neck back to allow him.

"Because you think I'm a better man than I am," he whispered into her ear. His heart stopped again, because that was the truth of the matter in one sentence. He wasn't good enough, and he certainly wasn't as good as she thought he was. But he wanted to be. He just didn't know how.

"And because you want to," he whispered again.

"Just one kiss," Angela sighed.

If it were going to be just one kiss, it would be just one kiss of epic proportions. Phillip was not going to stop at her mouth. Not when there was more of her to taste and to touch with his own mouth. Until she said *no*, until she said *stop*, he was going to be good in the only way he knew how: by being wicked and sinful, but pleasing all the same, so that there would never be another man for her that could compare to him.

Angela had been bold, more than she ever had been. Impending freedom must have gone to her head. How else to explain why she had just thrown herself at him? She had all but proposed to him herself. In another time, another place, she might have been mortified to expose herself like that.

But now, with Phillip pressing the sweetest kisses along her throat, that hot, overwhelming sensation taking over her was not embarrassment. She could have this forever, if only he could just stop being so damned practical. Because she could admit that he did have a point about them not having money or a home or anything. Really, of all the times in the world for Phillip Kensington to discover logic and good sense, it had to be now.

But they could have each other.

That would be enough, wouldn't it?

She slipped her arms around him, pressing the length of her body against his. His chest was warm and strong, like his arms that held her, and like his grasp on her waist. She could feel the unmistakable hardness of his arousal. With a wantonness that surprised even her, she wanted him.

He took a step back but took her with him. Then another, then another, until they reached the bed.

Thank God, she thought. Her legs were becoming too weak to support her.

"Just one kiss," she said to remind him but mostly to remind herself.

Phillip's hands fumbled slightly, shook a bit even, as he undid her dress. Soon enough the wretched garment was gone. He didn't stop there: her chemise went, too, and her undergarments, until she stood before him completely nude, save for her stockings. She might have felt silly, but it was impossible to do so with the way he was looking at her. Hungrily, lustily, longingly.

"I know. Just one kiss." Oh, that grin again. She would miss that. But would that devilish grin compensate for all the other things he said he lacked?

He guided her to sit on the bed. He slid off one stocking and then the other. Her feet might have been on the floor, but her head was in heaven. Because Phillip was making this one hell of a kiss. His mouth had left hers, moving to her throat then down to her breasts. They were covered by his hands and—oh, heaven—his mouth. He held them gently, with a little bit of pressure, enough to give her pleasure and enough to lift the weight she always carried around with her. He took one pink center in his mouth, and she moaned and arched her back. He did the other, and then back again. It was *almost* enough.

His hands had been clasped around her ankles, and they now traveled leisurely up the length of her legs, caressing her all the way. His hands were a little rough against her skin, but it only made her feel him more.

His mouth left her breasts and moved lower. And then lower still . . . across her belly, with a pause at her navel, and then lower still. Somehow, his intentions registered in her hazy brain. But he couldn't possibly mean to do what she thought he was about to do.

Just one kiss. He hadn't said where, though. But now she knew. She couldn't stop a little laugh of shock as his mouth found her most secret place. The secret place that ached at night, that kept her awake with demands she didn't know how to satisfy. That little laugh turned into a sigh, into a moan.

His tongue moved in lazy circles as if he could—and would—do this forever. And so she exhaled and closed her eyes and allowed herself to be completely and solely in this moment. It was overwhelming, for there were so many *new* sensations all begging for her attentions: Phillip's hair was soft against her inner thighs, his slight beard just a bit rough in that same place, the firm grasp of his hands on her hips, the warmth of the mouth, the gentle yet sure and determined movements of his tongue urging her to abandon all thoughts and surrender.

Phillip's tongue moved faster, creating a new pattern she couldn't follow but could only feel. And feel she did, everywhere. Waves of heat coursed through her, so that even though she lay naked with not a stitch covering her, she was not cold. She writhed a little, curled her toes, and arched her back, but Phillip's hands kept her from moving away, not that she wanted to. But something was building inside her, something she could not control, which demanded an escape.

Phillip did not stop, thank God. His mouth continued this tormenting pleasure, and then he also slid one finger inside her. *Oh God.* This was new, too. With what little ability for rational thought she had left, one truth occurred to her: I am an innocent at this. Maybe she hadn't known too much after all.

Angela gripped the bedsheets in one hand and ran her fingers through Phillip's hair with the other. She was almost there, almost on the verge of another little death that had the wondrous effect of making her more alive than she had ever felt.

Her sighs and moans echoed in the small stone-walled room. Phillip laced his fingers through hers. Oh, that hot, pulsing feeling was taking her over now. She pressed hard on his hand. She felt as if she would break or explode at any second. His open mouth covered the bud of her sex and sucked.

And that pushed her over the edge. Angela cried out. For a moment she felt neither alive nor dead but suspended in some magical place of pure pleasure. She cried out, because her body had finally discovered what it had ached for and demanded. And she cried out because in this moment everything was right, sublime, and perfect.

The feeling began a slow retreat, and she did not have the strength to do anything but lie there and enjoy the aftershocks. Phillip moved to lie beside her, to hold her, to kiss her mouth, and to run his fingers through her hair.

All she could do was murmur and try to smile as she returned his kiss. Angela pressed up against him and felt his arousal in his breeches pressing back against her. He groaned at the contact but made no effort to do anything or make her do anything. And she wondered if he was experiencing that same torturous pleasure of wanting with no way to satisfy the demands.

He moved his hips slowly against hers, and she placed her hand on his hip to still him.

"I'm sorry, I didn't realize," he murmured.

"I want to see you," she said, because for all of her experience with men, she had never had a glimpse of that part of a man. She placed her hand over the hardness, with the fabric between them.

"I want to touch you, too," she confessed in a whisper.

"Whatever the lady wants," he replied, with his voice low and rough. She began to unbutton his breeches and then moved them out of the way. His phallus was long and thick. The skin was pink and silky soft to the touch while hard at the same time.

She traced one finger along its length. He sucked in his breath.

She wrapped her hand around it and elicited a groan from his mouth.

Phillip wrapped his own hand around hers, guiding it up and down the length of his shaft. The movement was simple and repetitive, and the changes in Phillip were noticeable. He became harder still. His eyes closed, and he breathed heavily, burying his face in her neck.

After a moment, he took his hand away from hers and cupped her breast in his hand. With his thumb, he caressed the sensitive peak in the center. She arched her back and, without intending to, grasped him harder, all the while moving her hand up and down his length. It was hot in her hand, pulsing, and she knew it was because of her touch. Holding him in her hand made her feel powerful and in control in a way she had never felt before. She liked it.

His mouth crushed hers. And for a while there was nothing but hands here and there and everywhere, along with a scorching, fumbling kiss that stopped so he could murmur her name.

"Angela . . ."

His hips moved, too, now, mimicking the motions of her hand. His hand closed around her again, urging her to hold him harder and tighter and to move faster.

"Angela . . ." he murmured her name again and again like a plea or perhaps a prayer. She didn't stop, because she knew what he was feeling, that any second now he would reach his own release.

Phillip pressed his mouth against the skin where her neck curved into her shoulder. She felt him shudder. She felt him moan. She felt his climax.

And when it was all over, he held her until they both drifted off to sleep.

But in the morning, she woke up alone, having returned to her own bed in the middle of the night. She had not wanted their secret discovered; she wanted to keep it for her own.

She also did not want to be caught and to be forced into a marriage that he did not want. And she was a little sad to once again discover that a man did not want her or love her enough to even try to make a life together, in spite of all the obstacles in their way.

Chapter 11

Phillip had caught her at it again: watching him as he worked and scribbling in a little brown leather book. For three days now, he had felt that someone was watching him. He would look up, look around, and see her. For three days now, he had endured his curiosity about what she was doing because he hadn't managed to steal away from his working on the chapel to ask her.

And when he had seen her at the end of the day, well, he was far more interested in other things to remember to ask after a book. He took a moment now to lean against a tree trunk and wipe sweat from his brow with his shirt. He had never been so exhausted in his life. A long day of laboring under the hot sun was followed by long hours in bed with Angela. They had not made love, but they did find other ways to give each other pleasure. Despite his exhaustion, he managed to grin at the memories.

Those very same memories and experiences were making it harder and harder to imagine life without her. To never again hear her cry out his name in that bewitching voice of hers during a climax he brought her to was a very bleak future indeed.

So what if they were penniless and shunned by society? He dared to hope that he could make her happy anyway.

But at the moment, she was sitting at the base of a tree, for it was too hot at noon to be anywhere but in the shade. That book was open on her lap, and her eyes were closed.

He stepped quietly as he approached. She had definitely fallen asleep, sitting and leaning against the tree trunk.

"Hello," he said.

She opened her eyes, shocked, and stood quickly. The book tumbled to the ground.

"You scared me," she said.

"And you dropped something. Here, I'll get it."

"No!" She reached for it, and he couldn't help but hold it high out of her reach.

"*Please*," he said, giving her a pleading look. He would give it back if she really insisted, but now that he finally held it in his hand, he wanted to see its contents more than ever.

"I should have never taught you that word," she muttered.

"So is that a yes? Say yes, Angela." He grinned at her, because he was learning that she couldn't resist him when he did it.

"Fine. It's nothing that interesting anyway," she said dismissively.

He didn't immediately point out just how wrong she was, because he was too riveted by what he saw. He started at the first page and saw an illustration of a man sitting in some drawing room.

"Is that him?"

Angela nodded, and Phillip looked closer at the man who had ruined her. Part of him wished to beat that smug smile off his face. Or tear up the picture, erasing him from her memory forever. But he could see how lovingly she had drawn him, how well she had captured a moment before she had lost her innocence. He'd be damned if he damaged that drawing.

So he turned the page, and saw a drawing of the Virgin Mary holding Jesus as an infant. Angela had given her a serene smile and happy eyes. After a moment, he recognized it as the statue in the chapel, which had miraculously survived the roof collapsing around it. He knew it well, and that it was a heavy thing, since he and William Sloan had moved it into the abbey to keep it safe while the construction on the new roof was done.

He turned one page, and then another, seeing page after page of illustrations of the same thing: mother and child. But he saw more than the image; he saw why Angela had delayed in taking her orders. She longed for a baby of her own, and that slightly tired but happy smile and a plump child in her arms.

He flipped past a few more similar drawings, until a new subject caught his attention.

He recognized himself. Well, he recognized the features of his face, like his crooked nose and the cut and bruise on his forehead that had now healed into a scar. But the expression didn't seem like it belonged to him. He was peacefully asleep. And written below, *The Devil Sleeps*. That made him smile.

He turned the page and saw another illustration of the statue, this one done from below, as if she knelt before it, looking up to draw it. Idolizing it.

Phillip turned the page again and saw what she had been working on these past few days. It was him with his shirt off. Again, he did not recognize himself. He could not possibly be that impressive. She had portrayed him as practically heroic. There was no background, because her rendering of him took up the entire page. And she included details that spoke of their intimacy, like drawing in his scars in exactly the right places. She knew him, that much was clear, and in a way he didn't know himself.

But he could see now what he hadn't seen before. He could see exactly what she longed for, and by some miracle, it was something he could give her: himself. And a child. And that happy, sleepy smile.

"Are you going to say anything?" she asked.

He looked into her clear blue eyes and saw his future, his best chance at happiness; he saw her love for him and his own love for her.

"Marry me, Angela."

Her lips parted softly in what he guessed was surprise. That, he supposed, was fair. What was certainly not fair was that she had suddenly become speechless, leaving him standing there, with a marriage proposal unanswered.

"Are you going to answer?" he prompted her, because he was starting to get nervous now. His heart was thudding heavily and quickly.

"*Ask* me," she said with a hint of a smile at her lips.

Right. Asking, not commanding. Not very well done of him. Even *he* knew the proper way to issue a marriage proposal. And though dropping to one knee was incredibly painful after his injury, he did it anyway. Phillip took her hand in his and looked into her eyes again.

"Angela, will you please marry me?"

"Yes," she said with a laugh and a smile. "Yes."

He stood quickly and took her into his arms and kissed her thoroughly. He hadn't realized they had an audience until the shouts and calls of the other workers intruded. He had just compromised them both. Did it even count as a compromising position if it was after a proposal? For all his experience in the realm of being caught in compromising positions, he did not know the answer. But that didn't matter, because he was going to be with Angela forever.

And for the first time in the longest while, Phillip felt happy. Content. Proud. For once he had done something right.

～

"Well done, man!" William said, patting him on the back.

"Congratulations," Johnnie said.

"Thanks."

"Now I know why you weren't too keen on our advice about the local girls. Understandable," Johnnie added.

Phillip grinned and shrugged, which was as much confirmation as he would give them. The boys seemed to understand and went back to work, while continuing the argument they had been having all day, something about who had downed more tankards of ale the other night. Phillip didn't listen, so distracted by one thought: he was getting married. And oddly enough, he was excited about it.

Phillip was measuring and sawing planks of wood when he

had the feeling of being watched again. He looked around, expecting to see Angela, but she was nowhere to be found. Probably still with the abbess, telling her the news.

Out of the corner of his eye, however, he saw two men he didn't recognize. They weren't working but hanging around in the thicket, sharing a cigar. They looked like rather unsavory people, even from a distance. Certainly they could have no business with the abbey or anyone in it.

"Who are they?" Phillip asked William, nodding in the direction of the two men.

"Friends of yours, aren't they? That's what they said."

"I don't believe I am acquainted with them," Phillip said, although the sickening feeling in his stomach suggested that he was. Still, he did not know how.

"Oh, the one on the left is Pierre, and on the right is François. French blokes, they are. Not as forthcoming about the Parisian ladies as you were. Surly fellows, actually."

"Seem like it. How do you know them?" Phillip inquired.

"They've been staying at the tavern for a few weeks now. Said they were friends of yours and that they were waiting till you got better, since they said the three of you were returning to France. I reckon that might have changed, now that you're getting married. Or are you taking Angela to France with you?"

Phillip didn't answer at first. His brain was arriving at a very unwanted conclusion. He knew exactly who they were and, unfortunately, he was indeed acquainted with them.

"Angela and I are not going to France." He wasn't going without her, either. He caught the eye of the one William said was Pierre. There was no going back now. And so Phillip walked over to them.

"We've been waiting for you, Phillip," Pierre said with a revolting smirk that revealed the loss of more than one tooth. They pronounced his name the French way, *Fee-leep*. He did not correct him.

"I can't imagine why. You took all my money—all that I owed. And left me for dead. I should think we are even," Phillip said firmly.

"But you did not uphold your end of the bargain. For one thing, you are not dead," Pierre said. He was a short, stocky man with a full beard. A hat jammed onto his head hid his eyes.

"Easily remedied," the other one, François, added. He pounded his fist into his palm. A very big, fat fist, which belonged to a very big, fat man. He was easily twice the size of his companion . . . and Phillip, too.

"But first, you still owe us money," Pierre insisted, pushing his hat farther back on his head, revealing his eyes. They were bloodshot.

"No, I do not."

"But you do. We took your purse, and counted it—"

"Twice," François growled.

"And found it one thousand seventy-four pounds short," Pierre finished.

"How the hell do you figure that?" Phillip challenged. The seventy-four pounds, he knew, could be accounted for by his travel expenses back to England. He could make that up. But a thousand pounds? Impossible. And he knew he had won exactly as much as he had borrowed, and they surely had taken that.

"Interest, monsieur," François growled.

"Interest. I don't recall that being part of the deal I made with DeRue." Granted, Phillip couldn't remember much of the encounter. He had been drinking and needed funds to enter a high-stakes game of vingt-et-un at a gaming hall and brothel. Then he had requested another few thousand for wagering. Claude DeRue's offices were conveniently located in an alley a block away.

"Here is a copy. All the way from France. Maybe this time you'll notice the fine print at the bottom," Pierre said haughtily. He stroked his beard, and Phillip noticed bits of food stuck in it. Disgusted, he looked away and took the document offered to him.

For the one thing, the writing was in French. The words he knew in French were the kind used in the bedroom. Not in the dark, dank den of a moneylender in a seedier neighborhood. That was all irrelevant, because even if it had been in English, or even if he had been fluent in French, Phillip would not have taken the time to read it.

That sickening feeling in his gut increased. He gritted his teeth and ignored it, instead squinting at the minuscule script at the bottom of the page. He could understand a few words: *argent, empruntez, dix pour cent,* and *la peine capitale*.

"You're out of luck, gentlemen. I haven't a halfpence to my name," Phillip said, pocketing the sheet. He didn't think for a second that they would believe or even accept that, but he said it anyway.

They spoke rapidly in French to each other.

"*Bon.* OK," François growled again. It sounded like he had gravel stuck in his throat.

"Great. Glad we settled that."

"We're open to negotiation," Pierre said, stroking his beard again.

"I told you, I haven't got anything," Phillip insisted.

"The *belle fille* . . ." Pierre started, and Phillip actually gagged, the thought sickened him so much. *No. No. No.*

"She could be worth a thousand pounds on the right market, *bien sûr*," Pierre finished thoughtfully. What a sick, vile, disgusting specimen of a human. Phillip's hands balled into fists, and he only managed to keep them to himself because it vaguely occurred to him that throwing a punch would not keep her safe.

"Absolutely not," Phillip said so firmly, so quickly that even François looked interested by his vehement reaction.

"But you say you have not a single halfpence. And we are not going back to DeRue empty-handed." Phillip then saw the fear in Pierre's eyes. DeRue would make these two revolting creatures pay, probably with their lives or some limbs, if they returned without all the money.

Phillip would have just as soon sent them back to their fate, if he could have managed it. But he knew that their fear was fueling their determination. They were just as determined to get the money as Phillip was to keep Angela safe.

"I can get the money," Phillip said. He would have to ask to borrow it from his brother, though that thought, too, made his stomach burn. As did the knowledge that Devon most likely wouldn't give it to him. But that burn was not as bad as the thought of what they might do to Angela.

His past certainly was catching up with him and colliding with his future. It was only now that Angela's life was in danger, and thus his future happiness, that Phillip began to sorely regret every moment of his life until he had entered the abbey. Why did he have to borrow money from Claude DeRue? And for a stupid game of cards that he couldn't even remember playing? And why had he been so horrible to his brother? He had never thought that it would come to this.

"Ah, much better. Money is far easier to transport than an unwilling woman."

"When can you get it?" François demanded.

"A week," Phillip answered. It would take him a day or two to get to Cliveden. It would allow for some time if his brother was not at the country house but in London. And if Devon refused, Phillip would still have time to gather the funds. Surely he had some friends left in London who would help him pay. If they weren't broke themselves.

Hell and damnation.

"So where are we going to get this money?" Pierre queried.

"*We* are not—" Phillip started, and then caught himself. If these vomitous thugs traveled with him, they would be traveling away from Angela. He could endure their company if it meant keeping her safe. "We are going to call on my brother, the Duke of Buckingham."

"*Bon. Allons-y.*"

"Let's go," Pierre translated.

"Now?"

"The longer we take to return to Claude, the angrier he gets," Pierre said gravely.

"I just need to speak with someone. That bloke, right there," Phillip said, pointing to William, who was watching them. "And then I'll go with you, all right?"

"You think we are fools? Imbeciles?"

Phillip elected not to respond to that.

"You think we will let you give a message to the authorities or have help sent for you? No, you will speak to no one."

"Except for your brother, the duke."

"Aye, him you talk to. Beg if you have to," François said with a revolting, toothless grin.

"I promise I will not give word to alert the authorities. I promise that I will beg for the money if I must. I promise that you will get your funds. I just need to speak to someone first. I only want to relay that I will be coming back."

"Pfff. Who says you will return?" François said, pushing his jacket aside to reveal the butt of a pistol stuck in his waistband.

"Have you no mercy?" Phillip asked.

"You spent too much time in the abbey if you think that our kind has mercy for anyone."

Phillip looked over to William and Johnnie, debating if he should make a run for it. But Pierre was smarter than he looked.

"One step, one word, and I'll kill you and take the girl," Pierre said in warning.

With one last look at the abbey and a prayer that Angela would wait for him, Phillip turned and walked away with Pierre and François.

❦

"I'm getting married."

Angela told the abbess first. And then she told Penelope, who squealed with excitement and gave her a crushing hug. Helena was quiet for a long moment when Angela told her, and then she slowly nodded her head, smiled, and said, "Good for you," and gave Angela a hug. Angela was not sure if Helena was truly happy for her, but it didn't matter, because at least their argument had been quietly put aside.

And then Angela repeated, "I'm getting married," over and over to herself. She hummed as she walked around the abbey. She whistled as she helped prepare for dinner. Suppertime was approaching, when Johnnie and William Sloan stopped into the kitchen to say good-bye for the day.

"How did it go?" she asked. "Have you finished yet?" she teased.

"Not quite, but we've made some progress."

"Not such a thrilling day for us as for you. Congratulations on your engagement."

"Thank you. Will Phillip be coming in soon?"

"Dunno." The brothers exchanged awkward glances that Angela noticed but didn't bother to wonder about.

"I'll walk out with you then. I want to see him and make sure he doesn't work too hard. He's still not perfectly well, although he insists he is."

"Uh . . . well, he, um . . ." Johnnie stuttered.

"He left," William said softly with a pained expression.

"He left? When? And where did he go?"

"It was a few hours ago. He spoke with some French blokes who have been staying in the village for the past few weeks, and then he left with them."

"Did he say why? Or where he was going? Or when he was coming back?" Oh, she could not keep the panic and heartache from her voice.

"He probably just went to town for a pint with old friends," Johnnie said.

"Or maybe to buy something for you. An engagement present," William added, but Angela knew that was a lie.

"He'll be back," Johnnie said, and Angela knew that, too, was a lie.

⁓

By the next day, it was clear that he was gone. William and Johnnie had taken it upon themselves to inquire about Phillip in town. It was known that he rented a carriage and team of horses and left on the road west.

Twenty-four hours after Angela had stood before the abbess, joyfully informing her of the impending nuptials, Angela stood in the same position with considerably less feeling of any kind.

It was amazing, truly amazing, Angela thought, that one's world could crash and burn within a day. It wasn't amazing, actually. It was an unimaginable cruelty to have all you ever wanted just within reach, again, so close you could taste it, again, only to have it snatched away so suddenly, again.

Phillip had understood her and all her secret longings. She could see it on his face as he looked through her sketchbook. And she just knew that he comprehended that all she wanted was him, a child, and a Virgin Mary smile. And she saw the dawning in his eyes, the softening of his features as he realized, as she did, that he could give that to her.

He had to have understood that she loved him. Or perhaps he was as stupid as everyone said he was.

He left without a reason and without even saying goodbye.

She had been engaged and jilted within twenty-four hours. That had to be a record, even for Phillip Kensington. What, oh, what on earth had she been thinking? The man was legendary for abandoning women. He was the established King of all Scoundrels. And she was the Queen of Fools.

And now she was just another in a long list of delusional women who dared to think that he might come around. That he might love her. That he might, just might, this time, finally manage to walk down the aisle and say, "I do."

She had cried herself to sleep last night. Along with the tears she shed, she also relinquished any faith and hope she had ever had for finding a man who would love her back.

"He left," Angela said. The abbess spoke no words but opened her arms to Angela, and that said everything. She was pitiful, but someone still cared for her. Someone she was going to leave soon. *Queen of Fools.*

"You can stay. Forget about our bargain."

"Thank you, but I cannot stay here now." Not with so many memories of him clinging to every inch of the abbey. Every dark corner where they had kissed, every corridor they had walked down, his room, her room where she had lain awake thinking of him, the kitchen, and even the chapel. She could never enter that chapel again.

Besides, she had made a vow to the abbess, and unlike *some* people, Angela kept her word.

"Where will you go?" Lady Katherine questioned.

"I really don't know," Angela replied truthfully. She hadn't thought about that. She didn't really much care, either.

"What about returning to your home?" the abbess suggested gently.

"It's best for my sisters if I do not. I come from a small village, as you know, and it's doubtful that anyone has forgotten about what I did. And," Angela paused for a moment, "Mother told me not to come back."

The abbess nodded and then fell silent for a moment.

"Your aunt in London was a dear friend of mine. I'm sure she'll take you in."

"I have an aunt in London?"

"In a manner of speaking. Your mother's elder brother's widow. Your uncle died years ago; you must have still been a child. But I'm surprised that you do not know of her."

"No. My mother was never close with her family after her marriage."

"Nevertheless, you shall go to London and stay with your aunt."

"But . . ." Protests died on Angela's lips. She didn't want to impose, and she would certainly be an imposition, since she had no reputation and no money and no place to stay, if she did not go to pay a call on her aunt. She could stay there while she sought employment. Perhaps as a governess, and then she could mother children, even if they weren't her own. Angela wiped her eyes, finding she still had some tears left after all.

"I'll write a letter of introduction for you. I'm certain you and Lady Palmerston will get along famously." Angela wasn't, but at this point, that was the least of her worries.

"Thank you, Lady Katherine."

"I'll miss you, Angela, but I do think this is the right thing for you to do. You are always welcome to return here, of course. Now, one last matter to resolve: What shall I tell that scoundrel if he should return?"

Angela thought about this for a moment. She didn't think for a second that he would return. But if he did . . . well, he didn't deserve to know where she had gone. And if she left permission for the abbess to give him her address in London, then she knew she would always be half expecting him at every knock on the door. Thus she would be devastated on a regular basis.

But hope flared up. Perhaps there was a good explanation for his absence. Perhaps he would return. Perhaps, perhaps, perhaps . . . the flame of hope flickered and died as quickly as it had arisen.

"Please do what you think is best, if he should return. I no longer trust my own judgment on such matters," Angela answered honestly.

"Very well. I must say, before you go, that I have always admired your determination and your faith."

"My faith? But I am leaving."

"Your faith and determination that you will one day be blessed with whatever it is you long for. You keep trying, Angela, when others would have given up. I pray you don't lose that."

Angela didn't have the heart to say that her faith was already gone. It had left sometime yesterday afternoon and hadn't even said good-bye.

Chapter 12

The world outside the abbey felt like a foreign country to Angela. Everything was familiar and yet so different. Things had changed since she had last been waiting at an inn for the mail coach and then jumbled in with strangers for hours. Six years ago, it had been. And she had been ruined and brokenhearted.

So perhaps not much had changed.

After a few hours, the wonder faded, and Angela was bored. The mail coach was full, with six passengers, including herself. There was a family of four: parents and two daughters. She did not find them very interesting after the first hour. The father slept, the mother embroidered, the daughters read novels. The older gentleman across from her intrigued her.

His hair was jet-black, except for strands of silver at the temples. His face was worn and rough. It was a face that seemed as if it had seen things and been places. It was a thoroughly lived-in face. His clothes were clearly well made. At the last inn where the coach had stopped, she had overhead him saying something about his own carriage breaking and needing to get to London urgently.

Occasionally, she and the man made eye contact, but mostly

he read his newspaper. After hours in the cramped quarters, she was bored. Tortured. She couldn't stop thinking about Phillip—his eyes as he said, "Marry me, Angela," and how she had made him say it twice because she hadn't believed she had heard him right the first time. But the thought made her heart ache and her eyes get hot. She would not weep in front of strangers in the mail coach. She did not want to think about Phillip. She had to get over him and the hurt, eventually. It might as well be now, she told herself.

What she really wanted to do was draw the man across from her.

She opened her bag, which contained one spare dress and chemise, a letter of introduction, the money the abbess had been able to spare for her, and her sketchbook and pencils. She skipped over the pages with her previous drawings, not allowing herself to look at them.

She began to draw. She started with the outline of his face—just the bridge of his nose, eyes, and hair. The newspaper obscured the lower part. She kept drawing as the carriage hit a particularly bumpy stretch of road.

One particular jolt caused one sister to fall forward into the other, one of the men to swear, someone bumped their head, and Angela's sketchbook flew across the carriage to land in the man's lap.

He picked it up, and without asking for permission, began to look through it.

"Excuse me, sir," she said. He ignored her.

"I would like my property back, sir," she said loudly. That got everyone's attention, even his.

"You drew these," he said.

"Obviously," she retorted.

"They're good."

"Thank you?" she said, though it came out like a question. She accepted the compliment because she knew her drawings were good. She only questioned thanking him for complimenting something she had not given him permission to look at. He was eyeing her now, looking her up and down. She was suddenly ashamed of her old, very old and worn, gray dress and of her lack of possessions. She didn't even want to imagine what he thought of her.

"I'll hire you," he said in a gruff voice.

"I beg your pardon! I am not for sale!"

And then he laughed; the sound was low and rich.

"For your drawings, miss. I have need of an illustrator, and you'll do."

Her first thought was relief that he did not think she was a prostitute. Then she was simply stunned speechless.

"Nigel Haven, publisher of the *London Weekly*," he said, extending his hand. She took it but did not give her name. She did not know what sort of publication this *London Weekly* was, and the last thing her reputation needed was to be a known employee of some disreputable news sheet.

"Take my card. Call on me at my office. We'll discuss the terms of your employment."

"I have not accepted employment," she said. Women of her station did not work. And they especially did not work for surly men of suspicious publications. Although, she wasn't sure what her status was anymore, and if her aunt didn't take her in, she'd draw anything for anyone if it meant a roof over her head and food. She took his card.

"Yet, girl. Yet." He returned her sketchbook. And then he turned back to his newspaper and ignored her until the coach arrived in London.

A short while later, Angela was standing in the foyer of Lady Palmerston's town house, waiting to see if her aunt was at home to visitors. Even Angela knew that meant her aunt was deciding if she wanted to see her. Angela hoped her aunt would, if only for a cup of tea so that Angela might rest and refresh herself for a moment. She hadn't eaten or drunk anything since early this morning, and she so longed to sit on a stationary object.

She was trying to figure out just what, exactly, she would do if her aunt was not at home, when the butler, a stony-faced man of indeterminable age, gestured that she should follow him.

The drawing room was overwhelming. Everything in it was

obviously of the finest quality, and there was a lot in the room. The rooms were papered in a pale green pattern that Angela couldn't discern because so much of it was covered by paintings in ornate frames. Over the mantel was a large portrait of a man who could only be her uncle, the late Lord Palmerston. He had the same coloring as her mother, his sister. Dark hair and eyes. Angela took after her father, she thought with a twinge of remorse.

She continued to look around the room instead of dwelling on her painful past. There was a table at the far wall decked with dozens of fragile figurines. In the center were two settees upholstered in dark green damask. A low table bearing a tea tray was between them. Two tall French windows looked out onto the street.

There was a chair placed with its back to the fireplace, upholstered to match the settees. Beside it was another table stacked with newspapers.

Before it stood her aunt, Lady Palmerston. She must have been in her forties, but it was only her wise eyes and the way she carried herself that belied her age. Her features were a touch angular, strong but not mannish. Her hair was a pale blonde, pulled back loosely and arranged in a bun. She wore a crimson gown in what must have been the latest style. The color was vivid and bold, but the cut was simple. A gold and ruby brooch as well as a simple gold necklace provided ornamentation.

Angela thought she was magnificent. She was so stylish, so self-assured that Angela envied her, aspired to be like her, and yet she was also acutely self-conscious about her own plain, disheveled appearance.

"Angela Sullivan," Lady Palmerston said in acknowledgment. "I've been expecting you. Do sit, have some tea." She gestured to the tea tray. Angela sat and gladly poured herself a cup of tea, wondering how this woman already knew of her.

"Did Lady Bamford write to you? Because I do have a letter of introduction from her in my case."

"No. I've been waiting, oh . . ." Lady Palmerston touched

one finger to her lips and paused thoughtfully for a second. "About six years now."

"I'm sorry?" How had this woman been waiting six years for her? Six years ago was when she had been ruined.

"Your mother had written to me about your situation. So you chose life in an abbey over life in London? Interesting choice."

"I wasn't aware I had a choice," Angela replied.

"Nevertheless, you have finally come to your senses."

"I suppose that is one way of looking at it. Either that, or I have lost my mind," Angela said.

"Ha! Happens to all of us from time to time." She smiled wistfully, but her expression quickly became serious. "You'll stay here, of course."

"I couldn't possibly intrude . . ."

"Nonsense. I have plenty of room, and you, I suspect, have nowhere else to go."

"But the expense—"

"Is not something we talk about in polite company," her aunt said firmly. Angela did not dare contradict her. "But never mind that, I can afford it."

"Pardon me, but it's been so long since I have been out in society. I'm a bit rusty."

"Indeed," Lady Palmerston said, eyeing her plain gray dress now. "A trip to the modiste is certainly in order. I certainly cannot take you out in that."

"I can't go out."

"And why not?"

"I have been ruined. You know that."

"Six years ago. Practically a lifetime. You have no idea of the greater scandals that have taken place since then. I assure you, people likely won't remember."

"You did."

"I am gifted with an excellent memory. Something most of my peers are sorely lacking. We shall go buy you a new wardrobe—and don't go thinking it as charity; it's simply because I prefer not to look at that eyesore you are wearing. Then we shall go out and find you a husband."

"Lady Palmerston, I am not looking for a husband. I am absolutely finished with men."

"Recently heartbroken, are you?"

"How did you know?" Angela said, after sputtering on the sip of tea she had just taken.

"Because that is what we all say when we have been recently heartbroken. It happens to everyone from time to time. Never fear, it's not a fatal condition."

"Glad to hear it," Angela said dryly. "I should hate to expire right here in your drawing room."

"And I as well. Dreadful mess." Lady Palmerston took a sip of her own cup of tea. Angela's attention was drawn to the table of newspapers again. The title on one caught her eye.

"Is that a copy of the *London Weekly*?"

"Of course. 'Tis the bible of the ton."

"So it is not a disreputable publication?"

"Not in the slightest. It is only the most popular, most well-read newspaper in London. I suggest you begin reading it, if you wish to understand half of the conversations at parties."

"I was offered a job there, actually."

"*Really?*" Lady Palmerston set her cup down in the saucer with a clink.

Angela explained about her meeting on the coach this afternoon. Lady Palmerston laughed loudly.

"We shall pay a call as soon as you have a decent gown. Just think! My niece illustrating for the *London Weekly*! It is my favorite publication, you know. Yes, you must stay. I shall definitely keep you on. We'll convert a spare room into a workspace for you."

"Thank you, Lady Palmerston." It was all Angela could think to say—manage to say. A workspace? She had never had that luxury before. She had never even imagined it.

"Call me Dora. And you must show me your book of drawings."

Angela immediately obliged, so thankful for her aunt's benevolence. A place to stay. Gowns. A workspace! She didn't give a thought to the subjects of her drawings or what her aunt might think of them. That is, until Lady Palmerston opened to a page at random, her eyes widened, and one brow arched.

Angela looked closely to see which page her aunt was looking at. She winced. It was the portrait of Phillip without his shirt on.

"Oh, no, you did not," Lady Palmerston—Dora—murmured. She obviously recognized Phillip. Her eyes narrowed, and she looked closer, and Angela could see them taking in every last detail. Every muscle in his chest and arms. Oh, those arms.

"I did," Angela said with a sigh. There was no denying it. Not even the most gifted actor in the world could talk their way out of this one.

"But how? When? Where?"

"He was injured and brought to the abbey where I was living. I was assigned to tend to him and his injuries. I think I did too good a job of it."

"I'm sorry. But let me see if I understand you correctly. Phillip Kensington. In an abbey."

"Yes." In spite of her recent heartache, even Angela had to smile at that.

Lady Palmerston's lips twitched. And then her eyes started to water. And then she howled with laughter. It was a full minute—Angela watched the clock on the mantel—before Lady Palmerston was able to draw a breath.

"Oh, I'm surprised the place hasn't burned to the ground. It is still standing, is it not? That's not the reason you left?"

"Well, the chapel roof did catch fire in a thunder and lightning storm," Angela added with a wry smile.

"Hmmph," Lady Palmerston said, and it was followed by a chuckle. "That is *not* funny. But it is ironic."

"I suppose it is. At the very least, he did stay on to help repair the damage."

"He did *what*?"

"He worked alongside the men from the village to build a new roof. It was to be in exchange for the funds to return to London."

"Phillip Kensington *worked*?"

"Yes, I know," Angela said sadly. He had changed so much. Just not enough.

"Either hell has frozen over, or you have some sort of magical powers. I trust it was due to your influence that the man lifted something other than a flask of brandy."

"Well, we didn't have any brandy at the abbey. I could flatter myself and say yes. But it doesn't matter, because I wasn't enough. He left. Suddenly. He didn't even say good-bye." Angela's voice wavered. Once again, she wasn't enough of something—whatever that something might be—to keep a man.

"My dear girl, he leaves *everyone*."

"I know," she muttered, not feeling the need to confess that for a moment there, she thought she was special. The one that he wouldn't leave.

"You didn't fall in love with him, did you?" Lady Palmerston asked, eyeing her warily.

"Maybe," Angela confessed with a sigh.

"Talk about losing one's head from time to time. How you managed to fall in love with that dull scoundrel, I'd rather not know. But I must ask. Does anyone know of your relationship with him?"

"Just my sisters at the abbey."

"Good. Keep it that way. Merely conversing with him at a ball is enough to damage a girl's reputation."

"He said as much."

"You are not with child, are you?"

"No."

"Good. That would put a crimp in our social outings. I must also warn you that my niece, Emilia, is married to Phillip's twin, Devon. The resemblance is stunning. Even their own father had trouble telling them apart."

"I shall not confuse them. May I request that you do not tell them of my relationship with Phillip? I am starting a new life now, and I should hate for my past to interfere overmuch," Angela said.

"Of course. Your secret is safe with me. We shall tell everyone that you have been at home in the country all this time." And then Lady Palmerston returned to leafing through the sketches, saying they were quite good.

"Your relationship to this one?" she asked, pointing to the drawing of Lucas.

"The man who ruined me. The first time."

"Viscount Lucas Frost. His wife recently passed away during childbirth."

Oh. Angela braced herself to feel something at the news. He had gone on to marry, as was his duty, regardless of what he did or did not feel for her. That he carried on with his life did not affect her now. She merely felt the natural sadness she would upon hearing that any life had been lost.

But she could not ignore the fact that he was free now, and she was, too.

Lady Palmerston continued to flip through the book at random, until her eyes widened, then narrowed, but definitely lingered on the picture of the gentleman from the coach.

"Who is this?" Dora asked sharply.

"That is Nigel Haven. The man from the coach."

"Nigel Haven," Lady Palmerston repeated slowly, as if receiving the answer to a grand mystery. "The publisher of the *London Weekly*. Funny, that," Lady Palmerston said thoughtfully.

"Why is that funny?"

"Oh, never mind that. Groves will show you to your room. Just ring if you need anything. Supper shall be at eight o'clock."

"Lady Palmerston—"

"Dora."

"Dora. I can't thank you enough for taking me in. I promise not to be trouble for you, and—"

"Dear girl, I'm already glad you're here. As I said, I've been waiting for you to knock on my door. Better late than never, they say."

Two days ago, Angela had lost a fiancé. But now she had a fascinating and witty aunt, a place to stay (a really nice place to stay), and a job. If she had known that she could have all this, she might have left the abbey sooner. She might have even left before she ever met Phillip.

In her heart, she felt a hollow, empty hole that Phillip had almost filled. Did she wish that she had never known him? That she had never loved him?

Yes, she had fallen in love with him.

She had also loved Lucas, and lost him, and lived to love again.

Chapter 13

CLIVEDEN, BUCKINGHAMSHIRE

Phillip wanted to kill Pierre and François. Slowly. And painfully. He spent the long hours in the carriage with them alternately despising them and thinking of ways in which he might kill them. Slowly. And painfully.

They had taken him away from Angela. He could not imagine a greater offense. Unfortunately, he could not imagine that it was a suitable defense against murder. Twice. He couldn't be with her if he was swinging lifelessly from the gallows. That was the only reason why he did not kill them.

They also stank, argued incessantly in French, brandished weapons about as if they were merely sticks and not loaded guns, and, to put salt in his wound, refused to allow Phillip to join in their card games. He now understood the old matrons who complained about their nerves being shredded to ribbons. He was not in the slightest bit glad to have discovered empathy in that capacity.

He couldn't wait to arrive at Cliveden.

And yet, he had never dreaded anything more. He didn't know if Devon would be in residence. He didn't know if Devon would deign to see him, let alone lend him money. Before he met Angela, he would have died without a second thought rather than ask his brother for money. But things were different now. He was different now. He just hoped that Devon didn't make him grovel. Because Phillip would, even though he didn't want to. He would do it for Angela. He would do anything for her. Once again, he prayed that she would wait for him and manage to forgive him when he returned for her.

Finally, *finally*, the decrepit carriage they had rented was rolling down the long drive, flanked on either side by ancient oak trees. The house came into view, and even his imbecile traveling companions shut up upon seeing it. Cliveden was a marvelous house. It had almost been his.

"You stay in this carriage. I will be out shortly," Phillip commanded.

"With the money," Pierre added, stating the obvious.

"Yes," Phillip said wearily.

"I think we ought to come in with you," François growled.

"And I think that if you taint this house with your filthy, stinking selves, I will have all forty footmen and forty housemaids beat you so thoroughly that I could mail your remnants back to France in a snuffbox."

"We will wait in the carriage," Pierre said. "But if you are not out in an hour, we're coming in."

"Fine," Phillip said and slammed the carriage door.

And just as he was debating whether or not to knock, Marksmith, the family butler, opened the door.

"Lord Phillip," he intoned. The old man could not possibly be glad to see him. But his demeanor, stony as ever, did not show what he thought at seeing the prodigal son return.

"Is my brother at home?"

"Wait here, and I shall see."

Phillip waited in the hall, watching Marksmith enter the library. A moment later, the butler exited and said that Phillip might enter. It was strange, being treated like a guest in one's childhood home, and in the house he had expected to be master of. But really, now was not the time to dwell on such things.

"Phillip." His brother stood from where he had been seated behind the big, old mahogany desk. He could not hide his shock at Phillip's appearance. Presently, Devon looked like a cleaner, more genteel version of Phillip, for Phillip had not shaved in a few days, and the clothes he wore were obviously old and worn. No one would confuse them in this moment.

"Devon," Phillip said with a nod in greeting.

"Would you like a brandy?"

"Please," Phillip said automatically.

Devon walked over to the sideboard and poured two glasses, handing one to Phillip before returning to sit behind the desk and taking a sip.

"What brings you here?" Devon asked. Phillip looked at the clock on the bookshelf. One hour. He decided not to beat around the bush.

"I need to borrow money. About twelve hundred pounds, and I need it within the hour. Borrow, being the operative word. I swear I will pay you back however and whenever you'd like. Name your terms. I accept."

"Who is she?" Devon asked, catching Phillip off guard.

"What?"

"Who is she? The woman you are doing this for?" Devon always expected the worst of him, didn't he? So what if Phillip had given him and everyone else reason to believe it? It was time to put a stop to all that.

"It's not what you think. It's not like the other times. I need the money, because otherwise, they'll take her from me, to be used in the most despicable way. No woman deserves that, obviously. But especially her."

"I didn't think it was like the other times. But you certainly confirmed my suspicions," Devon said, much to Phillip's surprise.

"Really?"

"If it was like the other times, you would have said you needed me to fight a duel for you," Devon said, referring to an incident that had taken place years ago with the Duke of Grafton, involving Phillip's indiscretion with Lady Grafton and the duel that Devon had fought while masquerading as his twin, which resulted in Devon fleeing to America for five years. Devon continued: "Or you would have asked me to act as your second. Or you would have at least just asked me to give you the money to pay off some girl's family. You wouldn't have offered to pay it back."

"So things are different now," Phillip said with a shrug and another glance at the clock. He really did not have the time to talk about this.

"I'll say. You haven't taken a sip of your brandy, either. The brother I know would have been helping himself to more by now. You are my brother, aren't you? What have you done to the one I knew?"

Phillip wondered if that was a hint of a smile on his twin's face or a grimace.

"Damned if I know," Phillip responded.

"So who is she?" Devon asked again.

"I'll gladly introduce you later, but she's waiting for me, and I need to return quickly."

"Who is waiting for you?" Emilia, Lady Buckingham, interrupted, walking slowly and carefully into the room with a child in her arms. She stumbled slightly on the edge of the carpet, and Phillip moved quickly to catch her and the child before she could fall.

"Thank you," Emilia said, sounding rather surprised that he had caught her. The surprise was in her eyes, too—blue eyes, like Angela's. But Angela's eyes were a brighter, lighter blue. Did Emilia really think he would let her fall with a child in her arms? Had everyone thought so little of him?

"You're welcome," he said.

"This is your niece, Bella," Emilia said. "Dora is taking a nap. She's four." This child seemed to be about one or two years old and was not obviously a member of either sex just yet. But it was a girl, which meant that Phillip was still the heir to the Duke of Buckingham. Something had stayed the same.

"Take her," Emilia said, holding the squirming brat out to him.

"Oh, that's all right," he answered, looking at it—*her*, he corrected—warily.

"Please. My arms are tired from holding her. I swear, she gets heavier every day," Emilia said, thrusting the child into his arms and going over to collapse in a chair.

Phillip looked down at the child. She smiled at him—a big, lopsided, drunken grin—revealing two teeth.

"Da," she said.

"No. Can you say, 'Degenerate uncle'?"

"Da."

Apparently not. And then she pulled his hair.

"That is not acceptable behavior," he said sternly, feeling awfully stupid talking to this little creature. She kept trying to pull his hair. Annoying. Phillip shifted the child to hold her with one arm balanced on his hip, so that his hair would be out of her reach.

"Who is waiting?" Emilia asked again. "Is someone in that carriage parked out front?"

"Do *not* go near that carriage," Phillip growled. "In fact, you should probably go lock yourself in a room with a few loaded weapons."

"Who the hell did you bring here?" Devon thundered, looking warily at the door and then at his wife and child, who was now resting her head on Phillip's chest, though still trying to reach for his hair. Devon smiled at the sight of his wife and child, safe.

"Well, now I'm definitely interested," Emilia said with widened eyes.

Phillip explained about the debt, the collectors, and the deadline as quickly as possible. Another glance at the clock told him he had thirty minutes left.

"What should I do, Em?" Devon asked.

Oh dear God, Phillip thought. His fate—and Angela's— was now in the hands of a woman he had misled, lied to, and tried to compromise so that she would be forced to marry him instead of the man she loved, thus giving him access to her dowry.

He had only done it for the estate, his father's pride and joy. Well, he had really only gone so far so that his father might have expressed some approval at a match that would ensure the continuity and wealth of the estate. But his father was dead, and the estate looked a lot better than when he had last seen it.

But that reason was really rather weak, he knew. He had treated Emilia horribly. He had almost kept her from marrying his twin, the man she loved. And now his future happiness, and Angela's, too, was in this woman's hands.

"You want us to pay a thousand pounds—" Emilia repeated slowly.

"One thousand seventy-four, actually, plus our travel expenses," Phillip admitted, adjusting the child he still held in his arms.

"You want us to pay all that for a gaming debt?"

"Lady Buckingham—"

"Oh, for Lord's sake, Phillip, call me Emilia. We've been through enough that I think we can be on familiar terms. Besides, we are family." They were, weren't they?

"Emilia. Don't do it for me. Do it because they threatened to take the woman that I—" He stopped himself before he said "the woman I love." He wanted the first time he said it to be to Angela, not someone else. "Don't do it for me. Do it for my fiancée. They said they would take her if I couldn't pay."

"*Your fiancée?*" Emilia and Devon repeated this simultaneously. Phillip shifted the child again, because she was squirming now.

"If she'll still have me. I did leave rather abruptly. It was for her own good, but with my reputation, I expect a devil of an argument when I get back to the abbey, so if—"

"The abbey?" they both echoed again.

"That's where I met her. Stanbrook Abbey. But that's beside the point, and time is really of the essence. So—"

"An abbey? What the hell have you done now?" Devon asked, looking meanly at him.

"I have little time before they come in here. I promise I will tell you everything some other time. But don't do it for me, although I will pay you back. Do it for her. She doesn't deserve to pay for my mistakes." Plural. He had made so many.

"And if we don't?" Devon asked.

"I'll have to kill the two Frenchmen out in the carriage and bury them here. I'll really enjoy it; they are the most loathsome creatures. But then I'll hang. And Angela's friends at the abbey will say how they warned her about me and—"

"God, shut up, Phillip. You sound like the sentimental novels Emilia is always reading."

"You do," Emilia gushed. "It's lovely. And you, dear husband, have been known to enjoy hearing them read to you."

Phillip looked at Devon curiously, but his twin avoided his gaze.

"Hush. I'm writing a bank order. They do accept those, do they not?"

"Sure. And your terms for the loan?"

"Pay it back."

"At what percent interest?" Phillip asked, shifting the weight of the child in his arms.

"Since when do you know what interest is?" Devon looked up at him curiously.

"Since not knowing about it got me into this damned mess."

"What will you do when you pay them off and get your fiancée?"

"Haven't really thought that far ahead. I guess I'll go to Aston House."

"You'll need more money to fix that place up."

"You've seen it recently?" Phillip asked, shifting the squirming brat again.

"What's left of it."

"Bloody hell," Phillip swore and pushed the thought out of his mind. He'd deal with it later.

"Listen, I'll lend you the money to start on that, too. But after you dispatch with those thugs you have out there. Best if you don't let on that you have more funds at your disposal."

"You know this is killing me, don't you?" Phillip said plainly.

"Oh, yes." Devon grinned so widely Phillip feared his face would crack.

"That's why you're doing it, aren't you?"

"Pretty much, yes," Devon said, still grinning. "I've waited for years for this moment, you know. My older brother asking me for money. Splendid, really."

"But *you* are the older one," Phillip pointed out.

"I know," Devon answered with a shrug. "But I still think of you as my older brother."

"Touching. Truly. Oh, and if you haven't noticed, we now have one more identical feature," Phillip said, pointing to the scar above his right eye with his one free hand, the one that wasn't holding the brat. Devon's hand flew up to his own scar in the same place.

"You did that on purpose, didn't you? I had the scar first!"

"I told Angela you'd be livid when you saw it," Phillip said with a smirk.

"It's not funny," Devon said to Emilia, who was laughing.

"I'll just take that bank order, then," Phillip said, doing so and heading for the door. "Thank you. I'll pay you back. Promise. Oh—and take this back," Phillip said, transferring the child into his brother's arms. And then he left.

"Do you really think he will?" Devon asked Emilia.

"You know, I think he might try."

"Hell must have frozen over."

Three days later, Phillip personally escorted his despicable French companions onto a ship. He then waited on the docks until he saw it sail out of sight. Without taking the time to so much as sigh with relief, he turned and walked to the nearest inn. There he hired a horse (for Devon had given him plenty for traveling expenses) and rode off for the abbey.

He had been gone just over a week. It felt like a lifetime. His debt was cleared. His creditors were safely on their way to France, and he would have the funds to start fixing up Aston House. He and his wife would have a home.

Who would have ever thought that Phillip Kensington would put the words *wife* and *home* and his own name together in one sentence? Certainly not him.

He arrived at the abbey early the next morning. He wandered around, looking for her. She wasn't in the kitchen. She wasn't around the chapel, which was progressing nicely. He still didn't know which bedchamber was hers. He took to wandering the corridors.

Where was she? He was dying to see her, to kiss her, and to hold her. He wanted to hear her yell at him, "Where the hell have you been?" They would argue, he was sure of it, but that prospect didn't bother him, because that would mean she cared. About him.

Phillip knocked on the door to Lady Katherine's study, after an hour spent fruitlessly searching for Angela.

"I can't find Angela anywhere. Do you know where she is?" he asked, after Lady Katherine bade him to enter.

"Please sit, Phillip," she said in a tone of voice that reminded him of his dead father's whenever he was about to be lectured on one misdeed or another. He hadn't heard that voice in years. Phillip had been quite young when his father had given up on talking some sense into him.

So Lady Katherine would lecture him for leaving without an explanation and then tell him where Angela was. Fine. Though waiting any longer to see her seemed unbearable, he would manage.

"Angela left the abbey," Lady Katherine said plainly. It was a moment before Phillip could fully comprehend this.

"She left the abbey, or she left me?"

"You left, Phillip, suddenly and inexplicably shortly after issuing a marriage proposal. You have been known to—"

"I know what I've done in the past very well, thanks."

"Nevertheless, she has left, partly because you left her."

"I didn't leave *her*, though. I didn't want to go. But I had to, to save her and . . . It doesn't matter now, does it?"

Lady Katherine did not issue any sort of response, instead letting his question hang in the air. The problem was not that he couldn't fathom that this was happening but because it was all too believable.

He deserved this.

How many women had he left without an explanation or even a reason? A few. More than a few.

And it didn't matter, obviously, that this was the *one* time he meant to return, to do right, to give himself to her completely and forever.

And she didn't want him now, or forever. She didn't want him enough.

She was the only person who had ever believed in him or come close to loving him. And if she had lost her faith in him, well, he had lost it, too, if he ever even had it. *You disappoint me, Phillip,* his father always used to say. But he could hear it in Angela's voice now.

He deserved this.

He hated it, but he knew it was the truth. Phillip deserved to suffer, and he certainly did not deserve the happiness she made him think he could have.

But that knowledge did not make the pain less—not the tightness in his throat or the burning in his chest. There was a hot, queer, stinging feeling in his eyes, but he shut them for a moment, and the feeling abated. Slightly.

"You love her," Lady Katherine said gently with a touch of surprise in her voice, after a moment of silence. It may have been news to her, but not to him.

Phillip shrugged.

"Why did you leave if you love her?" Lady Katherine asked him.

"It doesn't matter anymore," he said firmly. She seemed to be waiting for him to contradict her and say that he hadn't loved her, but he couldn't lie about that. "I would have been a terrible husband. Likely I wouldn't have made her happy, and she would have come to regret it. But is she happy now, wherever she is?"

"If she is not happy now, I think she will be, if . . ." Lady Katherine let her voice trail off, but Phillip knew what she was going to say anyway. *She will be happy if you leave her alone, to forget about a worthless man like you.*

"She deserves to be happy. I'm just sorry I'm not the one to make her so."

BOOK 2

EIGHT MONTHS LATER

Chapter 14

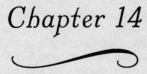

Phillip poured the contents of his glass into the fire. After a sudden, intense burst of flame, the fire settled into a slow, gentle burn. He set his now-empty glass on the mantel next to the letter.

Eight days earlier, he had discovered it in the cellar tied to a bottle of brandy. "*Lord Phillip Kensington, Marquis of Huntley*" was written across the front in a handwriting that Phillip didn't immediately recognize. The seal of the Duke of Buckingham, however, informed him that the letter was from his now-deceased father.

The placement of the letter told Phillip exactly what his father thought of him: a drunken wastrel. Which, to be fair, he had been when his father was alive. And for a few more years after the old man kicked it.

Phillip removed the letter to the mantel in the library, where he stared at it for eight days and nights, trying to find the courage to read a lecture from beyond the grave. His father had only ever lectured him. Though Phillip tried, he could not recall one word in the realm of pleasant ever uttered from father to son.

But tonight . . . tonight Phillip had nothing to lose.

That gray, nagging feeling that had followed him around, as consistent as a shadow, all of his life, was darker, more insistent than ever. If that dark and heavy shadow could talk—and Phillip was damned glad it couldn't—he knew what it would whisper: *You are a failure. You are a disappointment. You are not good enough.*

He believed it. He had spent his entire life going to great lengths to prove those whispers correct. Because he so badly wanted to do something right, even if it was to be as wicked and worthless as everyone expected him to be. He succeeded, yet there was no sweetness or satisfaction in his accomplishment.

Phillip hadn't felt this wretched since that first week in the abbey. He couldn't even manage to die when someone wanted him dead, because he couldn't do anything right. And so in his wretchedness, pain, and loneliness, he had made Angela's life a living hell. But when she was around, that damned shadow retreated just a little . . . and then more and then . . .

Well, it didn't matter now. He'd just get used to living in the dark. And he really couldn't stand to look at that letter any longer. He would read it now, and then burn it, and then . . . Well, he didn't know what he would do. He didn't really much care.

Phillip settled into his chair by the fire. The vellum was old but still spoke of quality. Phillip broke the seal and unfolded the sheet, and something fell into his lap.

A ring. Great. Jewelry. Just what he had always wanted, he thought sarcastically. Like he had any use for a woman's gold ring set with diamonds and pearls. Well, he could sell it for a nice sum. That settled, Phillip pocketed the ring and turned his attention to the page of perfect script.

April 1816

Dear Phillip,

If you have found this letter, it means that you have learned the truth of your birth order, of which I had only recently become aware, and which I had a duty to remedy. I have left the Aston property to you, because though you are no longer my heir, you are still my son, and it would not do to leave you with nothing. More importantly, it is my hope that owning something of your own will give you a sense of duty and devotion toward something other than yourself and your vices.

Aston House was purchased for your late mother, God rest her soul, in the event that she survived me. When she passed on during the birth of you and your brother, it became my intention to provide this unentailed property for my younger son. I must confess that it does strike me as more appropriate that the property go to you, for you were always just like her.

Your preferences were always the same: for company rather than solitude, for card games and wagers, for the social whirl of London, as well as the wildness and openness of the country. Your tempers are the same, too, stemming from the same passionate nature. Unlike you, however, she always knew when to stop before causing a scandal, or causing hurt to another, and when to walk away from a wager. Perhaps by the time you read this, you will have gained the temperance and restraint you did not possess in your youth. Oddly enough, I do have faith that you will achieve these things.

Your mother, Madeleine, was everything that I am not, everything I needed to feel whole. If I said to you as a child that you should be more like your brother, it was my own way of wishing you were more like me, or less like her. When I looked at you, I could only see what I had lost and not what I had gained. I am dying as I write this, although part of me thinks that I died the day your mother did. I was not fair to you or good to you. I am sorry.

Regret is a wretched thing to live with, Phillip. If I have one wish for you, it is that you never know the feeling as I do. If I could have a second wish for you, it

is that you do become truly like your mother and find
the goodness and love within you that she, too, pos-
sessed.

With Love,
Arthur Phillip Archibald William Kensington, Duke of
Buckingham

Included is your mother's wedding ring. Sell it, and risk
her wrath in the afterlife.

Well, if that wasn't everything he had ever wanted, right
there, wrapped around a bottle of brandy, resting in the cellar
of his house. And here he had thought it was what was inside
the bottle that would answer all those questions.

The irony of that did not amuse him.

He read the letter again to be sure it was real and to be sure
he had read it all correctly. It must be true and real, judging by
the tightness in his chest and that odd, hot, stingy feeling in
his eyes that he had only felt once before, on the day he realized Angela had left him.

Perhaps one day he would be glad to have found it. But tonight he only wished that he had found this letter years earlier,
because it was too late for him now. He already knew regret
like the back of his hand.

Duty to something other than oneself and one's vices.
Hadn't the old man realized, as Phillip had, that there was no
one but himself? No one and nothing so constant as his vices.
Except those had deserted him lately, too.

He hadn't had a woman since Angela, and he hadn't even
made love to her.

He hadn't had a drink since Angela.

He hadn't played a game of cards since that night at the
abbey, with Angela.

It all came back to the girl, didn't it?

Phillip looked out the window—or rather, in its general direction, since it was too dark to see what lay beyond. He saw
his own reflection in the glass, that of a lost and ruined man.

Beyond that lay a vast expanse of land that was his and which would one day belong to another.

He was only fixing up this old house so he might fetch a reasonable price for it and repay the money owed to his brother. Phillip had made remarkable progress in the past eight months. The house no longer looked in danger of falling to the ground. A good cleaning had done wonders; so had the fresh coats of paint that he had applied to the rooms himself. The tenants seemed hopeful for the next season, now that he had returned.

But still, he was in a very similar position to the one he was in when he met Angela: poor, indebted to others, and hopeless.

No, he could not go to her now.

Phillip scanned the letter once more, pausing on the last line about goodness and love within. His father thought Phillip might possess goodness and love. Phillip laughed.

The old man had been senile his last few years.

⌒

Phillip employed two servants, a far cry from the army of staff he had always been accustomed to. Samuels was approximately fifty years of age, looked like he was seventy, and yet had the physical strength and ability of a much younger man. He acted as butler, footman, and general repairman for anything that needed to be done, so long as it was not cooking. The latter, and all other housekeeping duties, were taken care of by Mrs. Samuels, who had maternal tendencies that had no outlet or object other than Phillip.

Samuels's other chief occupation was annoying the hell out of Phillip.

"Still staying up late brooding over the woman?" Samuels asked, while pouring Phillip's coffee for him in the kitchen the next morning. Phillip took his meals here, since heating the dining room was an unnecessary expense. He had never mentioned Angela to them, and yet they had assumed the truth. After all, what reason other than a broken heart would prompt a man to pour excellent brandy into the fire night after night?

"I was reviewing applications for your replacement," Phillip lied.

"Pfff. You're still pouring that fine brandy into the fire. If you want to get rid of the stuff, I can help you with that."

"No you cannot," Mrs. Samuels called from the far end of the kitchen, where she was cooking breakfast.

"Women," Samuels muttered under his breath so that only Phillip might hear. "You really want one?"

"I heard that!" Mrs. Samuels said from across the kitchen.

Phillip merely scowled at him. The truth of the matter was that he would never, ever replace Mr. and Mrs. Samuels—not just because they came with the house and had nowhere else to go, but because they were the closest things to parents he had ever had. Samuels set a newspaper, the *London Weekly*, next to the breakfast plate that Mrs. Samuels placed before him.

"You really ought to have a look at that," Samuels said gruffly before sitting down at the table. Mrs. Samuels brought over plates of food and joined them. When they started bickering about who snored louder the previous evening, Phillip focused his attention on the newspaper. He generally avoided reading them, but Samuels had suggested he do so, and Phillip wasn't in the mood to listen to the same argument they had every morning. Why Samuels still even tried to win an argument with his wife, Phillip knew not. Other than, perhaps, he enjoyed it. Phillip had once enjoyed bickering with Angela, but that wasn't something to be dwelt upon.

The first page listed the contents of the issue: theater reviews, fashion reviews, a gossip column, a different gossip column, recipes, and a list of the best dressmakers in London. It also contained the latest installment of the Darcy Darlington mystery series. Was that old story really still running? He recalled his days in London, when he still went out, and constantly overhearing young women discussing the story as if it were real. He hadn't been interested in it then, and he wasn't now.

But then he saw the illustration on page three. He swore.

The caption read: "*Is the Evil Lord Hartshorne the One to Hold Darcy Captive?*"

But Phillip's own face stared at him from the page. It was

not a drawing he recognized, but he knew the style. He knew it had been done by Angela's hand. She had drawn him and his grin, the one she always said was so wicked. The one she couldn't resist. But he was brandishing a knife in this picture, the sharp, slanting edges of the blade echoing the way she had drawn his cheekbones. Those lines made his crooked, broken nose stand out all the more. She had depicted him perfectly as if she had been staring at him as she did it. There was no mistaking it: Phillip was the evil Lord Hartshorne.

And in fine print below, he read: "*Drawing by Angela Sullivan.*"

He stared at her name for a long while, savoring even this small piece of news about her. He had wondered where she had gone. He had lain awake at night, worrying that she was in danger or in trouble. He had not known anything, other than she was better off without him. But this drawing gave him a peek into her world. He now knew that whatever her situation, she was earning recognition for and perhaps a living from her talents.

He had to admit the drawing was good. Excellent. He caught himself smiling down at her name, so proud of her for her accomplishment.

He smiled, too, because she clearly still thought of him. But his smile faded, because he could see that though he might be in her thoughts, he couldn't imagine he was still in her heart. With equal clarity he saw that Angela despised him, for she had portrayed him as the villain. Even he knew she had every reason to.

And yet it struck him as monstrously unfair that she could hate him while he still loved her. That she had a way to express her hatred of him while he had no way of expressing his love for her.

Wearily, he rubbed his eyes and then noticed Mr. and Mrs. Samuels had fallen silent. He closed the newspaper and looked up to find them staring at him.

"That's you, isn't it?" Samuels said excitedly. "I thought so, since it is the spitting image of you, right down to the broken nose. Now we can sue the chit for libel or slander or whatever it is folks sue the papers for, and then use the money to make repairs to the stables."

Phillip said nothing. He hadn't the funds to wage a lawsuit, even if he were so inclined. Which he wasn't.

"Unless," Samuels continued, "she is one of those chits you had a spot of fun with for a time, and this is her revenge. Any jury will take her side against yours if that is the case."

"It was not a 'spot of fun,'" Phillip stated firmly. He would not have his one love degraded to that. "It was . . . it was . . . something else. Something more."

"Ah. I understand. She is the woman you've been brooding over."

"I have not been brooding," Phillip protested, wondering why he even bothered. He brooded. He lamented. He held a glass of brandy that he didn't even drink, because the burn of remorse was plenty.

"Pfff. You have been acting like the very definition of a poor, lovelorn, brokenhearted sap. A blind man could see it!"

"Should be a pity if she were the girl you have been so distraught over," Mrs. Samuels said thoughtfully.

"Men do not get distraught," Samuels informed his wife. "That is purely a female ailment. We merely think deeply and rationally about troubling situations."

"You were distraught last week when you could not find your fishing rod," she pointed out.

"I was not. I was just thinking deeply and rationally as to where it might have gotten to."

"Yes, you were near tears because you didn't think rationally that I might have put it in the shed, where it belongs, rather than in the kitchen where you had left it."

"Mrs. Samuels, why would it be a pity?" Phillip cut in. They could bicker for hours.

"Why, she is being courted by another gentleman. It's right there, on page six in the society news and gossip section," Mrs. Samuels answered.

Phillip turned to page six and quickly scanned the page until he found her name.

Renowned *London Weekly* illustrator, Miss Angela Sullivan, was seen in an intimate tête-à-tête at Lady Carrington's ball with Lord Frost, who has recently returned to town after the death of his wife. Is he searching for a new bride?

No.

It could not be. The gossip columns were wrong often enough. And yet . . .

No.

It was intolerable.

There was a howl rising within him, from the very depths of a soul he had not known he possessed. *She is mine.* Frost was the one who had ruined her. Phillip would be the one to save her.

Or perhaps she would save him once again.

She had taken away his taste for drink, tainted his pleasure in cards with the bittersweet memory of one game, and destroyed his lust for other women. She had been someone to love, other than himself. And then she had taken herself away, too. She had made him, if not good, at least better, by taking away his pleasure in his vices.

Goodness and love. Goodness and love. Goodness and love. The words from his father's letter swam around in his brain. *Duty. Regret. Duty. Regret. Regret. Regret.*

She had taken his constant companions away from him. She had ruined him. She had left a big, gaping hole in him that he had no idea how to fill.

She was everything I needed to feel whole.

Or maybe, *maybe*, he did know how to fill that emptiness.

Phillip stood up quickly, knocking over the chair he had been sitting on, banging into the table and spilling the coffee. He could no longer deny that he *needed* her.

And if she was going to marry Frost—and Lord, he prayed she didn't—she was going to do so knowing that she had a choice.

"I am going to London. Now."

"You go ready the horse, dear," Mrs. Samuels said to her husband, patting him affectionately on the hand. "I'll pack a basket for Phillip. It doesn't seem like he'll take the time to stop for a meal on his way to London."

The old man grinned and shuffled off. Phillip stormed up the stairs, jumping over the hole in the third one from the top. He pushed open the door to the master bedchamber and packed the necessary items, including his mother's wedding ring.

Because among all of the things Angela had said and done, she had also agreed to marry him. He prayed she would forgive him for leaving and for taking so long to return. He prayed he would not arrive too late. For all he knew, it was already too late.

But he had nothing to lose, and he had everything to gain. Phillip had always been a gambling man, one who, for better or for worse, never had the ability to walk away from a chance to win.

Chapter 15

That drawing was threatening to be a scandal.

There were those to whom the detail of the evil Lord Hartshorne's broken nose was utterly lost; they assumed that the illustrator, Miss Angela Sullivan, had dared to insult His Grace, the Duke of Buckingham. This was considered odd, owing to the fact that she was his relation by marriage. What inner family turmoil had provoked her? Why had they not heard of it? And why did the duke not shun her publicly? These questions were fodder for discussions in drawing rooms all over town.

And then there were those who recognized it not as the likeness of His Grace, but of his twin, the notorious scoundrel Phillip Kensington, Marquis of Huntley. But how could she have known him? He had left town long before her arrival. And yet, the possibility of a liaison occurred to some; Miss Sullivan had portrayed him as the villain. Had he given her reason to? They, too, avidly discussed her portrayal of him, though their conversations were far more hushed and their suspicions much more salacious.

After all, what did anyone know of Miss Angela Sullivan? She was a recent addition to society, with few, albeit quality, connections. She was a young, unmarried woman who publicly

worked. And then there were those rumors about her past . . .
rumors about her and Lord Lucas Frost, who was most certainly not hiding his courtship of the young lady. Nor did he
deny that he had been previously acquainted with her. The
truth was forgotten or disguised and distorted and generally
not confirmable, due to the fact that whatever had happened—
something must have happened—occurred nearly a decade
ago in a small, provincial village far from London.

But who needed facts when one had gossip?

Angela had known that publishing that drawing was an
enormous risk. But drawing it—Phillip—had been a necessity
for her sanity and perhaps her soul. Eight months, one week,
and four days had passed since she had seen him last, and in
all that time, in spite of all the dramatic upheavals of her life,
she could not forget him.

Forget. Ha! The man positively haunted her dreams, and
everything reminded her of him. The sound of a bell ringing
always snatched her attention. She could no longer bear the
sight of something so mundane as fried eggs, because she was
reminded of the ones she used to cook for him. Men toiling at
construction work reminded her of him. Balls and waltzes reminded her of her wish to enjoy those things with him. Everything reminded her of Phillip.

She thought of writing to him, for she knew from Emilia
that he resided at Aston House. Words would not come to her.
And so she thought if she could just capture him in a drawing
on a sheet of paper, then she could remove him from her head
and her heart.

It was meant to be thrown away. But it was too perfect, too
sensational. Nigel Haven, her publisher, refused her pleas to
withdraw it after she had second thoughts. Instead, he doubled
her wages so as to keep her at the *London Weekly* rather than
lose her to a rival publication.

And so Phillip's likeness, portraying the evil Lord Hartshorne
holding captive the nation's beloved fictional sleuth, Darcy Darlington, was printed up and distributed all over England. When
she held the printed issue in her hands, she understood exactly
what her motive had been.

Like smoke rising from a fire, visible from a distance, she sent out the signal that she still burned for him.

She did not know what she wanted from him, other than an explanation for some vexing questions. Why had he left? Why had he not returned? Had he even loved her at all?

She had yet to receive the answers she needed.

As she entered the ballroom of Lord and Lady Finchleigh, her first public appearance since the drawing's debut, she would have had to be blind and deaf not to notice the sidelong glances, raised eyebrows, and whispers. She had searched for answers. Instead, she gave the ton far too many questions to ponder: aloud, in hushed whispers, and in heated conversations. She provided the gamblers new topics for a wager.

"What have I done?" Angela whispered to herself as much as to her aunt.

"You have created a sensation. Now is not the time to lose your courage, dear."

It took only a moment to find Devon and Emilia. Would her heart ever stop lurching every time she saw Devon? Since he was married to Lady Palmerston's niece, Emilia, Angela saw him often. She had no doubt that she would be able to distinguish the twins up close, but from across a ballroom, it was so easy for her heart to skip a beat before her head acknowledged the difference.

"We were just discussing your latest illustration," Emilia said, smiling slyly, once Angela and Lady Palmerston joined them. Angela and Emilia were quite friendly—but not too close, for Angela kept many secrets from her, simply because she couldn't bring herself to discuss them. Phillip, for example.

"People have taken to calling me the Evil Lord," Devon added, with a hint of amusement.

"I'm sorry, Devon. I had thought that people would be able to realize that it wasn't you. I drew the broken nose . . ." Angela let her voice trail off before she said more. She had already said too much.

"It's the perfect likeness of my twin," Devon said. It was such a simple statement with great implications. He and his wife exchanged a glance that spoke volumes. They may be ignorant of the details, but her past relationship with Phillip was no longer a secret to them, if it ever was. She wondered what Phillip might have told them. She dared not ask.

"It's best for your reputation if the ton thinks it is Devon," Lady Palmerston stated wisely.

Emilia and Lady Palmerston fell into a discussion about Lady Rutherford's ridiculous hairstyle for the evening. Angela found herself standing off to the side with Devon.

"Do you think he saw it?" She couldn't help but ask. It was an innocent enough question, and she was dying to know.

"Doubtful. He never reads the papers. But perhaps he has developed the habit. I haven't heard from him in months, since he went to Aston House. We're not very close."

"I know," Angela said truthfully, because Phillip had told her. "I am sorry that people are giving you trouble about it. I hadn't thought it through and—"

"I've spent my whole life being mistaken for my twin. I'm quite used to it."

"I know."

"I know, too, Angela."

"Whatever do you mean?" she asked evasively, having a very good idea as to his answer.

"He came to me, asking for money. He mentioned a fiancée in an abbey. I suspected that was you, when you arrived in London shortly thereafter. Your drawing confirmed it. I didn't think it was my place to broach the topic."

"You have discovered my secret," Angela confessed, feeling like some weight was lifted from her.

"You have my word that it will stay a secret," Devon replied. Angela thanked him, for it was only polite, but a horrifying thought occurred to her. What if Phillip, in his stubborn refusal to read a newspaper, never saw her call for him? What if she had thrown away her reputation for nothing?

"Unless," Devon continued, "you'd like me to enlighten him about the fact that one does not generally abandon their betrothed, which he seems to have done."

"If he can't figure that out for himself, then he does not deserve to have me."

Being seen in amiable conversation with Devon and Emilia seemed to give the other guests more to talk about rather than less. It apparently seemed to ward off a few people from joining their conversation. Except for one man.

Lord Lucas Frost, once the cause of her downfall, now stood beside her. He had courted her, undeterred by her reticence to receive his attentions, since they first reencountered each other in town a few weeks earlier.

She had stood frozen with shock once she saw him weaving his way through the crowd with the obvious intention of speaking to her at the Carrington ball two weeks ago.

"Angela, my darling," Lucas had said, clasping her hand in his. "Is that really you after all this time?" And then he treated her to the same smile that had once made her forget her own name and that had made the world seem like a brighter, more perfect place.

I am Miss Angela Sullivan, loved and left, not once but twice, she thought to herself. The smile she returned to him was bittersweet; she was pleased to discover that Lucas and his smile no longer affected her as he had when she was a mere girl of seventeen. And yet there was sadness there, for the loss of that girl she had been.

"Hello, Lord Frost," Angela said.

"Let's not forget our old familiarity," he murmured, as he lifted her palm to his lips. After pressing a kiss there, he said, "Call me Lucas. Just like old times."

"Hmmph," her aunt muttered from her place at Angela's side.

"May I present my aunt and chaperone, Lady Palmerston?"

"Pleased to meet you, madame."

"I wish I could say the same," Lady Palmerston replied smoothly, ignoring Angela's choked sound of shock and something like laughter. "But I do extend my condolences for your late wife and child."

"Thank you," Lucas replied graciously, ignoring her previous insult. He returned his attention to Angela. "A waltz?"

It would be rude to decline, she told herself. He offered his hand to her, and Angela looked at it for a moment before accepting. She saw her old hopes and dreams of being this man's wife. She saw a second chance.

And beneath the fine leather gloves were hands that had caressed and touched her intimately. They had not been the only pair of hands to do so. And given the choice, it was Phillip's hands her body craved to feel again.

But there was no choice.

Just one man, offering a waltz, and maybe more.

She accepted Lucas's hand, and they embarked on their first waltz together. His glacial blue eyes gazed down on her. He was different now—older, of course. His features had lost their softness and had become sharper. He looked like a man now, one who had loved and lost.

"You are just as beautiful as I remembered," Lucas had said. Angela simply smiled in return. It would not do to say what she really thought: that she wished his eyes were brown, his nose a little crooked, his hair darker, that he was taller, and stronger, and . . . well, a different man entirely.

That encounter with Lucas had occurred two weeks ago. Her thoughts as she waltzed with him now were the same. But now she was angrier. She had cried out for Phillip, and still, he had not come. And Lucas was always around now, acting as if their past had not occurred and throwing her into severe bouts of confusion. She couldn't forget that this was the man who had nearly destroyed her and her family. This was the man who had inadvertently caused the death of her father. Yet she also could not forget that she had loved him once.

Phillip, with his absence, was throwing her into the arms of a man that she wasn't sure she wanted. Lucas called upon her regularly. He sent her flowers. He waltzed with her twice at every ball. Lucas once dared to ask after her family, and she could see the guilt and pain in his eyes when she answered, "I don't know how they are faring." After that, they did not speak at all of their past. They spoke of how they enjoyed London, and Lucas described his estate, Bradley Park, at great length.

Lucas Frost's intentions were clear.

He meant to make an honest woman of her at last. But

would marriage to him right all those wrongs from so many years ago?

"You are distracted tonight," Lucas said, exerting a gentle pressure upon her palm to remind her to pay attention to him while they waltzed.

"My apologies," she replied.

"If you are worried about my thoughts regarding the object of your recent illustration, I can assure you, it matters not to me."

"How gracious of you to say so," she said, hoping to conceal the annoyance she felt. He thought she cared for his good opinion, and in this moment she realized she did not. Had a small part of her hoped, all along, that Lucas would realize it was Phillip and leave her alone? Maybe.

"But perhaps you might confide in me as to which twin you have portrayed," Lucas suggested with a smile. "I confess I am curious."

"Hmmm," Angela murmured thoughtfully. She was mad as hell at Phillip. He had hurt her horribly. But she had loved him truly, purely, and deeply. She would not degrade that by letting it be common gossip or using it as a convenient way to push Lucas and his affections away from her. And that was how she knew for certain that she loved Phillip still.

Even though she was mad as hell. Lord save him from her wrath if he ever did return.

"I fear your silence reveals everything," Lucas said.

"Does it confirm your worst suspicions?"

"To me, you are still the innocent, romantic girl you were at seventeen. I cannot see you any other way."

In other words, he was blind to the woman she had become.

"And what of you, Lucas? Are you still the man I knew?"

"No," he said sadly. "And I so wish I was. If we were together now, Angela, perhaps . . ."

The waltz concluded before he could voice the remainder of his thought. But she knew what he meant all the same. If they were together again, married at last, they could pretend the intervening years had never happened and be who they once were years ago.

Lucas certainly offered a second chance.

Or was it her last chance at marriage, a family, and something like love?

A FEW DAYS LATER...

Phillip looked at the address on the sheet of paper in his hand and then up at the town house before him: *Number Four, Berkeley Square.* His courage and determination started to fade. He knew this address. He knew this house.

Obtaining that address was easier than he had anticipated. By presenting himself as his twin, an absolutely enraged duke, to a hapless, terrified clerk at the offices of the *London Weekly*, he was able to walk off with Angela's address in mere moments.

He had come up with dozens of reasons not to go to her in the past eight months, among them: she likely despised him; what he had done was unforgivable; it was for the best if they went their separate ways; he would have made her miserable anyway. And, most of all, if she hadn't waited a week for him, why would she wait any longer? He could not see any reason to.

But something had changed. It may have been the letter from his father, and it may have been that illustration, or it could have been nothing more than the passage of time. That mention of her with Frost certainly had something to do with his arrival; that was undeniable. He loved her, and he could not let her make such an obvious mistake. Again.

And he had also come to the conclusion that if he was going to be a miserable failure—as he admittedly was—it was not going to be because he didn't try to be better. She may reject him thoroughly, soundly, and absolutely forever, but that was just a risk he would have to take.

Phillip checked the address again. It couldn't be. He knew this house; he had spent more time than he would have liked in the drawing room. His relationship with the lady of the house was one of mutual disdain.

And she was Angela's aunt, according to the clerk at the newspaper offices. He had courted, using the term loosely, another one of this woman's nieces before. That he should now need her favor to win the hand and heart of a different niece was a cruel, twisted joke for the universe to play on him. He did not find it the slightest bit amusing.

He could, of course, just walk away. But he had come all the way from Bedfordshire for this. In fact, it felt rather like he had walked barefoot across hot coals from the depths of hell for this chance at happiness. *Goodness and love. Duty and regret.*

No, he would not turn back now.

And who knows? Perhaps Lady Palmerston had moved. Phillip knew better than to hope that she had forgotten about him.

"Groves! Show him in." Phillip heard her voice from where he stood in the foyer. There was no mistaking Lady Palmerston's voice.

Phillip followed the butler into the drawing room. It had not changed since the last time he had been here, forcing a ring onto Emilia's finger in one last-ditch attempt to secure an heiress. It was still decorated in the same excessive manner. It still made a man feel like he was going to break something at any second. He grimaced and cringed at the memory of his last visit. If he had known then that he would need Lady Palmerston's favorable opinion one day, he would have gone about things a bit differently.

Lady Palmerston sat grandly in her chair by the fire, as if it were a throne. She looked at him with eyes that seemed to possess the ability to see right through his (and everyone else's, to be fair) carefully constructed social facade. That was why she terrified him. He knew she could see right through him.

However, that meant she could see right into his very soul and see his genuine longing for Angela. She was here; Phillip could sense it, feel it. And if she was indeed Lady Palmerston's niece, that meant that she was nearby, likely eavesdropping on this interview.

Phillip would not be cowardly when he faced the dragon.

Not this time. Not when it mattered. He stood a little bit taller, straightened his shoulders, and looked the dragon lady in the eye.

"Lord Huntley, we meet again," Lady Palmerston stated. "I find myself intrigued by your presence in my drawing room. But they do say there is a first time for everything, do they not?" She tilted her head slightly to one side, watching him closely to see how he would take her taunts.

"I did not come here to be insulted, Lady Palmerston, though I readily admit you have no reason to be kind to me," he answered evenly.

"Then why, pray tell, are you here?" Lady Palmerston asked, as if she simply could not fathom any other reason why he would come to call. It was an act; he was sure of it. Everyone knew that Lady Palmerston knew everything there was to know. And he discovered that that made it very easy to be honest with her.

"I need to see Angela."

"Need?" Lady Palmerston arched her brow.

"Yes, need. Want to, would like to, would love to, can't imagine a life worth living if I don't see her. *Need.*"

"What is it with you and my nieces, Lord Huntley?" Lady Palmerston wondered, abruptly changing the subject.

"I wonder the same thing."

"It's quite a coincidence," she remarked.

It was. How many young, unmarried nieces could one woman have? And how could Phillip end up crossing paths with both of them?

"Indeed, but that does not affect the fact that I need to see Angela."

"Spare me the speech again," Lady Palmerston said with a dismissive wave of her hand and rolling her eyes. "She's not at home."

"So she is living here, then," Phillip said, catching Lady Palmerston's slip and confirming that Angela was indeed residing here.

"You've gotten a bit sharper, haven't you?" Lady Palmerston commented, with narrowed eyes. He was not sure if he ought to take that as a compliment or not. He thought it best not to say anything.

"Of course she is staying with me, Huntley. You must admit it is the safest place in London for a young woman to be."

"When it comes to men with dishonorable intentions, you are more of a deterrence than a dozen armed soldiers," Phillip answered. And then he froze, because he had just insulted her, when he so needed her approval. But wait—Phillip noticed the *slightest* curve at the corner of her mouth. He wanted to shout in triumph. Nevertheless, he maintained his composure.

"I should think two dozen at least," she murmured. "But your intentions, Lord Huntley? Do I dare presume they are the same as ever?"

That was the question, wasn't it? He chose his words carefully and spoke clearly so that there could be no confusion.

"My intentions are as they ever were since Angela accepted my proposal. I mean to marry her."

"You know, Huntley, the last time you said you were affianced to one of my nieces, you were lying through your teeth." Phillip stifled a groan of utter frustration. Yet again, his past was catching up with him. The evening to which Lady Palmerston referred had been a low point, even for him.

But so far he had survived ten minutes in the den of the dragon. If she was going to skewer him alive, he would at least go down fighting.

"And if my memory serves me, you, too, lied through your teeth that evening, gravely insulting my masculinity. But I forgive you," Phillip said graciously.

"At long last my conscience is soothed," she deadpanned.

"I'm overjoyed to have helped. But as you said, I'm sharper now, so I do not expect you to take my word that Angela had agreed to marry me. But I trust you will believe her. You could ask her now, in fact."

"As I believe I mentioned, she is not at home," Lady Palmerston said firmly.

"I'll wait." He would. He would sit in this overdecorated drawing room until the apocalypse came and left, and then a little bit longer, if necessary.

"She could be gone for hours. Days. I have no idea," Lady Palmerston replied. They both knew she was lying.

"As negligent as ever, I see," he said. "Please tell her I called. And that I will call again tomorrow."

"And the next day, and the day after that, too, I suppose," Lady Palmerston said, saying the words for him.

"As long as it takes."

Phillip suspected she thought him a lovesick fool. He certainly was, and he had definitely been thought worse things than that.

⌒

Angela stood frozen in the dining room, behind the slightly open drawing room door, from where she had been eavesdropping.

When Groves announced that Lord Huntley had come to call, while she and her aunt had been enjoying breakfast, she was so shocked that she had dropped the piece of buttered toast she held onto her lap. And then her heart skipped a beat. Or two. He had come back. Her questions would be answered, and she could face her future with a full understanding of her past.

She frowned as she picked up the toast from her lap and set it aside. She didn't think she'd have to face her future with a stained dress and messy hair.

"Is he not aware that it is beyond the pale to call at such an hour?" Lady Palmerston asked.

"He seems rather impatient, madame. He wishes to see Miss Sullivan about an urgent matter."

"Perhaps he might return later," Lady Palmerston said, eyeing Angela's dress, which was a mess, even without the new stain from her buttered toast.

Of all the mornings for him to come to call, he had to do so when she had completely given up—and looked it. He had seen her in the awful gray, ill-fitting frocks she had worn in the abbey. He had removed those dresses to see her naked. But she did not want him to see her now in a plain morning gown stained with charcoal from her drawings and ink stains upon her fingers. She hadn't even so much as brushed her hair. And Angela wanted to be as stunning as she could possibly be when she saw him again.

Oh, she knew it was the height of vanity, and that such concern for her appearance went against all the teachings of the abbey. But the fact remained that she was a proud woman, facing the man who had broken her heart.

It only occurred to her in this moment that she might be facing a very, very angry man. He had confessed to her that the newspaper's portrayals of him bothered him. Her picture was not flattering, for she had portrayed him as the villain. He could be such a fool sometimes, and perhaps he didn't understand her intentions. She wanted his attention.

Her courage was evaporating by the second. Angela looked pleadingly at her aunt.

"I'll see him," Lady Palmerston declared. "You should listen, so I needn't repeat everything he says. If it's so important, he'll come back and tell you himself."

And so Angela eavesdropped shamelessly. Once she was sure he had left, she pushed the dining room door all the way open and stepped into the drawing room. She felt like such a ninny.

She had heard everything.

And she had understood less.

Lady Palmerston was grinning and muttering something about reformed rakes and it never ceasing to amuse her. Angela rang for tea and sat down on the settee.

"Hmmph," Lady Palmerston muttered. "Well, did you really agree to marry him?"

"Yes."

"Well, it seems he means to hold you to your word."

"So he says," Angela said bitterly. "Dora, what did you mean about him lying about that before? And courting your other niece?"

"Ah, that is quite a story. He had been very determined to marry Emilia, for her money, and she had been determined to marry Devon. His and Phillip's identical appearances caused some problems. But it all resolved itself before it was too late."

"Did he ruin her, too?"

"No. Not for lack of trying though."

"I thought he was rude to you, just now."

"Oh, to the contrary. The man has finally discovered his wits. And courage. For the first time, he did not bore me to tears. We could talk of it for hours, but the pressing point, Angela, is what you intend to do. For I quite believe he'll make good on his promise to call day after day until he sees you."

"I'll believe it when I see it. But if he does, please, do not leave me alone with him. Or any man," Angela added, thinking of Lucas's intentions to call and Emilia's stories of Lady Palmerston's unusual chaperoning methods.

"If you fear a man will harm you unless there is a chaperone present, I wonder why you would see the man at all."

"I don't fear being made to do something against my will. It is my own will, my own mind, my own judgment that I do not trust."

"I see."

"Do you? Lucas didn't force me. Phillip never forced me. And I have been ruined and heartbroken all the same. I chose them as much as they chose me. So do you see that I cannot be trusted, because I am a fool, a victim of my own poor judgment? I cannot be left alone."

"I understand, Angela."

"I'd better go change before we receive any more callers," Angela said, looking down at her gown once more.

She didn't take long and had just returned to the drawing room when Groves announced that Lord Frost was calling.

"*We* shall see him," Lady Palmerston informed the butler.

There was something about Lord Frost that Lady Palmerston did not like. She took the liberty of considering exactly that as he and Angela conversed about how they were enjoying London, the ball the previous evening, mutual acquaintances, and other such trivialities. The topic of the past, *their* past, was deliberately ignored and avoided, as were all the intervening years.

She thought it might be something about his eyes; they were such a pale blue, and the color reminded her of a sunny yet frigid February day. Bright, with the illusion of warmth. She could not fault his manners or his conversation. Frost was seemingly all that a gentleman ought to be, and all that was proper. Yet she couldn't shake the feeling that there was no depth to the man. Or that his behavior was all a carefully constructed act.

And Lady Palmerston couldn't help but compare Frost to Huntley, as he had been years ago, when he was courting her other niece. Huntley couldn't act to save his own life. Huntley had always conducted himself as if he were deliberately trying to be loathed, or at the very best, not trying to be liked.

And that was when Lady Palmerston could name the quality she did not care for in Frost: desperation. But whether it was desperation to please, to be liked, or for something else, she did not know. But it was there in the glacial blue of his eyes. She could sense a strain in his words and his actions.

And then Frost uttered the most peculiar thing.

"I saw Lord Huntley departing here as I arrived. Or should I say 'the evil Lord Hartshorne'? It is he, in your drawing, is it not?" Lady Palmerston pursed her lips. That was certainly odd. Huntley had left a good fifteen minutes before Frost's arrival. Obviously one of the gents had been skulking on the street outside of her house. She made a mental note to speak to Groves about that.

"I don't care to say whom I portrayed in that drawing."

"We needn't keep secrets from each other. Angela, I . . ." And here Frost glanced over at Lady Palmerston, holding her gaze for a moment. He obviously wished her to leave. He stared at her, issuing a command with his eyes. She merely raised her brow at him, and he looked away with a fleeting expression of annoyance. *Hmmph.*

"I should like to see you again, Angela," Frost spoke, his gaze upon Angela now. Her niece betrayed nothing in her expression. She either had acting talents previously unknown, or the girl felt nothing.

But permission was granted, and Frost took his leave.

"He is different than I remembered. Or perhaps I am," Angela remarked thoughtfully.

"I have no basis for comparison," Lady Palmerston said. But she could compare her niece's gentleman callers to each other, and oddly enough, she found herself preferring Phillip. Well, as she said, there was a first time for everything.

~

"Are you wearing my clothes?" Devon asked, eyeing Phillip's attire. Devon had just arrived in the foyer, and the twins were waiting for Emilia before departing to attend a ball. Phillip had, without Devon or Emilia's explicit permission, moved into Buckingham House. He had no money for lodgings of his own, or even his own clothes.

"Yes, I am. I can't thank you enough for lending them to me. I didn't really take the time to pack before I left." That was true; it was also irrelevant. Phillip no longer owned a set of evening clothes to pack.

"I don't think that I—"

"Isn't it great having a brother? Especially one that has exactly the same measurements. We are so lucky to have each other," Phillip said, grinning, and affectionately patting Devon on the back.

"Really, Phillip, did you suffer a head injury? You are not acting like the brother I know," Devon said, looking at him suspiciously. Phillip resisted mentioning that Devon was not the brother he remembered, either. For one thing, his twin hadn't beaten him again. His twin hadn't even asked him to leave— although he hadn't exactly offered to allow Phillip to stay in his home, either.

But something had changed between them. It might have been because Phillip had changed. Perhaps it was because they were no longer vying for their father's attention. Phillip did not care to examine potential explanations. All he knew was that for the first time in his life, he was glad he had his brother.

"I did hit my head, actually. Hence, the scar," Phillip replied, gesturing to the scar just above his right eyebrow.

"Stop pointing that out to me," Devon grumbled through gritted teeth. Phillip would have, if it didn't so obviously annoy his brother, and if that didn't amuse him so much. Some things never changed.

"Enjoy the fact that you had it first," Phillip conceded.

"I shall. Just as I also enjoy the fact that you are in debt to me by, what is it, six hundred pounds now?"

Phillip scowled. His brother had dictated the *worst* terms for the loan: he was to pay it back, without interest, but at the expense of Devon being allowed to nag, needle, tease, and remind him as much as he'd like, and Phillip was not allowed to taunt back. Although: "Five hundred and ninety-four, actually," Phillip couldn't resist pointing out. The collection of rent and the sale of some land had gone a long way toward paying off his debt.

"Good evening, gentlemen," Emilia said, finally joining them in the foyer.

"You look beautiful, Em, as always," Devon said, making eyes at his wife. Phillip looked away.

"Right. Shall we be going then?" Phillip asked.

"You are joining us?" Emilia asked.

"Devon was so gracious as to lend me a suit of evening clothes and to allow me to join you both as a guest," Phillip lied smoothly. As far as lies went, it was a small one and uttered for the noble purpose of searching for Angela. The fact that he hadn't an invitation, he assumed, would be overlooked. His mere presence after such a long, unexplained absence would be scandalous, thus giving the ton some gossip with which to amuse themselves. He considered it his gift to them.

Devon opened his mouth to reply to the contrary, but Emilia spoke first.

"Oh, Devon, that is so kind and thoughtful of you!"

Devon merely smiled at his wife. "Shall we be off then?"

Chapter 16

"*The* Duke and Duchess of Buckingham," the butler announced to the crowd at large as they all arrived at the ball. "And . . ." The butler took a second look at Phillip, "And the Marquis of Huntley?"

At first, only those standing in the vicinity took notice. Heads swiveled in his direction, mouths fell open, eyes widened, eyebrows were raised; all the typical expressions of surprise were present in some variation upon every face that saw him. Then the silence traveled through the ballroom like the plague, infecting one person after the next until even the orchestra ceased to produce a sound. More than one couple engaged in a waltz stopped short, bumping into their partners.

And then there were a few gasps of shock, which turned into whispers, until the room buzzed as if inhabited by a swarm of bees. That escalated into the roar of hundreds of people talking at once. The orchestra resumed playing. The couples returned to their waltz.

"I haven't lost my touch, it seems," Phillip joked. "I can still cause a scandal just by walking into a room."

"And yet the night is still young. I shudder to think what else might transpire this evening," Devon muttered.

And for a moment, as hundreds of people stood and stared, openly gaped and obviously gossiped about him, Phillip almost lost his nerve. He didn't feel like the greatest scoundrel of his generation but rather like a boy on the first day of school.

No one will like you. They are all going to laugh at you.

On that first day at Eton, he had stood a little taller, squaring his shoulders, gritting his teeth, and wordlessly daring them to say something to his face. Tonight, he did all of those things, except he added a grin. *Did you miss me?* his smile seemed to say.

One or two people couldn't help but smile back. But quite a few gasped at his audacity and turned their backs. Quite a few mothers stepped in front of their daughters, as a barrier between them and Phillip. They were safe from him now, for there was only one woman that he wanted.

If Angela was witnessing this, he hoped she at least understood now why he had hesitated so long to make her his wife. He badly wanted her at his side right now, as a source of comfort and strength. But at the same time, he was relieved that she did not endure this as well. And that was when he saw the flaw in his plan. He could not possibly speak to her tonight. He would not approach her. He would, if luck were on his side, catch a glimpse of her. And maybe, just maybe, she would seek him out. But he would not force her to endure his attentions. He could not taint her with his blackened, filthy reputation.

And like that first day of school, he had the backing of a duke, and he was still the heir to a dukedom. Devon stood at his side, still.

"You see now why I stayed away for five years," his twin murmured.

"The company does leave a bit to be desired."

And then it became apparent that someone was pushing their way through the crowd toward Phillip. More than one person turned to glare at the figure that so carelessly shoved them aside.

"Phillip! It is you. Good to have you back," Parkhurst said, grinning widely, once he had managed to survive the crowd. The happiness in his voice was undeniable, and Phillip was at once truly glad to see his friend yet also wary. Parkhurst had always been around, always enjoying the debauchery Phillip had surrounded himself with. What if that were the only basis of their friendship?

"Parkhurst. It's good to see you again," Phillip said, and it was the truth.

"We must have a drink to celebrate your return. Thank God you have chosen this ball to attend. I swear I was so bored that I was ready to drown myself in the vat of lemonade."

"I arrived just in time then," Phillip said, accepting a brandy from the footman. He looked at it and realized that he did not want it.

"Cheers!" Parkhurst said, raising his glass. Phillip did the same, though he did not imbibe.

"What the devil is that on your finger, Parkhurst?" Had Phillip taken a sip of his drink, he would have choked on it.

"Oh, that," Parkhurst said, staring at the wedding band on his hand with a mixture of annoyance and awe.

"Got yourself leg shackled, did you?" Phillip said, grinning. Parkhurst. Married. That was unexpected. What was the world coming to?

"Mother wore me down. But Lilly, my wife, she's sweet. Doesn't complain overmuch about how much time I spend at the club. She's around here somewhere tonight, off with her friends."

"Congratulations," Phillip said, raising his glass in cheers again but not taking a sip this time, either.

"I would have sent an invitation, but I didn't know where you were."

"Of course. You and I are not the letter writing type."

"No. The good thing about a wife, though—well, one of the good things—is that Lilly takes care of stuff like that."

"You could have hired a secretary," Phillip pointed out.

"But that wouldn't have gotten my mother off my back about getting married, now would it?" Parkhurst responded.

"No," Phillip agreed.

"Although," Parkhurst continued, "now she has moved on to to nagging me about providing her with grandchildren." Parkhurst as a father, Phillip thought. It was almost as unimaginable as Phillip being a father.

"And have you provided one?"

"No, but not for lack of trying. Which, the other day, I pointed out to my mother, and I managed to silence her for an entire thirty-seven seconds."

Phillip laughed. He could just imagine Parkhurst, stunned at his own minor triumph, counting the ticking of the clock hands above his mother's head.

"So does she still fill you in on the gossip when she's done nagging you about something or other?" Like Phillip, Parkhurst never read the papers. But unlike Phillip, Parkhurst had a mother who called thrice a week, without fail, and when she was finished lecturing him on this or that, she filled him in on every little *on-dit*. She had always been their primary source of information, particularly regarding all the wicked things Phillip was alleged to have done or, often enough, had actually done.

Phillip wondered if his own mother might have done the same. And if he would have complained to his friends about it, while being secretly pleased with the attention.

"Indeed she does," Parkhurst said, after gulping down a sip of brandy. "I think we both wish that she had had a daughter, who might enjoy hearing her babble on about all that nonsense."

"Nonsense it may be, I'm curious as to what has transpired in my absence."

"Where to start? Let me think. Well, Lord Derby over there . . ." Parkhurst began, and then he continued. Phillip only paid the slightest attention to his friend's gossip, as he looked about the room, searching for Angela.

She was not waltzing. She was not over by the lemonade table. She was not hovering on the periphery of the ballroom like a wallflower, nor, to his relief, was she in the middle of a large group of gents in the far corner.

But she was standing near the large French doors that led to the terrace.

Phillip's breath caught in his throat. He had imagined her every day and every night since he first met her. And the Angela of his fantasies had been so vivid that he could almost taste her and touch her. But this, this was something else. Because that was the real Angela, and she was closer to him than she had been in nearly a year. And yet she was still so very far away.

She was beautiful, more so than he had imagined. In fact, he had never imagined her like this. Her hair was piled atop her head in some elaborate arrangement that left a few honey-hued curls hanging around her face. He gazed at cheeks he had cupped in his hands, lips that he had thoroughly kissed, and eyes that had seen right through him and might have loved him anyway.

She wore a gown of violet-colored silk. At least, he thought it was silk. He couldn't tell from the other side of the ballroom, and really, who cared about fabric? He cared about what was under it. And her breasts. God. He could concede that it was the fashion for women to wear gowns with such low necklines, to have their breasts there on display. But he wanted nothing more than to cover her with his jacket so that no other man could gaze upon them. He wanted her all for himself.

He was staring. He couldn't look away. Helen of Troy had nothing on her.

And then she looked up and caught his eye.

She did not smile. Nor did she scowl. He could not discern the expression on her face. But she did stare back at him. One, two, three heartbeats. He counted. His heart was pounding so hard he couldn't help but notice it. Four, five, six, seven. She looked away.

But he did not look away. He watched her turn to the gentleman next to her. And his heart stopped in his throat.

"Phillip? Have you been listening?"

"Who is that?" Phillip asked, gesturing slightly to that man next to her. *Don't say it. Don't say it. Don't say it.*

"That fellow? Lord Frost. He's new to town this season,

likely looking for a bride since his wife died about a year ago. Seems to be a decent fellow."

Phillip did not want to know that Frost was a decent fellow. He couldn't possibly be. He had deceived Angela, ruined her, and caused the death of her father. God, the ton would have a field day if that rumor were to start circulating . . .

"Why do you ask?" Parkhurst questioned.

"I thought he looked familiar." It was the truth. Phillip recognized him from Angela's sketchbook. He also recognized the look on Frost's face as he spoke with Angela: it was an expression of adoration. And it would be sort of perfect, wouldn't it, if Frost was to make an honest woman of her, after all these years?

He sincerely hoped Angela didn't think of it like that.

"The woman he's talking to is Miss Sullivan," Parkhurst continued. "She does drawings for the *London Weekly*. In fact—" Parkhurst stopped short as he put two and two together. "It is you in that drawing! Now Lord North owes me twenty quid. Splendid. And that is why you have returned, right? Where were you, anyway, and how does she know you? And—"

"Are they . . . betrothed?" Phillip asked, cutting off Parkhurst. That was not a conversation he wanted to have at present. Fortunately, his friend was easily distracted.

"No. But according to my mother, they ought to be. She heard from her sister-in-law who heard from her cousin that Frost used to court Miss Sullivan, years and years ago. Everyone expected a betrothal announcement, but then he married another, and she disappeared for a few years. There was something about a small-town scandal, but I can't remember it. Either way, there are rumors about them. Wards off many suitors for her. So you'd think that she'd jump at the chance to marry anyone, let alone a viscount. *Women.* I swear they are impossible to understand."

～

"You look exceptionally beautiful tonight," Lucas said. *It's not for you*, Angela wanted to shout. She had suspected that

Phillip might be here tonight. She was determined to look her best for the encounter, not to please him but to show him just what he had given up, and because it made her feel better and stronger to be pretty.

She had been stunned by the reaction Phillip received just by walking into the ballroom tonight. It was then that she realized she hadn't quite believed him when he spoke of his reputation. *Society will not be kind to us,* he had said.

They were not kind now. "Did you hear about the orgies in Paris?" they whispered to each other in hushed tones. "What about all those ruined girls? Was it four? Or fourteen?" "He has a dozen illegitimate children starving in the streets." "No, I heard on good authority that it was at least twenty starving orphans." And then there was speculation as to what he had done during the past year, an unaccounted-for block of time in which no stories had surfaced about him. And those were only the things Angela had managed to overhear.

She, too, was among the gawkers. But she couldn't be the only one gawking at him because he was so outrageously handsome. He held himself like the duke he had been raised to be: strong and sure. And then he smiled, slightly amused at the reaction. Like it was just the welcome he had expected.

From her far corner in the ballroom, she searched his face for a clue of the man she had known. She was used to seeing him in the roughest garments, if any. And there he stood, in black-and-white evening dress. The clothing was different, but she could still see enough of the man she had known. And he could still make her heart beat double time.

Did you miss me? His smile seemed to say.

"Yes," she had whispered. But no one had heard, for they were too busy with whispers of their own.

"Did you hear me, Angela? I said you were more beautiful than ever tonight," Lucas stated.

"Thank you," she replied. Lucas kept staring at her. "What is it?" she asked.

"Your beauty has increased with time. And you were utterly ravishing when I first knew you."

"Ravishing," she repeated. Ravished was more like it.

"Angela—" Lucas murmured. But she ignored him, because she had the queerest feeling of being watched. *Don't look,* her brain urged. But it was no match for her desire. She saw Phillip, standing with some gentleman she didn't know. Phillip was watching her. He didn't smile, and neither did she. She couldn't, really. Every part of her was so overwhelmed with the heat of desire and anger. She wanted equally to slap him and kiss him. Instead, she stood where she was, frozen, and stared at him.

He had come back.

And remembering how it was said that he could ruin a woman with his eyes, she turned away.

"What were you saying?" she asked.

"I was asking if you'd like to take a trip with me this weekend to my house in Oxfordshire. Just the two of us. Alone." Lucas discreetly took her hand in his.

"Are you mad?" she hissed, snatching her hand away. Someone would be sure to see them, and that someone would talk, and before she knew it, her reputation would as black as . . . Phillip's. And where was Lady Palmerston? She had promised not to leave Angela alone with any man, and yet she had.

"You are not an innocent, Angela. The rules don't apply to you."

"Thank you for pointing that out," she said dryly. Was the heat in the ballroom tonight due to the masses of people? Or the mortification of what Lucas had just said? Or because she was sure Phillip was still looking at her? Where was her aunt?

"I never stopped loving you, Angela." She saw something in his eyes that made her think he might have spoken the truth. And she had waited years for those words, had she not? Wasn't this moment supposed to be grander? She spoke without thinking.

"And I never felt sorry for your wife, until now." It was the truth, she realized. She had never met her, so Angela couldn't hate her. But there was many a night that she seethed with jealousy. Another woman was married to Angela's husband.

"Do not pity her," Lucas said harshly, and his eyes darkened.

"Why not? Her husband was in love with someone else."

"The child she died giving birth to wasn't mine." If he had any feelings about that situation, they were not apparent in his voice. And she thought of his pride then, and what it must have cost him to admit something like that to her. She did not know how to feel about the stirring of tenderness she felt for him. Or was it merely pity?

"You have not been lucky in love," she observed.

"No. But I believe in fate. Could it be anything else that brought us together again, with no obstacles in our way this time? We have a second chance now, do we not?"

She hesitated in her response. She wasn't sure, and yet not one but two potential second chances were here in the ballroom.

"Ah, there you are, Angela," Lady Palmerston cut in. "We should go say hello to Lord and Lady Winsworth."

"Angela, think about my invitation," he urged.

"I will. Good-bye, Lucas."

For the next three hours, Angela danced with many men, none of them Phillip. When she wasn't waltzing, she was talking with many people, none of them Phillip. By the end of the evening, just one question burned within her: Why had he come back if he was not going to talk to her?

"What invitation did Frost want you to think about?" Lady Palmerston asked once they were settled in the carriage for the drive home.

"What? Oh. I had quite forgotten about that."

"You know, my dear, that I remember—"

"Everything, I know. He wanted me to go away with him this weekend to his house is Oxfordshire." After repeating his proposition, Angela laughed.

"Obviously you haven't given it much thought."

"No. It's outrageous. He obviously still does not have a care for my reputation."

"Unless he means to marry you this time," her aunt posited.

"I had that thought, too." They parted seven years ago under utterly devastating circumstances, and after a few weeks' reacquaintance, his intentions were clear. She didn't know how she felt about it. Sometimes she thought it was too soon. Unless it was too late.

"I can't even begin to imagine what might have distracted you," Lady Palmerston said slyly.

"Oh, hush Aunt Know-It-All. You know very well what has distracted me all evening."

"Quite an entrance the bloke made," she remarked casually.

"Indeed," Angela agreed. It would be the topic of every ton conversation for the next week, if not longer. The prodigal rake had returned.

"Well, are you going?"

"Where? Oh, right, to Oxfordshire with Lucas. It depends, I suppose."

"On Lord Huntley, I presume," Lady Palmerston supplied. Angela did not, nay, could not, contradict her. And in this moment, she felt another swell of hope. Her hope, like a child taking its first steps, tottered and then fell.

"Why didn't he speak to me tonight? After all those things he said this afternoon?"

"Probably because he didn't want his filthy reputation to tarnish your own good reputation that you have worked so hard to achieve. Touching, really. I never thought that Huntley had the mental space devoted to thinking of someone other than himself. Angela, what did you do to him?"

"I loved him," she said so quietly that she didn't think her aunt could hear.

But she did.

⌒

"You're still up. And still here," Emilia said, while pausing in the doorway to the library later that evening. Phillip was sprawled in a leather chair before the fire, which though dying down, still provided a decent amount of warmth and light. Even in London he maintained his evening ritual of sitting before a fire and brooding about Angela.

"I turned down Parkhurst's offer to go to a gaming hell. Where is Devon?"

"Upstairs, with the girls. He reads to them before bed. I guess I'll join them . . ."

"Join me, if you'd like. I could use a distraction from myself."

"OK." Emilia came in and sat in a chair opposite his. She bit her lip and drummed her fingers on the arm of the chair. She looked at Phillip out of the corner of her eye. A moment passed.

"Oh, just say it," he said.

"Angela is your fiancée from the abbey, right? The one you borrowed the money to save, right? And the reason you've returned to London."

"Yes."

"I knew it! Neither she nor our aunt breathed a word about you. I had no idea, until recently it slipped that she had spent some time in an abbey, and I couldn't help but put two and two together. And then that drawing in the newspaper . . ."

"Very well done of you."

"But you didn't even *try* to speak to her tonight! I thought you came here to get her back. And I can't see how ignoring her is going to accomplish that. Or is it because she wouldn't see you when you called today?"

"You women. Always talking," Phillip muttered.

"It's about time you learned that."

"Talking to Lucas Frost, of all the cads in the world."

"What is wrong with Lord Frost?" Emilia asked. "Is it because of the rumors about him and Angela from years and years ago? They are unconfirmed, you know. But they have become friendly of late."

"I cannot say. Will not say, rather," Phillip said. Emilia did not seem to know much about Angela's past. It seemed that Angela could keep a secret. But was it to preserve her reputation or an effort to pretend she had never known either of them?

"You are still in love with her," Emilia stated, filling the silence. Phillip decided to change the subject.

"Emilia, why are you being so kind to me after all I did to you?"

She smiled at him but didn't speak for a while, and Phillip began to feel sorry that he asked. She probably couldn't think of a reason to be kind to him and instead thought of twenty reasons why she should throw him out on the streets that very moment. But she surprised him.

"Because even though you haven't said that you are sorry, I know that you are. Because we're family now. Because someone has to warn my girls about the scoundrels of the world, and you are an expert. Because it makes Devon happy. All of that, and the fact that you need all the help you can get."

That last bit was particularly true, and it made him smile.

"I am sorry, Emilia. I wasn't before, but I am now. I know what it's like to be kept from the one you love. I'm sorry for the things I did that almost kept you from Devon."

"Thank you, Phillip," she said, and he could tell from her voice that his apology really meant something to her. *Goodness and love. Goodness and love . . .*

"You know, Phillip," Emilia said, leaning forward slightly, "I don't really like Lucas Frost, either. There is something odd about him, now that I think about it. He seemed so possessive of Angela, far too much so."

"Unfortunately, our opinion of him does not matter."

"I shall help you win her," Emilia said decisively.

"I don't like the sound of that," he responded warily. "Nor do I like the maniacal look in your eyes. In fact, you look quite like that dragon aunt of yours."

"Oh hush. If it weren't for my dragon aunt, you and I would be married now."

"Touché. Now, just out of curiosity, mind you, what would you do to help me win her back?"

"You will join me for tea at Lady Palmerston's tomorrow. If you are not announced, then Angela will not have time to hide."

"You are devious."

"You're welcome."

"Thank you, Emilia. For helping me, and for letting me stay here, and for forgiving me," Phillip said earnestly.

"I appreciate that. I should also warn you that you are

beginning to sound like some brooding sap from a *London Weekly* serial novel."

"What's wrong with that? I thought you liked those."

"I like to read them. I don't necessarily want to live with one." Emilia bade him good night and left him alone in the library.

Chapter 17

"*Are* you sure this will work?" Phillip said, desperately wishing he had a free hand to loosen his cravat. It was choking him. In each hand, he held a bouquet of flowers. The dragon must be pacified as well.

"No," Emilia said, before turning her attention to the now-open door. "Oh, hello, Groves. I'm here for tea. No need to announce us; we are expected."

"Lady Buckingham," the butler intoned. His eternally inscrutable expression cracked for a second, revealing obvious curiosity to see her with Phillip.

"Hello, Emilia," Lady Palmerston said when they entered the drawing room. She maintained her usual position on her chair by the mantel. "Are you quite yourself today?"

"I am. Why do you ask?" Emilia sat down on the settee opposite Angela, and Phillip sat next to Emilia. He wanted to look at Angela. To be near enough to steal even the slightest touch would undo him. That was not something that needed to occur in Lady Palmerston's drawing room.

"I just wanted to point out, in case you had become confused, that is not your husband," Lady Palmerston said.

"I am quite aware. I trust I needn't perform introductions?" Emilia asked innocently. No, she certainly did not. Phillip finally allowed himself to look at Angela. Her eyes were on him as well. Even with the accusatory and questioning expression on her face, she had never appeared so . . . pretty. Her long, wavy hair was let down, though pulled back with a ribbon. His fingers twitched, wanting to sink into that hair, which he knew was soft and silky.

She wore a simple morning dress in a shade of light blue to match her eyes. The dress suited her so much more than the dull gray ones she wore in the abbey. He could easily imagine her in the drawing room at Aston House. There it would be just the two of them.

His gaze dropped to the neckline of her gown. Though modest, it still did not conceal the luscious curves and swells of her breasts. He forced his gaze back to her face. Even he knew that now was not the time to be ogling her figure like a barbarian.

"Introductions are not necessary," Lady Palmerston said. "Phillip, what on earth are you carrying?" It was only then that he remembered the two bouquets he held.

"Flowers. Obviously. For you, Lady Palmerston," he said handing her a collection of purple hyacinths.

"Have you hit your head?" she asked, accepting the flowers and nodding in approval.

"I did, in fact," Phillip said, at the same time that Angela said, "He did." They looked at each other with half smiles.

"Hmmph," was Lady Palmerston's response. "Thank you, Huntley. You have managed to surprise me."

"These are for you," Phillip said, handing the other bouquet to Angela. It was an assortment of different-colored roses. The florist had tried to explain their various meanings, but Phillip was too impatient. He took a few of each: pink, white, yellow, red. Angela hesitated a second before accepting them.

"How are you, Angela?" Phillip asked once the butler left to put the flowers in vases, and once it was clear that no one else was going to initiate a conversation. That, and he did not have the patience to endure a discussion on the weather when he was finally with Angela again.

"Fine, thank you. And you?"

"I'm well."

A maid entered with the fresh pot of tea, as well as the two vases of flowers, which were set on small tables on either side of the drawing room doors. After everyone had tea to their liking, Phillip asked if Angela had any news from the abbey.

"I have, actually," Angela said, and her eyes lit up just a bit. He had said the right thing! He realized then that he, of all people, was the only person in London who knew of her old friends, and that she probably missed them. "Everyone is well. William enlisted in the army. He said it was far preferable to his other option, which was joining the clergy."

"I'll say," Phillip agreed strongly.

"Of course *you* would. Oh, and the repairs to the chapel have been completed."

"Thank goodness they managed without my help. I was worried about that," he deadpanned. He had to joke because he so very badly wanted things to be like they used to be.

"Oh, like you did anything other than stand about with your shirt off," Angela retorted.

"It facilitated all the heavy lifting I did. Besides, I didn't hear any complaints."

"You didn't stay around long enough to hear them," she said pointedly.

"That is true. And considering the companions—and I use the term loosely—that I left with, I would have gladly stayed and endured endless complaints about my naked chest. Or compliments, but we needn't argue over word choice."

"Well, who did you leave with?" Angela asked, setting her teacup down on the saucer with a clink. "And why?"

"Pierre and François, two of the filthiest, most ignorant brutes humanity has ever produced."

"You left me for *that*?"

"They had followed me on behalf of another stinking Frenchman, to whom I still owed money, which I was not aware of.

Rest assured, I will now read the fine print on contracts, particularly about interest on a loan."

"But you didn't have any money, or had you lied to me?"

"I didn't lie. I didn't have any money, which I pointed out to them. In their sick and twisted minds, they thought that *you* might be a fair trade for the thousand pounds I owed."

"Me? What could they possibly want with me?"

"You do not want to know of such things."

Her cheeks colored, and he could not read her expression. Some mixture perhaps of horror as she comprehended and relief, and yet still resisting forgiving him.

"No need to thank me, I know you are grateful," Phillip said casually. "Fortunately for both of us, I have a very wealthy brother who takes an enormous amount of pleasure in lending me money for the sole purpose of mocking me endlessly about it."

"Is this true, Emilia?" Angela asked.

"It is," Emilia answered. "And Phillip has endured Devon's taunts admirably. I myself have been tempted to hit my husband a time or two, having to listen to it."

"I, as well. Though I have not," Phillip said.

"Hmmph," Lady Palmerston said to fill the silence, and Angela knitted her brows together in thought. Phillip's heart beat a little bit harder. What did she have to say, now that she knew the truth? She parted her lips. Phillip held his breath. She opened her mouth again, to take a deep breath. He saw the color rise in her cheeks, and he braced himself for the explosion.

"You might have *told* me! You could have at least said *good-bye*. But no! You propose and then simply walk away as if nothing had ever happened."

"I wasn't given a chance to say good-bye. I asked. I tried. But I came back, and you had not waited for me."

"I was supposed to wait for you? Really? *Really?* After what I had been through and after all the other women you had walked away from, you really thought that I would believe anything other than the worst? Really, Phillip, *really?*"

"I wanted nothing more than to explain everything to you.

But by the time I returned, you were long gone, without leaving word of where you had gone. You left me, Angela, as much as I left you."

Obviously, she had not seen the situation as he did. Her only response was a choked sound of frustration. That, and chucking a teaspoon at his head. Phillip had been expecting that, so he ducked, and it went sailing past his head, hitting the wall behind him, and cracking the glass in a picture frame before clattering to the floor.

She was adorable. He loved her. This was the happiest moment he'd had since he last saw her. She cared . . . and cared enough to throw things at him, even if it was only a teaspoon.

"Do you think we ought to give them some privacy, Aunt?" Emilia murmured.

"Yes."

"Well, are you coming?" Emilia said, after standing to go. Angela stood as well.

"Oh, no. I wouldn't miss this for the world," Lady Palmerston stated. She remained comfortably in her chair, with a grin of pure amusement on her face. Angela had stood, so Phillip did, too, and she was now advancing upon him.

"But you returned anyway, Phillip. What changed? Or are you just here to complain about the drawing?"

"I'm here now because after nearly a year of pure misery and missing you, I gave up trying to stop loving you. Because I could finally find you again thanks to that illustration. I'm sorry that I left, sorrier than you'll ever know. But it couldn't be helped. You, however, fled at the first opportunity. You can apologize any time."

"*Me?* Apologize? To you? Have you hit your head again?"

"No, but not for lack of trying on your part."

She looked around the room then, and he knew that she was looking for something else to throw at him. He took a step back. Cowardly, perhaps, or an act of self-preservation. She smacked him on the arm anyway.

"You can thank me, too, for using my likeness to portray the villain in your drawings. I won't sue, though I could use the money," Phillip said, taking another step back. He was teasing her, teasing out her anger, so that she could stop being mad and start loving him again. But he, too, was hurt and angry.

He had always been the first to flee so that he wouldn't be the abandoned one.

And the one time he had loved and hoped and tried, his worst fear was realized. She had left him anyway. It was amazing he was here at all.

"Oh! You are impossible!" She took another step forward, and he took another step back, until his back was up against the wall. It reminded him of the first time he had tried to walk alone on his injured leg. When he had fallen on top of her, and when he had almost kissed her. He smiled at the memory. It seemed to make her angrier still.

"That's all that brought you to town, isn't it! Poor Phillip Kensington—always misunderstood and maligned in the papers. You are a horrible, selfish, shallow man, and if you ask me—" She punched him squarely in the chest. It didn't hurt in the slightest.

"I tried to tell you that I was horrible, selfish, and self-centered, but you wouldn't believe me."

"I've learned my lesson," she said dryly.

"But you also accepted my marriage proposal, so now I am y*our* horrible, selfish, self-centered man, soon to be hus—"

"Don't even say it!" Angela cried. "Do you really think I'm going to marry you now?"

"A man can dream," he said with an exaggerated sigh.

"That's about all," she said coldly while folding her arms across her chest. This resulted in her breasts being pushed up higher, and closer together, and if they hadn't had an audience . . .

"Well, Huntley," Lady Palmerston cut in, "I'm quite curious. Why did you come to town after all this time?"

"Because I couldn't stay away. And I arrived just in time to save you, Angela, from making a mistake. Don't go back to Frost."

Her only answer was to pummel him on the chest with her tiny fists.

"Woman, you are going break my ribs again!"

"Again?" Emilia and Lady Palmerston echoed him. Angela stopped hitting him, only to pluck up the bouquet of roses from the vase (thank heaven for small favors; that crystal looked like it might do serious damage), and she began smacking him with a dozen long-stemmed roses of every color and every meaning.

"You have no right!" *Thwack.* "You can't just leave me and then walk back into my life and expect that things haven't changed." *Thwack.* "And when I might just have a chance at happiness and making things right!" *Thwack thwack.* "You're probably just in it for the competition! As long as you win, who gives a damn about the prize?" *Thwack.*

"Oh, I want the prize."

"Which is why you ran off when you had it."

"We've already covered that, Angela," Lady Palmerston cut in.

"What can I do to prove to you that that I love you? That I am the one for you?" he asked plainly. Here he stood, his back up against the wall, not fighting the blows she showered upon him. He deserved those. But here he was, still, now covered in rose petals and thorns.

"When I figure it out, I'll let you know. Good-bye, Phillip." She threw the roses down on the table and walked out of the drawing room.

"That went quite well," Phillip remarked to Emilia once they were in the carriage.

"How on earth do you figure that?"

"If she didn't care, she wouldn't have been so blazing mad. Isn't she adorable when she's angry?"

"I think if you had said that to her, I might have had to have a footman carry your unconscious body home."

"I thought the same myself."

"Phillip Kensington shows restraint. I never thought I'd live to see the day."

❧

"Oh he is insufferable! He is impossible. I cannot believe no one has strangled him to death yet. I mean, the nerve! To just waltz in here and—"

"Walked. He didn't waltz," Lady Palmerston pointed out.

"Whatever. The bloody nerve to walk in here and—" Angela continued her pacing, as if walking back and forth in the drawing room would relieve some of her vexation. Lady Palmerston sipped her tea and watched her walk to and fro with a bemused expression.

"Tell you he loved you. The sheer audacity of it is mind-boggling."

"He didn't say that," Angela immediately retorted. "He just gave an excess of stupid excuses and—"

"Oh, he did say it," Lady Palmerston said, picking up a pile of invitations and letters, which she began to look through.

"He did not." Angela paused in her pacing.

"He did. You were too busy smacking him with the bouquet of flowers. Speaking of which, Groves!"

"Yes, madame." The butler materialized in a second. He was in the habit of standing just outside the drawing room doors, and likely eavesdropping when he wasn't called upon.

"Please have someone see to the mess."

"He probably only said it in self-defense," Angela protested, since now that she thought about it, she could recall the exact sentence he had uttered: *What can I do to prove to you that I love you? That I am the one for you?*

"Or you beat the truth out of him. Remarkable strategy. In fact, I don't know why more women don't employ it."

"He did take it all rather well," Angela said thoughtfully, thinking of how he never once told her she was overreacting or even tried to stop her. "But do you think that I was too hard on Phillip today? I missed him so, but I am so bloody livid that he left. Seeing him just reminded me of it."

"Gad, no, you were not too hard on him. He deserves no less. In fact, I'm inclined to think that he deserves the same treatment from all the girls that he ruined."

"He didn't ruin *me*, though," Angela said, knowing that it was the truth. Of all that he had done, he was not guilty of that.

"Right. He only broke your heart. You should have probably saved that rage for Frost then. Have you given him an answer to his invitation yet?"

"I will tell him tonight that I won't join him. For now, I'm going to go work on my sketches for an hour before it is time to dress for this evening."

"Very well. I shall tell Groves that we are not at home, for I am in need of a nap. I am simply exhausted from this afternoon's entertainment."

~

With his glacial blue eyes, Lucas Frost watched Lord Huntley exit Lady Palmerston's town house. He had watched as Huntley arrived, too, with flowers in hand. Lucas was pleased to see that he left covered in rose petals.

Lucas knew that Phillip had called the previous day. His footman, who had been assigned to watch the house, reported it. Some might call employing a footman for such purposes nefarious. He thought of it as protective. He had lost her once, and he would not relinquish her again.

It was her innocence that he had loved. He loved her naïve wonder at the world and her faith in him and his decency, even as he had deceived her. And he, cad that he was, though cloaked in respectability, had ruined it in one afternoon, due to one ill-conceived plan. He wanted all of that back.

Because of his father's debts, he had been forced to marry Beatrice Gilford. The daughter of a tradesman, she was plain, a bit crude in her manners, and frighteningly intelligent. But she was rich, and she traded her dowry for his title.

But she preferred books on antiquities to him. And then she preferred someone else to him. But it didn't matter, because Lucas had always loved another. He had loved Angela with every breath in his being. But he had to marry Beatrice, unless . . .

He had executed his plan to secure Angela, never anticipating the flaws. That her father would not offer more money than Mr. Gilford. That her father would call him out, rather than insist Angela go with him. Lucas shot wide, deliberately. Just to ensure he would miss, he had downed large quantities of brandy first. He just never anticipated the old man's heart giving out, right there on the dueling field. Technically, it was not his fault. But it was. He felt the incessant weight of guilt and the chronic ache of regret as if his bullet had gone straight through the man's heart.

Lucas had waited seven years for fate to provide this chance to make right what had gone so horribly wrong. He would marry her and make an honest woman out of her. And though this marriage would not bring her father back, it would in some way make it so that the old man had not died in vain. And it would soothe Lucas's own tortured soul.

He had been making progress.

And then Huntley had shown up.

Lucas had been suspicious when Angela's drawing featured Huntley. How had she known him? Had another man been with his woman (for after all this time, he still thought that she was his)? But Angela never spoke of him, and no one knew of Huntley's whereabouts. Still, Lucas wondered. How could one have competition for a ruined girl? And how could he lose that girl to a notorious scoundrel such as Lord Huntley?

But Huntley had shown up twice now. Thrice, if one counted his appearance at the ball the previous evening. Lucas had seen the way the man looked at his Angela. And he had seen her look back at him for far too long. He panicked. He proposed the weekend trip, and she had not yet accepted. It had been too soon, and he had startled his darling.

Or he had been too late.

She was clearly angry with Huntley, if the man's appearance as he left was any indication. Now might be the perfect time to pay a call.

"Miss Sullivan is not at home," the butler stated.

"But I . . . I've been watching, and I know she has not gone out." The words burst out of his mouth before he thought to censor them. It was only the slightest lift of the butler's eyebrow that indicated that he had said too much.

"You may leave your card."

Lucas did so, even though the butler very well knew who

he was. He had been calling regularly for weeks now, ever since the season began and Angela had by some miracle returned to him.

And now he was losing her. And he needed her, dammit! He needed her to marry him so wrongs could be made right. So that he might sleep at night without seeing her father's cold, dead eyes in his dreams. He was losing his chance at redemption, and he would not let that go easily.

Chapter 18

Angela did not have to look long for Lucas Frost. She had not been at the ball for more than five minutes when he found her, taking her arm in his and steering her toward a darkened corner of the ballroom.

She did, however, have to look for her chaperone. Lady Palmerston had been swept up in the crowd, and Angela had lost sight of her. And now, here she was in a darkened corner with a man. Alone. She acknowledged a twinge of irritation with her aunt for leaving her alone in this situation when she had deliberately asked not to be.

"You were not at home when I called this afternoon. Where were you?" Lucas asked, after the initial pleasantries of conversation had been covered. His voice was as light and smooth as possible, yet there was no mistaking the accusation there. It was as if he had expected her life to revolve around him, at his convenience. That might have been true once, but it no longer was.

"I was working on my illustrations," Angela answered truthfully.

"You should have seen me, instead," Lucas urged, and a

knot began to form in her stomach. She did not like the way he was speaking to her.

"Is there something you wished to speak to me about?" she asked directly, looking into his eyes. They were so cold, so blue. And she couldn't recall if that coldness had been there years before.

"No, I just think that I should warrant more of your attentions than your drawings. After all that we have endured together . . ."

She laughed bitterly. All that *we* endured *together*. What utter bullocks. The truth was that she had suffered alone. And she suffered pain now. Her laughter stopped abruptly.

"Let go of my arm; you are hurting me," Angela said coldly.

"I'm sorry. I hadn't realized." And all at once her pain was etched into his features. He loosened his grasp, but he did not let go. And she realized that he certainly felt strongly for her now. It also occurred to her that she did not feel the same.

"It's fine," she answered automatically, even though it wasn't.

"Dare I ask your answer to my invitation?" He was pleading now; she could see it in his eyes. And this is why she had not wanted to be left alone with him, or to rely on her own judgment. She was tempted to agree, if only to avoid hurting him.

But she looked into his eyes and found herself wishing they were warm and dark instead of cold and blue . . .

"I cannot go with you, Lucas. I'm sorry."

⌒

"Waltz with me."

Angela knew that voice. It was low, warm, and it belonged to Phillip. His words were murmured for her and her alone. And still, after all this time, he made her heart beat a little heavier, with a little more force.

Angela glanced to her left, to see that her aunt was engaged in conversation with Lady Stillmore, and thus not paying the slightest attention to her. Not that it mattered, she didn't need permission. She just needed to pause and note how her anger from the afternoon had faded slightly. Doubts, insecurities, and confusion remained. What had *not* changed was that no man before him or since him made her feel the way he did. He knew her in a way no one else did, and that terrified her and yet made her feel secure in equal measures. Phillip also had a way of looking at her, touching her, standing next to her, which made her keenly aware of every inch of her body. It was distracting.

Tonight, she wanted distraction.

Phillip lightly placed his hand on her lower back. She turned and looked up at him. His slight, tempting grin said it all: *Say yes; you know you want to.*

Lord help her, she did.

Angela hadn't gotten a good look at Phillip today, for her temper had clouded her vision. That, and she had been too busy beating him with a bouquet of roses. She drank in the sight of him now, as he held her in his arms for a slow waltz at the end of the evening. The candles were burning down, so the room was darker. The guests that were still present were quickly slipping into the more advanced stages of intoxication. But the orchestra played on.

She couldn't help but think of that afternoon in the abbey, after his shave, when she told him he looked *almost* civilized. And even now, in finely tailored garments and a perfectly folded and starched cravat, the emphasis was still on *almost*. Even as he led her in a waltz, with its routine steps set to elegant music, he still seemed almost civilized. The trappings of propriety were there, but there was still something so primal in the way he looked at her, and in the way his hand on her waist made her feel. As if at any second he would pick her up, throw her over his shoulder, and carry her off to bed.

She rested her hand on his shoulder, as she was supposed to do. But he felt stronger than she had remembered. Had he changed, or were her memories fading? Perhaps she was the wild and wanton one, because she wanted to feel his chest under her hand, to feel his hot skin under her palm, to feel the ridges and planes of the muscles there. She knew them so well, from her own experience, and from her own drawing that had captured them. The pencil-and-paper version had kept her captivated for almost a year. Now she wanted the real thing.

Instead, she slid her hand a little higher to rest at the nape of his neck. As if she could just apply a little pressure and his head would bend down to hers, low enough and close enough so that they might kiss. She trusted him to kiss her back, but she didn't trust him to kiss at the command of a vicar at the end of a marriage ceremony to signal that they were man and wife. The realization was disheartening, to say the least.

All it took was a little pressure from his hand on the small of her back, and she used that as an excuse to move a little closer to him.

"You're trouble, you know that?" he said, his voice husky now. She couldn't help a little laugh at that.

"*You* are calling me trouble?"

"I'm trying to be good, and yet you tempt me to be very wicked."

And then he lowered his head so that he might murmur into her ear. Phillip proceeded to tell her all the very wicked things he wanted to do. It involved the removal of her clothing, which he described in exquisitely vivid detail. Slipping the silk from her shoulders so that he might kiss and caress her naked skin. Buttons undone one by one. Her gown sliding to the floor. The unlacing of her corset, the chemise going the way of her gown. Her breasts free, and all the things he would do to her naked skin with his hands and his mouth. She bit her lip to stifle a moan.

Angela closed her eyes. She wasn't aware that she had moved closer to him, until she could feel the length of him pressed up against all of her. He was hard against her.

But not once did they miss a step, not even as her skirts tangled around their legs. And as if he had the same thought, he mentioned that it would be their legs tangled together, as they moved as one in the bedroom instead of the ballroom.

She wanted it, Lord knew she did. She wanted him.

But he didn't mention the morning after they made love.

She could easily see the vivid sensual images he described. Just as easily, she could feel the heartache of waking up alone the next morning. She could envision the imprint of their bodies on the bed, and the empty place where he had been, all in the cold light of morning. And that was like a bucket of cold water on her feverish skin, or rather, her thoughts, because her skin still felt hot. She was sure she was blushing from her head to her toes.

He had fallen silent, too, having described them making love until they succumbed to exhaustion. The orchestra played on, Phillip still held her close to him, and she still tingled with pleasure in all the places their bodies touched, which was to say, everywhere.

She wanted to ask him to keep talking. She wanted to ask him, "And when we wake up in the morning, then what?" But she just couldn't catch her breath. Fragments of thoughts and questions arose, but her mind was so muddled, melted, and distracted by those erotic images that she couldn't manage to find the words.

The orchestra concluded its song, and Phillip suggested stepping out onto the terrace. She nodded in agreement, feeling as if she had never needed cool air as she did now.

～

Lucas Frost was hot and bothered, too, but for a very, very different reason. It was rage that coursed through him as he watched another man act as if he owned Angela. But he couldn't possibly, because she belonged to Lucas.

The rage pulsed and throbbed through him as he watched his Angela waltz with another man. He had seen her eyes darken, and he had seen them close. He had noticed a flush creep into her cheeks and spread down to the edge of her bodice. He had watched as their bodies moved inch after evil after inch closer to each other, and farther from him. It was indecent. It was wrong.

She was his.

But he stood rooted to the spot because he didn't dare do what he wished to do, which was to march across the room,

without a care to those in his path, and pull her from
the scoundrel's arms. Huntley was bigger than Lucas. And he
couldn't marry Angela, and make right all that he had done
wrong, if he was dead, beaten to a pulp in a ballroom. He
would have to find another way to remove the obstacle from
his path.

He forced himself to take a deep breath, to calm down, to
clear his head. Fate had brought her to him again. He couldn't
let the opportunity get away.

The waltz was over now, and he saw Phillip lead Angela in
the direction of the terrace. He followed them.

He arrived a few steps behind Angela's aunt and chaperone, Lady Palmerston.

"Well, well," Lucas heard her say. "Lord Huntley alone on
the terrace with an unmarried young woman. I am shocked."
Her voice belied obvious sarcasm. Because Phillip was notorious for getting caught on terraces and in gardens with young
women, wasn't he? A plan began to form in Lucas's brain. It
made his heart pound with excitement.

"Angela, are you ready to depart yet? I feel a headache
coming on."

Lucas withdrew farther into the shadows, so that he might
not be seen. He left shortly after Angela and her aunt, for
there was no other reason for him to stay. Instead of having his
carriage take him home, he ordered the driver to take him to
the residence of Christine Grey.

∼

"Good evening, Frost. You haven't been around in a while,"
Christine murmured as she poured them each a drink. Lucas
couldn't help but notice that she wore not a stitch beneath her
red silk robe. The fabric did not have any adornment of lace or
beadwork or embroidery. Christine didn't need it, and she
knew it. But he was not intrigued or distracted from his reason
for calling. He had seen—and sampled—all she had to offer a
man. Lucas's late wife wasn't the only one who had been un-
faithful.

Christine was a courtesan. Her entry into that ancient

profession was all in thanks to Phillip Kensington's lack of honor. They had met in Italy, Christine told Lucas one night, and she had set her sights on him. He was young, handsome, rich, and drunk more often than not. Her devious plan to get caught with him had succeeded. The second part, their marriage, had failed. She had not counted on him fleeing the country.

"No matter," she was fond of saying. "My father wanted me to have a duke. Instead, I have had a dozen."

After handing him a drink, Christine curled up on the settee and indicated that he should join her. She placed her hand on his thigh and started to feel her way up.

"I didn't come here for that," he said, but he didn't make an effort to remove her hand.

"Then why did you call?" she demanded, digging her nails into his flesh. "It's three in the bloody morning."

"I came to talk." She rolled her eyes and leaned back. He took a sip of brandy.

"Talking. At this hour of the morning," she uttered with disbelief. "You know that is not why men usually call upon me."

"I have a proposal for you. Revenge." She licked her rouged lips and eyed him with sly interest.

"I'm listening," she encouraged him, eyeing him over the rim of her glass as she took a sip.

Lucas explained his plan.

"Easy enough. But why?"

"Because he's after the woman I mean to marry. I'm losing her, which can't happen. If she can just see what a scoundrel he is, then she won't marry him." Christine did not seem impressed with his emotional confession. He didn't care, so long as she helped him.

"I fail to see the revenge portion of your plan," Christine said pointedly. She wouldn't do anything unless she stood to gain from it.

"Don't you want revenge upon Huntley for ruining you?" Lucas asked, pushing aside a fearful thought that crept into his head: What if Angela wanted revenge upon him? He had hurt her as Huntley had hurt Christine. The idea added an extra degree of urgency to his plan. He needed to marry her with all haste.

"What makes you think I have any feelings of any kind for Lord Huntley?" Christine queried.

"Well, it is because of him that you ended up in this situation," Lucas said delicately. And he took a sip of brandy, because it only occurred to him now that he did not know how Angela had filled the intervening years, only that she had not been with him. He couldn't bring himself to ask. He just wanted things to be like they were *before*, and that meant avoiding the topic of their past and all the years until the present. If she had been occupied in the same manner as Christine, that might explain how she could have met Huntley. But she couldn't have done. Not his Angela.

"My situation?" Christine mused. "Rich and free to do whatever I please? Poor me." Her voice oozed sarcasm.

"Point taken. And what if I could increase your wealth?"

She leaned in closely to him, her breasts, cloaked in red silk, brushing against his arm, her manicured hand once again pressing firmly upon his thigh. And she whispered into his ear, "Then I am interested."

Lucas returned home at dawn. It took him and the utterly devious Christine merely an hour to concoct a flawless plan. It took them another hour to celebrate. But when he finally collapsed into bed, the burden he always carried felt lighter. Soon, with his marriage to Angela, he would be free of it entirely.

Chapter 19

ONE WEEK LATER...

Phillip stood with Parkhurst in the card room at Lady Derby's ball, watching, but not participating, in the games. At one table, Preston Drake was demonstrating exactly why he was known as the best gambler in England. After this evening, he would certainly be the richest. Phillip longed to join one of the other tables with an intensity that terrified him. He reminded himself that he was broke and his last incident with creditors was still too vivid. He was still dealing with the consequences. The urge passed.

He contented himself with just enjoying the sound of a shuffling deck and the low murmurs of wagers being made. It wasn't long before his thoughts drifted to one particular card game and one particular woman. Phillip looked at the clock and thought she must have arrived by now. He was just about to go in search of her when Devon found him.

"I believe this is for you," Devon said before handing Phillip a note.

"People are still confusing us, I take it," Phillip answered dryly, accepting the note. Each of them had always hated being confused for the other.

"Either that, or Angela has questionable intentions." Devon's voice belied his doubts about that. Phillip doubted that she did, as well, at least for his twin. But still . . .

"You read my personal correspondence?" Phillip asked, annoyed.

"The footman said he was told to give it to me. I thought it was mine, until I read it. You'll notice that it is not addressed to anyone," Devon said pointedly.

"Well, what the devil does it say, already?" Parkhurst cut in impatiently. Phillip quickly read the brief note, and he grinned. "It says that there is hope for me yet. Excuse me, gentlemen. I'll see you both in the morning."

Angela had been softening toward him in the past week. He had called on her at Lady Palmerston's every day. He brought her flowers to replace the ones she had destroyed. He also brought her a stuffed animal toy and explained that she could hit him as much as she wanted with that, since it would not result in damage to either himself or the toy.

"And here I was hoping you'd bring me *The Complete Works of Shakespeare*," she replied to that, but she smiled as she spoke. Instead, he brought her a new, soft leather-bound sketchbook. He had spent hours searching for the perfect one. It seemed he didn't have anything else to do these days besides figure out how to win her back. He couldn't think of a better way to spend his time.

Lady Palmerston was aiding him, too. Otherwise, the dragon would not have invented excuses to quit the room. Phillip didn't miss Angela's expression of panic at her chaperone's departure. So even though he thought he'd die from restraint, he did not kiss her or touch her.

After each day that Lady Palmerston returned to the drawing room to find Angela unscathed and unravished, she stayed away a little longer the next day.

And then today . . .

They made obligatory and proper small talk for the first few minutes of the chaperone's absence (Lady Palmerston had forgotten to review the menus with the cook), poorly pretending all the while that they had no idea what would come next. It was just so easy and so right to sit beside her and talk about the weather one second and lean in for a kiss in the next second.

Angela was hesitant at first, for she kept her lips closed. Phillip didn't force, urge, or do anything to persuade her lips to open to him. Because it had been so long, merely to be this close to her was like a taste of heaven. Her lips were even softer than before. The sensation of his mouth on hers was pure and sweet.

He took her hand in his, lacing their fingers together.

And then she responded to his touch, and his kiss, in the way that a man dreamed of.

Her fingers tightened around his. Her lips parted, and she was the one to take the lead, slipping her tongue into his mouth. He followed in kind. There were hints of the past in this kiss, as well as tempting, teasing promises for the future.

Angela placed one of her hands on his cheek, holding him to her lightly. Her touch was tender, and he felt as if his heart were breaking open in the very best way. For no one had ever been gentle and tender and sweet with him. And this, he knew, was the cure for that gray, aching emptiness that had always followed him around.

He was also certain that it was only *her* touch that could make him feel this way. He knew, surely and truly, that he didn't want it from anyone else.

Phillip reached for her, to pull her closer to him. But then, as if he crossed an invisible line, she shut down and turned away.

Something was holding her back, though, and he just didn't know what it was. Nor could he find the moment to ask. Lady Palmerston returned, eyeing them suspiciously before launching into a conversation about something or other that he was too distracted to pay attention to.

Phillip found himself wishing, as he often did, that they were still at the abbey, when he could see her as much as he liked. Or when, if he had been a cad, he could still count on her to be there the next day. Because something had just gone wrong, and he didn't know what, and he couldn't ask her now or be certain of having a chance to ask in the future.

Phillip slipped the note in his pocket as he entered the ballroom. It read, *"Meet me in the garden. A."* He was thrilled at the overture. Yet the thought of her awaiting him, alone, in the gardens was terrifying. Had she not thought of the danger? Suppose someone else with less honorable intentions found her first?

But the invitation could only mean one thing. Angela knew as well as he what happened in the dark, secluded corners of gardens and ballrooms. One needn't have firsthand experience in the matter, as they did, to know that. Devon had told him that he and Emilia became betrothed, thanks to a trap that sounded awfully similar to the one Phillip suspected he was walking into. He didn't think it likely that Lady Palmerston would repeat herself, but frankly, he didn't care.

He paid no attention to anyone as he passed through the stuffy ballroom. Hell, it was all he could do not to push and shove people aside. Every moment that she was out there alone increased the chances of something awful happening. He had to get to her first. He crossed the terrace in a few strides, resisted the temptation to jump down the stairs, and walked deeper into the shadows.

The only light came from the moon. Hedges and trees were planted in a formal grid arrangement, which provided many discreet corners. As he walked through the garden, along the gravel path, he noticed that many other couples had a similar idea.

An unsettling feeling stole over him. Something was not right. He quickened his pace.

Phillip didn't see her at first. She simply reached out and touched his arm as he nearly walked past her. He stepped closer to her, into the darkness. It took a moment before his eyes adjusted, and he clearly saw the woman before him.

"I've been waiting for you," she purred. She took a step closer and slid her arm around his shoulders, leaning her weight against him. The heavy scent of her perfume made his throat burn. At first he thought that she had confused him with another.

"It's time we finish what we started," she murmured into his ear, and then he knew who she was. "Don't you think?"

Phillip stood frozen. He felt nothing for this woman he once lusted for. Nothing. He took a step back, but she followed him, still draping herself all over him, like vines choking a tree.

"I'll even do it for free," Christine Grey whispered through painted lips.

"No," he said firmly. Phillip lifted her hand from his neck and placed it at her side. Her other hand stole around his waist. He managed to grasp both her wrists, and hold them away from his body. He didn't want her touching him.

"What the hell are you doing?" he demanded in a low voice.

Christine merely smiled, or smirked, but the effect was the same. A sickening twist of his stomach. She gave the slightest nod of her head in the direction of approaching footsteps on the gravel.

Phillip let go of her wrists, and took a step back. But by then, it was too late.

Christine wrenched one hand free, and pulled his head down to hers, pressing her lips firmly against his. He broke free in an instant, but the damage was already done.

He had ruined her once, and she had ruined him now.

Phillip understood everything in the instant in which that bastard Frost pressed a handkerchief into Angela's hand. Frost hadn't even retrieved it from his pocket but arrived holding it in his hand, as if he was prepared for tears. Or hoped for them.

Phillip had been set up. This was all a scheme to discredit him in Angela's eyes. And it only then struck him how much Frost wanted her. Phillip had been so blinded by his own desire, he hadn't seen his competition. He would not lose her because of this.

"Angela—" he started, and he took a step toward her.

She took a step back.

"It's not what you think."

"I don't know what to think anymore," she said coldly.

"If you'll excuse us," Christine murmured, "we were just taking care of some unfinished business." Her voice was heavy with innuendo, so much that it was unnecessary for her to trace her fingertips in a line from his cravat to the waistband of his breeches. Phillip pushed her hand away, but she did not keep her hands off him for long.

"Angela—" Phillip started, but Frost cut him off.

"Come, Angela," Lucas said consolingly, sliding one arm around Angela's waist, as Christine did the same to Phillip. "You are distraught. I shall see you home and leave these two to their business."

"Yes, do run along," Christine said lightly, as if speaking to a child. To further add fuel to this fire, she slid her hand across his chest, stroking him possessively. Christine's grasp on him would not allow him to move to follow Angela as she turned to walk away, with Lucas's arm securely around her waist.

He saw Lucas pull Angela to him. Christine clutched the front of his shirt.

He saw Lucas's mouth press against Angela's forehead. Christine grabbed the waistband of his breeches.

He saw Angela attempt to shrug off Lucas's touch. Phillip brushed Christine's hands away.

He did not wait to see any more.

"Bloody hell, woman, stop!" Phillip thundered. "You've made your point."

She pouted for a moment. And then she shrugged in defeat.

"You'd better go after her then," Christine said breezily and unnecessarily, because he had already gone.

⌒

Angela did not struggle against Lucas for long.

It couldn't have been more than ten minutes ago that she was in his arms for a waltz. Lucas had broken his monologue about the blessings of fate that allowed them to meet again, free to be with each other, to say, "My, that fellow seems to be in a hurry." And then he spun them both around so that Angela might have a clear view of Phillip eagerly making his way through the crowd and onto the terrace.

She did not think twice about quitting the waltz and following Phillip. If her suspicions were correct, she wanted to witness his betrayal. Let her remember that, when she thought of him. And here she had been on the verge of giving herself to him entirely!

Lucas had followed her into the gardens, uninvited.

And when she encountered the scene she feared and expected, her only thought was that she was well and truly trapped. She cursed herself for not thinking twice about rushing headlong into disaster. Again.

This was why she had asked her chaperone to never leave her alone, dependent on to her own devices and judgment. And where was her aunt now? Why hadn't she been there to talk some badly needed sense into her and to stop her before it was too late?

Her love for Phillip, coupled with a complete lack of trust, had led her out into the gardens and into a spectacle from which her reputation would never recover. Any hopes or plans she might have made for her future were now taken out of her hands. Even though she was in the thick of this scandalous scene, she saw it as if she was an outsider.

An unmarried woman with a questionable past, and the man she had been seen waltzing with just a moment before. A woman of obvious ill repute. A known scoundrel, oft discovered in compromising positions like this. The lot of them in a dark and secluded corner of the garden added up to one thing: scandal. If they were discovered . . .

She would have to return to the abbey. Oh, did her heart rebel against the vivid memories of the loneliness there.

Or she would have to marry Lucas. She could not love him, not like she once did. She could not endure a marriage to a man who had destroyed so much of her life. She had tried to convince herself that she could. But then Phillip had returned . . .

Or, she would have to marry Phillip. He would hurt her again and again, because she loved him, and he couldn't be trusted, for he had made that oh so clear. Really—in the arms of another woman at a ball where she, too, was in attendance! He couldn't even be discreet about his betrayal.

And then Lucas embraced her, and she struggled against him, because she heard footsteps on the gravel, and she did not want to be caught.

She did the only other thing she could think to do: flee, and pray that she was not seen.

But Lucas followed, catching her in his arms and pulling her against the length of him. She shuddered at his touch, panicked at the threat of discovery, and struggled to free herself from his grasp. She did not fight him for long, because he had not been the only one to follow her into the gardens.

Lady Palmerston had as well. She made her presence known by loudly clearing her throat.

"You may remove your hands from my niece," Lady Palmerston commanded. Lucas followed her order. Angela took a step back, massaging her upper arms where he had been holding her.

"Madame, allow me to explain," Lucas began. He did not continue, for the sound of heavy footsteps crunching on the gravel distracted them all.

"May I?" Phillip asked both Angela and Lady Palmerston. Angela didn't quite understand, but her aunt did.

"The pleasure is all yours," Lady Palmerston said graciously.

At the first crack of Phillip's fist against Lucas's jaw, Angela winced. At the second, her aunt took Angela's arm in hers and guided them away from the fight to return toward the ballroom.

"Two men brawling over you. How utterly romantic," Lady Palmerston mused.

"Indeed. So incredibly romantic I fear I might faint," Angela replied, forcing her voice to remain light.

Intrigued by the unmistakable sound of a brawl, guests started abandoning the ballroom and terrace in favor of watching the fight. Fortunately, very few people seemed to notice them walking briskly in the opposite direction.

Phillip found them a few minutes later as they were waiting for the carriage to be brought around.

"I'll escort you both home," Phillip said, grimacing and shaking out his hand. Angela felt the stirrings of pity. He had hurt himself, defending her. She wanted to take his hand in hers and, well, make sure it was well and truly broken, actually.

He was with another woman, when this very afternoon he had been with her. That doxy had left a smear of red lip paint on his cravat. That stain glared at her, taunted her.

Afraid that she might actually break his hand or strangle him with that stained cravat, Angela turned away. A footman opened the door to their recently arrived carriage. Angela entered, as did her aunt. Phillip climbed into the carriage after them.

"What do you think you're doing?" Angela demanded.

"Really, Phillip, you could just call tomorrow like a proper contrite and civilized gentleman," Lady Palmerston added.

"And give you a chance to run away from me again?" Phillip answered, looking at Angela. "I think not. No, Angela, you will hear me out."

She wanted to put her hands over her ears and repeat some nonsense word over and over so that she couldn't hear a word he said. But she would not act like a child because of him. Instead she clasped her hands in her lap and gave him her haughtiest look.

"Very well. Let us hear your excuse."

Phillip explained about receiving the note, simply signed "A," and assuming that it was from her.

"How could you think I would suggest something like that?"

"Attribute it to wishful thinking. It was an entirely different kind of trap that I expected to walk into."

"Interesting," Lady Palmerston murmured.

"And you," Phillip said, turning to glare at Lady Palmerston. "How could you let her wander alone in the gardens with someone like Frost? You are supposed to be her chaperone, which means you are supposed to stay with her and keep her away from the likes of—"

"From the likes of you," Lady Palmerston supplied readily. "And I was there the entire time. You were just too distracted to notice."

"Yes, I was too distracted by giving that bloody bastard the beating he deserves for hurting you, Angela."

"Angela, I do think Phillip cares for you," Lady Palmerston stated.

"He has an interesting manner of showing it," Angela retorted. "And the rest of your story, Phillip?"

"I was looking for you," Phillip continued. "But then Christine—"

"You know her," Angela gasped, losing the hope that it had all been a misunderstanding with a stranger. "How do you know her? Were you lying to me when you told me today that I was the only one?"

Her aunt groaned slightly beside her. Angela eyed Phillip through narrowed, suspicious eyes.

"I *knew* her," he said, shifting uncomfortably. "But I haven't had the slightest contact with her in years."

"How do you know her, Phillip?" Angela asked, though she feared she already knew the answer. He had ruined this Christine woman once. She was one of his many scorned and abandoned women.

"Go on, Lady Palmerston," Phillip said wearily, "I should hate to deprive you the pleasure of telling her yourself."

"How considerate of you, Huntley," Lady Palmerston said. "Christine Grey is the daughter of the former ambassador to Italy. Phillip met her there, after fleeing the consequences of another indiscretion here. He had been caught in the gardens with Miss Lila Althorp within the first hour of her debut ball. Anyway, Phillip was caught attempting to elope with Christine. Never finished that business, did you? And now she is one of London's most popular courtesans."

"The story seems to have lost some accuracy in its translation and in the six years it's been since it happened."

"Don't even dare to tell me you were misunderstood again," Angela snapped.

"I'll tell you the truth, even though it's probably worse. She offered what I wanted. I got a taste. But I didn't fully compromise her, because her father, his friends, and what seemed to be the entire household staff just happened to catch us first. The lot of them also just happened to have marriage documents drawn up. And Christine just happened to have all of her things packed."

"So you were set up. Just like you were tonight." She didn't need to say how bloody convenient that excuse was, not once but twice. Too convenient.

"I was young, rich, due to inherit a dukedom, and drunk more often than not. I was the perfect target for what she had in mind. And I don't know what her motives were tonight, but—"

"And now she's a prostitute all because of what you did to her." That could have so easily been her, had she not gone to the abbey instead. It was scary and heartbreaking to think of it.

"And richer than all of us combined, and more powerful than she would have been if she had been a duchess. She is still as devious as ever, too. Apparently, that Frost bastard is her accomplice."

"Why do you keep saying that? You don't have any proof that he arranged all of this. I think you might just be jealous of him," she challenged him.

"Well, was there another reason you were in the gardens with him?" Phillip asked. "Because, if so, then you have no right to be angry with me."

"Don't accuse me of that. He followed me, if you must know," she answered. And then she bit her tongue, because she wanted to add that she was innocent. But she wasn't. It occurred to her that Phillip did have some right to suspect something compromising between her and Lucas this evening. He had been courting her openly, after all. And Phillip knew about her past, more than anyone else.

"I'm not accusing you of anything, Angela. I don't believe that for a second," he said softly, and it broke her heart that he could believe her innocent when she couldn't return the sentiment. "But how did you know to find me there? And why was he with you?"

"I saw you run into the gardens."

"Yes, I was in a rush to ensure that you weren't waiting too long, alone in the dark and secluded garden, just begging for trouble."

"Well, you caught Lucas's attention. He merely pointed out what a hurry you were in."

"He just happened to notice, did he? Just as he just happened to have a handkerchief ready to press into your hands. You didn't shed a tear, though, did you? Because you saw what you expected."

Angela did not respond. Instead, she turned and looked out the window of the carriage, not that she could see much in the dark. Could Lucas really have set that up?

He did just happen to notice Phillip going into the gardens. He did have that handkerchief ready. And Lord knew she certainly hadn't sent that note.

But why on earth would Lucas do such a thing? If Lucas wanted her for himself, then he could have just *asked*. She would have said no, of course. But Lucas didn't know that . . . unless he did, and he had also arranged for some busybody to find them in a compromising position. No wonder he held her so firmly as she struggled to break free.

Angela sighed, because the evidence against Frost was damning. And because, once again, she had placed her trust in the wrong hands.

"You don't trust me," Phillip said, as if reading her thoughts. It was not a question. It was a statement of truth, and from the tone of his voice, it was a truth that just dawned on him. "That's what has been holding you back."

"You must admit, Huntley, your past hardly gives a girl reason to," Lady Palmerston added to the conversation, reminding them both of her presence.

"It's true," Angela said with a little shrug. She turned away, but not before witnessing the wounded expression on his face. But couldn't he understand that she was just trying not to get hurt once more? Wasn't twice enough? And couldn't he see that she *wanted* to trust him and give herself to him completely, without fear?

"Well, what the bloody hell do I have to do to prove to you that I want you, and you alone? That I will be faithful to you? And that I won't leave you? Because if there is nothing I can do, then tell me now." From his voice, his eyes, everything, she knew it was a plea. For better or for worse, she wanted to answer.

"Let me think," she muttered. To the sound of the carriage wheels clattering on cobblestones, she thought about how they might both put their pasts behind them. Because she did want to trust Phillip. She wanted to soothe her own fears, but she hadn't been able to do it alone after years of trying. If he did love her, he would help her.

And Angela thought of Lucas, yet again undermining her trust with his schemes. For tonight was not the first time he had concocted some plan to win her, with disastrous results.

Lucas was also trying to unite their future while denying their past. He couldn't even bring himself to acknowledge what had happened with them, let alone apologize . . . And then an idea occurred to her.

"You could apologize to the women you ruined," Angela said. "All of them."

"Could you explain what that has to do with us, or indeed anything?"

"Because it's the right thing to do, and you should have done it years ago. Because if you don't regret what you did, then there is nothing to stop you from doing it again. And because I can't have any more of your angry, scorned women making trouble for us."

Phillip didn't groan or even protest. He merely grinned.

"You *are* in love with me," he said, as if he had doubted it. The fool.

"Of course I am, you blockhead!" Angela burst out. "In spite of reason and better judgment, God help me, I am. But I don't trust you not to hurt me. Again. I have been too careless with my heart in the past, and I shan't be so again."

"If it means that much to you, I can write them all letters detailing my sincere, heartfelt apologies."

"And what shall you say? 'Dear so-and-so, my apologies for ruining your life. Best, Phillip.' "

"Something to that effect," he answered evasively.

"No, you must go and apologize in person."

"I doubt I'll be welcome," he said, now visibly uncomfortable. He shifted in his seat and looked longingly out of the carriage window.

"Well you can at least *try*, can't you?" she asked. And then he looked into her eyes and was silent for a moment before he answered.

"I can try, for you, Angela. But I'd like you to come with me. Please."

"Fine," Angela agreed. This way she could make sure he actually kept his word. And, now that she thought about it, she was curious about all these other women. They had much in common, and yet were strangers to each other.

"I shall be happy to join you both," Lady Palmerston volunteered, "since, Phillip, you so passionately defended the need for dear Angela to have a chaperone."

Angela bit back a laugh at Phillip's expression. He seemed like a little boy being given a present, only to have it taken away again. He recovered, though, and scowled, obviously because he could tell it would be futile to persuade Lady Palmerston to allow them to go alone.

"Now there is only one *slight* problem," Phillip said, obviously ill at ease. "I haven't exactly kept in touch with them, and it's been quite a while . . ."

"You don't even remember them!"

"I do, I just don't know—"

"Never fear, I know all their names, and shall have no trouble discerning their whereabouts," Lady Palmerston chimed in.

"Of course," both of them muttered simultaneously, as the carriage came to a stop. Phillip escorted them both inside. He kissed Angela on the cheek, bade her good night, and promised to call the next day.

And she dared to believe that he would keep his word about that.

"He does have a point," she remarked to her aunt as they ascended the stairs to retire for the evening.

"About what, dear?"

"You weren't there," Angela confessed, feeling wretched to confront her aunt. But she had promised not to leave her alone with any gentleman, and she had not kept her word, to nearly disastrous consequences.

"But I was, Angela," her aunt said softly. "I have no intention of allowing you to get hurt or suffer. However, you do need to learn to trust your own head and heart, and you'll never be able to do that if you always rely on someone else to do it for you."

"There could be a scandal in the morning."

"And there will be another scandal in the afternoon," her aunt answered dismissively.

"I could have been ruined again."

"We all fall from time to time, my dear," Lady Palmerston said with a faraway look in her eyes, and Angela knew her aunt was speaking of her own experience. "But we stand up again, too."

Chapter 20

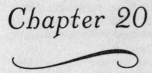

If sitting in Lady Palmerston's drawing room listening to his past sins was akin to the eighth circle of hell, then Phillip did not dare to think of what kind of torture it would be to actually call upon all these women.

He knew he wasn't guilty of even half of the things whispered about him. But that still left a lot to repent for. But if all Angela wished for was an apology, and if these women felt the same way, then he could do that. All he had to do was show up and say that he was sorry.

He very much was.

It only took one quick glance at Angela and the smile she gave him to remind him of why.

"The first was Miss Emily Preston, the seventh daughter of Baron Raglan. The last I heard, she had returned to the country. Oxfordshire, I believe," Lady Palmerston said. "She didn't last long in London. Not even a month, I think."

"How many years ago was this?" Angela asked.

"Nine, I believe," Lady Palmerston said.

"And the next one?" Phillip asked, urging her to continue to get this over with. Vague recollections began to filter through his mind, but he did not want to entertain them now.

"And then there is Lila Althorp, although she is a countess now," Lady Palmerston said, smiling fondly. "Prinny himself gave her and her husband the earldom. I was at their wedding."

"Really?" Phillip was surprised, and he thought that he wouldn't have been if he read the papers like everyone else. But she was married, and acknowledged by the king, so really, he couldn't have ruined her too thoroughly.

"Oh, I remember reading about this now," Angela added. "She had become a spy, as was her husband. The earldom was a reward for their service to the country."

"Phillip, she was the one you ruined within an hour of her coming-out ball," Lady Palmerston reminded him.

"Oh right. Nothing really happened to her. We were caught within five minutes of leaving the ballroom. Not enough time to—"

"But still, you were caught," Lady Palmerston cut in. "Then there is Christine Grey."

"We'll skip her, of course," Phillip said. If anything, they were even now.

"No. She obviously still harbors ill will toward you and demonstrated that she will act on it," Angela answered. "And furthermore—"

"Don't even say what I fear you are thinking," Phillip said wearily.

"I'm curious to see what a brothel looks like," Angela said with a shrug.

"I confess I am curious as well," Lady Palmerston added.

"Her sort doesn't live in a brothel. She likely lives in some grand apartment that some poor sop pays an arm and a leg for. And *we* are not going. Your reputations would never recover if you were seen."

"Oh, now you have an attack of propriety," Angela retorted.

"Just in time to ruin our fun," Lady Palmerston said, miffed.

"You think all of this is fun?"

"I think that you are not going to call on her alone," Angela stated firmly.

"The last one is Lady Grafton," Lady Palmerston contin-ued. "She lives in the country, alone, with her son."

His son, actually, if the rumors were true. He didn't think he needed to mention that. Judging by the silence in the room, Phillip knew they were all thinking of the same thing: Were the rumors true?

He had never seen the child and had never planned to. But what if he did have a son? The thought was too overwhelming to contemplate, so he ignored it, as he had always done.

"I made up an itinerary for us earlier this morning. I could have sworn that I brought it downstairs," Lady Palmerston muttered, while rummaging through the stack of newspapers and invitations on the small table at the side of her chair.

"Perhaps you left it on your writing desk upstairs," Angela suggested. She was a terrible liar, because she looked all too pleased with herself for having thought of a way to steal a mo-ment alone with him. Lady Palmerston gave her a look of an-noyance mixed with pride. She gave a look of unmistakable warning to Phillip.

"I shall be back in a moment," she declared, before step-ping out into the hall. The drawing room doors were left slightly ajar.

Angela knew that she was asking a lot of Phillip. But bro-ken trust was a hard thing to repair. Doubt was something not easily soothed. Heartache may not be fatal after the first bout, or even the second, but Angela did not dare risk a broken heart for a third time.

She didn't doubt that Phillip loved her. She simply wasn't sure if love was enough. She had trusted her heart and her happiness to someone else's care twice.

Both men had left.

But both men had returned.

She believed in second chances. But that didn't mean she needed to make the same mistake twice.

And she had to admit to herself that it wasn't just Phillip she didn't really trust. It was herself. And that was why she easily agreed to go with Phillip on this ridiculous errand. And she was glad that her aunt was coming with her. Lady Palmerston wouldn't let her give her heart and her body away too easily again, even if she gave Angela plenty of opportunities to do so.

"Phillip, thank you."

"Shhh."

He kept his finger over her lips to keep her from speaking, and she was glad. She didn't know what to say. And then he pressed his mouth to hers.

She couldn't help but yield to the pressure. She parted her lips, and he took full advantage. This was not a battle she wanted to fight. She surrendered quickly and easily, yet feeling like she still managed to attain the prize, a pleasure she had never quite stopped longing for.

And then thoughts surrendered to sensation. His breath became hers, and hers his. He was the source and the reason for the waves of heat she was feeling. Phillip was the reason her skin tingled, anticipating his touch. She had hungered for this, and he had, too; some things a girl just *knew*. Just as she knew that it was his kiss and no one else's that seemed to wake up all the dormant parts inside of her.

Just as she also knew that if this kiss didn't stop *now*, they would end up making love on the floor of Lady Palmerston's drawing room.

At the sound of her aunt descending the stairs, they both pulled back. When Lady Palmerston entered, she saw nothing compromising, although both Phillip and Angela looked a little bit happier.

~

Phillip left Lady Palmerston and Angela and walked to White's, since he had agreed to meet Parkhurst. Upon his arrival, he was pleased to discover that his club membership to White's had not expired in his long absence from town.

Phillip passed card games in progress. Though it pained him to do so, he declined offers to join in. He found Parkhurst in the back room, drinking a brandy and watching a billiards game. Once the last ball was sunk, a new group left their seats to take their turn wagering large sums of money on a mere game. Phillip longed to join them, but instead he and Parkhurst found two empty leather chairs.

A waiter brought each of them a brandy. Phillip still did love the feel of a snifter of brandy in his hand. And explaining to Parkhurst that he didn't feel like drinking would be a harder task than explaining why he didn't feel like breathing. It was easier just to place it on the side table and pick it up and hold it from time to time.

"Ah," Parkhurst exhaled after taking a sip of his drink, "a respite from the plague of females in my house."

"Your wife doesn't complain that you spend so much time here?"

"Hell no. I think it was written into the contracts that a portion always be set aside for my membership. Gets me out of the house and out of her way. It was only under the threat of my mother cutting me off that I married in the first place."

"How is the old woman?"

"Still calling three times a week. Just survived another session. You came up, in fact."

"I always do. But what have I done lately?"

"Your entrance at the ball merited at least ten minutes of discussion—almost entirely on her part. My contribution was that all you did was walk into a room, and it was not that interesting."

"I agree."

"But then you had to go and punch out that Frost fellow last night. That merited a lecture on the lamentable state of men's morals and inability to control their tempers and their fists. But what everyone, including my mother, is far more interested in is the reason you knocked him out. It was because of that Miss Sullivan, they say. A few people saw her leaving the scene. The saving grace is that Lady Palmerston was with her."

"Between you and me, Parkhurst, I did beat that man senseless because of Angela."

"Well, I'll be damned," Parkhurst said slowly, with an idiotic grin. "Never thought I'd live to see the day that you'd fight over a woman."

"She's not just any woman," Phillip said.

"Clearly. And I'm not the only one who finds the whole thing shocking. You should see some of the wagers in the betting book. I was having a look before you arrived."

"What is everyone betting on?"

"Well, since you and Frost were both seen following Angela out of the gardens, after fighting, everyone is betting on which one of you she'll marry. Because she has to marry one of you or leave town indefinitely, according to my mother."

"I'm guessing the odds are not in my favor," Phillip mused.

"Definitely not. But, damn, Phillip, if you bet on yourself, and won, you'd be filthy rich."

"Do you think, Parkhurst, that it's fair to wager on myself, given that I can control the outcome?"

"You can't, though. It's up to the girl, isn't it?"

"You do have a point," Phillip conceded. He picked up his glass of brandy, only to set it back down without taking a sip.

"For once in my life," Parkhurst muttered, though obviously pleased with himself.

"Do you think Angela will be angry if she finds out that I bet on our marriage?" Phillip asked, even though Parkhurst had absolutely no way of knowing.

"Who says she'll find out?" Parkhurst said with a shrug and then a sip of brandy.

Phillip gave Parkhurst a look of disbelief.

"If we have learned anything, my friend, it's that women talk."

"Yes, but they can't talk about what they don't know about." Parkhurst appeared smug, thinking he had made another point, and Phillip wished he had spoken the truth.

"First of all, they can and they do," Phillip began his lecture. "It's called speculation, which eventually snowballs into something 'heard on good authority.' And furthermore, all it takes it one idiot to comment on the wager a little too loudly to another idiot. A woman is bound to overhear, and she'll tell someone, who will tell someone else, all in the strictest confidence, of course, and that person will then—"

"Enough. I get it! Maybe Angela will think it's romantic,"

Parkhurst said with a shrug, and saying the word *romantic* as if for the first time.

She might.

She might not.

If he made the wager and lost, well, he'd rather lose all the money in the world than her. It wouldn't matter. In the end, though, he placed his bet because he couldn't resist betting on himself for the first time in his life.

Chapter 21

The following day, Lucas, still in his habit of keeping a watchful eye on Angela and Lady Palmerston's town house, witnessed the incomprehensible sight of Huntley arriving at Lady Palmerston's house. With luggage.

But that was not to be dwelt upon, because an even more wretched sight played out before his eyes. Footmen were securing luggage to Lady Palmerston's lavender-colored carriage. He watched as she entered the carriage, followed by Angela. Phillip joined the ladies, and two maids followed in a second carriage.

When the vehicles started to drive off, it was without a second thought that Lucas followed.

~

They would call upon Emily Preston first, a girl from so long ago that Phillip had trouble recalling anything about her except for her dark eyes, a lively disposition, and a hurried interlude in the gardens of Vauxhall.

He was not looking forward to this visit.

And yet after six hours in the carriage with Lady Palmerston and Angela, he was almost wishing to do anything, so long as he could leave the confines of this box. All he wanted to do was make love to Angela. And she was right there, just across the carriage from him, looking luscious and giving him secret smiles from time to time.

Mostly, however, she was thoroughly engaged in conversation with her aunt. He wondered if their topics of discussion were deliberately chosen to annoy him to the point of wanting to pull his hair out. Women's fashion was the reigning topic: hairstyles, hemlines, and hats. What was a more flattering cut for a bodice? Which fabrics and colors were the best for each season?

The topic then moved on to the particular fashion choices of nearly every woman of the ton. Their opinions ranged from scathing to adoration, to lamenting that it simply wasn't done to wear the same dress as someone else. Phillip wondered why but dared not voice the question, lest he endure an hour-long lecture.

After they paused at an inn for a brief lunch and to change the horses, Phillip elected to ride outside, with the carriage driver. The afternoon was spent in the pleasure of debating different racehorses, their lineages, their chances, their winnings, and their losses.

By methods Phillip preferred not to know of, Lady Palmerston had learned that Miss Emily Preston was now Mrs. Emily Andrews. She, her husband, and a small army of brats lived in a rather nice stone cottage on a decently sized parcel of land.

"Tell Mr. Andrews that we have callers," Emily Andrews née Preston informed a meek servant girl.

"Who should I say is calling, ma'am?" the maid whispered.

"My youthful indiscretion," Mrs. Andrews replied pertly as her children swarmed around her. "Billy, I said *no*! You may not have cookies before supper. Preston, what did I tell you about hitting your sister?"

"Only to do it if she annoys me," the young lad answered confidently.

"I said no such thing. Go outside, the lot of you, and try not to injure yourselves. Please don't mind them," Mrs. Andrews urged. "Come into the sitting room."

The sitting room was plain. The furniture was sturdy but slightly worn. The other items were not of the best quality but were very well cared for. The hardwood floors gleamed, and everything else was polished within an inch of its life. Windows looked over the front lawn, and Mrs. Andrews positioned herself so that she might have a view of her children outside. Her husband arrived and sat beside his wife. A servant girl brought a tea tray.

"Tea?" she offered.

"Please." Angela and Lady Palmerston said at the very same time.

"Well. Phillip Kensington. Lord Huntley. A lord and a lady in my drawing room. Mrs. Smythe is going to be beside herself with jealousy. What brings you here?"

"Mrs. Andrews, I have to come to apologize for . . ." Phillip paused, searching for the right words. He didn't want to say something too crude, or too specific, because it occurred to him that her husband might not know. The man could see fit to challenge him, and he did not care to duel.

"Ruining me in the eyes of polite society?" Mrs. Andrews supplied.

"Yes. Or in anyone's eyes. I'm sorry."

"Why . . . Oh, that is very considerate of you. I accept your apology, though if you must know, I am not entirely sorry as to what happened."

"Oh?" The three callers all expressed their interest simultaneously.

"I found society altogether too stifling, you see. My father had eight daughters, of which I was the youngest, and he treated the lot of us, me in particular, like the son he had lost in its infancy. That did not serve me well in polite society."

"Indeed," Lady Palmerston added to fill the silence as Mrs. Andrews paused for breath.

"I told as much to my sister, Lady Layford—she married Baron Layford. And she said that there were options to deal with it. The first was to develop a tolerance for it. The second was to go home. The third was to marry a duke, because duchesses, she said, can do whatever they wish. So I thought that *duchess* had quite a ring to it, and that I would go with option three."

"And that is where I come in," Phillip supplied. Had he been used? Had he been nothing more than a pawn in someone else's scheme, as with Christine?

"Not quite. Her Grace, Lady Hampton, and I struck up a conversation in the ladies' retiring room at a ball one evening, and she told me that being a duchess was a rather tedious thing, and that she certainly didn't have the liberty to do whatever she wished."

"Did you decide to return home then?" Angela asked.

"Yes. Because my mother, rest her soul, had written and said that John here was asking after me." Here she paused and patted her husband's hand affectionately. "I thought he was a fine-looking fellow and not so high in the instep as all the London gents I met. But my sister had other ideas. She would not allow me to go home, because I was to make a splendid match, which would show well upon her. My sister and I never got along, mind you . . ."

It was a long story that might have been summed up as: they never got along. In fact, they despised each other.

But as she rambled along, Phillip looked for the girl he had once known. He saw it in the eyes. Though time was taking its toll, her eyes were still bright and lively. She had been pretty, and that was still apparent. And he could see how a young rake, such as he, would have enjoyed her exuberance. She had an enthusiasm and vitality not often found in gently bred ladies.

He had been a mere lad of eight and ten, and the allure of wenching where he was supposed to was starting to fade. She hadn't stopped his advances. He was young and due to inherit an ancient and respected title. He thought himself above the consequences.

And in this case, he had been. No one had challenged him to a duel. No one had insisted he marry her. They talked about it behind his back, though, of how he ought to have married her. He couldn't regret that he didn't, especially considering just how much she talked. Phillip glanced over at her husband and wondered if the man was ever able to start, let alone complete, a sentence when talking to his wife.

"And then I met you, Phillip. I may call you that, still, right? Well, I still hadn't made up my mind about being a duchess or returning here, to Oxfordshire. And lud, you were handsome, still are, if I do say so myself. Anyway, we met at some ball or other, and waltzed a time or two. And then it was at Vauxhall that, well, we needn't go into details about that."

No, they didn't, Phillip thought.

"I'm a country girl, you see, so I had a clue what we were doing. And I went straight home and told my sister that I was going to be a duchess, and that I would walk into supper before her. And when I told her about you, well, she went off saying that you would never marry the likes of me. You were too young, thought yourself above everyone—"

"That was true."

"I was, I confess, rather disappointed the next day when you didn't call. Or the next day. Because you and I got along, didn't we? And, well, I shan't say it in proper company. Well, I was devastated. And then I was sent home. My father was livid at first. Threatened to beat some sense into me, and then to go after you, but he didn't because your father had sent him a personal letter and a generous settlement, provided he didn't challenge you, since you are reputedly a terrible shot."

"He did?" Phillip had known about the money. His father was always more generous with his money than his attention. And Phillip had known a woman would choose a thousand pounds and another man rather than marry him. What he had not known was that his father would plead to save his son in a letter that could have been made public. Too bad that the old man couldn't have told Phillip this.

"Yes. I saw the letter with my very own eyes. I can't recall the exact phrasing, but your father appealed to mine about the wretchedness of losing a son for men in their position. My father, having lost his one and only son, understood. That, and the sum your father offered was very generous, and our roof was in need of repair. Furthermore, a small sum was left aside for my dowry, and I could marry John. Now we have this lovely home and five wonderful children."

"Six," her husband added gruffly.

"Soon to be six," she said, resting a hand on her stomach.

"And how old are they?" Phillip asked nervously.

"Billy, the eldest, is seven . . ." Phillip pretended to listen after that. But he was too relieved by the fact that none of her children were his to fully pay attention.

"John, take Phillip for a tour of our land. I wish to discuss London things with the ladies."

Phillip and John Andrews exchanged looks of obvious relief at being dismissed. Once they were outdoors, Phillip discovered that the man was able to talk, just as long as his wife wasn't around. He spoke extensively of the condition of the land when he had acquired it, the changes he had made, some of which were failures, and some of which were definite improvements. Phillip made a note to himself to employ some of these strategies at Aston House.

They had just passed through the orchard and were heading toward the barn when Phillip paused.

"I owe you an apology, too."

"That's nice to hear," Mr. Andrews answered. "I was in a bit of a rage when I learned of what had occurred with you and my Emily. Didn't go with my notions of what my wife would be like. But then, you know, what is one night compared to a lifetime? I wouldn't have been good enough for her, if that hadn't happened. Her parents would have never let her marry the likes of me. Broke they were, with all those daughters, but still proud."

"She seems happy. Quite talkative."

"You can say that again," Mr. Andrews said with a grin. "My wife is a chatterbox. I don't mind, though. Keeps me from having to talk too much. And she doesn't mind if I don't really listen, so long as I pretend to. Let that lesson be my wedding gift to you. You are going to marry Miss Sullivan, aren't you?"

"I plan to."

"I reckon it was her idea for you to go around apologizing, wasn't it? Not something that occurs to a man to do."

"The things we do for women . . ." Phillip muttered, and Mr. Andrews agreed.

They ended up staying for supper, for Mrs. and Mr. Andrews would not hear otherwise.

"The food at the inn leaves much to be desired," she declared.

"The ale is good, though," Mr. Andrews added.

When the trio finally took their leave, Phillip noted that the visit had three pleasant consequences. First, Phillip had been forgiven. *One down, three to go,* he thought. Second, Mrs. Andrews had thoroughly exhausted Angela and Lady Palmerston's interest in discussing fashion. And third, Lady Palmerston claimed exhaustion and retired early.

Phillip and Angela secured a corner table in the main room of the inn. Though it was early, the room was rather dark. It was also starting to fill up with patrons, who were in the early stages of intoxication, and thus still fairly quiet and well mannered. Recalling Mrs. Andrews's warning about the food, and likely the water, too, they each ordered a pint of ale.

"I've never had ale before," Angela said, looking curiously at the pint set before her.

"After you take a sip, you might decide that you'll never have it again," Phillip cautioned. Angela tried it anyway and grimaced at the slightly bitter and definitely strange taste. Phillip laughed. "Look at you now. Sitting with me in a tavern, drinking ale—and without a chaperone, too. You've come a long way from your days at the abbey."

"You are a terrible influence on me. On everyone." To make her point, she took another sip of her pint.

"Or not. You heard Mrs. Andrews. I may not be entirely innocent, but I was certainly not the only guilty party."

"You were supposed to know better," Angela retorted. She took another sip of the ale and found it didn't taste as strange.

"I was eighteen years of age. I didn't know my arse from my elbow," Phillip answered, and she couldn't help but giggle.

"Imagine William Sloan with unlimited funds and no one to knock, or talk, some sense into him, and everything London has to offer just there for the taking."

"Oh dear God," Angela said. Her eyes widened in horror as she contemplated that.

"Exactly." Phillip lifted his own pint to his lips, but then set the glass back down before imbibing. "I never acquired a taste for ale," he said dismissively. "But you have to admit, she seemed happy. Things turned out all right for her."

"Yes," Angela sighed. "All those adorable children."

"Adorable? One of them flung peas at you from across the table throughout the entire meal. In fact, I think you still have a few stuck in your hair."

"Do I?"

"Allow me," Phillip said, reaching across the table. He brushed them aside, and settled for one caress of her cheek as he was taking his hand away. Angela smiled.

"He's just going through a phase. You must have done the same thing at his age."

"I did. But such antics were reserved for my brother or our governess. Having never dined with children before, I now understand why my father kept us stashed in the nursery until we were of age."

"Speaking of your father," Angela began, "you didn't know about the letter and the settlement, did you?"

"I knew about the money, and that she accepted a thousand pounds not to marry me. I didn't know about the letter."

"Well, it seems obvious to me that he cared for you. Otherwise, he wouldn't have offered them a settlement so that they might not challenge you."

"I was always aware that he cared for me as his heir, and by extension, he only cared about my transgressions if they reflected badly upon him, or the Buckingham legacy. I never thought he gave a damn about me as his son."

"If you think about it logically, that couldn't be the case. It's not as if you were his only son."

"Aye, that I know very well. I sure did make Devon look good in comparison. And maybe he did care. But I wonder

now if it would have been better that he hadn't interfered at
all. I might have learned to deal with the consequences of my
actions a little sooner," Phillip reflected. It made Angela think
of what Lady Palmerston had said about falling from time to
time and standing back up. The man before her was attempting, metaphorically, to stand up after a long, slow fall.

And if he could do it, so could she.

Angela reached across the table and placed her hand on
his. He took her hand, tracing his thumb over her palm for a
moment before interlacing their fingers.

"My father wrote a letter for me before he died," Phillip
said. "I only discovered it recently."

"What did he say?"

"He wished that I may not know regret as he did."

"And do you?" she asked. Phillip smiled shyly at her at
first, but it turned into that wicked grin she knew so well.

"Well, at the moment, I'm deeply regretting not getting a
private parlor. But not as much as I regret lecturing Lady
Palmerston about her chaperone methods, because otherwise
we would be sharing a room."

"I want you so much that I ache for it. But it's better this
way."

"Angela, why are you tormenting me like this?" His tone
was not angry, not quite desperate, either. Just plain. And the
plain fact was that she didn't mean to torture him. She was
simply terrified.

"Why? Because you habitually leave, and I am habitually
left. And I'm scared, Phillip. I lost you once, and I am not sure
that I could survive it again."

"But I'm not the man I was once was, Angela. Because of
you, I'm different. I may not be good, but I'm trying."

"Well, what if one of your other women love you still, and
you return the feeling, or suddenly have an attack of decency
and decide to make right what you once made wrong?"

"Doubtful. But this was your idea, mind you."

"I know," Angela sighed. "It's just that I need time. I need
to be sure because I am not."

"Oh, Angela," he murmured. "I don't know what to say." It

was the truth. If there were magic words, he would say them. But he wasn't sure even that would be enough. One thing that he was sure of, however, was that giving up and walking away was just not an option.

The number of patrons had increased by now, and the lot of them were all quickly descending into the more advanced states of intoxication. A group of men in the far corner erupted in a bawdy song, drowning out all other voices.

"You should drink more if you don't know what to say. There is something in it that makes me say too much. And those men, too." Angela took another sip of her ale and looked in the direction of the chorus of drunken fellows.

"It's called alcohol. C'mon, let's call it a night." He stood, and still holding her hand, urged her to come with him.

"So soon?"

"If you drink any more, you will get drunk. You will then make improper advances upon me, and I will be unable to resist."

That was almost exactly what happened.

They stood in the hallway before the doorway to the bed-chamber that she was sharing with Lady Palmerston, due to a shortage of rooms. Phillip intended nothing more than a brief kiss on her cheek after which he would bid her good night and lie in torment alone in his chamber. But Angela turned her head and captured his kiss on her lips.

He did not resist. When did he ever say no, anyway? And how could he now, when the woman he loved and longed for was warm and willing in his arms?

It was a kiss worth waiting for and one worth suffering for.

He cradled her head in his hand and wrapped one arm around her waist. Angela pressed all of her luscious curves against him. He groaned into her mouth as she, slightly unsteady on her feet, rubbed against his erection. Phillip took a step backward so that he could lean against the wall.

The woman was making his knees weak.

With one hand on the small of her back, and another just a bit lower, he urged her against him again.

The woman was melting his resolve and calling into question

his honorable intentions. She sighed and cupped his face in her hands so that he could do nothing but kiss her. Not that he wanted to do anything else ever again. Although . . .

Only the more primitive portions of his brain were functioning now, and they recognized two things. First, the woman he loved was willing in his arms. Second, there was an empty bed nearby. Was it the door to his room that he was leaning against, or was it the door on the left?

He couldn't. She was intoxicated, and not from his touch alone.

"I'm not scared when I'm kissing you," Angela confessed.

"Don't stop then," he murmured.

Of course he could. He was Phillip Kensington, notorious absolute scoundrel, with a willing woman in his arms and an empty bed nearby. He had done this before, he could do it again.

But he shouldn't. Not yet. And not like he had always done. She deserved more than that.

He would put a stop to this before it went too far. In just a second . . .

Reality intruded in the form of loud, drunken male voices, the shrill laughter of their female companions, and their collective footsteps stomping up the stairs. It occurred to Phillip that all he had to do was continue to kiss Angela until they were seen. Caught in a compromising position.

This time, after being caught, he wouldn't run. Unless it was *to* the altar.

But that was what they all expected of him, wasn't it? Phillip Kensington, caught in a compromising position. Again. And again . . . and a stunning thought occurred to him: just because everyone had low expectations of him didn't mean he had to prove them right.

He broke off their kiss, and not a moment too soon.

Lady Palmerston opened the door he had been leaning against. She raised one eyebrow in the direction of the group that was now passing loudly through the hall, eliciting their sincere apologies and silence.

Lady Palmerston gave him a Look.

Phillip bade her and Angela good night and retired to his chamber. Alone.

⌒

They had not taken the road to Gretna Green, Lucas had noted, which had been his first assumption upon seeing Angela, Phillip, and her chaperone embark on what would obviously be a long journey. Of course they hadn't. Who elopes with a chaperone?

He had followed them to this backwater village a day's drive from London. He could not fathom what purpose would bring anyone here, other than to spend the night before continuing on.

They had taken the last two rooms at the inn. Lucas seethed and secured lodgings at the seedier establishment a few miles down the road. He returned to the main village, and his discreet inquiries informed him that they had visited Mr. and Mrs. Andrews, a respectable couple with a passel of brats and lands that were the envy of more than a few of their neighbors.

He could not learn or imagine why they would have called upon some local farmers. But Lucas could wait and watch.

They left midmorning the next day. Lucas followed.

Chapter 22

At the rare sound of a carriage rolling up the drive of Grafton Park, Jane, Lady Grafton, ceased her writing and went to the window to see if she had well and truly gone mad and hallucinated the sound.

She had not. And furthermore, it was not her husband's carriage. It wouldn't be, of course. His Grace came to visit her and the child once a year at Christmastime. It was summer now. And that was definitely not her husband's carriage. Though she barely knew her husband, she was certain that Grafton wouldn't be caught dead in a lavender-colored vehicle.

"What is it, Mama?" Charles asked. The little boy abandoned his game of toy soldiers and came to peek out of the window beside her.

"Someone has come to call."

"Is it Father?"

Jane's breath caught in her throat as she saw a man step out of the carriage. He paused to help two women alight. She couldn't lie to her son, but he was too young for the truth. She looked down at Charles, six years old, with his nose pressed against the glass.

"It's not Father. Do you know how I know, Mum? Because the carriage is different, and it's not Christmastime."

Charles sounded so proud of himself for his deductive reasoning skills. Jane couldn't explain to him how that saved her—that note of pride in his voice instead of disappointment.

"Your Grace, there are callers." The butler had no trace of emotion in his voice, but that was unremarkable, because Farnsworth never did. But surely, he had to be just a little bit thrilled to utter the words "There are callers," for he so rarely had a chance to.

"Thank you. Please show them to the drawing room, and bring a tea tray. Please tell a maid to come up and stay with Charles. I shall be down in a moment."

Jane collected the pages she had been writing, placed them in her desk drawer, and locked it. She then fixed up her hair before the mirror, while explaining to her son that he should wait here while she spoke with the guests. She promised she would tell him all about it over lemonade and cake once they departed.

She forced her voice to be light and easy, so that her son might not know the panic bubbling up. What was Phillip Kensington doing here? And now, after all this time? She reassured herself that he had no right and no reason to take her son from her.

"You look pretty, Mama."

"Thank you, darling. I shouldn't be long. I love you, baby."

"I'm not a baby."

"Of course. I still love you."

She paused for just a second before entering the drawing room.

Phillip looked older than she had remembered, which was only logical. It had been years since . . . since she had seen him last. And it had been dark then.

He introduced his traveling companions, Miss Angela Sullivan and her aunt and chaperone, Lady Palmerston. Phillip did not explain their relationship to him nor why they were traveling together.

"You look well, Lady Grafton. How are you?" Phillip

asked. She searched his face to see what features her son might have inherited. The eyes, certainly, but only the shape and the dark brown color. Charles's eyes still had the light of innocence.

"I'm fine, thank you. Curious, actually, as to why you have come to call."

Phillip glanced at the young woman, Miss Sullivan, and she nodded her head, urging him on.

"Lady Grafton, I have come to apologize to you."

Jane did not take a sip of tea as she had planned. Instead, she replaced the cup in its saucer.

"I should have stopped as soon as I realized the mistake," he continued. "But by then it was too late. The damage had been done."

The damage to her virginity and to her marriage. To her life. It was almost laughable, what had happened. Almost.

It had been her wedding night, seven years ago. She and her new husband had stopped to spend the night at an inn on their way from London to Grafton Park. His Grace had elected to leave her in their room while he had a drink downstairs. Phillip had planned to spend the evening with a local trollop. He had simply entered the wrong room.

Her door had been unlocked for her husband.

In the darkness, the mistake was made.

She had been expecting her husband, a man of the same size and build as Phillip. She had been instructed by her mother *never* to question or contradict her husband. She was confused, but she followed the only directions she had been given. Do not question. Do not do anything other than lie there.

Grafton had entered with a candle to illuminate everything, after Phillip had finished with her.

She had been sent on to Grafton Park, while her husband chased Phillip to London. There had been a duel, though Jane knew her husband fought for his pride and not her honor.

They never spoke of it. In fact, they rarely spoke. Grafton certainly never, ever touched her.

"I'm sorry," Phillip said to her now.

"I am, too," Jane said. "What, may I ask, is your connection to each other?" she said, referring to Phillip and Miss Sullivan.

"She is my fiancée."

"If he apologizes to all the women he has wronged," Miss Sullivan added.

"Make sure you leave a candle burning on your wedding night, in case the wrong man happens to enter your chamber. You'll want to realize the difference before it's too late."

"*Hmmph*," Lady Palmerston muttered. "Your husband should have never left you alone in the first place. And all for ale in a roadside pub. The stupidity of men never ceases to amaze."

"You know what happened that night?" Jane questioned, again, with a wave of panic.

"Phillip explained—and don't be vexed at him. The poor man didn't have a chance, being trapped in the carriage with me and my curiosity all the way from London."

"Dare I even ask what stories people are telling in London?"

"It seems everyone has forgotten the incident," Lady Palmerston answered.

"Except for Grafton," Jane muttered.

"Mama!" Charles burst into the room. She couldn't help but smile, even though she had told him to stay upstairs. She opened her arms to him, and her son came and sat beside her on the settee.

"I'm sorry, Your Grace, he's just so fast . . ." the maid said, red in the face from rushing after the boy.

"It's all right. What is it, darling?"

"I wished to meet our guests." If her son noticed that she tensed, he gave no indication. Jane summoned her courage and met the gazes of her guests, with a plea in her eyes.

"This is *my* son, Charles." And then she performed the rest of the introductions. Her little darling conducted himself like the duke he would one day be.

Charles didn't seem to notice that the ladies were not

watching him but Phillip. To see them next to each other—a sight Jane never expected to witness—there was no denying that Phillip was his father.

Phillip shook the boy's hand and looked over his head to her. She could see the question in his eyes: *Does he know?*

Jane shook her head no, and Phillip merely nodded in response.

In that little exchange, she forgave him. This time, at least, he had thought to ask first before ruining everything for her all over again.

Neither Lady Palmerston nor Miss Sullivan said anything questionable, either, and their expressions said that they understood that this little boy was everything to her.

After Charles met their guests, he left with the maid without a complaint, reminding his mother about the cake she had promised him.

"We should go now," Miss Sullivan said. "We should hate to keep you from him any longer, and hate to keep him waiting any longer for the cake you promised him."

As Jane walked out of the drawing room, Lady Palmerston paused to speak with her. "Please write to me in London if you should ever have need of anything. Especially if that old fool of a husband of yours gives you trouble."

Good-byes were said, and the ladies exited, leaving Jane alone in the foyer with Phillip.

"He seems like a good lad," Phillip said, visibly uncomfortable.

"He is. Charles is everything to me," Jane said. She clutched her skirts, so afraid that Phillip would ruin something again.

"Is there anything I can do?" he asked, and this surprised her. She thought for a moment before answering.

"Perhaps one day you might explain to him why his father despises him. But it would be best for him, and for me, if you stayed away. And if this visit was not mentioned in town."

"Of course. You know, my father hated me, even though I was his. At least Charles has a mother who loves him. I wonder how things might have been different if I had that."

"I do love him. Very much."

"I am sorry, Lady Grafton, about our mistake—"

"I don't regret him," she said, and tears were stinging her eyes.

"No, I meant that I am sorry about what I have done to your marriage. But at least you have not been left completely alone. You have the boy."

"Yes. Please don't say anything."

"I will not do or say anything unless I receive instructions from you. But if he should ever ask after me, I . . ." Phillip's voice trailed off, and he looked off down the hall. "I will be there for him if you need me to."

"Thank you, Phillip."

Phillip elected to ride up with the driver rather than in the carriage with Angela and her aunt. He needed to think, and he desperately needed to avoid their pitying or questioning expressions for as long as possible. He sure as hell did not want to *talk* about it.

Rumors were easy to dismiss and ignore. But the small flesh-and-blood image of oneself was not. He had a child.

Or rather, he had sired a child. A brat that looked just like him, with an old duke to despise him. Of all the things he could have in common with his child, it had to be that, didn't it? And he would, one day, have to explain to the boy why his father hated him. And he would tell Charles that drinking and whoring may get his father's attention, but it wouldn't get his love. And he would tell that kid not to make the same mistakes he did.

But could he tell Charles that he was a mistake?

Maybe he was. Maybe he wasn't. But at least Charles had his mother. He would know he was loved, and that was more than Phillip ever had. One couldn't miss how protective she was of him.

One also couldn't miss how Phillip was dismissed.

And that was just as well. He had nothing more to give to them, even if he had wanted to. But he had given Jane someone to keep her company, since Grafton had abandoned her.

After arriving at the inn, finding a moment alone with

Angela was remarkably easy, and for that Phillip was glad.
Lady Palmerston left them alone in their private parlor to go
speak with some acquaintances she had encountered in the
hall.

The door wasn't even entirely shut when Phillip took Angela in his arms for a deep, hungry kiss. It was exactly what
he needed: a reminder of why he was going on this quest. He
needed a taste of the prize, and she gave it to him.

"Phillip, do you want to talk about it?" Angela asked.

"Of course not," he replied, even though he might have; he
just didn't know where to begin.

"Well, I do."

Of course.

"After Lucas, I was sad when I got my menses, even though
I should have felt relieved. I had thought that if something
good could come out of such a wretched situation, it might
somehow make it all better, or worth it. And I felt guilty, too,
because I wouldn't have been able to provide for it. But I would
have loved it, and the baby would have loved me. And Lady
Grafton loves her son, and he seems to be the only one who
loves her. She has something good from you."

"His father hates him. Just like mine hated me."

"But you don't hate him."

"I'm not his father. Not in any real sense."

"No, but you can explain things to him one day. And he has
his mother, who very obviously loves him and—"

"I'm as wicked as the stories say," Phillip said, cutting her
off, to avoid indulging in the fleeting surge of jealousy he felt
for his own child. Jealousy, and relief. Lady Grafton loved
their son, and Phillip hadn't had a mother's love.

"Perhaps. But you are not as heartless as they say you are."

"Angela," he murmured and drew her into his arms again.
He wanted so badly to see the good that she saw in him. He
wasn't heartless, not so long as she was around. She didn't just
own his heart, she was it. Dear God, since when did he think
such romantic drivel? He must be well and truly besotted.

Lady Palmerston entered their private parlor with the

newest a copy of the *London Weekly*, which was already a few days old. After supper, she had only read as far as the second page when she set down the news sheet and gave Phillip a long look.

He felt uneasy. He quite nearly felt like begging her not to show Angela. Because, though he did not know for certain, he had a very good idea of what the gossip column said about him now.

"Oh, go on then," Phillip said, resigned. He quit the room. He would be sleeping alone tonight. Again.

～

Lucas smiled when he saw Huntley exit the private parlor, alone, looking quite grim. He had been waiting for their return in the common room of the inn all day, imbibing all the while, and he waited while they dined. He went unnoticed by them due to the poor lighting and large crowd. He didn't know the reason why Huntley appeared so so grim, but Lucas suspected it had something to do with their call on Lady Grafton this afternoon.

That had been easy enough to figure out. He had no idea why they visited, but he suspected it might have something to do with the rumors from years ago. There had been a duel between Grafton and one of the Kensington twins; there was disagreement as to which one actually fought. But it was widely believed that Lady Grafton was the reason. She bore a child nine months later. For all anyone knew, the child was the duke's legitimate issue, but the fact of the duel and that Lady Grafton was last seen in London at her wedding was, for some, confirmation enough that the child was Huntley's.

He suspected they had verified it this afternoon. Angela couldn't possibly marry such a scoundrel now that she had likely seen evidence of his greatest sin. She probably told him such, which was why Huntley left their private parlor, alone, looking dejected and resigned.

Lucas ordered another drink from the barkeep in celebration. And he kept watch. Lady Palmerston emerged eventually, with Angela, who looked positively furious. He had consumed so much ale that he was seeing double, but not so much that he didn't recognize that now was not the time to press his suit.

The following morning he slept late and learned that they had left an hour before. He thanked the heavens for Lady Palmerston's unique carriage, for it was easy enough to be pointed in the correct direction.

By noon he had caught up with them at an inn, where they must have stopped to change horses. Lucas didn't have time to rest his mount, for he saw Phillip entering the carriage just before it drove off once more.

Lucas followed, of course.

He was getting bloody sick of following and never catching up. He was always watching her and waiting. After seven years he was still waiting for his chance to marry the woman he loved. He was still waiting for his chance to absolve his guilt. And every moment that Angela spent with Huntley was a moment in which his chance at redemption and marriage to the one woman he had always wanted slipped away.

He had tried to discredit Huntley. He had hoped that the scoundrel's own sins would prove to be an insurmountable obstacle. But no . . . Like the worst sort of vermin infestation, Huntley was proving impossible to exterminate.

Exterminate. That gave Lucas an idea. But no, he couldn't resort to that just yet. He did not want another lost life on his conscience. He just wanted *her*.

Chapter 23

The following morning, over breakfast, Angela read the cursed newspaper again. On this tenth reading, the words remained the same.

> After quite the scene at Lady Derby's fete, the betting books at White's are full of wagers on who will marry *London Weekly* illustrator, Miss Angela Sullivan. Odds are in favor of Lord Frost, and Lord Huntley is considered a long shot, although the notorious scoundrel did bet five hundred pounds in favor of himself. Whoever Miss Sullivan deigns to marry will be a very rich—and lucky—man.

"Do you think it's true?" Angela asked her aunt.

"I'd wager on it."

"You'd wager on a wager?"

"Everyone does it, my dear. But if you do wish to confirm the accuracy of the report, all you need to do is ask Phillip. Do let me know what he says; I should like to know if I am correct."

"Oh, I will ask him," Angela muttered.

"You do realize that he will be quite rich if you do marry him," her aunt pointed out.

"Or rather, I will be a very wealthy widow. I can't believe he did that! How am I to trust his motives for marrying me now? Is nothing sacred to him?"

"You know, you could completely ruin the man if you didn't marry him. If I am doing the sums correctly, he'll never be able to repay his losses. Not in this lifetime anyway."

"But then what will I win?"

❧

Lila Drake née Althorp had made headlines a year earlier when it was revealed that she was a spy. She had met her husband Sebastian Drake, also a fellow spy, when they teamed up to retrieve the Prince Regent's stolen coronation crown. As a reward, they were given an earldom.

"How a woman smart enough to single-handedly take down a ring of French smugglers and secure the coronation crown was foolish enough to get caught with you, Phillip, within an hour of her coming out, is quite simply beyond me," Lady Palmerston remarked just before they alighted the carriage.

The Drakes were thrilled to see Lady Palmerston again, for she had become acquainted with them at a house party the previous year. They had been pretending to be married for the sake of their mission. It wasn't long before their marriage was real.

After the introductions, Lila, as she told them to call her, focused on Angela.

"I've heard of you. You do the drawings for the Darcy Darlington stories, do you not?" Lila questioned eagerly.

"Yes, I do," she replied, liking Lila already.

"They're quite good. You are certainly very talented."

"Thank you."

"I'm rather determined to uncover the author's identity," Lila said pointedly, and Angela stifled a groan. It was fair to assume that she might know the secret author of the stories she illustrated, but in truth, she had no idea. Nigel Haven had been clear that he would not tell her, and she didn't argue, for she really didn't need another secret to keep.

"You could spare me a tremendous headache, Miss Sullivan, if you would just tell her," said Lila's husband, Sebastian Drake, the Earl of Diamond.

"She's a vault," Lady Palmerston replied. "I've been trying to get the answer out of her for almost a year now, to no avail. I have even considered, dear niece, opening your correspondence, if it weren't sealed."

"Oh, I know a trick to help you with that," Lila said breezily, as if they were merely discussing housekeeping remedies and not interfering with personal correspondence.

"I can't tell you anything simply because I don't know the author, nor do I know what is going to happen in the story. I am simply told what to draw."

"How vexing," Lila said, biting her lower lip.

"It's a relief, actually. I'm sure I would have accidentally slipped by now if I knew."

"But I can't imagine you have come all this way *not* to tell me a secret. What does bring you here?"

Angela and Lady Palmerston turned to Phillip.

"I have come to apologize to you, Lady Diamond," Phillip said.

"Really?" Lila seemed surprised, of course.

"Yes. I'm sorry for ruining you in the eyes of society," Phillip said sincerely.

"Thank you. Rather late in coming, but better late than never, they say."

"Lila, is there anything else you'd like to say?" her husband, Drake as she called him, added. That piqued everyone's curiosity.

"Well, I suppose I should apologize on behalf of my brother for challenging you to that duel . . . and years after the fact, too. Is it true that you fell and shot yourself?"

"To my eternal annoyance and mortification, yes."

"Lila . . ."

"Yes, Drake?"

"Isn't there something else you'd like to tell him?"

"Husbands are such a bother. Are you sure you want one?" Lila addressed Angela.

"I'm considering it, and I thank you for your warning," Angela said, with a pointed look at Phillip.

"What my husband wishes me to tell you, Phillip, is that I probably owe you the apology."

"Interesting . . ." Lady Palmerston murmured, with a smile.

"You were set up, Phillip. I did not care for my father's marriage plans for me, so I decided to get myself ruined. You were very obliging. It was almost too easy, really. So thank you, for your assistance."

"You mean you got ruined on purpose?" Angela asked, incredulous. The very idea was unfathomable to her.

"If you had met the lecherous and revolting Baron Montrose, to whom my father arranged an engagement without consulting me, you would have done the same without a second thought."

"He was a nasty creature," Lady Palmerston added.

"But why did you choose me?" Phillip asked.

"Your reputation, of course. I heard all the rumors about that Preston girl and all the speculation as to what else you might have done. I would only have to be seen with you in order for people to suspect the worst."

"Madame, a caller," the butler intoned from the doorway.

Lord Lucius Rothermere, an elderly gentleman with bright blue eyes and a shock of white hair, was introduced to Angela and Phillip. Apparently, he and Lady Palmerston had been introduced at Lila and Drake's wedding.

After politely discussing the day's lovely weather, it was decided they should all take a walk in the garden.

They all ended up pairing off and wandering down separate paths: Lady Palmerston with Lord Rothermere, Drake and Phillip, Lila and Angela.

"Please forgive my boldness, but after years of being sly and subtle, I can't quite manage it any longer. I'm very curious: What is your relationship with Phillip?" Lila asked.

"I think I am going to marry him," Angela said. "Or at least I said I would."

"You don't sound sure of yourself."

"I'm trying to be. I love him, but trust is another matter entirely. And I've been hurt in the past—"

"Again, forgive my boldness, but were you ruined as well? You must know there have been rumors."

"Yes, a long time ago. Gossip lives a long life and dies a slow death it seems," Angela remarked.

"But look at us now," Lila urged, linking arms with Angela. "We are supposed to be shriveled up, bitter old spinsters. Or dead. But here we are, showing that there is life after being ruined. I am happily married, and you could be. And to handsome fellows, too. If more young women knew about us, I daresay more would follow our paths."

"But weren't you utterly miserable at first?" Angela asked.

"Oh, of course. Rothermere saved my life by giving me something to do."

"The spying."

"Yes. And you have your illustrations."

"And now if I may be bold," Angela started, "how did you come to trust your husband?" Though they had been acquainted for no more than an hour, Lila's straightforward demeanor encouraged intimacy. Furthermore, they had too much in common not to find an immediate bond. And for the first time, Angela realized one of the things she had been missing: someone who could be truly empathetic to her situation.

"I kept pushing him away, and yet he came back every time," Lila responded, and Angela could relate. "I knew very well how to be alone, but I did not know how to be with another person. And it didn't hurt that he saved my life from an armed and dangerous highwayman. Of course, I would have managed perfectly well by myself. But I didn't have to, and that was nice."

"I'd rather not have my life in peril, if I can help it."

"Well, there is another way. Keep in mind that occasionally, when one employs this method, they learn things they'd rather not. But every once in a while, one hears exactly what one wishes to know."

"What is it?" Angela asked.

"Shhh," Lila whispered with a mischievous gleam in her eyes.

They fell silent, walking along until they heard the murmur of men talking. Lila pulled Angela behind a hedge with her and indicated that they should remain silent.

"I bet she put you up to this, didn't she?" They overheard Drake say.

"Traveling all over England to apologize to scorned women certainly wasn't my idea," Phillip responded.

Drake chuckled. "Every man's nightmare. It never ceases to amaze me what sort of devious schemes females come up with. Is it as horrible as I think it is?"

"Pretty much, although I must admit it could be far worse."

"Best to let them all think you are suffering horribly. For whatever reason, women seem to love the brooding, tortured routine. They'll go to great lengths to soothe our wounded souls, etc. etc. . . . ." Angela and Lila both rolled their eyes and smothered their laughter.

"It shouldn't be too difficult to act as such in the carriage ride back to London. All they ever talk about is gossip and fashion. I can't imagine anything more torturous."

"Oh, they wait until they think we are asleep to start discussing the good stuff. Trust me on that one."

"This has been an enlightening conversation. Why have I not learned these things sooner?"

"Because you didn't marry a spy. Speaking of marriage to a spy," Drake muttered in a lowered voice. When Drake spoke again, his words were loud and clear.

"Your apology is not necessary, Huntley, though I appreciate it," Drake said loudly. "It is *I* who should be thanking you. For if you had not compromised Lila, I might never have met her, let alone married her. She has been such a constant source of joy in my life, and it would be a fate worse than death to live without her."

Phillip grinned, understanding what Drake was up to. He stifled a laugh at the unmistakable sound of a female scoffing in disbelief from the other side of the hedge.

"Why, that sounds like my lovely wife," Drake remarked.

"My dear husband," Lila said sweetly after reappearing from the other side of the hedge with Angela in tow. "I need to have a word with you. Privately."

Drake needed no encouragement. He winked at Phillip and sauntered off with his wife. Phillip grinned. For the first time since the previous evening, he had a moment alone with her. He could tell that she was upset about the wager, but he rationalized that a good, deep, passionate kiss would make her forget all about it. He drew her close to him.

"So you are not going to at least act brooding and tortured to elicit my sympathy?" Angela asked sharply, stepping away from him and folding her arms over her chest.

"Not when I am so happy to have a moment alone with you," he said, reaching out for her so he could kiss her and make her forget her anger. When he placed his arm around her shoulders, she shrugged off his touch.

"Lady Palmerston could be eavesdropping," she said by way of explanation.

That was a chilling thought. But still . . .

"She might not be."

"You are hoping that we will get caught in some sort of compromising position, aren't you?" She kept her voice low, but her anger was undeniable.

"Now that you mention it, the idea does have some merit. I'm going to marry you, Angela. Why not sooner rather than later?"

"Oh, you are impossible!"

"*I* am impossible?" he echoed. "I have done everything you asked me to, and it's still not enough to please you, is it?"

"Do you really want to make me happy? Or are you just trying to win a wager?" Angela retorted.

Phillip looked up toward the heavens and thought now might be a good time for God to show some favor for him. In his silence, she spoke first.

"You stand to win a lot of money if we marry."

"And I'll spend it all on you, darling."

"But how could you make a sport of us? A wager on whether we'll marry. Really, Phillip. I'm not some racehorse."

"That is quite obvious."

"You're not even sorry about it, are you?" she accused. And then something just broke within him. Phillip couldn't stop the surge of feelings that suddenly crashed upon him. Frustration at never being able to do enough or to do right. Fear that she might not love him and that she was taking some perverse pleasure in making him jump through one hoop after another. He had been patient. He had been steady. He had been repentant and devoted. And it was insufficient, and he no longer knew what in God's name to do about this impossible woman.

She was the impossible one. He loved her anyway. But still . . . enough was enough.

"I'm sorry you're upset about it, Angela," he said firmly. When she opened her mouth to reply, he didn't give her a chance to utter a sound. "But no, I'm not sorry I placed that wager. You made me believe in myself, Angela. For the first time in my life, I'm betting on myself."

"And if you lose?"

"Who says I'm going to lose?" He was emboldened now, taunting fate and fury, and this angry angel. But he could not restrain himself.

"You could at least apologize for making a mockery of what we have together."

She had a point. He could just take her hand and look her in the eye and say that he was sorry, and this would all blow over, and they would live happily—and richly—ever after. But suddenly he was overcome with a new, strange feeling: that of pride and confidence in himself. For once, he knew his own mind and heart, and he could see the truth that she was avoiding.

"Angela, it's one thing for me to apologize to women I've wronged, and should have made amends with before," he said calmly and patiently. "I can, and have, sincerely apologized to them. But I am not going to apologize for the wager, because it would be a lie. I have never lied to you, and I will not do so now."

"But still—"

"I think the one apology you want most of all is the one I

can't give you." That was the truth that she was running from. The other truth was that they didn't have a chance at happiness if either of them kept running from the past. He had faced his, and she had to do the same.

"He has nothing to do with this."

"He has everything to do with this. You may have moved on with your life, but you have not forgiven him or yourself. I can't fight your demons for you, Angela."

"This has nothing do with me. You're the one—"

"Yes, I am the one. I love you, Angela. Why isn't that enough?"

⟳

"That is Lila with Drake," Rothermere pointed out. The earl and countess were strolling arm in arm ahead of them on the path.

"So it is," Lady Palmerston replied.

"That likely means, Dora, that your Miss Sullivan and Huntley are alone somewhere in the gardens. Alone." She did not miss the double suggestion in his tone. She glanced slyly at him, and he raised one eyebrow in return. She smiled and looked away.

"What an astute observation for you to make, Rothermere. You must have been an exceptional spy," she responded. He had told her of his former employment when she asked how he was acquainted with their hosts. She could not deny a shiver of excitement at knowing a spy. Or was it that he smiled in response to her teasing?

"Correct me if I am wrong, but are you not trying to make a match between them? To discover them in a compromising position would ensure a marriage."

"You daft old man, this is Phillip Kensington we are talking about. Catching the man in a compromising position is as easy as breathing. It's getting him to the altar after the fact which is the challenge of a lifetime."

"Lila has an exceptional gift with weaponry, if that should aid your endeavor."

"I shall make a note of that, thank you. But I daresay no

woman wants to marry a man who has a pistol pressing into his spine as he recites his vows."

"That would not be romantic at all," Rothermere said, linking their arms. "Or perhaps it shall not be so easy to catch him after all."

Ahead of them, Angela came storming out from behind a hedge, quite nearly running. Phillip followed in hot pursuit, calling her name. She did not turn around.

"Fools, the lot of them," Lady Palmerston muttered.

"Women do tend to overreact to even the most insignificant matters."

"I was referring to men, actually, and their uncanny ability to always say the wrong thing. I thank you for just proving my point."

"Anything to please you," he murmured. "Now, what are we going to do about the young lovers?"

"Give them time to cool their tempers and plenty of opportunities to make amends. Come, let's return to the house. I expect Angela wishes to leave."

Angela did wish to leave and return to London immediately. Lila and Drake would not hear of it. Everyone was to stay for dinner and spend the night. After all, they had plenty of rooms, the local inn could not compare, and they were sure to have a splendid evening together.

After supper, a pleasant affair during which the Drakes regaled their guests with stories from their spying days, the ladies adjourned to the drawing room for tea, while the gentlemen remained in the dining room to drink port.

Phillip accepted a glass and strongly considered drinking it, along with the entire bottle.

"Things don't look good for you winning that wager," Drake remarked.

"You saw it in the paper, too?" Phillip assumed.

"No, I overheard your argument with Miss Sullivan this afternoon. My wife is not the only one who eavesdrops," Drake replied with an unapologetic grin.

"I may be a fool, but I hope there is still a chance," Phillip said. He had seen Angela lost in thought yet still glancing at him throughout dinner.

"You'll be paying off half the ton for the rest of your life if you lose," Drake stated. "You need more than hope, my friend."

"It's not the money I'm afraid of losing. I've already lost every penny. I just don't know what I'll do if I lose her."

"Besotted, are you?" Drake teased. "Happens to the best of us."

"What you need is a plan to win her for certain," Rothermere contributed.

"Right. Grand gesture, and all that nonsense," Drake said.

"Does that really work?" Phillip asked skeptically.

"Did for me," Drake answered and took a sip of his port.

"What did you do?" Phillip asked.

"Saved her from an armed highwayman," Drake answered. "Any other ideas?"

"I'll offer my services as a distraction to the young lady's chaperone," Rothermere suggested. The two younger men eyed the elderly gentleman curiously for a moment.

"You sly old dog, Rothermere," Drake said, breaking into laughter.

"Anything I can do to help," he answered.

"Right. So we distract Lady Palmerston. And then what?" Phillip said, thinking that between the three of them, they were sure to come up with a good plan. After all, two of them were spies, with years of practice at devising plans and saving the day. There was hope after all.

Or not.

They all fell silent for a moment. A very long moment. Drake supplied cigars. Rothermere accepted another glass of port. Drake leaned back in his chair and began to whistle. Phillip rested his head in his hands, elbows on the table.

"Did you, uh, tell the lady of your affections for her? Tell her you loved her, can't live without her, etc., etc?" Drake started.

"Repeatedly."

"Flowers?" Drake suggested.

"Yes, and she beat me with them."

"Perhaps a serenade from outside her window?" Rothermere contributed.

"But only if you can sing well," Drake added. "Because if you can't, then I'd rather not hear it."

"You can't put your comfort aside for your guests?" Rothermere reprimanded him.

Drake scowled. "Admit that you'd rather not hear it, either."

"I will not be singing outside of her window. I only know bawdy, grossly inappropriate drinking songs. I doubt that's very romantic."

"What about composing a poem for the lady?" Rothermere said.

"My efforts would probably embarrass us both," Phillip said, certain of that. He could feel his hope slipping away.

"There is always jewelry," Rothermere said. "That usually works like a charm."

"Where is he going to get jewelry at this hour?" Drake retorted.

"I do have a ring for her," Phillip said, suddenly feeling a lot less hopeless. He had brought his mother's ring along, with the intention of giving it to Angela as a wedding ring. But why not an engagement ring? Really, he should have thought of this sooner.

"That's good! You'll give her the ring and make some romantic speech," Drake said. That sounded like something he could do. Although . . .

"Great. Now what does one say in a romantic speech?"

The gentlemen, once again, fell silent.

"This is really something you should have female counsel on," Drake suggested.

"Yes, but they will tell, as they are women and thus unable to keep a secret, thereby ruining the element of surprise, which is, in my understanding, essential to the efficacy of the grand gesture," Rothermere said, reminding them of an important truth.

"Well then, can either of you give me a few thousand pounds?"

~

When the gentlemen rejoined the ladies in the drawing room, Angela was not present. Phillip was informed that she had retired for the evening. Lila declared she had a headache, and Drake insisted on escorting her to their chamber. Rothermere gave Phillip a look, which Phillip immediately comprehended. He claimed exhaustion and bade them good night.

He trailed Lila and Drake on the stairs.

"So, my dear wife, I trust you have seen that our guests are comfortably settled in their chambers."

"Of course."

"I'm sure you gave Lady Palmerston and Angela rooms with views of the garden."

"You have the subtlety of a herd of cattle," Lila retorted.

"Well, are you going to help out a poor besotted man or not?"

Lila paused at the top of the stairs and turned to Phillip, looking down on him menacingly.

"Phillip, I have a gift with weaponry. My aim is exceptional. I once shot a man in the knee from twenty yards, not paces. It goes without saying that I hit what I was aiming for."

"Help him, Lila, don't threaten him."

"Hush, you," she said to her husband. "Phillip, you did me a tremendous favor once, so now I shall help you in return. Angela's room is the second one on the left. But if I hear that you do not do right by her, I will hunt you down and—"

"I promise you will be invited to the wedding," Phillip said quickly.

"Excellent. Good night then."

Phillip knocked softly on the second door on the left.

~

Angela had been deep in thought throughout the evening. She excused herself from tea with Lila and her aunt so that she might go over her thoughts once more, in private. And so she mulled over everything as she waited to see if he would knock on the door.

The things Phillip had said this afternoon were echoing endlessly in her mind. She wondered if he might be right.

The guilt and shame that Lucas had left her with were threatening to ruin her life all over again. Phillip could apologize to every woman in England, and it wouldn't change her feelings. It might lessen her fears, but it wouldn't erase them completely. Lucas was the one who should apologize to her.

He should say that he was sorry for taking advantage of her innocence and ignorance. He should be sorry for his part in her father's death. And if Phillip was right about his scheme in the garden at the ball, then he should damn well apologize to her for trying to ruin her second chance at love and happiness.

She might grow old and die waiting for this apology. A bleak prospect indeed.

Or she could hunt Lucas down and demand it. But that would take time and would require facing him again, and she wasn't sure she wanted to. And for all she knew, he could apologize until his dying breath, and it might not make her feel any better.

But all Phillip had to do was take her in his arms, and that made everything seem right and perfect in the world. At supper this evening, like every other time she looked into his dark eyes, she felt that now-familiar hum in her body. It wasn't any less thrilling than the first time or all the other times since then. With his eyes on her, or even with him near, silk felt softer against her skin. She felt warmer. She would swear she could feel her blood coursing through her veins.

She couldn't stop imagining making love to him. She knew what his hands felt like on her skin, his mouth upon hers, and his kiss. And she could imagine how he would feel inside her. And that was the problem. She knew things she shouldn't.

She wasn't perfect. But neither was he.

And Angela thought of her old prayer that she recited every night before bed when she lived in the abbey. Her prayer was for a second chance at love with a good man whom she could love and who would love her back. And, now that she thought of it, she hadn't recited that prayer since Phillip had arrived.

Perhaps God had answered her after all.

There was a knock at the door.

To hell with the past, she thought, when she had a chance at heaven, here on earth. Love was enough.

She opened the door.

"Promise me that you will be here in the morning," Angela said, after Phillip entered her chamber and shut and locked the door behind him.

She stood tall before him. In the candlelight, her hair, like spun gold, was unbound and falling over her shoulders. He pushed one lock aside, allowing his hand to skim across the soft skin of her cheek. With one fingertip, he traced along the curve of her neck, the curve of her shoulder, the swell of her breast. And he noticed that her hands were anxiously grasping the silken folds of her skirt. She was nervous. He took her hand in his.

He was the lucky one. The one who would get to kiss away her fears, the man who would erase her pain and give her pleasure instead.

"Promise me, please," she whispered. It was a plea. She thought she was asking too much. But she might as well have asked him to breathe, for to promise her that would be the easiest promise to fulfill.

"I promise, Angela, that I will wake up with you for all the mornings of all the days of our lives."

And then he sank down to one knee and looked up into her eyes. As far as grand gestures went, this one might not even count. There was no poetry or pageantry, no public to witness the promise. There was nothing, nothing at all, but the plain, honest truth. And on bended knee, with a ring in hand, there was no mistaking his intentions and his promise.

"Will you marry me, Angela?"

"I already said I would. But . . ." Angela pulled him up to

stand again. "I am not an innocent. You have to know that you will not be my first. But I can promise you that you will be the last man. And I do love you. So if you will still have me—"

Phillip pressed a fingertip to her lips.

"Angela, I already know. And I still love you. I can't imagine not loving you. And I hope that I am the last man for you, just as you are going to be the last woman I ever make love to. But what matters more is that you are happy. Oh, don't cry. Say yes and let me love you tonight and forever."

"Yes," she said in a voice that was sure, certain, and steady. Phillip slipped the ring on the fourth finger of her left hand. He gave her a second to admire it, with a smile as dazzling as the diamonds.

With his ring on her finger, the truth spoken, and hope in her heart, Angela knew she was ready. Though she had done this once before, she was still a little nervous. Like her second first kiss, this would be her second first time. Did she remember what to do? Had she even known before? Did any of that even matter? It would be different this time, she was sure. She knew that he could pleasure her, and that she could do the same for him.

And they were in love.

And they had waited long enough.

She pressed her mouth to his. And if she had any lingering doubts, Phillip kissed them away. With his hands, he pushed her hair out of the way and cupped her cheeks. He held her, as if drinking her in. She parted her lips, and he did the same. The kiss deepened.

Now that this moment was finally here, it became impossible to wait any longer. The months of longing, of loving, and of losing were finally over.

She began to push his jacket off of his shoulders. With his mouth never leaving hers, he shrugged and pulled it off, while she grasped and tugged buttons free.

His coat fell silently to the floor, followed quickly by his shirt. She pressed her palms against his chest. His skin was hot to the touch, and she could feel his heart pounding. She caressed the muscular contours and ridges of his abdomen and felt the soft, slight covering of hair. But it felt different than she remembered, different than before.

She opened her eyes and took a step back so that she might see with her eyes what she had felt with her hands. Oh, yes, he was stronger now. The sun darkened his skin. It was impossible not to imagine him shirtless and working outdoors in the sun, with a breeze cooling his heated skin.

Yes, he had changed. He was different than before. Stronger and bigger, but still hers. The hair on his chest narrowed into a line, leading to below the waistband of his breeches. His arousal was obvious. She didn't bother to even try to look away.

And she couldn't help but smile, knowing that his desire was for her. She could remember the way he felt in her hand, incredibly hard and strong, yet the skin there was silky soft and hot. She didn't care anymore that she wasn't supposed to know what his erection looked like and felt like. She knew, and she was glad of it, for once, because she didn't have to fear the unknown. She could simply enjoy.

He groaned, and she raised her gaze to his face. His eyes were dark. His jaw was set in a firm, hard line.

"And they say that I can ruin a woman with my eyes. But your eyes . . . looking at me like that . . ."

"Look at me," she whispered.

Phillip reached out, placing his hand at the back of her neck, sliding it down her back and up again. With both of his hands he quickly and easily took care of the buttons on her gown. She shrugged it off. He pulled her chemise over her head. And the lacings on her corset were removed with practiced ease.

And she was glad of that. He had done this before; he knew what he was doing. That meant there were not extra agonizing seconds of fumbling. She could be free of her coverings and restraints sooner. And then she stood before him, clad in nothing but her stockings with a pile of clothing at her feet.

Angela watched him as he stared at her. His eyes focused on her breasts first, and her nipples hardened from a look alone. His eyes darkened, and looked lower, to the gentle roundness of her stomach, and lower still to the thatch of hair between her legs. He bit his lower lip.

His desire for her was so clear, so undeniable, that she suddenly felt very bold. She turned around to walk toward the bed, after first casting a glance at him over her shoulder.

She sat down on the bed.

He stood before her.

She raised her hands to the band of his breeches, and began to slowly and carefully push the buttons through the holes. It was little more than a second later that he stood naked before her. Angela reached out to touch his arousal. His hand enclosed around hers.

A wicked thought occurred to her. Phillip sucked in his breath as she pressed a gentle kiss to its tip. She parted her lips around his erection, and his hand tightened on hers, and he moaned.

"Not. Yet." Phillip groaned. She stopped and looked questioningly at him. She had thought he liked it. He urged her to lie back on the bed, and he covered her with his body.

"You first," he whispered in her ear, as he stroked lightly between her parted legs. "And when it's my turn, I want to be inside you."

"Mmm," she murmured, for it was all she could manage. How had she ever managed to live so long without his touch?

He shifted above her and began to feather kisses in a slow, teasing trail from the hollow of her throat down to her breasts. His mouth closed around one pink center, sucking the peak and eliciting a gasp from her, and then another, as he pressed light kisses in a line from one breast to the other. All the while, his fingers kept stroking her in a steady rhythm of increasing pressure.

Phillip's attentions moved lower still. He pressed his open mouth on the curve of one hip, and then the other, and all the bare skin in between. Back and forth and up and down, there wasn't an inch of her skin that he didn't lavish his kiss and his touch upon. Sometimes she laughed when he came across a ticklish spot, but more often she sighed with pleasure. Angela ran her fingers through his hair, holding him to her, even though he showed no intentions of pulling away.

And then his mouth moved lower still, and he stroked the bud of her sex with his tongue now instead, leaving his hands free to caress the delicate skin of her inner thighs. She began to writhe under his loving touch. Her movements and her moans were involuntary. She knew she could not silence or restrain herself if she tried.

But she didn't try to.

She knew she was on the verge of that explosive pleasure he had given her before. As if it were only yesterday, she remembered the heat that spread through her like wildfire, burning hotter, and brighter, and completely unstoppable. She remembered this tingling feeling that started from his mouth and that magical place that he kissed thoroughly.

And then her entire mind and every inch of her body was possessed by a wave of pleasure so explosive, so wonderfully overwhelming that everything in the world vanished except her and him and this amazing feeling.

She hoped that no one else heard her cry out his name as she climaxed. And then she didn't care if the whole world heard her.

And before the pleasure faded completely, she was treated to the marvelous feeling of Phillip lowering his weight upon her. Angela also felt his rock-hard erection pressing urgently between her legs.

"Angela . . ." he whispered, looking into her eyes.

"Yes," she whispered back.

Phillip entered her slowly, inch by hot, hard inch.

He never once took his eyes away from hers.

He was gentle, slow, and restrained, as if it was her first time. But the truth was so much better: it was their first time together.

She pressed her fingertips into his back and raked them slowly down that long expanse of hot, muscled skin. With both hands splayed on his buttocks, she urged him to enter her completely. Because she was beginning to feel almost whole and almost at one with him. She wanted the feeling to be complete.

And when he was totally sheathed within her, he laced his fingers with hers and pressed his mouth to hers for a deep, hungry kiss. His hips began to thrust, slowly at first. He moved inside of her, and she moved with him. And then a little bit harder, and a little bit faster.

She felt desperate for more yet so utterly complete at the same time. He gasped out his love for her, and she opened her mouth to say the same, but her second climax caught her by surprise, and she could only cry out his name.

Angela felt his final thrusts, rougher than all the others, and beyond his control as she brought him to release. His mouth pressed firmly against her shoulder, and she felt him groan in pleasure and completion.

"I didn't know it could be like that," she whispered a while later after she caught her breath.

"I didn't know, either," he said, wrapping his arms around her and pulling her close to him. He kissed her again. And again. They made love many times that night, only closing their eyes at the first light of dawn.

⌒

They were the last to arrive at breakfast that morning.

"Well, is there a need for a special license?" Lady Palmerston asked, ever so bluntly.

"No," Phillip said, enjoying their shocked and murderous reactions. "No one will believe that *I* am married, unless they witness the ceremony. So we will be having a very big, proper wedding."

"As soon as the banns are read," Angela added.

"That leaves us three weeks," Lady Palmerston said briskly. "We'd best return to London today so that we can start planning."

"There is one last visit we have to make first," Angela said.

"Oh, right. I still have to apologize to one other woman," Phillip grumbled.

"A note will suffice for her. You are not to be in her company."

"Don't tell me you still don't trust me," Phillip said, wounded.

"It's *her* I don't trust," Angela replied, and they smiled at each other.

"Who are we to call on then?" Lady Palmerston asked.

"My family," Angela said, beaming, "I'd like to invite them to the wedding in person."

∽

After spending the night in the woods near the stately home of the Earl and Countess of Diamond, Lucas finally saw Angela emerge late the following morning. He saddled his horse as they packed the carriage. He was starving, exhausted, and desperate.

But he didn't think twice about following them.

All day he rode a discreet distance behind them. As dusk started to fall, Lucas noticed the surroundings were becoming familiar. He felt himself break out into a cold sweat. *This cannot be,* he told himself. *You are imagining things. You are out of your mind with thirst, hunger, and fatigue.*

He was not feeling well. But he could not deny what he saw. Angela was returning home, and on the way, they passed the dueling field where her father had fallen. He wished once again that he had been the one to fall that day. But this time, his wish was intensified by the guilt and remorse of seven years.

For six of those years he endured a marriage he could not bear. Every time he had looked at his wife, he wished she were someone else. Beatrice knew he loved another. But she never once complained or made the slightest effort to gain his affection. She carried on a long affair with another. He was unwanted, always taking second place. To see Angela with Huntley made him feel like more of a cuckold than Beatrice's actual infidelities.

He did not mourn Beatrice. He saw that his marriage was yet another mistake he had made, all because of his idiotic plan to gain the money he needed and the woman he wanted. He should have been less of a coward, he thought now, and lived in poverty with Angela. At least they would have been together.

Lucas felt dizzy, so he tightened his grasp on the reins. His head hurt horribly now, and the relentless drumming of his horses' hooves on the dusty road was exacerbating the pain.

But the physical pain was nothing compared to the torturous regret he had lived with every day for seven years. It was more than a mortal man could endure. Lucas wanted to either fix what had gone so horribly wrong or die.

Angela was his last hope, his only hope. He would do anything to secure her and her forgiveness. And if he couldn't have that, then he simply did not want to live any longer.

When their carriage turned onto the drive up to her family's home, he paused. For a moment, he allowed himself to remember that lovely and pure anticipation he had felt every time he had ridden to her home. To her. For a moment, he felt as if he were a young man, in love and loved, and that he had his whole life ahead of him, full of hope and happiness.

He would do anything to feel that way again.

Chapter 24

～

As their carriage turned into the long drive that led to the house, Angela was struck by a surge of homesickness. Seven years' worth, all at once. Returning now, she saw not the site of her fall but all the happy memories of the seventeen years she had lived before everything changed. *Home.* Why had she waited so long to return?

Her sisters, Samantha and Claire, burst out of the front door with nearly deafening shrieks of unmistakable joy. Angela was nearly knocked to the ground by the exuberance of their embrace. She hugged them both back fiercely, feeling like such a fool for not coming home sooner. But she had finally come to her senses.

"Look at you both! You're all grown up now."

"Never mind us. Who is that?" Samantha demanded. She was just as blunt as she ever was.

"Oh, it's the evil Lord Hartshorne!" Claire gasped, recognizing Phillip from the drawings in the paper. Her eyes were wide with excitement or horror; it was hard to tell. Claire was always quieter and more reserved than her sisters.

"His name is Phillip Kensington, and he is my fiancé."

"*The* Phillip Kensington?" Claire asked suspiciously, unsure of how to accept him.

"Yes. It's a pleasure to meet you both," Phillip said, smiling almost shyly at them. Angela realized that he was nervous, of all things.

"And this is our aunt, Lady Palmerston. She's been my chaperone in London."

"Since you're getting married now, does that mean we can have seasons, too?" Samantha asked, and it broke Angela's heart that their lives had been so affected by what she had done.

"I don't see why not. Is Mother home?"

"Yes. And Damien, too! He only returned from his grand tour last week," Samantha said. They all entered the house, and Claire showed Phillip and Lady Palmerston to the drawing room, while Samantha accompanied Angela to their mother's private sitting room.

"Angela!" her mother gasped in obvious shock. And then, rather than smile as Angela hoped she would do, her mother frowned. "Did anyone see you arrive? It should reflect poorly on your sisters if you were seen here. I thought we had agreed that you were not to return here."

"I have stayed away for seven years. I couldn't stay away any longer," Angela answered. She was no longer running from her past but determined to make amends for the sake of her future.

"And in all that time, you seem to have forgotten how the neighbors gossip here. They still haven't forgotten what you did," her mother said cruelly. Angela felt Samantha squeeze her hand in support.

"Oh, Mama, no one mentions it anymore," Samantha said. "And it wouldn't matter if they did, since Angela is engaged."

"You are?" Ah, the hint of a smile on her mother's face.

"Yes. And we are in love," Angela said. Her mother was not impressed.

"He's a marquis," Samantha added, and her mother suddenly seemed much happier.

"He's downstairs, along with Lady Palmerston."

"Oh! I haven't seen her in years! How did you ever connect with her, my dear? And do tell me how you met this marquis . . ."

For the first time in seven years, the Sullivan family was assembled in one room. Added to that was Angela's new family, Phillip and her aunt. They all dined together, of course, with seven years' worth of news to share. It was late by the time the ladies left the dining room for the customary after-supper tea.

Phillip remained in the dining room with Angela's brother. Damien was younger than him, but years of acting as the head of his family had given him an air of authority that made him seem older than he was.

"Cigar?" Damien offered.

"Thanks." Phillip accepted.

"So you mean to marry my sister."

"Yes. We are planning to marry in London next month."

"I'll be there to walk her down the aisle," Damien said. Phillip knew that would mean the world to her. Damien fell silent, looking at Phillip thoughtfully, before continuing.

"You are aware, obviously, that we have not had contact with Angela for some time."

"Yes, and I can tell that you are too much of a gentleman and care for her too much to ask if I am aware of her past. I do know, and I do love her."

"Thank you. My sisters and I never wanted her to leave. It was my mother's insistence, mostly due to grief at the loss of our father. She's proud, my mother, so she never admitted regret, but I could tell she missed Angela. We all did. And if she were hurt in any way, we would stand behind her."

"I promise I will not hurt her, and that I will love her as she deserves."

"Good. Brotherly warnings and threats are finished now. But before we rejoin the ladies, we ought to discuss her dowry."

"She has one?"

"You didn't know that?"

"No. She never mentioned it, and frankly, it never occurred to me."

"Well, that eases my mind that you were marrying her for her money," Damien said. "She probably expected that she no longer did. But she does. My father set aside portions for all my sisters."

"But you might have—"

"I didn't," Damien said. "I figured that if she didn't marry, she might need the money anyway. Knowing her, I can't believe she lasted as long in the abbey as she did. We'll draw up the wedding contracts tomorrow. Cheers," Damien said, raising his glass.

"Cheers." Phillip raised his glass in toast.

"Ah, one sister settled. Two more to go," he said, taking a sip of his drink. "If they have their way—which they always do—they'll be going to London with our aunt, and I should have to deal with this again."

"They'll be married within their first season with Lady Palmerston as their chaperone."

"Why does that make me feel concerned?" Damien queried.

"Because it should. And she'll have you married off, too, if you're not careful."

∽

Lucas watched as they all enjoyed a long dinner, full of boisterous conversation and laughter that carried to where he waited in the gardens. *That should be me,* Lucas thought. *Huntley is in my place.*

Lucas could only think of one way to get rid of his rival and thus to secure his place at Angela's side.

Chapter 25

There was really only so much that a man could endure, Phillip thought warily. He looked at his watch again. Lady Palmerston and Angela had been discussing wedding plans for the past three hours. He stifled a yawn and leaned his head against the window.

Every time he tried to nod off, they woke him to ask his opinion.

"Phillip, what do you think of roses?"

"I don't."

"You don't like them? I know, it's such a predictable choice, but they are so lovely."

"I don't think of them. I want whatever you want."

"And, at the moment, he hopes you want an elopement to Gretna Green, I wager," Lady Palmerston said.

"She said it, not me," he replied to Angela's questioning look.

"Oh, go to sleep. We have to talk about my gown, and I want that to be a surprise for you."

"Thank you," he said and closed his eyes. His respite was short-lived, however. Their carriage came to a stop a few moments later. Phillip looked out the window and saw absolutely nothing . . . nothing but open fields and blue sky, and no reason to stop, unless there was a problem.

"I'll see what this is about. Stay here," he said and stepped out.

There was another carriage stopped at an odd, diagonal angle in the road ahead of them. Phillip couldn't imagine why someone would park it thus, or what circumstances had caused it. But that vehicle did look familiar, or perhaps it was that it seemed more suited to town than country.

"We can't get through, unless we help them move their carriage," the driver, Frank, commented.

"Hello, there!" The driver of the other carriage stepped out. "Have a bit of a problem. Per'aps you might lend a hand?"

"Sure. What is the problem?"

"Something with the door on the other side. My master started off for town about an hour ago, to get help. But if I can fix it up, then I reckon I could catch up to him."

This struck Phillip as odd. Usually, the kind of man who owned that kind of carriage would not undertake to walk miles to the nearest village in the hot midday sun when he could send the driver. But to each his own, Phillip thought.

"We'll have a look at it," Phillip said and walked around to the far side of the carriage. And there he stopped when he saw—

Silently, Phillip offered up what was likely to be his last prayer.

He didn't need to see what transpired behind his back, for the sounds alone told him all he needed to know. Someone took a blow to the head and then fell to the dirt. Someone else was dragging that body into the carriage, through a door that had nothing wrong with it at all. Phillip noticed that out of the corner of his eye, it was Lady Palmerston's driver who was now unconscious.

"Tie up his hands," Frost said to the driver. The rope was ready, and Phillip's hands were yanked behind his back and tied tightly with a length of rope.

"Thank you; you may go," Lucas Frost said. "Wait in the carriage and keep an eye on the other driver."

"I presume that was not addressed to me," Phillip said, staring at the pistol Frost had aimed at him. The driver, presumably, had followed orders, leaving them alone by the side of the road, on the far side of the carriage so that neither Angela nor Lady Palmerston might see.

"The only place you are going is the afterlife," Frost said coolly.

"Ah. I've never been," Phillip remarked in an effort to stall for time. Chances were slim to none that anyone would come across them and save him. Thus, he needed a plan, and he needed a moment to think of something. In the meantime, he would bide his time.

"There is a first time for everything," Frost said.

"Indeed," Phillip said, focusing his eyes on the man and not the gun in his hand.

"First, we are going to take a walk," Frost said. "It wouldn't do to leave your carcass by the side of the road."

"No, it would be far too easy for someone to discover it," Phillip replied, thinking of how the Sloan brothers had come across him in the ditch alongside the road. Really, was he going to be left for dead by the side of the road *again*?

Only this time, it was likely Angela who would find him. It was a sight he prayed she'd never see—that of his dead body, or any dead body. He had to protect her from that. He had to protect her from all of this. For what if he did die this morning? And then she and Lady Palmerston would be left at the mercy of this madman. He would have to do something.

But he didn't know what. Bloody hell, it was hard to think with a pistol aimed at one's face.

"Exactly," Lucas answered, stepping closer and closer. He pressed the pistol against Phillip's throat. "We wouldn't want your carcass discovered, now would we?"

"You wouldn't, no," Phillip said. "But I'll be dead, so I won't care one way or another."

"Not that I give a damn about your cares or wishes."

"Obviously not," Phillip said, wincing as Frost jammed the gun a little harder into his throat. "But perhaps you would condescend to tell me why you are doing this?"

"Because she belongs to me, and because I have to marry her. It's the honorable thing to do."

"I'm not sure I understand completely," Phillip said, though he certainly had a clue. He just wanted Frost to keep talking.

"It's his eyes," Frost said cryptically, and Phillip was lost. "Wide open, but he can't see anything. Have you ever seen a dead man's eyes?"

"No."

"I see them all the time. I can't sleep because of it."

"I'm sorry, but whose eyes?"

"Her father's. I missed, deliberately. But he died anyway. And it's my fault. And now I can't sleep because I see his dead, open eyes. Like he's watching me, to make sure I do right by her," Frost whispered. At that, Phillip knew that the man would stop at nothing to marry Angela. The realization was no consolation.

"He's watching to make sure that I marry his daughter, so that he didn't die in vain. But she won't have me as long as you are alive, you see?"

"And what if my eyes remain open after you kill me?" Phillip asked.

"Oh, I brought a blindfold for you. I have learned from my mistakes."

"Good thinking," Phillip said, nearly choking on the words.

"Yes. I've thought this out completely," Frost said cryptically. Phillip decided to let it go. He decided to let go of everything. The man was obviously completely and utterly insane, and thus, it would be impossible to reason with him.

With his hands tied and a loaded pistol pressed into his throat, it was impossible for him to fight back. He could run, but he wouldn't make it far. Any sudden movement, and Frost might pull the trigger in panic.

This was it for him then. His throat was tight, and it was

suddenly too hard to manage what would be his last breaths. He could blame it on the dust in the road, but it seemed pointless to deny the truth at this point.

He did not want to die. Not now. Not when he finally had a reason to live. Not when he had promised Angela forever.

Phillip could see no way out for himself, but one chance that Angela might manage to escape. If he could lead Frost far enough way from the carriages, then she might have a chance to drive off after hearing the gunfire. He prayed that she and Lady Palmerston would display the common sense to leave him and flee before Frost could return to them.

"Shall we be off then?" Phillip offered.

"Yes. Go," Frost said, indicating the direction with a wave of the pistol.

"After you," Phillip replied graciously. He would have gestured, but his hands were tied.

"I think not," Frost snarled. And then he cocked the pistol.

"Hmmph." Lady Palmerston's unmistakable voice interrupted. Phillip never, ever thought he'd be so glad to hear it. And yet he could not move, not when his body was the only thing between a gun and a woman.

"Angela, I think we shall arrive in town a little later than expected," Lady Palmerston said, and Phillip's heart broke to learn that she was here, so close to this madman who wanted to marry her and then do God knows what else.

"It does appear that way, Aunt."

"Don't worry, ladies, this shouldn't take too long," Frost said.

"It might, though," Angela remarked. "Phillip is really rather difficult to kill. Lord knows how many have tried and failed already."

"The lady does have a point," Phillip grumbled.

"I will not fail," Frost said so certainly and so coldly that it suddenly seemed as if the temperature had dropped twenty degrees. The man was deadly serious. Phillip wanted so badly to turn around and look at Angela one last time, but he didn't dare.

"Angela, go back to the carriage," Phillip said. "You, too,

Lady Palmerston. *Please*." He tried, and failed, to keep the desperation out of his voice.

"Come along, Angela," Lady Palmerston said quietly and firmly.

Phillip did not hear the sound of her retreating footsteps.

"Now," Lady Palmerston barked.

"No," Angela said firmly. She took a few steps forward and stopped when she stood between Phillip and Frost. And the loaded gun.

"What do you think you are doing?" Phillip demanded.

"I'm saving you," she replied without turning around to look at him.

"No, Angela, you are putting yourself in mortal danger. Please don't do this."

"Lucas won't kill me," she said gently, looking into Lucas's eyes. "Because I am want he wants. Isn't that right, Lucas?"

Over Angela's head, Phillip could see Frost nod in agreement.

"And you think, Lucas, that you can't have me as long as Phillip is alive," Angela continued speaking calmly.

"You belong to me, Angela," Frost stated. The man seemed enchanted by her.

"If that is true, then it doesn't matter if he lives or dies, does it?"

"I don't—wait—where is she going?" Frost asked, noticing Lady Palmerston turning to walk away. He craned his neck to look, but his pistol never wavered. It was still aimed at Angela's heart. Her attempts to distract him had hit a snag.

"Oh, me?" Lady Palmerston replied. "I was just going to wait in the carriage. This heat is a little much for a woman of my advanced age."

"How old are you, anyway?" Phillip asked, to queer looks from Angela and Frost. But he was certain, knowing Lady Palmerston as he suspected he did, that she was not going to go wait in the carriage. She may be negligent, but she was nobody's fool and not a coward. She alone seemed to understand what he was getting at.

"Really, Huntley. You are about to die and you want to know my age?" Lady Palmerston said, playing along.

"I'll take your secret to my grave," Phillip said, with a slight nod in the direction of the pistol. "Whisper it to me."

Lady Palmerston did so.

"I would have never guessed," Phillip said, sounding impressed. "Advanced years indeed. You have aged remarkably well." She glared at him so meanly that the look was almost as deadly as the damned gun in Frost's unshakable hand.

"Now where were we?" he continued. "Oh, right. It doesn't matter if I live or die, so long as Angela goes with you. So I guess this is good-bye then, darling." He tried to keep his voice light and that flicker of hope alive, but he truly feared that it might be the end.

"What about a kiss good-bye?" Angela asked Lucas. "And then I will go with you, Lucas. Please, Lucas. I did not get to say good-bye to my father." At the mention of her father, a strange look came across Frost's face. The hand holding the gun wavered. Her words had hit a nerve.

"Allow me a proper good-bye this time, and I will forgive you for the past, and then I shall be yours completely," she said in that intoxicating, bewitching voice of hers. Her voice worked its magic now, and she pushed it for all it was worth. "Forever," she murmured, her voice low and husky, daring to step closer to Frost. She reached out, slowly, and touched his heart. "Allow me this, and I shall be yours forever."

"Just be quick about it," Frost mumbled, oddly enough. He looked away.

Under the hot sun and on the dusty road, with a gun at her back, Angela turned around and pressed her mouth to Phillip's to kiss him good-bye.

"I love you," he mumbled against her lips.

"I love you, too," she responded. Her hands stole around his waist, and she busied herself with trying to untie the knots there. He could feel her fingers fumble with the ends of the rope, grasping and tugging. The pain of the rope moving slightly, digging deeper into his raw flesh, yet never yielding, was agonizing. But it did not compare to the pain of plans gone awry, of dreams of future happiness dying by the side of the road. The rope was tied too tightly, and her hands could not accomplish a task that needed a knife.

"I can't do it," she whispered, panicked. Cheek to cheek, he could feel her tears. "I can't do it. I can't get the knot out, and I can't let you go, and I can't go with him." She was truly panicking now. He could hear it in her voice and feel it in the way her fingers frantically grasped and tugged. And Phillip wanted nothing more than to take her in his arms and tell her everything would be fine.

But he couldn't.

"Shhh," he urged. Lady Palmerston would return any second, wouldn't she? But he couldn't say that. And he couldn't be sure that it would matter. He wanted to tell Angela that it would be all right, but he had already broken enough promises to her.

He closed his eyes so he could savor all the more the sensation of her being near. For the last time.

She gave one final, desperate tug, and it loosened.

"What the—" Frost had comprehended what was happening. Angela kept working frantically.

And then she freed him.

"So your hands are no longer tied," Frost sneered. "But I still have a loaded gun. What the hell are you smiling for?"

"Turn around and see for yourself."

Curiosity got the better of Frost, and he turned only his head at first, and then turned completely around. He swore.

Lady Palmerston held a pistol of her own, aimed at Frost. She merely arched one eyebrow, and Frost lowered his own weapon.

And then Phillip seized the moment and threw himself at Lucas. They both hit the ground with a thud. The gun was knocked out of Frost's hands and ended up just out of his grasp. Lady Palmerston kicked it away with her satin slipper.

Frost struggled. Phillip fought back.

Eventually, Phillip managed to grab both of Frost's wrists, and he held them tightly, pressed into the dirt road. Angela hurried in with the rope and began tying his hands. Frost gri-

maced as she tied them tightly. She showed him no sympathy
but stood beside Phillip.

"This isn't over," Frost panted up at them, still struggling.

Lady Palmerston gingerly handed Phillip both pistols.

"Really?" he asked with a pointed look at Frost and then
dropping his eyes fleetingly to the weapons in his hand.

"Are you . . . ?" Angela started to ask the question, but
couldn't finish it.

Phillip, with two guns in his hand, stood over Frost, who lay
on the dusty road with his hands tied behind his back. There
was nothing to be discerned in Frost's eyes: not fear, not defi-
ance, not guilt, nothing resembling a plea.

Phillip could kill him here and now. Put the man out of his
misery and ensure that Frost would never bother Angela and
him again. He was a terrible shot, but even he could hit the target from this short a distance.

But Phillip thought about what Frost had said about the
cold, dead stare of her father's eyes. And Phillip thought about
what he held in his hands. It was not merely weaponry but
power to take away a man's life. And he thought of the pleasure he could give to Angela with these hands of his.

And he could not imagine touching Angela with hands that
had murdered a man. He could not imagine denying them
pleasure for the rest of their lives.

"Well?" Frost taunted.

If it were up to him, Phillip would not kill him. But it was
not entirely his choice to make. Phillip looked up to Angela,
asking her silently with his eyes what she wanted him to do.

Angela looked down at Lucas. He lay bruised, battered,
and tied up before her. And she couldn't help but think of the
first time she had seen him, when his blue eyes were bright,
his face free of pain and full of love and promise.

And she thought of all the loneliness and heartache she had
suffered in the years after Frost had done what he had done. She
had, in truth, fantasized about this moment, when she could
make him suffer as she had done, when she could have her
revenge. When she could finally and completely put her past
life behind her and make it disappear forever.

But her past had brought her to her future: Phillip. He took her hand in his. Together, hand in hand, they stood over Frost, now lying patiently as they decided his fate.

She looked up at her aunt. No words were exchanged between them. Lady Palmerston stood tall and sure. And she remembered what her aunt had said to her that one night: *Trust your head and your heart.*

She knew that this was not the end, no matter what her choice would be. She also knew how a little love, mercy, and forgiveness could go a long way toward soothing a tortured soul.

Her own heart and soul had suffered enough. She would not have any more of it.

She would let him live.

And so Angela suggested that they take him to the magistrate in the next town—alive. Phillip breathed an obvious sigh of relief, and she knew that they were of one mind on this matter.

He emptied the bullets from the guns and let them fall onto the road. He dropped the guns, too. His hands were free to hold her, now and forever. Angela threw her arms around him, and he held her tightly to him. It wasn't long before their lips touched for a kiss, but it was quite a long while before they stopped.

A few hours later, Frost was left in the care of the local magistrate, and the trio continued on their way back to London.

"Now, where were we?" Lady Palmerston asked. "Oh, yes. Angela, for your wedding gown, I think a cream-colored satin would work best with your complexion."

Chapter 26

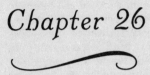

Five hundred people were invited to witness the wedding of Miss Angela Sullivan and Phillip Kensington, Marquis of Huntley. Not one person declined to attend.

Phillip stood at the altar of St. George Hanover Square, with his twin by his side. Neither of them felt the need to mention that this was the last thing either of them had ever expected.

This moment was all their parents could have ever wished for them: both of their sons in love and loved, and with their old sibling rivalry set aside.

Mostly.

"This is your last chance to live up to your reputation," Devon suggested.

"I'm not walking out of here without Angela," Phillip replied.

"Good. Just checking."

"Shut up."

"How dare you speak to your older brother in such a manner!"

"Did you not hear me the first time I said to shut up, or are you so much older that you're going deaf?"

"I'm older by a mere minute, so if I am so old as to—"

Devon did not get to finish his reply, for the organ sounded, and all five hundred witnesses to the unexpected nuptials of Phillip Kensington and Angela Sullivan stood and turned to watch the bride walk down the aisle, escorted by her brother.

Angela wore a gown of pale gold. She carried a small bouquet of pink roses. And even though her face was partially obscured by her veil, Phillip could see that she was smiling.

She ought to be. She was the one woman who had managed to reform the greatest scoundrel of a generation. He was far more than merely reformed.

Because of her, he had become the man no one, least of all himself, ever expected him to be.

He was loved.

He was *in* love.

And he vowed to love, honor, and cherish her; he had never spoken words he meant more. Except for when he told her he loved her. Which he did, constantly. He even suspected he was starting to annoy her with how often he told her. But if that was her only complaint about him, he'd take it. Lord knew he satisfied her in other ways. Well, perhaps it was best if the good Lord didn't know about that . . .

And somehow, by some miracle, this beautiful, amazing woman was pledging to love, honor, and obey him. Even though they both knew that she would obey when she felt like it. He didn't realize that he had feared she would come to her senses and back out at the last moment, until he caught himself exhaling a deep breath he had been holding. And he felt, as she slipped the ring on his finger, that gray, nagging feeling of never being good enough just . . . go away. Maybe he wasn't good enough. Maybe he wouldn't be. But he would try. No one would ever fault him for not trying.

And maybe he didn't deserve this happiness. But maybe, just maybe, he did.

"And now, if anyone has any reason why these two should not be joined in holy matrimony, speak now or forever hold your peace."

That could *not* be the sound of someone clearing their throat and saying, "I have a reason."

It was *not* the sound of five hundred people gasping and shuffling in their seats to turn and see who had dared to interrupt, or even ruin, this miraculous, historic event.

It was.

Lord Lucas Frost, who had *not* been invited and had apparently managed to avoid a suffiently lengthy incarceration, was standing at his seat in the middle of a pew, in the middle of the church.

"I have a reason they should not marry."

Angela muttered a string of words no one should ever say in a church, let alone a bride on her wedding day.

"Don't worry, darling. I'll take care of this. And I'm coming back." But first he kissed the bride.

And then Phillip turned to Devon. They nodded at each other and started toward Frost. Phillip took the center aisle, and Devon took the aisle on the left side of the church. Angela's brother Damien followed as well.

Frost could try to escape—which he did, damaging shoes and dresses in his haste—but it was futile.

Frost arrived at the aisle and, with two murderous-looking Kensington brothers after him, and the angry brother of the bride who had been hurt by him as well, turned and ran for his life.

They caught him in the vestibule.

"You don't have a good reason. You don't have any reason at all," Phillip growled, holding the man up by his cravat and using the cold stone wall as support.

"I do," Frost gasped.

"She made her choice."

"She has to marry me. Otherwise I won't be able to sleep at night."

Phillip understood, but as he said, the lady made her choice, and he was not going to argue with it. Somehow with a diminished supply of air, Frost managed to keep rambling on. Something about needing to make right a wrong and that was why

Angela had to marry him . . . God, the stench of whiskey on the man's breath was almost enough to make Phillip drunk.

But because Angela had changed him, Phillip knew regret was eating this man alive. And oddly enough, Phillip saw how he could help. And it did not involve strangling this man, though a part of him considered it.

"Shut up," Phillip told Frost, who obliged.

"You will apologize to her. Trust me, it'll go a long way toward making you feel better."

Frost agreed, reluctantly.

Phillip marched down the aisle, holding Frost by his collar, and ignoring the stares and whispers. Devon and Damien followed.

Angela stood at the altar with her spine straight and with all the dignity of a queen, Lady Palmerston by her side. Phillip could see her expression change from confusion to understanding.

"I'm sorry, Angela," Lucas said quietly, standing a few steps below her.

There were tears in her eyes, and she didn't speak for what seemed like an eternity.

"I can forgive you, Lucas," she whispered. She bent down and kissed him on the forehead. "But you must leave us alone now."

"If you don't mind," Damien said, "I'd like to escort him out. Out of the country, to be specific."

"Please," Angela and Phillip said simultaneously. Damien received assistance from Nigel Haven and Samuels, who had traveled to London with his missus to meet "the woman that made a man pour perfectly good brandy into the fire."

"Where were we?" the priest asked, once the interruption was over. "Ah, yes. If there are any other reasons these two should not be married, speak now or forever hold your peace."

There was a very tense moment of silence.

"You may now kiss the bride."

And because part of him was still a scoundrel, Phillip gave Angela a *real* kiss. A kiss that left no doubt in anyone's mind that he was in love with her. A kiss that was a small scandal and the talk of the ton for weeks.

Of course, everyone said they never thought they'd live to see the day that Phillip Kensington kissed his own bride. Neither did Phillip. But there were no words to express how glad he was that he did. And it was all because of Angela, his angel.

Epilogue

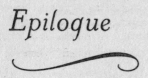

"*Where* is Madeleine?" Phillip asked, looking around for his oldest daughter.

"I have her with me," Lady Palmerston answered. Phillip felt a stab of panic that he would turn around to find that his aunt-in-law would have his daughter betrothed, when the girl was merely six years of age. But there she was, his mother's namesake, discreetly going through Lady Palmerston's reticule looking for the peppermints she knew she would find there.

"Madeleine, I see what you are doing." Somehow, it had come to this: an absolute scoundrel catching his child sneaking candy. She looked up at him with his eyes—and his mother's eyes, so he was told by those who knew. He would give her all the peppermints in the world, and then some. And she knew it.

"You must be sneakier about it, moppet," he whispered. "Don't let your mother see."

She nodded and popped a candy in her mouth.

"And Katherine?" Phillip asked after his next-oldest child.

"Relax, Phillip. All your children are accounted for," Lady Katherine answered, holding the hand of her namesake, a five-year-old girl with her mother's blonde hair. She was so well behaved that Phillip might have questioned her paternity. But he trusted Angela, and besides, he knew better. He knew very well that Katherine was his, because he could remember the night she was conceived . . . He should not be thinking such thoughts in a church. In front of children. But once a rogue, always a rogue . . .

"Two out of three," Phillip said with some relief. "Where is James?"

"I have him," Angela said. "Really, Phillip, you are such a worrier."

Oh, his darling wife had no idea. He didn't know how he had ever managed to sleep before he married her. He needed her within arm's reach, if not closer, to be able to sleep through the night. But only after checking on their three children.

He took his son in his arms. Technically, this little one wasn't his first son. Lady Grafton had given birth to, raised, and loved his first. But they were both his, and that was all that mattered. And when he held little James, named after Angela's father, he knew it didn't matter who was born first or second. They were all different but equally loved.

But this one was trouble already.

God, this one was trouble.

James had his mother's eyes, and stared at him as if to ask, *Really, Father, do you know what you're doing?* But for once, Phillip knew exactly what he was doing. And he told his son exactly that. And the little one yawned as if to say, *If you say so.*

"I know so," Phillip whispered.

"Are we ready, then?" Angela asked. They were all gathered in the chapel at Stanbrook Abbey for the baptism of their third child. Their third child to be baptized here. As per their ritual, they lit a candle for their newest child and placed it at the foot of the statue of the Virgin Mary and her baby.

Angela often had a similar smile as Mary did: sleepy and satisfied.

After the baptism and after ensuring that their three children were watched over by their thankfully vast number of relatives and friends, Phillip and Angela escaped for a moment to themselves.

"I never got to show you this," Angela said, pushing open a door.

"It's a room," Phillip said, looking at the four stone walls that contained nothing more than a narrow bed, a table, and a chair.

"This was my room," Angela said.

"How can you tell?" he asked. It looked the same as the room he had stayed in.

"Well, I'm not exactly sure, but it really seems like it."

Phillip grinned and laughed.

"You know, I used to pray that I would find a good man to love me."

"And then I arrived."

"An unlikely savior, I admit."

"I think you were the one to save me."

"Does it matter who saved whom?"

It didn't, really, so long as they had each other. Phillip told her he loved her—again. And she told him she loved him—again. Neither of them ever tired of hearing it. And then, because he was a scoundrel, he couldn't help but notice that he was in an empty room with a bed and a beautiful woman. There was only one thing to do. Phillip did what he did best: he locked the door and made love to his wife.